# "If you point a gun, you had better be prepared to use it."

With unblinking eyes, he stood erect. Hands on his hips. Legs apart.

Sabrina held his gaze and knew his rigid stance was a dare.

Aiming the pistol to the right of Kenilworth, she pointed at a lone birch. "Don't move, milord." As she lowered the hammer, his body stiffened. "Now, look to your left. Should I try for the left or the right branch?"

"To your right. It's farthest from me."

Gritting her teeth, she focused and fired. Wood crackled and snapped. Birds squawked. She smiled, feeling an odd satisfaction. Somehow, the act replaced the dignity Kenilworth had stolen.

"Luck," Kenilworth murmured, eyeing the severed branch.

Feeling the challenge in his single word, her blood started to hum. She shifted her gaze to just below his waist and adjusted her aim.

"If *that's* where you want to shoot me, go ahead…!"

Dear Reader,

Entertainment. Escape. Fantasy. These three words describe the heart of Harlequin Historical novels. If you want compelling, emotional stories by some of the best writers in the field, look no further.

We think Janet Kendall is one of the best *new* writers in the field. Her debut book, *Hunter of My Heart*, is a captivating tale set in Regency England. Here, the heroine's powerful and dangerous grandfather is so desperate for an heir that he'll stop at nothing to get one, namely forcing a marriage between his granddaughter and the mysterious duke of Kenilworth. But when their unexpected passion turns to love and trust, they triumph in the end!

*Maggie and the Maverick* is a heartwarming new Western by Laurie Grant. With the help of newswoman Maggie Harper, Garrick Devlin, wounded in the Civil War, finally learns to love again. And don't miss Cassandra Austin's *The Unlikely Wife,* the story of a handsome officer who falls for his commander's flirty daughter during a journey to an army fort.

Rounding out the month is *The Welshman's Bride* by award-winning author Margaret Moore. Forced to marry after being caught in a compromising position, a roguish Welsh nobleman and a demure chatelaine learn to appreciate their differences and fall in love.

Whatever your tastes in reading, you'll be sure to find a romantic journey back to the past between the covers of a Harlequin Historical® novel.

Sincerely,

Tracy Farrell
Senior Editor

---

Please address questions and book requests to:
Harlequin Reader Service
U.S.: 3010 Walden Ave., P.O. Box 1325, Buffalo, NY 14269
Canadian: P.O. Box 609, Fort Erie, Ont. L2A 5X3

# Hunter
## of My
# Heart

## JANET
## KENDALL

# HARLEQUIN®

TORONTO • NEW YORK • LONDON
AMSTERDAM • PARIS • SYDNEY • HAMBURG
STOCKHOLM • ATHENS • TOKYO • MILAN • MADRID
PRAGUE • WARSAW • BUDAPEST • AUCKLAND

ISBN 0-373-29060-8

HUNTER OF MY HEART

## JANET KENDALL

graduated with a bachelor's degree in sociology from the University of Colorado and worked there as a personnel counselor.

She was born and raised in Durango, Colorado. With not a lot to do in a small mining and tourist town, cowboys, eastern gents and Native Americans stirred her imagination. They became heroes. This, coupled with a Texan husband and a mother-in-law whose family is from England, fueled her love of history more. So she began to write in her favorite genre. Romance. When she's not writing, reading romances, or doing research, she tends her other passion, her flower garden and rare orchid collection.

She and her husband live in the Chicago suburbs. Janet would love to hear from her readers. Please write to her at: P.O. Box 3003, Naperville, Illinois 60565.

To my loving husband, who believed in me and
supported my writing from the first day.

To my mom and dad, the best parents a child could have.

## ACKNOWLEDGMENTS

To Jean Newlin and Laura Renken for their thoughtful
critiques as I was writing the final version of this book.

To the best den mothers in the world:
Susan Elizabeth Phillips, whose advice challenges me as
a writer, Cathie Linz, who taught me to persevere and the
real meaning of "creative," and to Jimmie Morel writing
as Lindsay Longford, whose keen sense of direction
kept me on the right path.

Finally to my editor, Margaret O'Neill Marbury,
who took the chance.

I thank you all.

# Prologue

The unmistakable smell of sweat and passion greeted Hunter Sinclair as he opened the door.

The butler had been right. Hunter's father wasn't alone and thus had broken his word. To witness the infidelity would give Hunter proof and another reason to sever their bargain.

Silently he entered the bedchamber and picked up a robe, his hands crushing the velvet fibers. Groans, muted by the satin hangings surrounding the bed, made his stomach turn. Drawing a quiet breath, Hunter parted the drapes and dropped the robe onto the lovers. "The study in two minutes," he said flatly.

The young woman gasped.

As his father rolled off the lithe body, he pulled a sheet over the woman's naked form. He gave Hunter an unrepentant smile. "You show yourself at the most untimely moments."

"No. I believe I arrived just in time," he said, and left.

A few moments later, Hunter entered the study his mother had lovingly decorated years ago. From the ebony cellaret, he poured himself a drink. He settled in a chair and propped his feet on a gilded table, then lifted the crystal goblet to his mouth. Before he took a sip, the heady bouquet told Hunter the pale amber liquid was cognac—but then his father always demanded the best.

As Hunter took a huge swallow, the smooth liquid scorched a trail down to his stomach and settled in a hot pool. Since his mother's death last week, nothing had erased the pain curled around his chest. Hunter downed the cognac to seek warmth, but the burning quickly died. When he started to fetch another drink, he stopped. No. He *wanted* to feel cold and without heart when he confronted his father, Randall Sinclair, Baron of Wick. That's exactly how the baron had treated his wife during their years of marriage. Randall had merely coveted the luxury her family's wealth provided. Long ago, he had emptied his own coffer on extravagant comforts and mistresses.

In exchange for keeping his affairs discreet, Randall had demanded a huge allowance from Hunter, who had agreed in hopes of protecting his mother from more shame. But now the time had come to end his father's unscrupulous life-style. By seducing a lady in their family home, his father had gone too far—he had severed the agreement. Furthermore, Hunter no longer had to shield his mother in life, only preserve her honor in death.

Leather slippers brushed the study's Oriental carpet and Hunter met his father's arrogant green gaze. An ageless panther, Randall looked ten years younger than his forty-eight years. Women found him irresistibly attractive. Of course the "Sinner," as the ton called him, took every advantage of his good looks.

"Stalked another one?" Hunter's tone was very dry.

"Are you referring to the talented lady upstairs? I have a voracious appetite." Smiling arrogantly, Randall sat and smoothed his robe's velvet collar.

Hunter steeled himself. "Aren't you curious about my arrival?"

"I thought you were out of the country managing one of your business enterprises. So why are you here?"

"Your wife, sir, is dead." He managed an even voice but

his throat tightened. Rising, he removed his greatcoat and un-
veiled the mourning band tied around his arm. He waited for
his father's reaction.

Randall stared at him. "I do not believe you. Your mother
is as strong as a man."

"She died five days' past."

Would his father ask for details about the quick funeral?
Did he feel a shadow of remorse? Did he care how she died?

"I am a widower?" A trace of concern crossed his face.

Suddenly Hunter realized Randall's problem. "Marriage no
longer protects you. Worried about an angry father marching
you off to the preacher?"

"I will manage. Mourning serves as an excuse not to re-
marry for at least a year."

He gave his father a lean smile. "Still, I've decided to cut
your allowance. Paying for the upkeep of this house, food and
a reasonable amount of clothing is all you'll see of my money.
With Mother's death, our agreement ends."

Randall gripped the chair's arms. "The devil you will. I
haven't an income, while you're wealthy as Croesus!"

"You're in mourning. What good is money? Attending
quiet affairs is all society will permit you." Hunter untied the
silk strip. As he dropped it onto his father's lap, he felt a
sense of morbid satisfaction that he could finally give Randall
his due.

His father gave the mourning band a fleeting glance. "You
will continue to pay the sum upon which we agreed," he
demanded. Pausing, he gave Hunter a nefarious look. "You
look like me. Tall. Well muscled. Handsome. Undoubtedly
virile. You have my green eyes and black hair…remember
Diana?"

Every muscle in Hunter's body tensed, rejecting the foul
memories of that tragedy, but he managed a look of indifference. From experience, he knew his father had some scheme
in mind. "What about Diana? You left her carrying your
child. I should have let her father call you out."

"Like a good son, you did not reveal the truth. Once I

announced your engagement to her, I thought you would honor it. Diana and I thought the idea brilliant. Ah—but you could not summon the chivalry to marry her. You surprised me by preferring a scandal to marriage. In the end, she took her life. I did not have to fight a duel and you are still a bachelor. Does your conscience have room to carry more guilt?''

Hunter clenched his jaw. He had refused to comply with his father's scheme and offered Diana some money—but not his name. When she ended her life and that of her unborn child, Hunter held himself accountable for the deaths.

He eyed his father warily. ''What have you done now? Have you ruined another lady's life?''

''Nothing. I have satisfied the hunger of a few ladies, but no woman is bearing my child.''

''Then why bring up the past?''

''Well, you may have refused to marry Diana…but unless you continue the payments, *you* will be married within the month. After all, you are twenty-seven and should have a bride.''

''Married?'' Hunter repeated in a low voice. ''I don't plan to marry.'' After witnessing the faithless wives and brainless innocents who had succumbed to his father's seductions, Hunter never wanted to marry. His fingers tightened around his glass as he walked to the cellaret and poured himself another drink.

''Would you like me to pass myself off as you? A little silver nitrate in my hair would hide the gray. In dim light, a lady would easily mistake me for you. I *might* even allow you to pick your bride. Bedding an innocent is a delicious thought, and afterward, you would *have* to offer the lady your name. She would believe that *you* seduced her. I would make sure of it.''

Simmering blood tangled with his grief, but he presented an unaffected facade. ''Is that a threat?''

''Would you care to put it to the test?'' Randall gave him a smug smile.

Hunter knew the baron's heart proved as empty as his coffers and would do anything to continue his lavish and decadent existence. A thread of control drew Hunter's emotions taut and he sipped the cognac that numbed his conscience. His father's threat was nothing short of blackmail.

*No more blackmail,* Hunter decided, *no more payments.* Could he allow Randall to ruin other lives and not stop him? With bleak choices, Hunter settled on a plan. Moral justice counted for something.

"You win. I have money on my ship so come with me now. Tell the lady my coachman will drive her home."

Randall inclined his head in acquiescence.

As they neared London Docks, the stench of the Thames grew, smelling of human waste and rotting fish. Hunter peered out the window of the hackney toward the warehouses. Beyond them, hundreds of masts and fluttering sails rose above the roofs. Fading slashes of violet and orange on the horizon signaled fair sailing weather. On the poop rail of his ship *Priscilla,* four lanterns created oblique shadows that moved with the water and changed with the wind.

Sailors waiting the next watch rose from their hammocks while others were busy at their duties. Hunter spoke with the ship captain, then returned to his father.

"The money is in my cabin below. Shall we?"

Hunter showed Randall to a small cabin with two narrow bunks, one above the other. A sea chest filled the opposite corner. Atop a small table sat a ditty box, a copper bowl and an oil lamp. Tucked underneath was a chamber pot and stool. After Randall entered, Hunter leaned against the doorway.

"This is your cabin?" Randall asked. "I imagined it to be bigger, given the ship's size."

"Oh, it is. My cabin's much larger. This one's yours." Hunter felt the ship sway.

Randall swung around. "What the devil are you saying?"

The sails unfurled like the sound of dull drumbeats. "I promised you a home, food and clothes. You will get all three—in Australia.'' As Hunter stepped back into the hall, he pulled the door closed and locked it.

"Damn you!" Randall pounded on the door. "I'm your father!"

Father, hell...only by the misfortune of the same blood.

The rhythmic sound of the waves slapping against the hull drowned the voice.

*No more scandals.* Hunter promised himself that no one would ever blackmail him again.

# Chapter One

*Scotland, September 1830*

"Shabby reporting! The *Times* said you'd be here! Why aren't you?" As Sabrina's words faded into the wind, she looked up and saw no lights in the second-story windows, or the third, either.

Keir Castle's four towers rose above the mist, a billowing white gauze that occasionally dipped and caressed the ground. Moss and shadows painted the stone structure. A seagull flew overhead. Slowly Sabrina "Beaumont" dropped her gaze. Interrupting this solitude was the light coming from the kitchen windows, the only evidence of life stirring on the massive estate.

The kind housekeeper, a lone servant, had answered the door but didn't know when her master would arrive. Slapping the stone wall, Sabrina willed Lord Kenilworth to appear.

"Everyone is speaking about his return from Barbados. Rumor says he distrusts strangers," Marga Beaumont said.

Turning to her aunt, Sabrina made a face.

"Do you think we have committed a faux pas by not sending word? Maybe he instructed the housekeeper to turn away visitors."

"She looked honest. Faux pas or not, we've waited months

to collect the debt. The *Times* portrayed him as fair and honest. Surely he'll understand our lack of propriety. The man the newspapers described wouldn't allow us to go to the poorhouse." Despite her hopeful words, his absence weighted her heart. The *Times* was quickly losing credibility.

"Possibly he is with a paramour, *non?*"

"Paramours." Sabrina scowled to hide her emotions from Marga, a petite lady of thirty-eight years who still managed to look fashionable despite their dire financial circumstances. Her moss-green traveling gown accented her hazel eyes and chestnut hair, coifed in artful curls above her ears. Marga always took pride in her grooming. Her fashion sense and creativity had made the partnership in their dress shop possible.

Marga cleared her throat. "The on dit on him varies. Some say he is unlike his father. The newspaper says he's been in Barbados. At least monseigneur supported the paramours during his absence. I feel certain he will pay us."

Caring little for gossip, Sabrina jabbed a finger to her chest. "*We* supported his mistresses! He owes *us* money for their gowns!"

Marga sighed. "Quaintly put, but true."

With her emotions running rampant, Sabrina leaned against the structure and ignored the stones pressing into her back. "I apologize for raising my voice. Yes, I do believe he'll pay us once he realizes a debt exists. I'm just worried about the twins." She paused, thinking about her four-year-old siblings. "Do you think they're all right?"

"Ha! Christine never lets her brother out of sight, and you know how mad Alec gets when we pamper him. He is weak in body but strong in spirit. They will be fine with Thomas for another few days." Marga squeezed Sabrina's hand.

She managed a smile. "Father was lucky to have Thomas as a friend. He's gone beyond friendship to watch them. But we've never left them alone for so long. What if…"

"Ah! You are thinking about more than just the little one's

health. *Oui?* That wretched man, your grandpapa, worries you. Rest assured, Sabrina, no one will discover our secret."

"I can't help it. He's probably furious that I didn't meet with him three days ago." Instead, she'd burned his missive and fled to Scotland.

"*Oui.* He is probably searching for you all over London."

"There! You see? What if he followed us? And, *you're* not the one he wants for a brooding mare." She groaned, knowing she was his last chance for a male heir. With political reform stirring, he loathed the idea that upon his death, the Crown would sell his title. God forbid that a wealthy commoner might buy it. Her only solution was to reveal Alec.

She refused to do that for fear he would separate the twins. Christine would be of no use to him. By alienating Alec from the only family he knew, the duke would harm him emotionally. Christina, too. Her sister was healthy though, whereas Alec, in a fit of anger or tears, could easily provoke an asthma attack. He could die.

After giving Sabrina a thoughtful look, Marga wandered to the nearby herb garden. "The world believes Alec and Christine are mine. Our purpose is to shield them. You are old enough to give your grandpapa a good fight. The twins are not."

Guilt accompanied Marga's mild scolding. Her aunt had agreed to the deceit when Sabrina conceived the idea. "My apologies. Yes, you're right. In a few months, I'll reach my majority. He'll have no control over me. Won't that be a joy?"

The thought brought a measure of relief, but fear lay coiled in her stomach. Sabrina had lived in dread that her grandfather would discover her whereabouts. Now he had.

*"If we do not meet again, you must do everything possible to insure the twins' safety,"* her mother had pleaded.

Sabrina's throat thickened at the recollection and of her vow. After learning from her parents what her grandfather had done to them, she never wanted to meet or claim him as kin.

"Marga? Aren't you afraid he'll discover you worked for Queen Josephine, too? What would I do without you if he…"

"Accused me of being a French spy like he did your mother?" Marga let out a wry chuckle. "The war was fresh in people's minds then. Too much time has passed. I was just the queen's couturiere, an assistant. What can the authorities do now? Browbeat me until I reveal the queen's measurements?"

"How can you jest? He could accuse you of instigating the deception. Of kidnapping his heir! I can't bear the thought of you in jail, or God forbid, hung. Or the nightmares the children will suffer if he rips them from the only mother they know."

Marga's olive skin paled but she raised her chin. "I considered all those things before I agreed, but I had to take the chance. If we remain mum, he will not learn anything."

"Mother was innocent, too. Yet he caused enough ruckus to make the authorities believe she was a spy." Sabrina breathed deeply. "We'll get our money and then take the twins someplace safe."

The duke had somehow found her, and that brought him one step closer to Alec. Lord. She wished her brother's health was better. Living in the shadows had left her stomach permanently knotted.

Every Sunday for the past four years, the *Times* last page had contained a small paragraph, one with nothing to identify the advertisement's owner. Three facts identified her and she had discounted coincidence long ago. *Still searching for Derek's daughter Sabrina, now twenty.* She guessed the notice would no longer appear now that he'd found her.

Drawing a cleansing breath, Sabrina smelled the ripeness of the herbs intensified by the sea air. Tears threatened and she summoned the same courage she had relied on since her parents' death four years earlier. She buried the dark thoughts and focused on the immediate problem. Opening her reticule, she pulled out her father's pocket watch. Four-thirty.

"It looks like rain. We'll wait several more minutes to see if Kenilworth arrives."

Marga smiled, kindness warming her eyes. "Patience, *ma chérie*. In a few days, we will return to the little ones. This business, *fini!* Thomas will give us shelter until we make other plans. He need not know the truth about the debt or why we closed the shop."

Sabrina latched onto Marga's optimistic words. For months, Kenilworth was just a name, but a week past, the *Times* featured an article on him. The newspaper described him as a man intent on helping the populace and reforming the government. Surely, the *Times* couldn't be wrong about everything.

A neighing horse and rumbling of a wagon jarred her thoughts. She spun toward the sound. In the distance, the Scottish mist obstructed her view as it meandered over a browning heather field. A breeze divided the fog and revealed a rider beside the loaded wagon. "*That* must be Lord Kenilworth!" Her heart drummed with expectation.

From atop his black stallion, the man spoke to the wagon's driver and then sang a Scottish ballad of a lad marrying a lass. Laughing, the driver turned the conveyance toward the castle. The man and horse disappeared inside the stable.

Sabrina glanced at the horizon, now frosted with thunderclouds, and back to the stable. Turning, she handed Marga a small valise. "Watch for the mail coach. Ask the driver if he'll wait for us. I must learn if that man who just arrived is Lord Kenilworth."

Marga fumbled with their baggage. "*Mon Dieu! Alone?* How do you know if either is his lordship?"

"I don't, but he looked aristocratic by the way he sat in the saddle. He looked confident! In good humor!"

Her aunt frowned. "I should accompany you."

"I'll be cautious. We can't be in two places at once."

Without waiting for a reply, Sabrina lifted the skirt of her gray wool gown and ran down the garden path. The pebbles jabbed her feet through the soles of her half boots. As the wind parted Sabrina's cloak, the clasp dug into her throat and the brisk air stung her cheeks—but those little irritants paled to her rising hope.

After bursting into the stable, Sabrina took a steadying breath and smelled the pungent odor of moldy hay. The man's tune drowned out her entry, and though she couldn't see him, she followed the rich, baritone voice. Suddenly the tune stopped.

"What the devil?" Surprise laced his words.

Taking small steps, she edged closer to a stall. A pair of black-gloved hands broke her line of vision as they helped a filly stand. Sabrina craned her neck. He sat on the straw-hewn floor and stroked the black animal still wet from birth. When the foal's hind legs wobbled, he steadied and guided her to the mare.

"You're a surprise. What shall we call you? The marking on your head says that stallion of mine is a lusty one." Turning, the filly tried to suckle the riding crop tucked under his arm. He laughed, a deep rumble coming from his chest. "Oh, no. You'll get no nourishment from this thing. You want this." Placing the crop on the floor, he gently guided the filly to the mare's udder.

By claiming the filly, Sabrina felt certain she had found Hunter Sinclair, Earl of Kenilworth, the estate's owner. His softly spoken words and gentle touch reinforced the newspaper's accounting of him. Bless the *Times*. "Lord Kenilworth?"

Swinging around, he stared at her with wide green eyes. "Yes?"

"May I speak with you?"

His brow creased. As he stood, he picked up his riding crop and brushed the straw off his buff trousers. "If you're looking for a position, speak to the housekeeper."

The motion of his hand drew her gaze to his muscular thighs. Quickly she reversed her perusal. His towering height and broad shoulders, emphasized by the short cape layering his greatcoat, made him look formidable. She gripped her braid and finally pushed it over her shoulder.

From her reticule, she retrieved a folded paper and handed it to him. "I'm Sabrina Beaumont, from Maison du Beaumont of London. This bill explains everything."

He snapped open the parchment and read. "I owe you six thousand pounds for women's frippery? I pay my debts, Miss Beaumont, and this one isn't mine." Kenilworth flicked the paper between his fingers and held it beneath her chin. "Besides, the last time I wore a nightgown, I was a babe." His smile didn't quite reach his eyes.

Her mouth parted and closed before she wrested her gaze from his well-shaped lips. "Your lordship, you or your man of business approved these expenditures. You've been in Barbados. Perhaps you're unaware of this debt or didn't receive my letters. Or forgot! I have something else."

Digging into her reticule, she produced his promissory note. She cautiously held the paper close to her chest as he read. Unease prickled her skin. "*Sir.* How long does it take to absorb one line?" She slipped the evidence into her reticule.

Kenilworth's green eyes narrowed, emphasizing the high bridge of his nose. He pointed a finger at her. "That's a forgery. What deviousness are you plotting? Who sent you?"

With his accusations ringing in her ear, she stepped backward. "What are you talking about?" She couldn't keep the disbelief from her voice. This was *not* the man the *Times* described.

His eyes turned cold and hard. "I dislike surprises, Miss Beaumont, but welcome justice. I'll give you one minute to tell me who concocted this alleged debt. Otherwise, I'll take you to the authorities for trespassing, forgery and extortion." From his waistcoat pocket, he retrieved his gold watch.

The set of his chiseled jaw conveyed no sign of compassion, but his hard look fueled her determination. "All I know is that *you* owe me six thousand pounds."

"Thirty seconds."

She considered a strategy but knew she couldn't execute it. "If you won't listen, I'll take this issue to court!"

Exasperated, she turned as if to leave, but an iron grip caught her wrist. His touch made her heart jump. Still she raised her chin and pulled her arm from his hold.

Kenilworth slid his crop through his fingers. "Go ahead. Take me to court."

His frigid timbre sent a chill down her spine, but from the ruffians she occasionally encountered on her errands, she had learned to show a tough demeanor. She glared at him. "The populace will think you made false promises. That you're cheating a poor merchant. My accusations will taint your reputation, hurt your political aspirations."

He whacked his thigh with the whip.

She winced.

Kenilworth pointed his riding crop toward the barrel next to her legs. "Sit and start talking. Don't spin a tale."

What happened to the gentle man who cooed to a newborn filly? Sabrina sat, but only because he granted her a chance to speak. "The debt is eight months old. As you saw for yourself, the note said to contact your man of business for payment. I couldn't find him."

"How did I accumulate such a debt?" His tone was very dry.

Shifting, she bunched her cloak in her hands. "The debt is for the gowns you allowed your three mistresses to purchase."

"I *doubt* that I'd forget one mistress let alone three. You should have given your tale more thought. Right title, wrong man. Until recently, my grandfather on my mother's side carried the title."

She gave him a tight smile. "*Sir,* your family history is of no interest to me, only the money you owe me."

"A *lesson* in my family history is exactly what you need. Seven months ago, my grandfather died. He was seventy-four years old, bedridden for the past two, and incapable of satisfying a mistress."

The implications made her heart skip. "I've three letters of promise signed by Lord Kenilworth. You hold the title and must honor the debt.''

He slipped the paper she had given him into his frock coat pocket, then patted it. ''Evidence for extortion. I'll not honor a debt that isn't mine, but I'll seek justice.''

''You'll pay me, or I'll…'' What could she do?

''You will *what?*'' Kenilworth tapped the whip against his palm. ''So far, I could charge you with trespassing. Extortion. Swindling. Exploitation. Forgery. Defamation.'' He paused. ''Do you know what those words mean?''

Sabrina straightened and thrust her chin forward. ''In four languages.'' She enunciated the words. ''*Five* if you count English!''

Kenilworth looked unimpressed. ''They also mean that if you're guilty, you'd go to prison or hang.''

Thunder boomed.

The thought sent a chill down her spine. Anger and frustration clashed. Clutching her reticule, she sought mercy in his cold eyes. They appeared like green ice chips. Afraid for the twins' well-being, Sabrina pressed her point. ''Milord, you might have reason to be suspicious, but I swear, I speak the truth. I used *my* savings to pay *your* bills. I'm in quite desperate financial straits.''

He frowned. ''Would *you* give the money to a stranger?''

So the rumors were true. He distrusted outsiders. ''No, but—''

''Nor will I. Now. Leave and I'll forget this affair.''

At his dismissal, she heaved a frustrated breath but wouldn't retreat. Her father, who had been a military strategist, said no one won a battle until one side stood alone. She wasn't dead yet. She had no choice but to continue with her feigned strategy. ''I'll go straight to court.''

He pressed his face close. For a fleeting second, she noticed an emotion not spawned by arrogance. Fear?

''Really? *If* you're telling the truth, who and how will you pay for a defense?''

Sabrina couldn't seek more legal help for lack of funds and

because of her false identity. According to her solicitor and the only other person who knew her secret, she would commit perjury if she used the Beaumont name. Now if she used her real name, her grandfather would find her again because of the publicity. Despite this, Kenilworth's staunch refusal fueled her ploy.

"Maybe I'll request that *you* pay the legal fees."

"You want to use every opportunity to demand money from me, is that it?"

She pursed her lips. Perhaps he disliked the notion of settling in court. Could she goad him into paying her where honesty and reason had failed?

"Imagine the *Times* headline. 'Earl of Kenilworth Cheats Poor Merchant.' Now, *that* would be a scandal in these unsettled political times. Parliamentary reform has England in an uproar. The news would contrast with their recent portrayal of you."

He stared at her hard, then rammed a hand into his trouser pocket. "An investigation should settle this matter. I'll start with some questions and forward what I learn to my solicitor."

*Investigation?*

A tremor skipped down her spine. What if he succeeded in revealing her heritage? What would happen to the twins?

Maybe answering a few questions would satisfy his curiosity. What choice did she have if she hoped to get the money? She said a quick prayer and asked forgiveness if she had to lie for the twins' sake. "If I can answer them, I will."

He nodded and slowly walked behind her. "You're a couturiere? I've never seen one dressed in such plain attire."

"I usually work in the back of the shop. Ledgers. Organizing the fabrics for orders. Why spend money on expensive clothes?"

When he snorted, Sabrina sensed his closeness and edged forward. Why did he cause her pulse to race? He had been so gentle with the filly. Though calmed by the thought and feeling no cause for alarm, she wanted to bolt off the barrel.

Instead, she rose with her back straight. She felt like a rabbit running from a fox, all cunning, sleek and too sure of himself. How could she convince him he owed her the money without an investigation?

"Pray that you're not lying. They hang people for lesser crimes than those I've mentioned. I'd hate to see a noose around that lovely neck." With the crop, he traced an arc beneath her chin.

The smooth leather felt cold against her skin and caused gooseflesh. Sabrina had an irrational urge to pull up the collar of her cloak. His hooded eyes reminded her of a bird of prey scouting for its next meal. "Noose? I'd hate it more."

Although he smiled faintly, his eyes remained cold. "Well, I don't need the court to decide if a debt exists. Nor do I need them to order me to pay if it does. I'll decide both issues based on my investigation. Justice, Miss Beaumont. I want justice." He retraced the arc.

She touched the clasp at her throat. A rope…he was serious! Her palms grew damp.

"So, you intend to play a judge." She batted the whip away. "Threats and intimidation won't change the truth. I'm no simpleton." Their eyes locked in a battle of beliefs. His shadowed jaw remained resolute, not a stubble of black hair moved.

"Are you a courtesan?"

Stinging warmth ebbed into her cheeks. She grasped her cloak to keep from hitting him. Recalling his insults, she said in French, "I don't care if you're the *tenth* Earl of Kenilworth." In Italian, she added, "You owe me the money." She continued in Portuguese. "I'll prove it!" With a flowering Spanish finish, she asked, "Is that clear?"

"Unusual. A couturiere more educated than most men I know. Who are you? What do you really want of me?"

Suddenly she realized her error. Anger had overwhelmed caution and she had revealed too much of herself. "The money."

In French, he said softly, *"Baizer moi, Sabrina."*

Her body grew hot from spinning emotions. *Kiss me, Sabrina!* "For six thousand pounds plus interest," she replied in French.

"Really?" Kenilworth drawled.

"Well..."

His mouth curved into a baiting smile. "Well?"

As she considered the enormity of allowing him one kiss, she immediately berated herself. Perhaps his threats and speculations had been for naught but to somehow lead to this moment. Despite his handsome facade, she couldn't kiss a man who thought so ill of her. She narrowed her eyes. "You can go to the devil."

Thunder rattled the windows of the stable.

He shrugged. "You're becoming more interesting by the moment."

The whip's rhythmic tap against his solid thigh reminded her of a drum in a death march. Rain pelting the roof created a chorus. She fought for a nonchalant look. "So are you."

"What else can I learn about you, Miss Beaumont?"

What if he learned that she was the granddaughter of the powerful and wealthy Duke of Sadlerfield? Or maybe Kenilworth wouldn't learn a thing. She had been born in Paris, and her mother had birthed the twins aboard ship and no records existed. When they arrived in London, Marga had lied to the minister at Wesley's chapel. He entered her aunt's name as the twins' mother in his records. Sabrina had hidden the evidence of Alec's heritage in a place no one would think to look. When her grandfather died, then she could take steps to help Alec claim his birthright.

*Protect the twins.*

"Depends what you ask."

## Chapter Two

Hunter regarded Miss Beaumont's pale blue gaze, a fiery one that swept his face and stabbed his uncertainty. Innocent? Actress? He didn't know, but her desperate and sincere tone gnawed at his conscience.

As thunder clapped, something nudged his leg. Startled, he looked down and suppressed a grin as the filly licked the end of his crop. "Still hungry? Go back to the stall. Your mother will get anxious if she can't see you."

"See to your animal, milord. Surely your questions can wait."

Her soft voice caused him to glance up. Miss Beaumont's piercing eyes had melted to a different emotion. Sadness? Panic? Damn his conscience. Quickly reaching for the filly, he guided her to the mare, now shifting with unease. With a few strokes, he calmed her, wishing something could settle him as readily.

Had his father found a way to leave Australia? Who else could or would impersonate Hunter? Had he coerced her into this scheme? Despite the cold panic knotting his gut, caution warned him not to speak of his father. Discussing him might lead to questions he must avoid, for in the legal world, he had committed a crime against the blackguard. Hunter had taken justice in his own hands. What could he do now? Leaning, he secured the stall's rope closure.

"*Ma chérie!* The fool raced by me!"

Hunter whipped his head toward the stable door and quickly joined his guests. The intruder, a comely woman, curtsied. Water rolled off her hat brim and onto his boots as Miss Beaumont introduced them. "Oh, not an accomplice?"

Frowning, the newcomer fumbled through her valise as water dripped off the tip of her nose. "*Monseigneur?* What are you saying? *Accomplice? Mon Dieu.* Where is my handkerchief?"

Hunter reached into his frock coat pocket and offered his. "May I save you the trouble?"

"Thank you, sir, but I'll give her mine. You might accuse us of stealing if we forget to return it."

Shrugging, he tucked the cloth into his pocket. "A handkerchief hardly compares with six thousand pounds."

Rolling her eyes, Miss Beaumont unbuckled her bag and snapped it open. "Marga, what happened? Please don't tell me the mail coach left. Didn't you wave?"

"Of course! I stood near the trees to stay drier. The idiot had his head burrowed into his collar like a turtle and never saw me. We're stranded!"

As Miss Beaumont searched her bag, a gardenia scent drew his gaze downward. He caught a glimpse of a pistol. His pulse beat out of time. Had she come with dark intent?

Only one person harbored enough contempt to wish him dead. What if the debt was just a prelude of blackmail to come? Would Miss Beaumont use the gun as inducement? He watched her hands, but now she held a garment that might be a pair of drawers.

Although his concern that Randall might harm another innocent person continued to grow, the gun heightened his uncertainty and curiosity about Miss Beaumont. Why would she carry a pistol? Did someone threaten her? Who sent her? Who was she?

Rain pelted the slate roof and water gushed down the interior pipes into the horse troughs. Should he offer them shelter? As fast as the thought came, the words flowed. "You've missed the coach. Consider staying here."

Briefly, Kenilworth wondered if, during the night, he would find himself facing a pistol. But his worry that they might be his father's victims concerned him much more.

"No, thank you, milord. We'll walk." She pressed a handkerchief into her aunt's hand.

As Madame Beaumont dabbed her face, she turned to her niece. "Walk to Edinburgh? We will drown!"

"His lordship refuses to pay us. I'll not spend one night with that—" Miss Beaumont threw him a glacial look "—tyrant."

His goading and authoritarian manner had not affected her in the least, yet to show a softer side would be disastrous. If he didn't stay alert, her beseeching eyes could weaken his resolve. He whacked his thigh with the crop. "That's nothing compared to what I can be if you're lying."

Madame Beaumont dried her brow then looked up at him with narrowed eyes. "*Mon Dieu!* Look at her young and honest face!" Cupping her niece's chin, she turned it side to side.

"His imagination blinds him to all else. Isn't that so, sir?" Miss Beaumont smiled thinly.

He arched an eyebrow. True, she possessed an innocent's look, too young to let life harden her incredibly beautiful eyes, or etch lines on her porcelain skin. Her plaited mink-colored hair only added to her aura of youth. He had, however, learned to look past a lady's appearance. Her connections and mind interested him more.

"First, I need to confirm your story and identity. Are you acquainted with a person who might do so? Someone of repute?"

Miss Beaumont chewed her plump bottom lip until she worked it to a rosy hue. For some reason, the chaste act seemed like something a child would do and stirred his watchful nature more.

Finally she looked up with her white teeth still gripping her lip. "Geoffrey Norton. He's our solicitor."

"Stay. I'll send a message by ship to my man of business. With good wind, I might have an answer in a few days."

"So you really plan to be judge and jury, milord? We decline your offer. I've no wish to visit with the executioner too."

He narrowed his gaze. "The truth decides your fate."

"I think *monseigneur* is very generous, *ma chérie*. We will accept his offer."

Her pale blue eyes grew round. "Aunt Marga! An *investigation* might take longer. Investigation! We can't afford—"

Madame Beaumont shook her head, and a look passed between the ladies that Hunter couldn't decipher. "*Monseigneur* might use the time to reconsider. Especially when Geoffrey proves our story."

Desperation flashed in her eyes, but she raised her chin a notch. "Considering my aunt's condition, I might agree…if you promise to pay us before we leave."

"No assurances, Miss Beaumont. Confirming your story and identity is a beginning. Questions regarding the debt require a deeper investigation. Your aunt's right. I'm being generous. You *could* spend the night in prison."

Her mouth opened and snapped shut. "I've no words to express your hospitality."

He threaded his crop through his fingers. "Scots are famous for it. You're staying?"

She glanced at his hands then looked up. Her dainty nostrils flared. "Only because of my aunt."

"Wise choice."

A short time later, his housekeeper ushered the ladies up the servant's staircase. With his mysterious guests comfortable, he marched down the hall, which looked ghostly due to the sheets covering the furnishings. Miss Beaumont's untimely demand irritated him anew and he yanked the covering off a Queen Anne side table. He threw the sheet onto another macabre heap.

As he entered his study, the air still smelled musty, but at least the housekeeper had cleaned this room before his arrival.

His oak desk and worktables gleamed from beeswax. After removing his greatcoat, he threw peat bricks into the hearth and lit a fire. Within minutes, he penned a note to his solicitor.

Suddenly his foster brother, Gavin MacDuff, entered. A frown heightened the sun-etched lines on his face. Water matted his blond hair. Gavin's rolled sleeves and smudged trousers reminded Hunter that he had promised to help unload the wagon.

"I worked and ye entertained a lass. Hardly seems fair. Now we've guests, I hear. What's this about?"

"I wish I knew. I need you to take this note to London." He folded and sealed the parchment.

"Now?" Gavin asked incredulously. "It's raining! We're supposed to be opening the castle. Hiring staff! What of me wedding plans?"

After handing him the letter to Jonathan Faraday, their solicitor, Hunter explained the situation. "You're the best captain I know, and the only man I trust to do this."

"Bloody hell! Fine time for Randall to concoct another scheme. We could wait. He might show his face."

"No. You helped me! A kidnapper. You were the ship's captain. I don't know the punishment, but transportation comes to mind."

Gavin drove a fist into the air. "I'll strangle him myself if he ruins me wedding!"

Hunter shook his head. "I've already brought enough trouble into this house. If he reveals the reason he's been in Australia, my esteemed peers might charge me with kidnapping. The Tories would embrace any chance to stop reform!"

Gavin let out a disgruntled sigh. "You think Parliament would take the case to trial?"

"I'll not chance your life or my ruination."

"What about the things he did to you? Were they not crimes?"

Hunter combed his fingers through his hair. "True. My word against his, and you're my only witnesses. I doubt the law would heed an accomplice's word. Even in a land full of criminals, Australia has a small fashionable society now.''

''Ye think he opened his bloody mouth and announced he's the Baron of Wick? He'd risk his freedom to leave the estate!''

''Maybe he's testing me to see if I would do as I threatened. Maybe he lied to explain his presence. He's made me look like scum before. I must learn if he's behind this debt.''

His friend scowled. ''He's always liked to play games, yer father. I'll go, but watch yer back while I'm gone. This wouldn't be the first time a desperate lass allied with the Sinner.''

Hunter lowered his face in his hands. ''I've the worse feeling that he found a way to leave Australia. You're the last person I want to hurt.'' He pounded his desk. ''Damnation! I should have found a better way to stop him. If asked, I'll say I held a gun to your head, and demanded you sail my ship.''

''Nay! You'll not lie to save me hide! Do ye hear me?'' Gavin threw him a determined look. ''In yer place, I would've done the same thing, and asked ye to help me.''

Despite his knotted stomach, the words warmed Hunter's heart. ''I would have agreed.''

Gavin moved forward and squeezed his shoulder. ''As lads we pledged that we're brothers, that we'd watch out for the other and share equal blame for everything. Don't break our vow.''

''We were children!''

''Say it! No sacrifices!''

He swallowed the emotion that rose to his throat. ''No sacrifices. Go now. May God be with you.''

After Gavin left, Hunter untied his cravat and leaned into his leather chair. For years, he'd rationalized his actions because he had prevented an offense against an innocent person. In doing so, he had committed a crime against a member of the peerage. He'd involved Gavin, a man with no title—although Hunter's grandfather had raised him like his own—to help him. The thought reminded him of his mother and the loving way she had nurtured Gavin, too.

Hunter closed his eyes and tried to shake away the memories and dark thoughts. Short of another crime, he would do anything to keep his past buried. The questions remained. Had his father returned to London? If so, what did he want?

Yawning, Sabrina closed the door to her room and crept down the dimly lit hall toward the tower. Her head felt numb from worry and no sleep. She hoped the housekeeper was awake and would offer her a cup of tea.

In the turret, dawn's light flowed through a small window and softened the stone staircase, one smoothed by time. The steps seemed to shimmer with history. Each step bore a slight indentation, proof to the numbers who had used them. With a light touch, she traced the curved wall and coolness kissed her fingertips. Even to her untrained eye, she knew the turret had breathed for centuries while the main section of the house boasted Georgian architecture.

For some odd reason, the heritage the turret represented mocked her situation. She missed the twins! Blinking away the tears, she continued down the stairs. Until the time was right, she must keep her and her sibling's ancestry a secret.

If Kenilworth paid her when she left Keir Castle, the money would curb some worries. She hoped the messenger returned quickly. Lord, she needed the money.

As she reached the lower steps, she blinked at the surroundings. The staircase had spilled into the foyer and not the servant's hall. She stared at the crystal chandelier that graced the domed entrance, the carved oak door and the sheet-covered furnishings. The appointments told her that riches filled the house, yet the contents didn't matter. She was lost.

Due to her worries last evening, she had paid no attention to the route. She glanced behind her. Should she retrace her steps? Gooseflesh covered her arms. Suddenly she realized the earl might take offense to her wandering and she eyed the door. Maybe she could walk around the castle and find the rear.

"Going somewhere?"

With her heart pounding, she swung around. "I'm looking for the servant's hall. Actually, I'm lost."

Kenilworth leaned against the doorway of a room off the foyer. As he regarded her with a raised brow, he threw his frock coat over his shoulder and fingered his untied cravat. The motion drew her gaze to his throat, unshaven jaw and the exposed portion of his chest. Without his toilette, he looked…savage.

Suddenly a knock sounded and his lordship glanced at the door. "Early for callers. More of your friends?"

She produced a wry smile. "Perhaps just a traveler needing aid. If so, they'd do themselves a favor by looking elsewhere."

"A man could shave with your tongue." With long strides, he crossed the foyer and opened the door.

A servant dressed in indigo livery whipped off his hat. "Beggin' yer pardon for the hour, milord. The Duke of Sadlerfield wants a word with the earl."

Sabrina's pulse raced. *Her grandfather!* He must have followed her! She had to leave. Grabbing her skirt, she climbed a few steps, but curiosity urged her to look to the door again.

"I'm Kenilworth."

Stepping into view, the man dismissed the servant with a crisp nod. "Splendid. May I come in?"

Kenilworth gestured for him to enter. "Sadlerfield. I only know you by your politics. Did you come to sway my reform efforts?"

Sabrina climbed a few more steps, but a sudden need to see this man made her peek over her shoulder. Maybe he hadn't come because of her. The thought didn't calm her thundering heart. If she moved beyond the banister, the curved wall would hide her.

"That is a subject for later. Right now, I am looking for a young lady."

No! Spinning around, she raced up the stairs. Despite his longer nose and leaner build, the man resembled her father, only with white hair and a determined set to his jaw. She had to alert Marga!

"A moment while I see to my guest. Miss Beaumont?"

Sabrina halted but didn't turn. Only three more steps to the wall! "Milord?"

"Young lady! Come here," Sadlerfield said.

Sweat trickled down her back. What could she do? Slowly she turned and managed an unaffected look. "Yes?"

"Sadlerfield, do you know Miss Beaumont?"

The duke let out a disgruntled breath. "Beaumont! One look and I know she is my granddaughter. Sabrina Barrington!"

Kenilworth's dark eyes demanded answers. "Barrington, is it?"

Holding his gaze, she raised her chin. A powerful urge to deny her grandfather's claim skipped across her conscience. Despite his discovery, a tiny part of her was glad she could emerge into the light and fight him. Maybe this was the reason she hadn't run. However, this didn't mean she would acknowledge him as her kin. "So what if it is?"

"One of you. Start explaining." Kenilworth marched toward her. His steps resonated off the marble floor, bounced off the stucco ceiling. "Who's it going to be?"

"In time, Kenilworth, but I will not discuss this matter for all to hear! Come down at once, young lady!"

For one second, Sabrina considered appealing to Kenilworth, but his cold gaze held no mercy. Where were the servants' stairs? When she glanced over her shoulder, an iron grip captured her wrist. An indignant cry whispered through her lips. She tried to yank her arm from his hold, but Kenilworth's large hand imprisoned her fingers. His breath, hinting of brandy, brushed against her cheek and filled her ear.

"This time, I want the truth!" Seizing her elbow, he escorted her into the room from which he had emerged earlier.

Her heart thundered. "Let go of me!"

"Sit!" He pointed to a leather chair and motioned Sadlerfield to take the seat beside her. Standing in front of her, he leaned against his desk.

"Undoubtedly, you have questions, Kenilworth. First, I must properly introduce myself to Sabrina. Look at me, young lady! I am your grandfather."

Her line of vision ended at Kenilworth's taut stomach and broad chest, one that vibrated with anger. She trembled and laced her hands. Shifting her gaze to her grandfather, she suddenly realized he had remained silent during Kenilworth's tirade. Was that a look of satisfaction brightening his blue eyes? She pursed her lips. In that moment, she didn't know which man frightened her more.

To hide her emotions, she summoned her most insolent manner. "Have I passed your examination, your grace?"

"Quite. You have your father's eyes. I will not go into the reason you have avoided me these past years. Not seeking me out and avoiding the meeting I requested conveys your feelings. However, I did spend considerable funds searching for you."

How much did he know? Despite the dread that threatened to steal her breath, she managed an unaffected facade. "A waste of money, I assure you, but I'm curious. How did you find me?"

He placed his ebony cane between his legs and rested his hands on the gold knob. "Bank clerks receive little recompense. That is irrelevant now."

"Bribery! How dare you!"

His eyes gleamed. "My men informed me that you came to Scotland. One sailed with you. So, of course I had to follow."

She fought for a steady voice. "How long have you had someone trailing me?" Guessing she would run, he had undoubtedly completed his plans before he approached her. Had he found the twins? What horrible fate did he plan for Marga?

A white eyebrow rose. "A very short while. I needed time to decide the best course for your future. Dashing off to Scotland changed my plans naturally.'' He shifted his gaze to Kenilworth. ''She stayed the night here. You realize her reputation will be in ruins if society learns.''

Kenilworth's eyes turned hard. ''I offered her *and* her aunt shelter from the storm. Don't make anything more of my generosity.''

Refusing to consider the dark thought that blew through her mind, Sabrina willed her pulse to calm. ''Your grace, I came here about a debt.''

''I know you are in financial straits. Your bank account and closure of that shop are proof.''

What else did he know? To hide her concern, she slapped her knee. ''Did you hear that, Lord Kenilworth? Surely, you'll believe the duke. The debt put me in my current position.''

''Odd. Despite an obvious estrangement, you embrace his words. His affirmation doesn't mean I'll pay you.''

''But now you have proof of my story and identity!''

The earl's black eyebrows snapped together. ''Do I? That was before I learned your real name. You lied.''

She bit her lip. ''Barrington doesn't suit a couturiere. Beaumont is French. You know the English relish Parisian fashion.''

''Trade!'' the duke scoffed. ''We will discuss that and your finances later. Your reputation concerns me more. Already you have sullied it by dabbling in commoner's work.'' Her grandfather turned to the earl. ''I must speak to you alone.''

''If this conversation concerns me, I'm staying.''

''Kenilworth. Put her somewhere.''

''Wait in the secretary's office.'' The earl looked at her hard and pointed to a small room off the study.

When she remained in her chair, his arm shot out. Strong fingers captured her hand. She tried to dig in her heels as he pulled her across the room. ''This isn't fair!''

''Right now, I don't care what you think.'' He dragged her inside and retreated quickly.

''Lock her inside, Kenilworth.''

To her dismay, he did as the duke ordered. As she pounded

on the door, she pressed her ear to the wood, but the thick oak muted their voices. She squeezed her eyes shut. Imprisoned like her mother! As old stories emerged, hot tears rolled down her cheeks.

When Sabrina's father had refused to abide the duke's demands, her grandfather stealthily created circumstances to make the English government believe her mother was a French spy. He even pretended shock when the authorities arrested her as a war criminal.

Worst of all, the powerful duke did nothing after Thomas's barrister father saw her in jail, nearly dead from starvation. She hadn't fit into the duke's plans. He had used his power to keep the affair quiet. Thank heavens for Thomas. He and her father had managed to smuggle her mother out of jail.

The black recollection reminded Sabrina of her own situation. How long would Kenilworth keep her imprisoned? Fear and anger mutated to determination. She ran her sleeve over her damp cheeks and vowed to never show any weakness or let her grandfather rule her life. His cunning had ruined her parents' lives, and she'd not forget his strength on this score or forgive his sins. He had indirectly killed her parents. Cursing, she kicked and pounded on the door.

What were they talking about?

## Chapter Three

Hunter curled his fingers around the key and slowly turned. He could not shake the disturbing feeling that the duke had planned his arrival, early hour and all. "What do you wish to speak to me about?" Behind him, the doorknob rattled and pounding followed.

The duke looked at the door and then threw him a dispassionate glance. "She stayed here with you. You are a bachelor."

"Her aunt chaperoned."

"Was she ever alone with you?"

Hunter threw Sadlerfield his darkest look. "I haven't touched her, but I can't vow for her innocence."

Sadlerfield pounded his cane on the rich carpet. "Do not be insolent with me, young man. Now, tell me about yourself. Start with the time you left Oxford until your recent return."

Surprised, Hunter glared at the duke, but to learn the answers, he sensed he must comply. As he rubbed the key between his fingers, he spoke about his years in India where he owned a sapphire mine. He discussed his plantation in Barbados and included every unconventional business maneuver he had ever employed. "Satisfied?"

"Almost. You left out your little trip to Australia."

Hunter gripped the key and managed an unaffected facade. What kind of game was he playing? "A good businessman should always see to his interests. Why shouldn't I see to my warehouses and estate?''

''I know about those, too. I am a good friend of Australia's governor.''

Hunter planted his fists at his waist. ''Why ask me anything if you know the answers?''

Sadlerfield straightened. ''I am just confirming the facts. A man of my years and experience assumes nothing. You will do.''

''For what?''

''To marry Sabrina, of course.''

The key dug into his flesh. ''You're out of your mind.'' He said the words, short and succinct.

Sadlerfield's chin rose. ''I know exactly what I'm doing.''

The duke's shocking demand stirred a question, one that seemed improbable. ''You want an heir? Go look for a stupid buck! Did you plan the debt? Did you force her into a situation so she had no choice but to come here?''

When the pounding continued, Hunter glowered at the door. Despite her beauty, a wife was the last thing he wanted, and an impertinent, lying chit only made matters worse.

Sadlerfield remained stoic. ''Outrageous. I am merely a concerned guardian who spent years searching for my only kin.''

''You left out planning and scheming.''

''*If* I have, so what? She was still here. A man of my position must assure the title will continue. Why allow such revered heritage to revert to the Crown?''

''I refuse to marry her.''

''I think not. You transported your father against his will. The governor conveyed that amusing story. A man in his cups can tell a great deal.'' The duke's blue eyes gleamed.

Hunter forced a harsh laugh. Did Sadlerfield know all? ''You believe a drunken man's tale?'' he asked in an icy tone.

''Whether I do or not is irrelevant. The governor believes it. However, he has more sympathy for you than he does your father. The fact remains, if you do not marry Sabrina, I will ruin you. I will tell the world what you did.''

The blackmail fueled Hunter's anger and he searched for ammunition against the duke's well-planned assault. Yet, like a man who held bad cards, he had to try to deceive his opponent. "My father has a tainted reputation. No peer will take his side.''

"Society might not believe Lord Wick. However, they would believe me if I conveyed the tale. Are you willing to chance it?''

Hunter stalked to the hearth. ''Bringing a Sinclair into your family could sully the Barrington name. Is that what you want?''

"If I ignore Lord Wick's despicable reputation, your lineage is satisfactory. Besides, linkage to the Barrington name will improve your social standing. The connection might even help you in Parliament. What is your answer?''

Hunter understood the threat. Marry the wench or suffer personal and political ruination. He slammed his palm against the stone mantel and wished it were the duke's face. He had no choice. ''Damn your pompous hide.''

"I gather that means yes?''

"One day I'll see you in hell for this.''

A corner of the duke's mouth rose. ''My felicitations.''

"Don't expect me to ask for her hand.''

Sabrina kicked the door. ''Let me out of here!''

Now she could truly understand the reason her mother had begged her to hide the twins, having aptly described the duke. Sabrina would do anything to keep them from this cold, ruthless man! His heartlessness alone would kill her brother.

As metal grated in the keyhole, she stepped back. Suddenly the door slammed against the wall. Kenilworth's piercing look could splinter rock.

For a second, she stood paralyzed, but rage and pride forced her chin up. ''Move aside, milord!''

"Enjoy your moment of freedom," he drawled, and stepped away.

She stomped past him but suddenly realized the men were glaring at each other. Warily she looked at her grandfather.

He held her gaze with unmoving eyes. "I am by rights your guardian and have arranged for your future."

Horror rocked her heart. "I've managed on my own."

"You are the granddaughter of a duke. I control you." He slanted a glance at the earl. "That is, until you marry. Sabrina, meet your intended."

His words hit her like a hurricane, at once stealing her breath and fueling her anger. She jabbed her arm toward the earl. "Him! Never! I refuse to marry to him!"

"Don't dream that I'd ever ask for you." Kenilworth scanned her with cold eyes.

She let out a deep breath at the earl's refusal, but simultaneously his rejection tweaked her pride. The humiliating situation was the cause, wasn't it? "His lordship and I agree. We don't want to marry. We don't even like each other!"

"It is what I want that matters. You will marry him. You stayed here, and he has agreed to do the honorable thing!"

Kenilworth sneered. She could feel the anger emanating from him, sense his restraint, see the fury hardening every muscle. Like a cornered animal about to pounce, he seemed suddenly...primitive. He walked to the hearth, planted his hands on the mantel and stared at the cold ashes.

Sabrina couldn't explain her sudden compassion for the earl, a victim like herself. "Your grace. You can't insinuate that he compromised me. He didn't."

The earl slapped the mantel. "When do you want the marriage?"

Surprised that he would relent without a fight, she twirled around. He had held his ground about the debt. "Milord! Are you a coward? If we both refuse, he can't force us!"

"Well, he has." Fury burned in his eyes.

Sabrina pursed her lips. Her grandfather must have somehow threatened to use his power, just as he had persecuted

her mother. This thought didn't ease her tumultuous emotions.
"Really, milord. I expected you to give a better fight."

"Oh, he tried. You will marry within a month. I've a paper
that will secure a license."

Kenilworth marched toward the duke. "What paper?"

Her grandfather reached into his tailcoat pocket.

She jabbed the air with her fist. "A month! Never!"

Keeping his eyes on her, the duke started to hand the paper
to the earl. "Is that shop important to your aunt?"

Sabrina threw him a vicious glare and grabbed the paper.
"Just like you to take away our livelihood!" As she read the
letter, her hands began to shake. *I will help you in any way
regarding the personal matter we discussed. William Howley,
Cantuar.* "You went to the archbishop!"

Kenilworth snatched the paper from her hand and read. His
jaw worked. "So, you paved a path to God just to see your
granddaughter married," he drawled.

"I will do anything for a male heir. The Barrington name
must continue."

She knew his title and deeds to property came from Nor-
man times. By royal decree, the lands were entailed and the
deeds stipulated that only a male heir could inherit. Yet, out
of this mess, Sabrina felt a ray of hope. The relief made her
limbs weak and she sank into a chair. She was certain—well,
almost sure—that the duke had not learned of Alec's existence
or he wouldn't have planned her marriage...that is, unless he
knew about Alec's poor health and wanted a spare heir.

What could she do? She glanced at Kenilworth, whose dark
look didn't invite camaraderie. A niggling thought rooted
deeper. Even her grandfather couldn't force a man like Kenilworth to do anything unless the duke had some power over
him. Perhaps her instincts were right. Dark, wild and powerful
emotions inhabited the earl's soul, something primal and un-
tamed. She could not imagine being married to the man, who
didn't want her anyway.

Suddenly a thought came to mind. Perhaps she could turn

the disaster to her advantage…and help the earl, too. "Kenilworth? May I speak to you alone?"

As Hunter closed the door to the small office, he stood with his back to Miss Barrington. He grasped the knob.

He knew now that the duke had long considered a union between him and his granddaughter. Damnation! Had Sadlerfield investigated every eligible peer? Of the lot, he must have the darkest past. Lucky him. Obviously he was the person most likely to succumb to blackmail and still meet Sadlerfield's requirements.

Curious, Hunter turned, but cursed himself a thousand times for even considering her innocence and welfare. She appeared to dislike a forced marriage, too, but she was still a liar. His measure of kindness made him angry with himself. When would he learn?

"I should have had the authorities take you to jail. Neither of us would be in this fix if I had. I vow this, Miss *Barrington*. You'll never make a fool of me again."

Straightening, she slid her palms down her skirt. "That was never my intent, milord. I only omitted a slight detail, but because I've used the Beaumont name for a long time."

He snorted. "I wonder. What else you have excluded?"

"Nothing important to you, milord. The reason I asked to speak to you should help both of us."

"You've sparked my imagination again. What do you want, Miss Barrington? A grand affair with jewels as a wedding gift? Forget it. You're not getting a thing from me except my name."

She chewed her bottom lip. "I only want one thing from you, sir. Unless you agree, I won't marry you."

He narrowed his eyes. That innocent thing she did with her lips wouldn't make a fool of him again. This announcement shouldn't have surprised him but it did. Sadlerfield had made his position clear. Total ruination. Even if he didn't consider his own survival, he had to think about Gavin's life, and the lives of his workers in Barbados. Many were counting on his efforts in Parliament to help free friends and family members who toiled on other plantations.

"We don't have a choice."

"I think you agreed only because he knows something about you. I'm sorry he used such coercion. I won't question your actions if you don't ask me mine. My terms, sir. I will refuse to speak the vows…unless you give me a bank draft for six thousand pounds."

"That is a separate issue."

"The money or no vows."

He stepped closer. "You're a scheming little wench."

Sabrina swallowed hard but remained rooted to the floor. "I'm sorry you feel that way. If you consider everything, I'm helping you. You're in some kind of trouble. Without my vows, you'll be in a real fix."

The determination in her eyes and the tilt of her chin told him she would do as she said. Damnation! He had no choice. "Blackmail. It must run in your family."

Her dainty nostrils flared. Looking away, she eyed the bookshelves. "I'm only asking what I'm due. Keep your fancy wedding. The show would only be a farce. Why give the duke such satisfaction?" Her voice quavered.

With her back turned, he didn't know if she experienced a spurt of anger or remorse, however, he did appreciate her low regard of the duke. "Of course, why should we?"

Slowly she moved to the wall and fingered a book. "Will you accept my condition?"

Hunter pulled his frock coat from his shoulder and retrieved his leather pocketbook. Walking to the desk, he found a pen and ink. After a second's pause, he drafted a banknote. If he accomplished nothing else in his life, he vowed he would learn everything about his bride-to-be. Rage hit him in the gut. He was about to enter a loveless marriage, one that could easily resemble his parents'. The reality left a bitter taste in his mouth.

He walked up behind her. "The money, Miss Barrington." Turning, she pinched the banknote, but he didn't release it.

Panic flashed in her eyes. "Aren't you going to give it to me?"

"We've a deal. You set the boundaries, and that includes more than saying the vows." He released the banknote.

"What do you mean?" Folding the draft, she tucked it into her pocket and then looked up.

"Let me refresh your memory." Planting his hands on the books, he bracketed her.

She moved backward, her heels clicking against the oak shelf. "What are you referring to?"

"*Baizer moi,* Sabrina…for six thousand pounds."

Her eyes grew wide. "*What?* That discussion has nothing to do with this!"

Leaning a little closer, he caught her gardenia scent. "Oh, I disagree. You're a scheming liar. Show me you can keep your word."

She frowned and suddenly she tilted back her head and closed her eyes. "Kiss me then and be quick about it."

Lowering his mouth, he brushed his lips across hers, but her rigid posture challenged his pride. Surely he could get some reaction from her. After all, she would be his wife…a cold, stony one. This thought urged him on, and he kissed her again, this time pressing his body against hers. Suddenly her closeness and soft lips stirred his base needs. Her gardenia scent aroused all his senses more. Although he cursed himself for reacting, something inexplicable made him want to taste her sweetness again. As he deepened the kiss, she let out a mewing sound and her lips quivered beneath his. Her lips began to melt, mold against his.

Suddenly a knock shook the door. Deliberately Hunter continued to kiss her and lifted his head long enough to bid the intruder to enter. He captured her lips again.

"Good God! What are you doing?" the duke roared.

Hunter raised his head, felt a small fist grind into his midriff. Giving her a cold look, he backed away. He could never let either of them know that the kiss had affected him. "Sealing our promise to wed," he drawled.

''Barbaric! Nonetheless, your display does not surprise me. You both come from parentage with lust in their veins.'' The duke shook his head. ''However, your natures will give me an heir sooner.''

Her piercing blue eyes flashed from the duke to him as she tried to sweep past them. ''I must go speak with my aunt.''

The duke held up his hand. ''You are not leaving. We must discuss your finances. I cannot have you embroiled in a scandal now. Once you wed, I will settle them for you.''

She slid her hand into her pocket. ''No need, your grace. Aren't husbands responsible for their wives' debts?''

Despite her faults, her refusal revealed an admirable trait. Hunter could even admire her spirit, but he had let compassion overrule caution, an act that led to this moment. ''She should come to me with no debts and a dowry.''

Using the duke's money for himself or her dowry wasn't what he intended. He had plenty of his own. Instead, he could use the funds to help the Scots, and that would irk a Tory. The compensation seemed a small price for losing his freedom. He knew the man would use Hunter's past as control, but only in private. In public, the duke would never tarnish the Barrington name.

''Yes. On the up-and-up. Say, one hundred thousand pounds?''

''Two hundred thousand.''

The duke arched a white eyebrow. ''Fifty thousand after you wed and one hundred fifty when you produce me an heir. After your display, I have no doubt that you will do so quickly. Furthermore, I expect you to turn Sabrina into a befitting countess.''

''I don't think that's possible.'' Curious about her silence, Hunter looked down at his bride-to-be. Pink washed her cheeks. However, he didn't know if she was angry or anxious about the marriage bed. A pang of guilt nudged his conscience for kissing her the way he had, and giving Sadlerfield reason to speak so bluntly.

"Of course it is." The duke turned to his granddaughter. "I will also give you funds to see to your personal needs."

Her frigid gaze swept from her grandfather to him. "If it's money that spurs you to this agreement, you should have bargained harder, milord. He will pay any price to get an heir."

Pride and anger collided. Hunter could and should defend himself, but he wouldn't. Let the minx believe as she wanted. No man had a pristine past. He refused to live his life under the continued threat of blackmail, and thus must learn of their weaknesses. With the marriage a month away, he had time to consider his approach to an unwilling bride. Slowly and deliberately, he skimmed her length. "I'm sure I'll get my money's worth."

# Chapter Four

The cool air numbed Sabrina's cheeks and the earth crunched like thin wafers beneath her feet. Occasionally a drift of Scottish mist brushed the black landscape and a cloud shuttered the light of the moon. Despite the desolation, she and Marga headed toward Edinburgh. "Do you think they've discovered we're gone yet?"

Marga hurried her stride. "*Monseigneur* never considered we would use the servant's stairs. A man too sure of himself. After checking on you twice, he might have left you to pout."

"Pout! I still can't believe they bargained over me as if I were a horse!" Nor could she forget Kenilworth's angry kiss, one that branded her lips and stirred an odd sensation in her stomach. Just thinking about the encounter renewed the tingle.

"A month we must wait for your wedding? Ha! My little ones will think I abandoned them."

As they walked in silence, tears pooled in her eyes, but Sabrina refused to let them fall. Her mother always said a rainbow followed a storm. The squall that had killed her parents left her three rainbows—the twins, and money her father pushed into her bag at the last moment. From that tragedy, her shop had emerged. Where was her rainbow now?

*Do what you believe and follow your heart, not what others want you to do.* Those were her father's last words. When she was sixteen, Sabrina tucked away his sage advice; now, the words fed her purpose. She had promised her mother she would guard the twins and nothing would break that vow.

To keep her word, Sabrina needed a thriving shop. But it was more than a livelihood. No other employment could give her independence, something she required because of the twins. Now they must start anew. At the thought of her bleak future, a chill tunneled to her bones and eroded her confidence. She summoned her strength, and, with an effort, she considered the immediate future.

"Are you all right, *ma chérie?*" Marga shifted her valise to the other hand. "If you curse *monseigneur* or your grandpapa, I'll not mind. I might spit a few choice words myself."

Sabrina managed a smile. "If Alec's health is better, should we move to France or back to South Carolina? The French population in Charleston was vast enough to shield us before."

"I detest the idea of running and hiding. Poor Derek. Your father spent every spare shilling on legal fees. In the end, Thomas paid the remaining balance and loaned your father money, too. I do not want to find myself beholden to another as Derek was."

Sabrina frowned. "Father never told me he was indebted to Thomas."

"You were a child. Revealing your grandpapa's perfidy was hard enough."

Now Sabrina understood that her father's dream to start a shipping business wasn't the only reason he had wanted to return to England. Honor and repaying a debt were important to him. Her heart ached. Deaths. Debts. And Kenilworth.

Fury burned inside her. "I detest Lord Sadlerfield."

"With reason. Now I worry he will discover the twins aren't mine. They resemble you." Marga looked at her with sadness in her eyes. "Alec's health might force us to stay in England. If so, you must marry *monseigneur*. Then we pray your grandpapa will not poke his nose into my life."

"If nothing else, I need time to learn the truth. Lord Sadlerfield blackmailed Kenilworth into the marriage."

"*Oui?* How will that help us now?"

"Kenilworth paid me the debt money so I would marry him. Maybe if we learn his secret, he'll reconsider."

"*Ma chérie!* Blackmail him into removing his offer?"

"I don't recall him proposing."

"You intend to ask Geoffrey to help us?"

"Of course. Kenilworth had the audacity to investigate me. Why can't I do the same?"

"Use the money *monseigneur* just relinquished to pay Geoffrey? We need that in case we must flee."

Sabrina smiled. "Lord Sadlerfield offered to fund my personal needs. I consider an investigation a *personal need.*"

"*Très bien!* Learning his secrets might be a way to keep you from marrying! You have your uncle Philippe's blood. He too was clever in his work as an intelligence officer." Marga let out a disgruntled sigh. "If we do not learn what *monseigneur* is about, you know what you must do."

"Unfortunately, yes."

A distant rumble caused Sabrina to tilt her head. She grabbed Marga's elbow. "Listen! Horses! Quick! Down the brae!"

They rushed down the slope until brambles stopped their descent. When Sabrina pushed the branches aside, the thorns punctured her hand. She bit her lip to stifle a cry. Quickly she and Marga passed through the opening.

As they lay belly down, Sabrina smelled the moist earth, and the vibration of thundering hooves rattled her insides. Kenilworth or highwaymen? Sabrina rummaged through her valise until her skin touched the cold steel of her pistol. Foreboding constricted her lungs. Although Kenilworth's banknote and every shilling she possessed lay in the bottom of the bag, she almost wished the horses belonged to thieves. When the pounding of the earth ebbed, Sabrina expelled a long breath and relaxed her fingers.

"*Soyez tranquille.* I did not live through Napoleon's war to die now. We will get home safely."

Marga's brave words calmed Sabrina's thumping heart. "I'll try not to worry. I don't know what I'd do without you."

"*Mon Dieu!* We are family! We take care of our own. After Philippe died, marriage no longer bound me to your parents. Where would I be without your father's support? I would have starved during the war. Derek's generosity is something I will never forget." Standing, Marga grabbed her umbrella and valise.

They returned to the road and continued to walk. Sabrina rotated her shoulders to ease the ache in her arms, but the thorn impaled in her left hand continued to throb. Every discomfort reminded her of Kenilworth. If he had paid her immediately, the duke might not have found her so quickly or put the twins in a vulnerable state. At least she wanted to think that were so.

Although she feared Kenilworth or her grandfather would search and eventually find her, she wanted to prolong, even prevent that fate. Her own welfare and the twins' aside, she worried about her aunt. Would he harm Marga? When Sabrina envisioned the duke supplying twisted evidence for an imaginary crime, she lengthened her stride. Her spinning emotions urged her toward the twins.

As they approached a bend in the road, plodding hooves broke the silent night and banners of mist veiled the rider's identity. Her heart jumped. Quickly Sabrina looked for a place to hide, but the flat land dotted with birch trees dimmed her hopes. Her pulse raced. After retrieving her double-barreled pistol, she placed her thumb on the hammer but hid the weapon in her cloak's folds.

A heartbeat later, she sucked in her breath as Kenilworth and a coach emerged from the mist. Panic, followed by anger, shot through her veins. He stopped his horse in front of them, and the coach, adorned with glowing lanterns, pulled up next to him.

Kenilworth straightened. "Well, Miss *Barrington,* going for a stroll? Or did you forget the agreement we made?" His tone was very dry.

"I changed my mind. I refuse to marry you." She moved her hand to her side.

"Miss Barrington..." He gazed at the pistol in her hand. "Put that bloody thing away before you hurt someone! The last thing I need is for you to blow a hole in your foot."

Tumbling emotions turned her blood hot. Yes, she even wanted to experience a touch of revenge because he had insulted her integrity and, in part, ruined her life. His actions threatened those she loved. Irrational thought overcame sensibility.

She wanted him to experience the loss of control and helplessness she felt. With a tight grip on the pistol, she summoned her darkest look. "We've left your property. You can't tell me what to do."

"You're still *on* my property. Now put that gun away and get in the coach. We have a deal." He started to dismount.

"*Mon Dieu!* Are you deaf? She does not want to marry you!" Using her umbrella, Marga speared his swinging leg.

Kenilworth glared at her aunt and then tied the horse's reins to a birch tree. When he turned, he stared at the pistol she aimed at his stomach.

"I'd at least wait until after our marriage. You'd be a wealthy widow."

She motioned with the weapon. "I've no intention of even being your bride. Now, move and let us leave."

"If you point a gun, you'd better be prepared to use it." With unblinking eyes, he stood erect. Hands on his hips. Legs apart.

Sabrina held his gaze and knew his rigid stance was a dare. She couldn't shoot him. Deep in her heart, she knew she would eventually have no choice except to marry him. Until then, she refused to relent.

Aiming the pistol to Kenilworth's right, she pointed at a lone birch. "Don't move, milord." As she lowered the hammer, his body stiffened. "Now, look to your left. Should I try for the left or right branch?"

"To your right. It's farthest from me."

Gritting her teeth, she focused and fired. Wood crackled and snapped. Birds squawked. She smiled, feeling an odd satisfaction. Somehow, the act replaced the dignity Kenilworth had stolen.

"Luck," Kenilworth murmured, eyeing the severed branch.

Feeling the challenge in his single word, her blood started to hum. With her arm raised, she sighted the other branch, but the fluttering of his greatcoat cape caught her eye. She shifted her gaze to just below his waist and adjusted her aim.

"If *that's* where you want to shoot me, go ahead." He didn't budge.

"*Ma chérie!* You proved your point!"

Sabrina ignored her aunt, cocked, shifted her arm and fired. Marga shrieked and the horses neighed. The air smelled of singed wool. The reality of her act reached her conscience. What if he had moved? What if she had shot him *there?* Blood rushed to her head and her hand shook. Despite this, she couldn't let Kenilworth see her despair or guilt and reached for words of bravado.

"I wanted to clip your wings two minutes after I met you."

Without examining the shredded tip of his cape, Kenilworth shortened the distance between them. His gaze held hers. A triumphant look made his eyes gleam. "Now, your gun's empty, and I won't need to worry about your life."

The telling sign in his eyes scorched her like lightning. He'd used mockery as a trick not a challenge. Instead of pruning his arrogance, she'd boosted it. The blow grated her pride and added to her careening emotions, but she clung to her bravado. "How do you know I won't shoot *you* *next* time?"

"You had the opportunity and didn't. Just in case, give me the pistol until you cool your temper." He held out his hand.

Quickly she hid the weapon behind her back. "You don't own me or my possessions yet, milord."

Despite the huge difference in their size and social class, Marga rapped Kenilworth's arm with her umbrella. "That is *ma chérie's* only weapon! Besides me, of course!"

"What are you going to do? Spear me again with your umbrella?" Kenilworth glowered.

A click sounded. "I could do more than that, *monseigneur!*"

Startled, Sabrina glanced at the winking knife that protruded from the umbrella, and she quickly searched her valise for her bullets. A knot formed in her throat. She knew Kenilworth would force her to go with him. Tears threatened to fall.

"Madame Beaumont, how clever. So, you too carry a weapon. Give it to me."

"I will not! This was my husband's umbrella! I have little of his but this."

After muttering a curse, he thrust his hand in the air. "Keep the blasted thing!"

Sabrina glanced at Kenilworth, who turned and marched in her direction. A tear rolled down her cheek. As she pawed deeper into her valise, her fingers finally found the bullet pouch. Too soon, he stood beside her.

"What? Tears?"

Slowly Sabrina lifted her gaze. Was that concern or mockery in his eyes? The angle of his head shadowed his face so she couldn't tell, but displaying weakness was unwise in this arrogant man's presence. Still she needed a reason for her damp eyes. "I have a thorn in my hand."

"Annoying varmints, aren't they? I've just experienced a few myself. They've a knack of working themselves deeper."

A second passed before she realized he'd called her a thorn. Perhaps he considered himself one, too. "We should both heed what we touch then, shouldn't we?"

The corner of his mouth twitched. "Now that you've spent your anger, are you ready to return to the castle?"

His faint conciliatory tone didn't soften her stance and if she agreed to return with him, she would admit defeat. "No."

Kenilworth's black brows snapped together. "I don't like this situation any more than you."

"I doubt that."

"Are you going into the coach willingly, or do I throw you inside?"

She took a step backward. "Don't touch me."

"Do you realize I could charge your aunt with assault? Would you like to see her in jail?"

"You wouldn't!"

He narrowed his eyes. "Try me." His tone exuded confidence.

Sabrina swallowed hard, knowing how horrible jail would be and that the twins needed Marga. He'd faced a bullet and remained adamant about their marriage. Perhaps she could escape again. Carefully she put her pistol back in her valise. "I should have shot you in the chest."

"You had the chance and...missed."

Her fingers itched to prove him wrong. "Your puffed-up chest makes a broad target, but a bullet wouldn't have done any damage."

"You don't consider a hole in my flesh a serious injury?"

"I would have aimed at your heart, but you don't have one."

He jerked his thumb left, then right. "Which direction, Miss Barrington? The castle or the authorities in Edinburgh?"

She lifted her chin. "Maybe I'll continue my stroll another time."

"Not without me, you won't."

Taking their valises, he escorted them to the coach and opened the door. A figure loomed inside. Every muscle in her body tensed.

"Good evening, Sabrina," Lord Sadlerfield said, and turned to the earl. "Well done, Kenilworth. My granddaughter obviously has her father's temperament."

Sabrina pursed her lips. "I'm proud of the comparison."

Her grandfather looked at Marga, and Kenilworth quickly made introductions. "So you are her kin. Madame Beaumont, you will stay until after their wedding. First to serve as witness and second to prepare Sabrina for the consummation."

Given the duke's stoic composure, Sabrina couldn't tell

what he knew about her aunt. She prayed he knew nothing but couldn't take the chance. "Your grace, if I must marry him, you should at least let me decide the place. I choose London."

Marga grabbed Sabrina's hand. "*Monseigneur.* Your grace. I have responsibilities in London. My shop and children need my attention. To stay another month is impossible!"

"You have a servant watching your whelps," the duke replied dismissively.

"I can't let her travel alone." Sabrina's heart stopped but she held her grandfather's stony glare. How much did he know? She prayed that he didn't see through the excuses. All they wanted was to return to the twins. The shop's future was as nebulous as her own.

"Young lady, after your act of defiance, I have decided you will wed within three days."

Two days later, Sabrina stood outside a tiny brick chapel on the castle's grounds. To the side, a cemetery lay with neat rows of headstones but she could almost hear her pounding heart amidst the serene setting. Behind her, the Sadlerfield barouche squeaked and footsteps approached. Marga dabbed her eyes with a handkerchief. Her grandfather wanted the ceremony to begin.

Tears crowded Sabrina's throat. "Even in my worst nightmares, I didn't imagine things happening this way."

Marga straightened. "We will talk after the ceremony. I have an idea that might ease the situation a little."

The reassuring words lifted Sabrina's spirits. "You always know the right thing to say."

As her grandfather moved beside her, he nodded to his footman to open the door. The hinges creaked and stale air hit her in the face, further reminders that this affair would hold no cherished memories. Terror lodged in her throat. As the only guest, Marga entered, her merino wool gown stirring the dust on the floor. She wiped the bench with her handkerchief and sat.

Sabrina fought the urge to run, but the duke took her arm and escorted her toward the altar, dark for the unlit tapers. Seasons of grime stained the windows and the dim light painted the interior gray. The brightest thing inside was the preacher's shiny head.

Her knees threatened to buckle, and her uneven stride echoed off the wood beneath her feet. Near the altar, Kenilworth stood erect. The pale light failed to hide the grim set of his jaw. He stuck a finger down his snowy cravat as if it were too tight. Considering the surroundings, his white linen shirt and ebony frock coat of superfine looked out of place.

The occasion didn't deserve finery. Sabrina touched her white pelerine collar and simple gray wool gown with pride. When she met Kenilworth's dark look she shortened her stride. Nothing or no one had prepared her for this moment or what might follow.

Lord Sadlerfield handed her to the earl then sat. When she hesitated to place her fingers in Kenilworth's, he pinned her with a black look. She slapped her hand against his broad, warm palm. The instant his long fingers curled around hers, she recalled the power they possessed. With only pride to rely upon, she thrust out her chin. She couldn't turn back.

Leaning toward her, Kenilworth smiled, but darkness clouded his eyes. "I take it you'll say the vows with the same intensity," he whispered, and tucked her hand on his arm.

"With the same sincerity as you will."

He turned to the clergyman. "Do the shortest version, sir."

The preacher's eyes darted from bride to groom. "Yes, milord." He cleared his throat. "Sabrina, will you have this man..."

Their hollow words resonated off the stone walls. Within minutes the ceremony ended. In that second, she realized he had failed to give her a wedding ring and sensed the blatant omission was a protest. Despite the forced marriage, the lack of a ring galled her.

"You may kiss the bride, milord."

Something urged her to deny him, and Sabrina stepped back.

Kenilworth seized her hand. "I think I will."

Suddenly he pulled her close, crushed his lips over hers, and that same odd sensation made her stomach churn. His clean-scented clothes heightened her senses. As his mouth grew softer, her mutinous body arched against his hard form. Warmth seeped across her skin, but when she realized she was returning his kiss, she snapped her head back. He was only kissing her for the audience and punishing her for her slight.

"That's enough, milord."

"My dear countess, that's just the beginning."

She stared into his green eyes, ones that glittered with dark promises. "Beginning?" The word came out a whisper.

Planting his broad hand on her back, he urged her up the aisle. "I made a devil's bargain with Sadlerfield. I accepted your scheming deal and made a vow to God. Do you know what that means?"

She licked her dry lips. "No."

"I'm your husband. You're my wife. As distasteful as that is to you, I intend to see you play the role well. A perfect countess. Is that clear?"

"I've no experience."

A slow smile matched the promise in his eyes. "I intend to teach you. Everything."

She shivered. "Dare I ask for specifics?"

He laughed.

The echo of Kenilworth's mocking laugh still rang in Sabrina's ears. "Marga, this marriage is going to be awful. He'll be here any minute. I'm sure he'll want to consummate the union."

As Sabrina conveyed Kenilworth's demand, she paced her new bedchamber, one that adjoined his. She moved around her Queen Anne dressing table, slid her finger over its mahogany surface. Taking several steps, she planted her hands on the back of the wing-backed chair where Marga sat. Sabrina wrinkled her nose at the wallpaper. Peacocks. A male with his pompously fanned tail hovered over a hen, it reminded her of Kenilworth.

Suddenly a tremor rippled through her. He exuded overpowering maleness, which caused her stomach to flutter during his kiss. Then as now, she dismissed the urge to examine the feeling. More important things needed her attention.

As she stared at the rose-patterned carpet, Sabrina realized her words had drifted into silence. "I must think of a new plan. I can't stay married to him."

Marga gasped. "We agreed you must do this for the twins."

Moving around the chair, Sabrina faced her aunt. "Remember we considered investigating Kenilworth?"

"*Oui.* Blackmail him. What good is that now?"

"Blackmail is an ugly word. Consider this! If we learn his secret through an investigation, he might consider an annulment."

"What about your *grandpapa?* He will never allow it."

"If I can convince Kenilworth, we could keep our plan secret. Once I reach my majority, Lord Sadlerfield loses his legal right to dictate my life. My birthday is just a few months away."

Marga tapped her nails on the brocade upholstery. "Then you must think of ways to stop him from bedding you."

Heat crept up her neck. "This is what you planned to tell me?"

"*Oui,* you might avoid the act until you know him better. It might not seem so distasteful to you then."

Loath to admit it, his kiss was anything but unpleasant. She frowned. "Why is that?"

"Not all women enjoy coupling. At least he is an attractive man. Once you acquaint yourself, you might find pleasure in sharing a bed. Did you forget the *Times*? They said he was a good man."

"Shabby reporting! Probably not a word of truth!"

"Possibly, but he did not ask for this marriage. You cannot fault a man who tries to turn a bad situation into good."

Sabrina snorted. "I want to return to London, speak to Geoffrey and at least consider an annulment. What if Kenilworth happens to meet the twins?"

"I doubt he will pay much notice. Your grandpapa is paying him money to produce an heir. His interest will be bedding you."

She pressed her palms over her ears. "Don't remind me! I can't give the duke an heir! Unless I reveal Alec, the babe would usurp my brother's rights." Yet, when she considered lying next to Kenilworth's hard form, the odd tingling sensation returned. She disliked her body's reaction. Sinking onto the bed, she ran her hand across the emerald velvet counterpane. "Can you think of anything to keep him from me?"

"Your monthly. A headache. Inebriation." Marga grimaced. "They are the usual excuses, but he will know what you are doing. If an annulment is the goal, you must invent new reasons."

"I'll think of something. Surely we can return to London before I run out of excuses. Then I'll ask for Geoffrey's help."

"Pray your grandpapa never learns what we are doing."

She groaned. "A chance exists to nullify my marriage. I want to explore the idea at least. What if Alec's health is better? We have money now and could leave! I can't do that if I'm married."

"You have a point. I wish we could take the twins far away from here. A place where your grandpapa would never find us."

Sabrina's heart ached, for she and the twins had never been apart. Suddenly she realized how much she took for granted—their incessant chattering and their rebuke of authority. She missed their cherub smiles and bright blue eyes, Alec's mischievous nature and Christine's thoughtful demeanor. She also worried Alec's health would worsen. "Do you think they're all right? Do you think they miss me? I don't like being separated from them.''

"Nor I. I miss them, and they are too young to understand if we are absent too long. With the ceremony over, we can finally return to London.''

A knock sounded on the adjoining door.

Sabrina started and wrung her hands. As she looked at her bare fingers, an idea burst forth.

# Chapter Five

Gripping the brass doorknob, Hunter knocked again. He glanced at his bed, a massive structure sitting atop a dais, anchored by four turned posts. Gold satin ropes secured the blue velvet drapes that hung from the canopy. No one had ever slept in his bed but him.

Fury burned his insides. Why did he bother knocking? She belonged to him, bought and paid for with his life. No one blackmailed him without punishment. If he were noble, he would thank God for sparing his life and turn his cheek, but he didn't believe he could. He refused to be a stone beneath Sadlerfield's feet. Or his wife's, either.

When no reply came, he cursed. This was his home. She was his wife, and he intended to make Sabrina his in all ways.

He had no choice.

Hunter kicked the door and it bounced against the wall.

''Your lordship!'' Sabrina spun around, her hand still on the outer entry.

As he leaned against the doorway, he crossed his arms over his chest. He gave her a casual perusal, one intended to stir his interest more than anything, but to couple under the duke's command seemed to stifle his base needs. Pushing away from the portal, he stepped into the room, one smelling of gardenias. He eyed the two crocheted buttons at her throat and walked toward her.

Her arm shot out and she took a backward step. "Wait! We should discuss our, uh…situation."

There was nothing to discuss. She'd blackmailed him and used him for target practice. If circumstances had been in her favor, she would have run from the altar. What was she up to now?

"Anything your aunt didn't explain, I will."

Panic flashed in her pale blue eyes, and the determined angle of her jaw put him on alert. "We didn't start our relationship in a good way. I'd like to feel better about us before…"

"We seal our vows?"

Pink spread across her cheeks. "Yes."

Pausing, he picked up the bottle of perfume from her dressing table and sniffed the heady scent. "What do you have in mind?"

She let out a long breath. "When we spoke the vows, we were both angry. I want them to…mean more."

Hunter laughed harshly. "You want to hear endearing words? We've one purpose in this marriage. To give your grandfather an heir."

"A ring might help. I don't feel that we're quite married."

Disbelieving her quiet words, he slammed down the bottle. "You've my name. That's enough. Don't expect me to spout Lord Byron's romantic prose or give you sentimental baubles."

She cast him a solemn look. "Won't people wonder about my lack of a ring?"

"Don't use society to blackmail me into giving you a trinket." Unfortunately, she had a point. With long strides, he closed the distance between them. He reached for her hands, studied her blunted nails and long slender fingers. They trembled in his palm, but he didn't know the reason. Her skin was rougher than he imagined, and something made him look at her palms. Calluses scarred each, suggesting she hadn't led a pampered life. He checked his thoughts. Feeling sorry for her had gotten him into this mess.

With his thumb, he rubbed a circle on her third finger. He dropped her hands. "The last time we made a deal, you ran with my money."

She flashed him a look that appeared to be regret, but then blossomed into desperation. "A little impulsive on my part. Only because my aunt needs to return to her children."

A man with half his wits could lose himself in her incredibly beautiful eyes, but he had his faculties and disliked caving in to her demand. Moreover, if he refused, he would never learn what she was thinking...or scheming. "Even if I wanted to postpone consummating our marriage, that's impossible."

"Have you no compassion? We're strangers. Is it that easy for you to bed a woman?"

"Do you want your grandfather standing over us? He promised to do just that if our sheets are clean. Would you like an audience?"

She flushed crimson from her cheeks to her neck. "Of course not."

When she lowered her head, Hunter thought she would succumb, but then she jabbed her fist in the air. He caught her wrist, but she twisted it from his hold.

Fury blazed in her eyes. "Impotent! That's what you are! If you were man enough to stand up to him, you'd think of a way to avoid this! You don't want me any more than I want you."

The accusation hit his gut like a lead ball and whipped his temper like nothing else she'd said or done. He quickly realized he disliked her rejection of him. After all, he possessed a title and wealth. Considering the situation, what more could a lady want? She might think he was doing nothing to strengthen his stance, but hell if he'd tell her his plans. He glared at her hard. "So you think me impotent, do you?"

She bumped up her chin. "Yes, I do."

In a lightning movement, he clamped his hands around her shoulders and crushed her lips with his own. Her sweet taste beckoned. Abruptly he released her. She took a gulping breath of air. He couldn't let her soft lips lure him beyond his anger.

With a swift flick of his wrist, he yanked her collar off her shoulders. Her eyes grew wide. The crocheted buttons bounced on the floor. "Get undressed. When I come back, you'd better be in my bed." Turning, he opened her door and slammed it behind him.

Hunter flew down the stairs, grabbed a lantern from the foyer. When he opened the door, Gavin stood on the other side.

"Bloody hell! Where are ye going?"

"To the conservatory." He motioned Gavin to join him and asked what Jonathan had learned. His solicitor had confirmed what Sadlerfield told him, but would need time to investigate the debt and Sabrina. In turn, Hunter explained the events during Gavin's absence.

The moonlight revealed Gavin's grim look. "Blasted! Ye sacrificed yourself. Why are ye going to the hothouse? Ye should be talking your scheming bride into bed."

"Looking for a red dye."

Gavin's blue eyes widened in understanding. "Ooh. Wouldn't it be simpler if ye just pricked your skin?"

"They've already stolen my life. Why should I give her my blood? Besides, that smacks of honor, and the last thing I feel is noble." *Impotent!* He snarled.

"Ye've the right. Just take her."

Hunter's blood ran cold. "A willing bride appeals to me more. If a few days will make her more agreeable, I won't have to live with guilt. Besides, I want to find out what she's planning. She ran away, and now seems almost…biddable."

"Aye, something doesn't quite ring true."

A few moments later they entered the conservatory. A rush of hot, humid air, smelling moldy and fragrant, hit Hunter in the face. The housekeeper cared for his mother's flowers, but they still looked neglected. Nostalgia wrenched his heart. How often had he watched his mother tend her plants and explain which ones provided good dyes for her paints? Shaking away the memories, he scooted around the wooden benches. Now wasn't the time to bask in her warmth.

"Damnation. Do you remember which one had sap that resembled blood?" Hunter scratched his head.

"Bloodroot?"

"Yes. Help me find the damn thing." As Hunter searched and pinched, he realized he'd accumulated a nosegay.

"Found it!" Gavin handed him the pot.

Taking the sprigs, Hunter added them to his bouquet. "She wants Lord Byron. She's going to get him." He paused. "I plan to give her a well-deserved lesson."

Kenilworth was torturing her with his absence. Sabrina sensed she would pay for her impulsive words. Would he demand his rights as a husband? She glanced at her cotton nightgown, one with ribbons lacing the front. With trembling hands, she tightened the bow at her neck.

She'd never seen a man in such an angry state. Beneath his fury, passion simmered. The taste of him lingered on her lips and made her tremble again.

She had no choice.

Without a doubt, she knew Lord Sadlerfield would hover over them as they…

Closing her eyes, she willed away the horrid image of such a spectacle. If she agreed to the consummation, her…husband might let her return to London with Marga. She had to believe he would be more agreeable once they finished the union. Dread and anticipation dampened her skin. She'd try to talk to him first. If all else failed, she would succumb.

Slowly she entered his bedchamber, which smelled of his clean scent. She glanced at his bed, rising like a blue sphinx in the room. Sheraton furnishings carved from mahogany graced the room. Stopping in front of a cheval mirror, she regarded her nightgown again. One powerful grip and he'd split the cloth from neck to toe. The image sent a tremor down her spine.

A creak in the hallway made her dash for the bed. She burrowed beneath the covers, and with only her nightgown hugging her, she searched for her rainbow. Unfortunately, nothing surfaced amid her surroundings. Kenilworth's clean scent clung to the bedsheets, a clear reminder of the man who could, with a touch or word, send her senses and emotions into a whirlwind.

Suddenly the door swung open and a mixture of fragrances filled the room. Stifling a cry, she pulled the counterpane to her chin. Kenilworth's flash of white teeth glowed brighter than the sconces lighting the room. She clung to the sheets.

"No need to look like a mummy." Closing the door, his gaze traveled from her feet to her hands and then to her face.

"The air's chilly."

"We'll warm the bed."

She forced herself to breathe. "I want to wait to consummate the marriage."

"Let's see if I can ease the situation."

"Does that mean you will?"

"I brought you some flowers." With a light step, he strolled to the bed and presented her with a courtly bow.

She narrowed her eyes. "What are you doing?"

Plucking a flower from his hand, he tucked it behind her ear. "Let go of the sheets."

When she ignored his command, he yanked the bed linens and dropped them at her feet. Alarm shot through her as she covered her bosom with her hands. A corner of his mouth curved. As he sat, his hips pressed against her thigh, their clothing forged a bridge between their flesh.

Fighting for a calm look, she tried to scoot away, but he planted his left hand on her other side. "Why did you bring me flowers?"

He placed the bouquet on his lap. After selecting a carnation, he stuck the stem through a lacing hole of her nightgown. "I've always liked it when a lady smells sweet." He bent and sniffed.

His face was so close to her breasts that she knew one movement would cause them to meet. She dared not breathe, but his warm breath filtered through her gown and a prickly sensation moved across her skin. When he straightened, she drew a quiet gulp of air. "Do I look like a vase yet?"

A slow grin broke the angled lines of his jaw. "Not quite."

She pursed her lips. "Why are you decorating me in flowers?"

"Smell this one." He pulled a lily from his lap and waved the petals beneath her nose.

The heady scent thickened the air around them. Taking her hand, he wrapped her fingers around the stem and held them in place. He brought the flower to his nose, looked down at her with half-lowered lids. Trembling, she desperately tried to hide her fear.

Releasing her hands, Kenilworth put the bouquet on the bed, then shrugged out of his frock coat. He tossed it onto the floor. Belatedly she realized that he no longer trapped her, and slid a good foot away from him.

He untied his cravat and threw it on the sheets. "Keep going. You're in the middle of the bed. I need a little more room than that." He eyed the space between her and him.

Her pulse soared. "Milord, you're exercising your rights?"

Sitting, he pulled off his boot and the mate followed. "You haven't moved. I'm coming to bed."

Angst mutated to anger and she punched his back. "Answer my questions! I've a right to know what to expect from you!"

Flinching, he looked over his shoulder with narrowed eyes. "I could say the same of you."

He padded to the fireplace and threw in kindling and peat. Flint grated and flames crackled to life, sending another sweet scent into the air. Moving from the lantern on his bureau to the one atop his secretary, he blew out the flames in each.

Sabrina captured a calming breath. She'd never lost control before, and this man possessed a powerful aura that sent her emotions careening. His lithe movements resembled a predatory animal stalking a fledgling.

He moved to the sconces. "Would you put out the candle on your side table? I'll get the one on my stand."

Glancing to her right, Sabrina grimaced as she moved. Her weight crushed the flowers. She put out the candle, but after laying down the snuffer, she curled her fingers around the silver candlestick. For one second she considered crowning him on the head. Suddenly she experienced a pang of guilt. He'd brought the flowers as a peace offering. Hadn't he?

"Don't even consider it."

"I'm trying to curb my impulses." Turning, she reached for the flowers beneath her. When she brought the destroyed bouquet to her nose, she drew a sharp breath. Red liquid covered her fingers.

"Did you enjoy our consummation?"

Slowly she realized what he had done. She should have been grateful. "You lout! Letting me believe you were going to do it."

With an unreadable expression, he crawled into bed. "I might yet. Can't say what will happen between now and morning."

She whacked him with the bouquet. Petals flew like leaves in the wind. "You're cruel! This wasn't funny!"

He grabbed her wrist, held her gaze with stony green eyes. Their breath came short and hot, stirring the clove scent that hung between them. His clasp made her fingers go numb. The flowers dropped on his chest.

"Cruel? You want to know what that would be? I'd have ripped off your gown and not prepared you for anything."

Warmth invaded her flesh followed by another surge of guilt. She didn't fully understand his words, but his harsh tone said enough. He could do anything he wanted. He owned her. Resentment bubbled anew, and she had to force a conciliatory smile. "You're right. Let's talk about something else."

Releasing her hand, he looked down on his flower-covered chest. Swipes of red and green stained his shirt. "About what?"

"Have you booked passage for our return to London?"

"I've arranged your aunt's. My friend Gavin will escort her."

"You have friends?" The second the words flowed, she wanted them back. She didn't want to rile his temper again.

The muscles in his neck tightened. "Go to sleep."

Slowly she gathered the flowers off his chest, taut as a board. "What about us? Why can't we return to London with Marga? She's the creative one. I'm the one who manages the business side."

"You don't own the shop anymore. I do."

As his words slowly registered, anger burned her insides. By marriage law, her share of the shop now belonged to him. He was controlling her life. "What do you want with a dress shop?"

"The records. Someone swindled me out of six thousand pounds. I think I should know the source of the debt. Don't you?" His eyes turned as hard as granite.

Deuced. He was a man who didn't like to lose, and she'd blackmailed him. "I can't change your mind about London?"

Taking the bouquet from her hand, he dropped it on his side table. "No, but unless you go to sleep, I might change my mind about consummating our vows."

She dropped back. "Will the flowers work? Are we safe from my grandfather? Why did you do this?"

"I'm emulating Lord Byron."

# Chapter Six

A group of stevedores walked between Sabrina and Kenilworth. Chains and winches groaned as workers hauled sails and moved crates for shipment from Leith to their destinations. Welcoming the intrusion and din, Sabrina grasped Marga's hands. "You've Kenilworth's banknote?" she whispered.

Tears filled her aunt's eyes, but she quickly brushed them away. "*Oui.* It is unfortunate your grandpapa insists on remaining here for Mr. MacDuff's wedding. I dislike leaving you alone with the duke and *monseigneur,* but I have no choice. The twins need me more. Do you have qualms about our plan?"

She slid Kenilworth a surreptitious glance. "No. When you and I came to Scotland, we discussed the side trip. Your request will have merit. Go. Ask him now." Sabrina urged Marga with a nudge.

Kenilworth was speaking to the blond man named Gavin, Marga's escort. When his lordship had introduced them earlier, the captain had been coolly polite. She wouldn't find a friend in him. Behind them, the schooner *Priscilla* bobbed in the water and that ship would take her aunt to London. Sabrina hoped they'd not encounter rough weather. She planned to write Geoffrey so he could make her the twins' guardian, just in case Marga died at sea. She swallowed hard, unwilling to consider the dark thought. They must plan for accidents, too. With linked arms, she and Marga closed the ten paces between them and the men.

"*Monseigneur.* I have a favor to ask you before I leave."

Kenilworth glanced down with unreadable eyes. "What is that, Madame Beaumont?"

"The delay in Scotland has prohibited me from going to Dunfermline. I had planned to purchase some linen there. Would you be kind enough to take Sabrina?"

"Today if possible. We've lacked a supply for over a month because of our—" Sabrina's throat closed "—predicament."

"*Monseigneur,* I must open my shop, and I haven't the goods I need."

His green eyes assessed her aunt's face. "I don't know if I should allow you to resume business. Did you forget the debt and records? My solicitor intends to look at them."

Sabrina stepped in front of her aunt. "Look here, sir. My aunt was—*is* the most sought after couturiere in London. The shop makes money. Don't you care about your *investment?*"

He surveyed her from head to toe. "I'm looking at it."

With fists clenched, she forced a conciliatory smile. Yes, he owned her, too. "The events of the past week have been trying. Consider the request."

His smile didn't reach his eyes. "All right, Madame Beaumont. I wouldn't want your niece to think I've no mind for business. We'll get your cloth."

"*Merci, monseigneur.*" Her aunt had the grace and foresight to bow her head.

Sabrina let out a huge silent breath. "Thank you." Showing appreciation couldn't hurt, especially since she needed him to trust her just a little for her plan to work. "May we go today?" Suddenly she realized she sounded too anxious. "We're already at the docks, and Dunfermline is just across the firth."

He nodded curtly. "We've an errand in Edinburgh first."

A few moments later, Sabrina waved to her aunt. Already

air filled the sails, resembling giant pillows against a gray counterpane. The air smelled of rain. As the storm that had killed her parents unfurled in her mind, a prickling sensation inched down her spine. No! Everything was her grandfather's fault. They wouldn't have been at sea had it not been for him. Dropping her trembling hand, she whirled away and hurried toward his lordship's coach.

Although Kenilworth was on her heels, she beat him and the driver to the door. She yanked it open. Plopping down onto a leather squab, she laced her fingers tightly. "Let's attend your business."

"No curiosity about why I agreed to take you to Dunfermline?" He slid into the seat across from her and eyed her steadily.

"Your affairs are your own."

"I only agreed so we'd have some time together."

Sabrina's blunt nails dug into her hands.

Hunter's long, heavy stride kicked up amber leaves. He and Sabrina walked down Edinburgh's Princes Street where well-heeled citizens observed the gardens and entered fashionable shops. Smelling faintly of Scotch whiskey, the air teased Hunter's nose, and, despite the early hour, he considered indulging in a tankard of ale himself. Yet, he didn't dare. The letter she just tried to post would have been a bullet to his gut. He still couldn't believe she would pursue an annulment behind his back.

Now, besides preserving his own hide and Gavin's, he also needed to stay alert. Hunter thought he had passed the worst moment of his life by entering into an unwanted union. Taming her was his mission…that and to investigate her and Sadlerfield's past. He wanted to gain the upper hand. The person who caused the debt weighed on his mind, too, as did his father's whereabouts. Dissolving the marriage never entered his mind. He should have learned from her past actions.

Sabrina's recent deed in the goldsmith's shop proved she'd

continue to defy him, thwart his intentions. Planning his caveat pumped his blood. He tightened his hold.

Just when they reached his coach, a little boy ran beside them. "Milord! Pansies fer yer lady?"

Hunter's heart twisted, sending a thick lump to his throat. Gooseflesh riddled the lad's exposed arms, and his toes curled and flexed against the cobblestone walk. Drooping violets provided a color relief to his faded garb.

Hunter released Sabrina's arm. "Take the flowers."

She threw him an uncertain glance, then accepted the bouquet. Pausing, Sabrina looked down at the urchin who appeared no more than half-a-dozen years old.

Reaching into his pocket, Hunter retrieved a handful of shillings and pressed them into the lad's upturned palm. "Find some warm clothes and a cobbler. Winter will arrive soon."

The boy beamed, and his amber eyes turned round and shiny as the coins. "Thank ye, milord!"

Sabrina brushed the child's cheek with a trembling hand and her eyes glistened with tears. Suddenly Hunter saw her as just a woman with a tender soul, and something odd tugged at his heart that further stoked his sympathy. Looking abashed, the boy made an awkward bow and dashed away.

When Hunter moved to take her arm, Sabrina's letter to Norton rustled in his pocket. He straightened, suppressed his emotion for the child, for the unnamed feelings her tears evoked. Grabbing her arm, he pulled her upright. How could he be so stupid as to show his compassion? He forgot Sabrina's keen eyes and quick mind.

Hunter helped Sabrina into his coach and it dipped as he seated himself. The interior quickly captured the mingled scents of gardenias, violets and rich leather. He rolled up the shades.

Sabrina adjusted the skirt of her dark brown traveling gown and gave him a wavering smile. "You were very kind to help him."

His jaw worked. "I purchased the flowers to get rid of the

lad. Don't make my act into anything more.'' He nodded toward the violets she still held in her hand. ''You wanted romantic baubles? You have them. Flowers and that ring on your finger.''

As she hit the leather seat with her fist, the violet petals flew helter-skelter. ''More cynicism? Isn't one jest on me enough?''

''Perhaps when you quit fighting our marriage.'' From the pocket of his gray frock coat, he removed a missive. ''Slipping the goldsmith a letter to your solicitor? Do not try to contact him again. Is that clear?'' He threw her a piercing look.

Mutiny glimmered in her eyes. ''My father told me never to submit to a man's demands unless I agreed with them in my heart. I *cannot* wear this ring.''

''No more foolishness like this. No more ideas about annulments.'' He held the letter she'd written to her solicitor.

She looked down at her tightly clasped hands. ''The missive wasn't just about that. My aunt has…children. If something happened to her, we needed to arrange for my guardianship.''

''Nothing will happen to her.'' As they passed St. Giles tower, Hunter ripped the letter into shreds and tossed it out the window.

She glared at him. ''I had no idea you're a prophet. Your visions should tell you that we've no future together.''

''Say it,'' he said in a commanding tone. ''Say you *will not* write him again or we'll return to Keir Castle.''

''All right. I'll not pen him another missive.'' She furrowed her brow. ''Why haven't you considered an annulment?''

If only he could. To admit it, though, would only encourage her rebellious nature. ''We'll discuss our marriage.''

With compressed lips, she started to take off the newly purchased ring. ''This will never work. I don't even like you.''

Hunter pressed his hand over both of hers. He realized her demand for the ring had been a deterrent, a way to avoid consummating their union. She wanted to end their marriage. "You asked for the ring. You got it. Now wear it."

As if she recalled her own excuse for not consummating the marriage, her fingers tensed and suddenly grew warm. Her reaction to his touch invited a carnal urge more hazardous than his stupidity. Suppressing the untimely feelings, he released her hands.

"Our marriage isn't a matter of liking, but of showing more enthusiasm. People know me in Edinburgh. Unless you want them to ask questions, you'd better change your attitude."

"I said I wouldn't ask the reason you are beholden to my grandfather. That is the only motive you have for staying in this marriage. No one will believe we're…happy…no matter what I do."

"Our job is to make people trust with their eyes. Addressing me as Hunter will help. A smile wouldn't hurt. A couple should act informally. Can you manage that? Try it."

She smirked. "Hunter."

As he summoned his shredded patience, he shook his head. "You said it as if you are ill. Say my name without wrinkling your nose."

Heaving a deep sigh, Sabrina rolled her eyes. "How can we explain how we met?"

"The truth. You came to see me about an account. Then, to add credence to our union, I'll kiss your palm and cheek. That's socially acceptable."

"Oh?" Sabrina jabbed a finger to her chest. "I don't accept it!"

"Don't fight my physical attention. The more you display your unwillingness, the more you'll force me to curb your defiance. Cooperate and you might find a little enjoyment from our charade."

With disbelief in her eyes, she snorted. "Enjoy? Never!"

The shadowed interior of the coach didn't hide her suddenly pink cheeks or the tip of her tongue wetting her full lips. Was hers the reaction of an innocent, or one who fleetingly considered the enjoyment his attentions might bring? He preferred to think the latter. Despite his plan and authoritative words, he didn't want to unnerve her.

"Thou protest too much," he said lazily. "Like it or not, I'll teach you to act like a properly married lady before we return to Keir Castle."

"I won't."

"You will."

The cragged hills of Edinburgh flattened as they neared Leith again. Hunter glanced at Sabrina as she stared out the window. Women and sailors laughed at private jests. A seaman grappled a whore's breast, and in return, she reached between his legs. Sabrina's cheeks turned rosy. Hunter snapped the shades down.

Starting, she fixed her gaze on him. "Why did you do that?"

"Saving you from life's vulgarities." Though the marriage would shield him from ruination and scandal, he felt an urge to prevent her from harm. His father was somewhere...

"Hear ye! Attend thy meetin'!" a man yelled from outside.

"What about a voice in Parliament?" another fellow said.

Hunter raised the window flap and swore silently. If Sabrina hadn't disrupted his life, he would be at this assembly supporting the Reform Bill. The proposal would help the Scots obtain a voice in Parliament and end slavery in the West Indies.

"What's the ruckus?" She drummed her fingers on the leather squab now littered with the shriveled pansies.

"Abolitionists."

"What are they abolishing? Arrogant lords of the realm?"

He drilled her with a sharp look. "Slavery in the West Indies. Never mind. You probably don't read the newspapers."

A flash of indignation brightened her eyes, but then a mocking smile curled her lips. "Then I'm right! They *do* want to abolish lords of the realm. People aren't pleased with Parliament. Raising taxes. Deplorable working conditions. Low wages. No voice in government. That crowd is using the slavery issue to show Parliament's unfairness.''

Speechless, Hunter stared at her for a long moment.

"The newspapers say you're a Whig, but undoubtedly, you're a Tory. They oppose reform, and don't give a wink about the common people. Or freedom for the slaves, either. I should join them. After all, I'm your prisoner for life.''

His blood raged just to find a suitable retort. "Your knowledge of languages and politics is commendable. But neither matches your ability to scheme. What else are you skilled at? Inventing numbers?'' His tone was very dry.

Suddenly the coach came to a jolting halt.

"Out of me way!'' The driver's whip sliced the air.

"Hey fellas! See the crest?'' a person said.

The coach started rocking.

Hunter glanced at Sabrina. "Stay here.'' As he stepped outside, shadows from the placards fell over his face.

"Ye'r one of 'em. What excuse does Parliament 'ave? Eh? When do we get a voice?''

"Tell 'em 'tis not the Middle Ages!'' said another man. "We're no better off than the slaves are. No voice. No vote.''

As Hunter gazed across the sea of placards and people, he searched for Dr. Ramsay, the leader. Some faces carried a look of hope while others carried the look of hate. Hunter pulled a leather pouch filled with gold sovereigns from his frock coat pocket.

A man edged forward wearing a cleric's collar. His hat brim flew back, exposing white hair. "Aye! Your lordship. Glad to see ye home!'' A smile deepened the creases in Dr. Ramsay's sun-weathered cheeks.

"I'm glad to be home.'' Hunter started to hand him the pouch. "This is for our cause but I can't stay.''

The minister's brows arched. "Well! Who's the bonny lady?''

Turning, Hunter saw Sabrina approach.

"I'm his pri—''

"Princess. She's my little princess. My wife.'' He gripped

her elbow hard, smiled and warned her with the darkest look he could manage.

The minister's questioning gaze shifted from Sabrina to Hunter. "Your wife?"

"Of just a day." Hunter introduced them.

The cleric bowed. "My blessin'."

"Dr. Ramsay, I'm—"

"She's delighted to meet you. Take this." Hunter dropped the pouch into the minister's palm. Turning, he threw her a hard look, demanding silence. Anger flushed her face. "Princess, do you want to return to Keir Castle?" he asked in a dangerously soft tone.

Sabrina shook her head slightly.

With his eyes fixed on the pouch, the minister jiggled it and the metal scraped a rich sound. He raised his head. "Obliged, your lordship. I'll see that the crowds lets ye pass. See you at Gavin's weddin', Lady Kenilworth."

Hunter quickly helped Sabrina into the coach, then followed her inside. Closing the door softly, he pounded on the roof. His princess came very close to causing a scandal. With prim innocence, Sabrina sat with her hands folded on her lap.

Pulling his cravat off his neck, he twisted the ends of the silk fabric around his hands. "If you attempt to thwart me again, I *will* stuff this in your mouth."

She flinched and spared the cravat a glance. "Bribing them with coins to let us leave won't take away their problems."

"Do not pretend innocence or change the subject. We're going back to Keir Castle." He yelled instructions to the driver.

"No! Wait! What about my linen? What about Dunfermline?"

"Too bad."

"Wait. What if I promised—"

"Not to tell the world you're a 'prisoner' for life? Have you forgotten your grandfather?"

She licked her lips and looked undecided. "All right."

"Say it." He pointed at her.

''I promise I won't tell anyone I'm a prisoner.''

''Should we meet anyone else I know, who are you?''

''Sabrina...Sinclair.''

''And you're my?'' He arched his brow, a warning that his question had one answer.

''Your wife.'' She spit out the words. ''Hunter! Have your driver turn this—''

''My little princess, we're not finished.'' He twisted the cravat around his hands again. ''You don't listen well, do you? If I say 'stay,' you do not move. Announcing this marriage on the docks of Leith isn't what I planned.''

She arched a delicate eyebrow. ''What *do* you have planned? Don't I have a right to know?''

He leaned toward her. ''No.''

''Well, if someone asks us why we decided to marry, *you* answer. I can't think of one reason, unless we tell the world my grandfather forced us.''

Inexplicably, her words stung and presented a challenge. Hunter threw the cravat over her head and, though she struggled, he pulled her to his seat. ''Oh, I can. Can you?''

''Anything I say is a guess.'' She tilted her head away from him.

Warm breath from her softly parted lips touched his face. His mouth went dry. He skimmed the pad of his thumb over her lower lip. She inhaled a sharp breath. He found ignoring her gardenia scent impossible, something that had plagued him for miles.

''I'll show you a reason people marry,'' he said in a tone mingled with fury and desire.

Sabrina started to rise. ''Let me go!''

Yanking on the cravat, he brought her down. She struggled and planted her palms against his chest. When Hunter lowered his lips onto hers, they quivered with anger. Or was it anticipation?

As he brushed his lips against hers, he absorbed the soft texture and gentle contours. He stroked her back as if each movement would tame her defiance. Yet she squirmed beneath his palm. Anxiety or fury?

The pressure of her hands eased, one moving to his shoulder while the other dropped to his thigh. He sucked in his breath, let out a silent groan. His blood grew thick. When she arched closer, her body softly molded against his chest.

Desire warred with his plan, but a satisfied sigh still escaped. He liked taming the minx in this manner. Hunter shifted his legs to ease the discomfort in his loins. With his tongue, he traced her mouth with a feathered touch and gently dipped it between her softly parted lips. Her tongue retreated as if inviting him to plunder further. When her hand slid up his thigh, every muscle tensed, forcing his heart into an erratic beat.

Damnation, he wanted her. The realization made heaven crash. Quickly releasing her, he pretended nonchalance.

"I can think of another reason people marry," he said with dry mockery. "Would you like a demonstration?"

With the back of her trembling hand, she wiped her lips. The passion drained from her eyes. She raised her chin and flared her delicately sculptured nose.

Her silent insult made him feel low, pricked his pride. Guilt thinned his blood. Yet whether she would admit the truth or not she responded to his kiss. As he waited for a verbal denial, he held her gaze in a silent challenge. The movement of her arm caught his eye, and before he realized her intent, her palm met soundly with his cheek. Wincing, he caught her arm, but the slap chafed his self-esteem more than his flesh.

"You'll never seduce me enough to get me into your bed. So, if anyone asks why we married, you explain! Now, turn this coach around!" She tugged the bottom of her pelisse and pulled her matching cloak squarely on her shoulders.

"Besides your grandfather's demand for an heir, I gave you one. Passion. People do marry for passion, and don't tell me you didn't enjoy my kiss. Passion doesn't lie." He smiled devilishly then yelled at the driver to turn the coach around.

Her pale blue eyes glowed with anger, and for a moment,

they sat in silence. Sabrina gazed out the window and he stared at her. What was she thinking? Her mind was too quick to let it sit still for long. After this latest encounter with her, he didn't believe for a minute that she just wanted linen. What did she want in Dunfermline?

Sabrina finally faced him. "When's Gavin's marriage to occur?"

Hunter shrugged. "Three weeks. Maybe four. When the castle is in order."

"Weeks! What about my aunt? She can't manage alone for that length of time. If you'd just let me leave, neither of us would suffer this charade. Wouldn't you like that?"

"The matter of allowing you to leave isn't negotiable. I thought you understood that. You'll attend Gavin's wedding."

She scowled at him and fell back into the squab.

Hunter couldn't deny the desperation in her voice, but Sabrina had proved her cleverness more than once. She wanted out of their marriage. What besides the shop was so important to her? He'd find out, even if he had to kiss the secret from her lips.

"Our trip to Dunfermline will be our whirlwind wedding trip. We'll use the time to learn about each other."

"Haven't you listened to anything I've said? I need to go home!"

"Unlike you, I listen very well. However, you did agree to acknowledge yourself as my wife." He leaned close to her. "That means playing the role well."

She sat straighter. "You won't always win." With folded arms, Sabrina tapped her fingers against her pelisse.

"On that score, you're wrong. I always win." He gave her an arrogant grin. Most women would plot to become his wife. All she wanted was to leave. With every drum of her fingers, he imagined her concocting a way to thwart him. Little did she know that he possessed vast experience unraveling and destroying schemes.

*   *   *

They boarded a two-mast schooner for Dunfermline and
Hunter took the helm. His white linen shirt rippled across his
back and emphasized its broadness. Sabrina's fingers twitched
as she remembered his solid legs, now poised in a sailor's
stance. Midnight hair brushed his shirt collar, and he looked
more like a pirate than a nobleman, more like a rogue than a
gentleman. He made her feel like a fool.

As she recalled her wanton behavior, heat embedded her
cheeks. How could she succumb to his kiss so willingly? She
paced the deck and could still feel her lips quivering from his
persuasive mouth. If she didn't watch herself, she'd find herself in his bed. That couldn't happen.

He had humiliated and bruised her dignity countless times,
but the sea air cleared her head. The cold wind against her
cheeks sharpened the marriage to stark reality. Attending a
society wedding didn't fit her plans. For her part, fooling a
soul would be blind luck. Her social inexperience aside, she
didn't want a man who made sport of kissing her to initiate
her into womanhood. Eventually he would. When?

Any guilt she experienced for breaking her promises to him
died quickly. She must focus on standing up for the twins.
Passion and a conniving husband claimed no part in her future. Inexplicably, the thought made her feel a little empty.

No matter. The ring wouldn't stay on her finger for long.
She had a plan that any military strategist would envy.

# Chapter Seven

"A wig maker could make a fortune from the hair of those cattle." The pungent smell of wet animals made Sabrina's stomach turn. Though she held her breath and fanned her face, she gained nothing but a second of relief.

Shifting, she faced the city. Like floating goose down, smoke from the coal and peat fires spiraled up the chimneys in Dunfermline. The drovers waved in silent appreciation for giving them the road.

"Those shaggy beasts are highland cattle. Put this over your nose." Hunter pressed a handkerchief into her hand.

Without hesitation, Sabrina accepted the offering and covered the lower part of her face. For some reason, the sandalwood scent reminded her of his brash kiss. More, his small gesture suggested he possessed some compassion and regard for a person's discomfort. This stole a bite from the resentment she harbored. She didn't want to think he possessed any goodness, for this could hinder her plan.

She must take advantage of his mood and convince him to reconsider their marriage. The trip from Dunfermline to Leith would be her last opportunity. If she failed, she'd have no choice but to continue with her ruse to escape.

"The beasts are gone. Are you all right? You're very quiet."

Turning, she held out the handkerchief. "Thank you."

"Keep it. We might encounter another herd."

She twisted the cloth in her gloved hand until the square became damp and wrinkled.

The two other wagons driven by hired men began climbing the hill. As the hoofprints and wheels formed rivulets, seeping moisture created prisms in the road. Hunter flicked the reins and harnesses groaned. The Clydesdale horses breathed white clouds, and, with lowered heads nearly touching their massive chests, the beasts obeyed. As they dug their hooves into the sodden earth, mud clumped on the animals' white fetlocks. After the rain had stranded them in Dunfermline an extra day, Sabrina was going home if things went as she planned. She hoped...

"Tonight we'll arrive at Keir Castle. You've not come to terms about our marriage. We should have spent these past few days learning about each other." Hunter turned, looking down at her.

"Why do you want a wife who doesn't want you? I know you didn't marry me just to save my reputation."

Suddenly he cupped her chin and pressed his strong, gloved fingers against her flesh. "Imagine living your life with an undeserved reputation. You wouldn't like it. Once lost, no amount of money can buy back your respectability."

Sabrina held her breath and wondered what caused the bitterness in his voice. As he lessened his grip, the coldness in his gaze evaporated and mutated to a dusky green hue. When she realized the darkness in his eyes carried the same sultry look they had before he kissed her, she cautiously pulled her chin away.

The recollection caused an unwelcome tremor, not from panic, but from the strange sensations the kiss had evoked. She recalled her shortness of breath, her pounding heart, the way her insides seemed to take on a life of their own. Sabrina shook away the memory. Since she knew Hunter married her under duress, she doubted that her reputation was important to him.

"Once you even thought I was a courtesan. You can't like me very much if you thought that."

"That's not important now, but if you're still thinking about an annulment, forget it."

Disappointment weighted her soul. "Why would you accept anything I say about myself?"

"Maybe I just want you to try to convince me."

Although she'd avoided discussing herself, she recalled his earlier vow. "Are you still planning to investigate the debt?"

"I already am."

A cold chill ran through her. Undoubtedly he was investigating her, and Marga, too. "Did you learn anything before we left for Dunfermline?"

"Are you afraid I'll learn why you blackmailed me?"

Her pulse raced. "No. And I don't regret what I did."

He shrugged. "I never thought for a moment you would. But I might learn to live with it if you'd start acting like a wife. That's what you promised me in exchange for the money."

"I'm not after your fortune. Haven't I offered to return this ostentatious ring though I know it costs a veritable sum?"

"Too often to count."

"Would a truly dishonest individual offer to return valuable jewelry? Of course not. That person would *never* give the ring back to you. In my case, all I wanted was what you owed me, nothing more. Consider the logic of that."

"Maybe you're not a thief, but you still schemed to get that ring."

Sabrina's face warmed. "I did no such thing."

He raised a brow. "Well, giving the ring to you was *my* choice. If you're telling the truth about the debt, then someone else is responsible. That's not my choice. Don't you want to find out who tricked us?"

"Of course!"

"Then until I learn something, I'll put your little blackmail scheme aside. We're husband and wife now." He leaned close. "Act like it."

Her heart plummeted further. The request for the ring seemed the basis for the farce, but was he concerned about her reputation? She pushed away the chivalrous thought. Her emotions for him would hinder her plans. "My mind is on business. Perhaps once my fabric is safely aboard a ship, and en route to London, I can think more about the marriage."

"Just remember your grandfather awaits us. And unless you want him to observe us in bed, you'd better decide to accept our union."

She swallowed hard. "He wouldn't have to know if we ended the marriage. In several months, I'll reach my majority. He won't have any control over me."

He let out a harsh laugh. "Can't you let the idea of an annulment go? Your age won't stop a man like Sadlerfield. Even now, he's probably pounding his cane because we left Edinburgh without him."

Her throat went dry. "Did you send him a message?"

"A brief one. I told him our marriage bed was too crowded. You, me, Lord Byron and himself."

She brought the handkerchief to her brow and cheeks. They were entering a dangerous territory. Over the delicate edge of the linen, she glanced at her...husband.

At first a bland look veiled his face, but then the corner of his mouth curled and his green eyes sparkled with mischief. She pressed her knees together. Her anklebones rubbed from the wagon's sway and jolts. Since he wouldn't consider an annulment, she must pretend acceptance.

Suddenly his closeness made her very aware of his maleness, of his arm and thigh rubbing against hers as the wagon rocked. The cadence of her pulse ticked out of time. Since their wedding night, he'd slept with her but hadn't touched her. She knew now he still intended to validate their marriage. A horse shook his head, jangling his harness, and if not for the sound, Hunter might have heard her pounding heart.

She considered her plan and decided it was now necessary. "I'll need to find a ship that's nearly loaded. Paying for the whole vessel isn't something I can afford."

"Perhaps I can help." Again he leaned close. "Remember our marriage makes me your aunt's partner. I know the harbormaster. He'll need a freight list."

A wheel hit a rut, and she grabbed the wagon's arm. Sabrina kept forgetting he owned her and everything that she considered hers. She grasped the wooden arm so tightly that her fingers began to cramp. "Of course. I know that."

"Are you accepting my offer of help?"

"How can I refuse such a generous overture?" Although her voice didn't quite have a sincere ring, she met his eyes. Was that a look of relief on his face?

"Then no more discussing annulments or business. Let's have a proper conversation. How do you entertain yourself in the evening?"

Sabrina pretended to be accommodating. "Tell me what you do during your evenings?"

A mischievous glint brightened his green eyes. "Take care where you direct this conversation. You know what I think we should be doing of an eve."

She hoped the sun answered for the warmth in her cheeks and scrambled for a different topic. "Do you play the piano? I do."

He chuckled, apparently enjoying her discomfiture. "I'll play for you sometime."

"Fine. Shall I tell you about my friend Geoffrey? He's my solicitor."

"Why not?" he asked in a clipped tone.

She slid him a measured glance but didn't stop to question his mood change. Discussing anything was better than their consummation. "I met him when I was sixteen. Besides being a *wonderful* person, he's warm, compassionate, reliable and he loves children." The wistful recollections of Geoffrey playing with the twins made her smile.

"Your friend sounds like a well trained dog," Hunter said with dry amusement.

"Well, he's nothing like you! Geoffrey's smarter!"

The humor in his eyes faded. "He can't be that intelligent.

He doesn't even know who you really are. And he should have investigated the debt so you didn't have to come here.''

His defacing words made her wish to defend Geoffrey more. "He gives me sound advice and helps at the shop. Our friendship goes beyond helping with legal matters.''

"I see. Norton's counsel isn't sound if he advised you to seek my audience. If a lady were important to a gentleman, he would never allow a lady to visit a bachelor. Why did Norton suggest such a trip? Perhaps he isn't a gentleman.''

Before coming to see Hunter, she had believed *she* could resolve the situation. Until now, she had always managed to control her life despite the odds, and never failed at anything if she set her mind to the task. The reminder made her sit straighter.

"Well? Why did he allow you to come?''

Sabrina slapped the wooden arm. "Geoffrey *is* a gentleman! He trusts and believes in me. He will not like it that I've been gone so long.''

"Are you insinuating he'll come looking for you?''

Sabrina smiled innocently. "He might.''

"A little late to rescue you from the altar, don't you think?''

She bumped up her chin. "Geoffrey knows I have no wish to marry. When he learns, he'll think I've lost my wits.''

"He obviously doesn't know you like I do. So why do you oppose marriage?'' His tone was very dry.

"I've a *special* dislike for men in Parliament. They're pompous idiots.''

The corner of his mouth curved. "All of them?''

"Every one of them.'' Sabrina looked into his eyes, now twinkling with light, but his unnerving smile sent an odd sensation rippling through her stomach.

"Why is that?'' he asked in a tone that curiously bore a hint of disappointment.

"They're selfish beyond measure and—''

Suddenly grating wood made her look over her shoulder. She gasped. A linen-filled crate protruded from beneath the canvas cover and was hanging over the edge of the wagon. "The rope's loose!"

"If we stop, we'll get stuck. Can you handle the reins?"

"I can drive a carriage."

"Good enough. Don't let the horses stop." Hunter thrust the reins into her hands then scrambled on top of the crates. On his hands and knees, he edged toward the back of the wagon and pulled the crate forward.

Sabrina experienced a surge of gratitude. She didn't ask for his help, and he didn't offer, but acted on instinct.

Wood scraped against wood and the wagon dipped. When she glanced over her shoulder, she held her breath. The crates had slid toward the rear with Hunter lying on top. A chill slithered down her spine. What if he lost his grip? What if he fell and the crates crushed him? Cold sweat glazed her skin.

For one insane second, she envisioned herself a widow.

She pictured her grandfather presenting her with another candidate for a husband.

"Don't hurt yourself! Are you all right?"

"Keep going!"

The canvas flapped like a sail, and crates grated with an eerie crescendo as he uttered oaths. Rhythmic puffs of air bellowed out of the horses' nostrils. The other two wagons disappeared over the ridge. Splintering wood, a thud, and a string of expletives followed his declaration. Hunter!

Sabrina twisted around and let out a deep, calming breath. Though the pitch of the wagon threatened to send him over the edge, he was safe. In one hand he held a lid, while his other hand held a crate. Her heart sank when she noticed several bolts of cloth lay impaled in the mud. When they reached the crest, Sabrina reined the horses to a stop.

"What the devil are you doing?" Hunter yelled from his precarious position on the wagon bed.

Sabrina looped the leather ribbons around the wagon arm. "Getting my cloth!"

He bolted to his knees. "Leave it!"

Sabrina ignored him and looked at the cloth. Shades of

brown slowly crept up the pristine linen and dyed the fabric in hues no one of sound mind would wear. But still…

Tucking her skirt and cloak hem in her belt, she climbed off the wagon. When mud oozed over the top of her half boots and the damp, cold dirt coated her ankles, Sabrina grimaced. Sodden earth threatened to suck off her shoes with each step.

Splattering mud and heavy strides echoed in her wake.

Hunter stood beside her with his hands on his hips. "That cloth isn't fit for a nappy. Why do you want it? Cattle just relieved themselves on this road."

"Oh. Cattle dung. Well, obviously you've never changed a nappy. Maybe if I wash the fabric, and let the sun bleach it for a few days, the stains will fade. If not, I can still use the linen for petticoats. No one will see the marks."

His eyes grew round. "You're joking."

"No, I'm not! Maybe my aunt can make something from it. A nightgown for me or my cousins."

He waved a hand at the linen. "You'll never get the filth out of the cloth. And no wife of mine will wear something stained with manure." He spoke the words with soft authority.

Her body turned rigid and her arm shot out with an accusing finger. "Have I no say in anything? Even soiled cloth has worth!"

"Sabrina."

"*Don't say anything!* You wonder why I had no wish to marry? Once wed, the laws allow the husband to take ownership of everything his wife possesses! Furthermore, the laws allow the man to control everything. The moment she says, 'I do,' the woman becomes deaf, dumb and mute. That's what I meant when I said men in Parliament are pompous idiots! I'd love to see them live under the same laws they issue for women."

As if he understood, he nodded slightly and stared with a thoughtful look on his face.

Disliking his regard, Sabrina retrieved the cloth and tried to shake off the mud, but the motion drove her feet deeper into the ground. Hunter's silence stirred her curiosity and she gave him a surreptitious glance.

A smile played at his lips. "Leave the cloth. I'll replace it." He extended his hand as if offering peace, but his eyes offered comfort and something more.

Sabrina didn't dare accept; instead she clung to something she understood. "Who says I want your platitude? You sound just like a husband! I want *this* cloth."

"I sound like *what?*"

"A *husband!* He decides everything because suddenly, the wife no longer has a brain. A husband—a man who has *all* the money and gives it back to his wife in shillings, but only when he feels particularly generous!"

"I *am* your husband and can give you a lot more than a shilling."

In the moments she had stayed in one spot, the earth seemed to have consumed her feet. Their conversation was on as precarious ground as she. "What? A cravat stuffed down my throat!"

In three long strides, he reached her side and captured her arm. "At this rate, you'll take all day to reach the wagon."

She twisted from his hold. "If you want to be helpful, take this." Sabrina slammed the cloth against his chest. "Well?"

He looked down at the front of his muddied frock coat. "If you want a dog to do your bidding, I'll buy you one," he said.

Walking away, Hunter turned his attention to securing the crates. Sabrina lifted her chin and hugged the fabric to her chest. They smelled of wet earth. She didn't care. With slow, sinking steps, she returned to the wagon.

Silence followed, broken by snorting horses and the wagon's groans. They were tiny mocking sounds, as if telling her she'd acted a bit too peevish.

"What are you thinking about now?"

Sabrina shifted her gaze to Hunter, then back to the road. "The classics. I'm particularly fond of Homer."

\* \* \*

Dressed in a cloak and traveling gown as dull as dusk, Sabrina blended into her surroundings. After the daylong trip from Dunfermline, Hunter still wanted their marriage, for her to act like a wife. She prayed the heavens were with her now. They had been in Dunfermline when she asked the merchant for the extra crate. This was a feat since Hunter was usually by her side. Yet, he had left her alone for a few minutes when he spoke to the hired drivers.

When a nail squeaked, Sabrina winced but remained in her crates' shadows. Homer. Bless his creative soul. Besides being built of wood, the Trojan Horse and rough-hewn shipping container had something else in common. According to the Greek tale, warriors hid inside the massive horse that carried them through the gates of Troy. Her Trojan horse, a wooden crate, would carry her back to London.

As Sabrina glanced around the docks at Leith, her muscles tensed with each passerby.

Sailors in wide breeches and workers dressed in tough homespun trousers listened to the reformist organizers gathered dockside. Many faces possessed expressions as wrinkled and worn as their attire. The murmuring crowd blended into the night din of whining cranes and raucous laughter from nearby pubs. Everything provided the perfect cover for her escape.

Sensing their hope and despair, Sabrina's heart tightened with sympathy. With only a few to represent them in Parliament, the Scottish people had little rule over their fate. She wanted to recapture the control of her life like the Scots.

Using Marga's special umbrella, she pried. Another nail squeaked. Sabrina's heart raced in anticipation of her impending freedom. As the umbrella handle grew slippery, she wiped her palms. This was the only chance to escape. She glanced at Hunter again.

After Sabrina had insisted that she supervise the loading of the crates, he had finally agreed. He wanted to speak to Dr. Ramsay. Every few minutes, Hunter looked in her direction.

He stood several dozen feet away speaking to some abolitionist reformers, including the clergyman.

Using her darkest hair ribbons, Sabrina fashioned a handle on the cover so it wouldn't shift. The workers would truss the crate like a goose. A few days in the ship's hold and she'd be home.

After glancing at her again, Hunter turned back to Dr. Ramsay and handed the minister a pouch. Had Hunter just given the cleric more coins? He had accepted the offering with a nod of appreciation. A few days ago, had Hunter given him gold for the cause and not as a bribe to let the coach pass? This wasn't the time to think that her arrogant husband did any good deeds.

With her eye on him, Sabrina lifted the lid and tossed her valise and umbrella inside. Quickly she scanned the docks. No one was watching. She stepped into the crate. In a hunched position, she closed the lid, but the movement produced a sound like a lumberman's saw. Sabrina gritted her teeth. Except for muted slivers of gray light filtering between the boards, swollen blackness filled the interior.

A thud on the crate's top made her heart jump and Sabrina grabbed the ribbon. When the wooden box tilted a little and the rope vibrated beneath her, she knew they'd just secured the crate. A clanging chain came from above.

Apprehension coursed through her body. When Sabrina shifted, cloth ripped, and she realized the lid had snagged her petticoat. She grimaced, but a tear was a small price for freedom. The rope whined as she edged skyward, and when the crate began to swing, she knew the crane had moved over the ship. With the abrupt movement, the container started to spin. Her heart lurched. Quickly she planted her hands on the rough wood and braced her feet in the corners.

The trip down seemed to take longer than going up. Was it her imagination or anxiousness? "Please, Lord, let my plan work."

Expecting the workers to untie the crate, she wrapped the ribbon around her hand. When she landed as softly as an autumn leaf, she drew a calming breath. Suddenly the click of heavy heels sounded. Her heart bobbed. She held her breath.

Rope scraped against the crate. Suddenly something pulled on the lid and forced the ribbon from her hand. She stifled a cry. Fierce green eyes stared down at her.

Sabrina cringed. Her body went rigid. Disappointment choked her breath. "Hunter," she whispered.

# Chapter Eight

For one long moment, they stared at each other.

The emerging stars seemed to mock her with their winks. As if aiding in her capture, ribbons of Scottish mist wove like a net above her head.

Suddenly Hunter lunged. Grabbing her hand, he forced her to stand. His arm whipped around her waist like a hemp rope, squeezing the air from her lungs.

Would she ever outwit this man? The thought turned her dampened spirits into determination. Given time, she would think of a new plan, one that would enable her to shield those she loved.

"Do not utter one word. Step out of the crate, or I'll throw you over my shoulder."

His low, ugly tone reminded Sabrina of the time he had kissed her in the coach. Then, too, he had been in a black mood and used angry passion to humiliate her. She regarded the implacable line of his jaw, the dark promise in his green gaze, and his rigid body, projecting power even in its stillness. Nothing moved except the soft flutter of his cravat and his black hair, now curled by the sea air. When he tightened his iron grip, she let out a choked breath.

With sailors in their midst, Sabrina preferred the more dignified choice. Lifting her skirt, she stepped onto the deck, but when she tried to distance herself, his strong hand held her elbow. A dull pain traveled up her arm.

In bleak silence, Hunter ushered her below deck and into a dark cabin. After he lit a lantern, he gestured to a pair of commodore chairs opposite the door. "Sit." He spoke the word softly but with authority.

His ominous tone made her recoil yet the amber glow revealed that although his face was pale, it was not mottled with anger. She chanced that he'd spent his fury. "I've tried to explain. Our marriage has no future."

As he walked toward her, his face possessed a feral look. He resembled a magnificent beast, powerful and sleek, sure of his moves and confident of victory as he cornered his prey. Her heart started to pound. Forced to retreat, Sabrina bumped into a chair and had no choice except to sit.

The beast hovered over her with his hands riding his hips. "Have I treated you so badly that you'd risk your life to leave me?" he asked harshly.

She bit her lower lip. "No, but you've intimidated and threatened me with prison and consummating—"

"All with good cause, I might add. This attempt at escape surpasses everything you have done. My God, you could have killed yourself!"

"If you hadn't succumbed to my grandfather's demands so quickly, I'd almost think your concern sincere." Was he concerned? He *had* shown compassion to others. Recalling this, guilt rooted deep in her conscience, but what was his real motive for marrying her?

"What kind of person do you think I am? Never mind." He took a deep breath. "You obviously weren't *enlightening* me with your preferences in literature."

"Homer's poems aren't popular today. I should have mentioned Lord Byron." She managed to inject a saucy tone.

He threw her a sharp look. "So, you conceived the stupid notion of sending yourself home in a crate like the fabled Trojan horse? You shouldn't have tried that idiotic stratagem at all."

Shifting, she produced a sassy smile. "In truth, I thought the idea was very clever. I vowed not to send Geoffrey a letter. Sending him 'me' wasn't part of the promise."

"Sabrina, I'm not a fool like the Trojans, and I don't believe you have the power of the Greeks. Your act was foolish beyond comprehension."

"I understood everything I did. If I hadn't mentioned Homer, would you have known that I was inside the crate?"

Bringing his palm to his face, he rubbed his temple. "No," he whispered, and paled visibly.

Sabrina didn't understand his sudden look, which oddly lacked the same anger as his voice. "Judging from your pallor, you possess a weak stomach. Are you dizzy from watching me spin?" She clung to her fleeing wit. "I assure you that I didn't feel indisposed, not for one second."

*"Weak stomach?"* He looked at her as if she had stripped away his masculinity. Inexplicably, his apparent weakness made him appear vulnerable. She thought about Alec and the way his asthma frustrated him; he denied his physical ailment, too.

She smiled. "You shouldn't feel shame for a physical weakness. I'll never whisper you possess the affliction."

*"Silence.* Don't you realize the rope could have snapped?" He rubbed a palm over his shadowed jaw. "And..."

His tone warned her to be prudent. "And what?"

For a second, sadness engulfed his dark eyes. "And accidents happen," he said quietly. "The last thing I want is to fish you out of the water."

"I didn't plan this without observing how workers load goods aboard a ship. I never felt as if I were in danger."

"I've wasted enough time with you."

Hunter planted his hands on the chair arms and regarded her with an intense gaze. Enveloped in his masculinity, Sabrina pressed into the leather cushion. Her stomach rippled. She breathed deeply to quiet the unnerving sensation, but instead, tasted the sea air and smelled his distinct male scent, flavored by a whiff of bayberry.

''Are you interested in making a deal?'' he asked softly.

His calmness unsettled her more than his rage, but her heart drummed with hope. ''You'll agree to an annulment?''

''Never.''

Lowering her eyes, she fought the swelling in her throat. ''What kind of deal do you have in mind?'' she asked quietly.

''Act like a wife or your aunt's efforts to reopen the shop will be for naught. I'll keep it closed.''

As she snapped her head up, her jaw dropped. ''You wouldn't.''

''Try me. Furthermore, I'll hold your cloth here.''

''*What?*'' He'd stood against a bullet. What made her think he wouldn't do as he said? ''You can't use your anger against me to harm my aunt!''

''I own this ship. I own the linen.'' He leaned closer and his nose nearly touched hers. ''I own you.''

His arrogance stunned her for a second. She held her breath. Then his bayberry scent stirred her like smelling salts. ''That quite sums it up, but you'll never have my heart.''

''Lord Byron again? Romantic dribble.'' A mocking grin etched his face. ''I'm not finished. You've forgotten our bargain. Shall I refresh your memory? You will act as my wife, convincingly. You're not a prisoner for life. But if you try to escape again, I'll hunt you down.''

Sabrina pursed her lips. He was determined to control her life. As she forced herself to relax, she tapped her nails on the leather arms. ''Must I answer now?''

''You have one minute to decide.''

He gazed over her head in the direction of the clock. Its rhythmic click resembled an army marching in unison, guards escorting a prisoner to the gallows. Her stomach knotted.

In a rush, she considered the facts. She had to take precautions. Assuming her grandfather hadn't found the twins, she couldn't destroy Marga's livelihood. The marriage seemed the only way to insure that her grandfather's focus would remain on her and on no one else. ''What if I don't agree?''

''Your shop will never reopen and I will take you to bed

right now." His face was rigid, and his dark green eyes held her gaze.

He'd lost his patience with her.

Her heart ticked out of time.

Rot! She needed to change her strategy. As his wife, wasn't she entitled to make some demands? How would she know unless she tried? "You're very determined. Perhaps I underestimated you. I'll do as you ask. We have a deal?"

Hunter straightened and for a second a look of relief crossed his face. "For once, you're using your brain. We have a deal." Taking her hand in his, he kissed her palm.

His soft lips, a contrast to the slight roughness of his hands, sent tingling heat up her arm. Her mind warned her to be cautious, though the woman in her delighted in the sensations he evoked. Still she didn't like succumbing to the intimacies of a proper wife.

Both knew her grandfather wanted their consummation, yet she couldn't explain the surge of excitement, nor did she like the emotion. Tender feelings had no place in their relationship as Hunter so bluntly said. Besides, he had made a fool of her once.

This aside, she usually had control of her feelings but felt powerless when he kissed her. Anywhere. Admitting this was one thing, but if she showed her weakness to this virile man, he might take advantage. Slowly she pulled her hand away and managed a look of indifference.

Furthermore, he'd thought her a courtesan. Did he still think she was wanton?

"Perhaps I was a little hasty. Since our minds work dissimilarly, would you define 'convincing' for me? That is, would you clarify my duties?"

Hunter shrugged. "You'll entertain my guests when they arrive for Gavin's wedding. I'll do the same."

"Would you define 'entertain'?"

As his black brows met, his arms shot out from his sides. "Deuced! Do you think I would use you in that manner?"

"Answer my question."

He drew a short breath. "I expect fidelity, on both our parts."

Inexplicably, the confession warmed her heart. "I'm glad you no longer think I'm a courtesan."

A corner of his mouth lifted slightly. "Though free with her favors, a true courtesan is a lady in all other ways. And she would never use her potential sponsor for target practice."

Heat moved across her cheeks. Loath to admit it, on occasion and with very good reason, she defied the confines of a true lady. However, she didn't think less of herself despite her lapses in propriety. She decided not to pursue the conversation. Undoubtedly, he would mention her other shortcomings.

"Continue with your explanation of wifely duties." Hiding her embarrassment, Sabrina waved her hand airily.

"A friend agreed to hostess Gavin's wedding. Now you'll do the honors, but she can still help with the arrangements. Dinner parties, dances, card games. She'll be glad to lend a hand."

"That seems reasonable. However, I do not know how to do *any* of those things. You should keep her as your hostess."

He looked at her with utter disbelief. "You can't withdraw from our agreement by making excuses. The wedding is one reason your grandfather insisted on our quick union. He stayed because he wants to introduce you to Scottish society."

She narrowed her eyes. "You'd never allow him to stay without a good reason. What aren't you telling me?"

He shrugged. "What hound doesn't like to catch a fox?"

Who was the fox, the duke or her? Instinct warned her to avoid the topic for now. "Back to your request. I speak the truth. I've no hostess skills. Furthermore, I do not know how to dance, ride or play card games." After revealing her lack of social graces, she didn't know if she wanted to laugh or cry.

His black brows snapped together. "Impossible. You speak five languages and are well-read. You're of noble birth."

"An accurate summation," she said in French. "I play the

piano, but I cannot read a note of music,'' she added in Portuguese. With an exaggerated sweep of her hands, she said in Spanish, ''That's the extent of my leisure skills.''

''Most unusual. What were you doing when you should have been learning those things? Climbing trees?'' he asked dryly.

Sabrina felt the pang of self-pity at losing her late childhood but never dwelled on it. The twins needed her more than she needed social graces.

The sweet memories of her life in America invaded her heart and stirred the love she still felt for her parents. Sabrina recalled her father's handsome face when she helped him with his ledgers, and the warmth of her mother's laughter as they toiled in the garden. A smile tugged at her lips.

''You think this is humorous?''

Proudly raising her chin, she swallowed a thick lump in her throat. She refused to share the memories. He'd taken enough from her already. ''Social things didn't matter. My family was close. I worked. We lived in very humble circumstances, seldom entertained, and didn't attend balls or hunts.''

For a moment his eyes hinted of compassion and he looked as though he believed her. ''All right. Then we can't lose time in teaching you. I'll help, and perhaps Countess Darlington has arrived at Keir Castle.''

Sabrina looked at him wide-eyed. *''Who?''*

''My original hostess. Her Excellency is quite harmless.''

Suddenly she felt like a barnyard chicken next to an exotic bird. His friend was the epitome of what society thought a lady should be—refined, well connected, superbly attired and stunningly beautiful. ''This will not work!''

''More excuses?'' He sounded equally frustrated. ''You're very reckless, but you do possess *some* intelligence. Learning these things won't be difficult.''

Sabrina flashed him an indignant glance and couldn't even appreciate his backhanded compliment. ''Your friend is one of the shop's customers!''

''That's of no consequence.'' His countenance remained resolute.

''She will recognize me. What will she think of our marriage? She'll know it for what it is. A sham!''

''Pamela, the countess, that is, might be a little curious.''

Sabrina started to tell him that Countess Darlington was the shop's *best* customer and realized she couldn't. The more he knew, the more he could use against her. One sullied word from him to his esteemed friend and Maison du Beaumont could lose the countess's business. Hadn't he threatened to change his mind about reopening the shop?

''You look doubtful. Trust me.''

''*Trust you?*''

As if she had offended him, Hunter rolled his eyes and took a deep breath. ''All right. I understand that you distrust me because I thwarted your escape.''

''I'm wary because I don't understand why you insist on remaining in the marriage.''

''One earns trust.''

She didn't regret her actions but his desire to remain married still puzzled her. ''I've done what I had to do, and so have you.''

Suddenly she realized that as his wife, she had access to his property and personal papers. Servants gossiped, too. If she could just learn the reason he had buckled to the duke's demand, an annulment might be possible. Why hire Geoffrey? She'd investigate herself.

Her father had been a military strategist, and Geoffrey employed legal cunning in his work. From them, Sabrina knew that every defense had a weak spot. What was Hunter's? How could she penetrate his hardened veneer?

He stared at her with an unreadable gaze. ''Do we have a deal? Will you play the gracious hostess and dutiful wife?''

''Before I agree, I have some conditions.''

''Yes?'' he asked in a low voice.

Rising, Sabrina paced the cabin once for effect and stopped

in front of him. "One. I want freedom. No hovering over me."

He arched a dark brow.

"Two. You will not censor my letters." She had to write her aunt that the escape plan had failed.

His brow crept up a fraction.

"Three. No consummation until...we both agree." She wouldn't, but he didn't need to know that.

He crossed his arms over his chest.

"Four. You will not kiss me. *Anywhere.*"

"Five. I want to familiarize myself with your affairs. If you want a marriage, we should share everything." Consummation flashed in her mind. Her heart rapped against her chest. "Posh on what society thinks a woman should do. I think your work is a good way to acquaint ourselves first," she amended.

"You have lofty demands, Sabrina. The answer is no."

She brought herself up tall. "Then I will not agree to anything. Let the countess act as your hostess."

His jaw ticked as if he were considering her ultimatum, but she didn't expect him to change his mind about the conditions he had set forth earlier. All she really wanted was to do a little investigating of her own. Would he agree? She started to pace again. A tug on her skirt and ripping cloth made her stop short. She looked at the linen trailing from her petticoat to Hunter's foot. "Oh no! See what you've done? Go get my valise. I've scissors inside."

"We must do something about your attire," Hunter muttered as he left.

Sabrina arched a brow and for the first time in days, she welcomed her new challenge. "You're hiding something, and I'll find out what it is."

Hunter hadn't gone a dozen steps when he realized he should not leave Sabrina alone. He didn't know if she was sending him on a fool's errand or not, but today, she put the fires of hell in his veins. Turning, he marched back to the cabin.

"We don't need your valise." He produced a knife from inside his boot. With a flick of his wrist, he started slicing the ribbon of cloth and continued around the hem.

"No! Not like that! You oaf! My aunt can fix the tear!"

"Stand still or I'll rip the thing off you."

*Oaf?* Hunter gnashed his teeth and wanted to do as he threatened. He loathed the things she had called him. He continued to slash. She had accused him of being a Tory, a degenerate member of Parliament—and implying that he sounded like a *husband* didn't bode well with him, either. None of the comments should bother him, but coming from her, they did. Why? Perhaps he felt bested by her cunning and wit. Damnation. Between her exquisite eyes and sharp mind, a man had no place to hide…or relax.

She also suggested he possessed a weak stomach. He wrapped his fingers around the linen and yanked. Perhaps she was partially correct. His insides had knotted when he realized the crate was carrying her. Even now, his heart pounded. She had more blind courage than sense. When she had stepped out of the crate, she looked as if she had just finished a ride in a well-sprung barouche.

Giving in to her demands wasn't something he wanted to do. However, if learning about his affairs occupied Sabrina's time, maybe the task would keep her from engaging in another foolish act. Other than his experiences with his father, he had no secrets to hide. Thinking about all the things she had done stirred his blood. He shouldn't care, but he did.

Furthermore, he had entered into the charade of making their marriage appear harmonious to teach her a lesson. Damn the ring. No one blackmailed him without punishment. When had he begun to care about her as a person? The unanswered feelings irritated him as much as her actions. He cut the fabric mercilessly.

In the process, he got a very good peek at her slender calves and well-turned ankles for the second time that day. An unbidden desire surged through his loins and reminded him of her conditions. *You will not kiss me anywhere.*

When he stood, furious blue eyes glared at him. He didn't understand the reason, but her passionate nature and expressive eyes always fueled his carnal instincts. Sliding the knife into his boot, he tossed the earthy-smelling cloth on a chair.

"Now, we were speaking of conditions," he said in a tone that sounded curiously low. "I'll compromise. You must not draw away from me when I greet you with a kiss."

She took a step backward. "Kissing my cheek or hand will not convince anyone that we're happy."

"On that I disagree. Like your parlor skills, we'll practice kissing until you've learned the art adequately."

She paled. *"Practice!"*

"Until the act becomes second nature." He placed her cool slender hands in his, but again he noted the faint calluses on her palms. As he recalled her humble life, compassion engulfed his heart. Why did he feel such emotions? How could he accept her words for truth? He didn't know this woman and realized her presence was beginning to cloud his thoughts and emotions. She was a schemer, too. Given Sadlerfield's threat, Hunter had to save himself. Pushing the feelings aside, he resumed his lesson.

With exaggerated slowness, he kissed her right palm, then rubbed his thumb over the spot as if to seal the kiss. She gazed at their hands and did not withdraw hers. Hunter repeated the intimate greeting on her left hand, and though it quivered, she allowed him to continue.

"Was that adequate?" She met his gaze, her tone as controlled as her pale blue eyes.

"This time. Now, present your cheek to me," he said softly.

For a second, her eyes grew wide, then slowly, she tilted her head toward him. As he lowered his lips, he caught her gardenia scent. Years of nurtured control and propriety kept him from kissing her as he had in the coach.

Suddenly she pulled her hands away. "Now, you see? If

ordered to do so, I can do as you ask. I see no reason to practice.''

His fingers itched to touch her. No woman had ever scorned his touch or considered his kiss an ''order,'' and for some reason, Sabrina's rejection nipped his pride. ''Oh, I do. You have a very bad habit of forgetting our agreement. I've other conditions. First, I asked you to address me as Hunter. Next, you need some new gowns. I can't have my wife dressed like a street urchin.''

She dropped her jaw. *''An urchin!''*

Taking her hand, he dragged her to the mirror hanging above the toilette chest. Clumps of dried mud clung to the front of Sabrina's gown and cloak.

The reflection in the mirror showed her pale blue eyes glinting dangerously. Her delicate nostrils flared. ''Nothing is wrong with my clothes! Brushing will fix them!''

''On the contrary, I'm well nigh sick of the drab colors you wear. Furthermore, they're unsuitable for the coming occasion. So, if you want your conditions, you must agree to a new wardrobe. I will bear the cost, of course.''

Turning, she looked at him with barely suppressed rage. ''You are acting like a husband again! Telling me what to do! What to wear!'' Sabrina started to brush her cloak furiously.

The accusation hit low like a blow to the gut, but he ignored the feelings he didn't want or understand. ''Then calling me Hunter should not be difficult. Besides, *any* woman would appreciate a few new gowns. They will add to the credibility of our marriage.''

The icy look she slipped him could freeze a man's heart. ''I'm not just any lady.''

''No, you're my wife. Well? Have we come to an agreement?'' For fifteen minutes, they bartered on issues that each deemed important.

''Our pact rivals the Magna Carta,'' he concluded.

She raised her chin. ''Just remember the details.''

Fraudulent or not, he intended to make sure she appeared

to be his wife. To him, Gavin's wedding was more than an exchange of sacred vows and a social occasion. After purposely avoiding society for ten years, the affair was a beginning for him, a chance to bring honor to the Sinclair name.

More, he would learn what Sabrina was hiding. She wanted to return to London for something. What?

# *Chapter Nine*

Through the study's mullioned windows, light angled off the oak furniture and bathed the room in autumn warmth. The drapes fluttered, and again, the gardenia scent taunted his senses. When Hunter gave Sabrina a surreptitious glance, his hand stopped on the letter he was writing. She flipped another paper onto the table where she sat and sorted his shipping invoices.

When he again eyed his correspondence, he noted that the ink from the quill of his pen had spread on the vellum and ruined another letter. He cursed silently. Yesterday they had agreed on a deal more complicated than the Magna Carta, but he hadn't realized her presence would distract his work. Imagining Sabrina attired in a more elegant gown than the gray wool dress she wore didn't help, either. Most disquieting was the anticipation of his "once a day kiss," his contribution to their "treaty." He felt like a schoolboy.

"Hunter?"

He felt as if she had caught him committing a sin. Guilt ridden, he reached for more papers. "Finished with those?"

"You've never mentioned your father."

Slowly Hunter glanced at an empty spot on his desk and shifted in his chair. "What are you talking about?"

"I just read the business report on your warehouses in Australia. The last page is for your father's expenses."

Rising, Hunter lifted the papers from her hand and placed them on his desk. "Obviously, I put them with the others in error."

"Will you tell me about him?" Curiosity and expectation filled her wide blue eyes.

Hunter swore silently but managed a bland facade. Beyond telling her things that were common knowledge, he would do just about anything to avoid discussing his father.

"Since society knows, you'll undoubtedly hear gossip at the wedding. I suppose I should tell you. My father's a rogue. Beyond that, I have little to say about him."

"I see," she said softly. "I've also heard other gossip from the housekeeper."

He curled his fingers. "What did Mrs. Finlay say?"

"Something estranged you from your father, and that your parents didn't suit. In the end, he left you in your mother's care."

Despite the compassion in her voice, he let out a bitter laugh. "Didn't suit? Servants' gossip. Lies."

"Then tell me your side of the story."

He reached into a crate for more papers and placed them in front of her. "Don't you have some sorting to do?"

Keen interest replaced the sympathy in her eyes. "For days, you've *insisted* on learning more about each other. I'm merely satisfying the bargain we made."

"Since when did you decide to be so solicitous?"

Her sassy smile emphasized the determination in her eyes. "Well, since our Magna Carta, as you called it, I'm to play the role of your wife with conviction. How can I do that if I know nothing about you? Or, do you forget our bargain when it suits you? What will your father think if he arrives and finds his son married?"

"He wouldn't show his face here, or care what I was doing."

"Of course he would," she said with a dismissive air. "He's your father, despite your estrangement. What caused your differences?"

A life of deceit, dishonor and schemes, he wanted to say, but as shame, old memories and hurts surfaced, Hunter turned and gazed out the window. Below, birds let out indignant chirps as the gardeners worked among the hedges. Hunter glared at Sadlerfield as he walked toward the conservatory. That was his mother's domain. At least the duke wasn't bothering them for the moment. He stared beyond the garden at the rolling hills. A vision of his mother sitting against a birch tree came to mind, and the old ache crushed his heart. With only her paints for company, she appeared so alone.

He buried the image. How could he escape Sabrina's inquiries? As his wife, her questions had merit, but to answer them would be like putting his head in a guillotine and releasing the rope himself. Her incredibly beautiful eyes hadn't totally blinded him to his purpose, and her questions stirred his unease. Was his father behind the debt? Had Sadlerfield paid him to commit the deed?

"What if people ask me why he isn't here?"

Hunter tasted the bitterness rising from his stomach. "Tell them the truth. He's in Australia."

"Doing what?"

Turning, he stared at her for a long moment. "You won't let this go, will you?"

The tilt of her chin exuded determination. "I'm just trying to understand your family. For instance, the day I arrived, I asked if any kin knew your whereabouts. Mrs. Finlay didn't know how to reach your father and said your mother had died five years ago. Losing her must have been difficult for you. I'm sorry."

The compassion in her voice touched a place inside him that he opened to few people. Instinct warned him that trusting her with his darkest secrets or deepest hurts would be folly. He might as well hand her a pistol and ask her to blow off his head.

She didn't want their marriage, so why give her reason to seek an annulment? One whisper from her sweet lips and she'd ruin him. She'd tell everyone he was a criminal. Blackmail ran in the Barrington blood. He must remember that.

Rising, Sabrina moved beside him and gently placed her hand on his arm. This was the first time she had willingly touched him, and instantly, the carnal part of him wanted her to explore more than his arm. He didn't move. Waiting. Wishing. His heart drummed a little faster. She was so close he could kiss her, and he hated that she affected him in such a private way.

"Discussing your father bothers you, and I think I understand the reason. Your belief that he abandoned your mother is painful."

Her words stopped his errant thoughts. Memories, smothering and cold, rushed forth like a tidal wave—his mother weeping, his father disappearing for days, a little boy with his face pressed against the window as he stared at the empty road, and of a young man who no longer cared. Hunter drew a deep breath to erase the recollections, to ease the unbidden ache in his heart that was surely for his mother.

As much as he wanted to ignore the remark, something deep inside urged him to speak. "You're listening to lies. I know he deserted my mother."

She creased her brow. "Well, I heard another version."

"I'm sure there are many."

Her face turned a rosy hue, a sign that implied she had been absorbing the housekeeper's words with relish. "According to Mrs. Finlay, your father wasn't a saint or the devil on earth, either. Your mother loved the country life, and he preferred the environment London offered."

Memories nipped at old wounds and he flinched as if he were receiving the hurt for the first time. "Why do you think he preferred London? For the culture?"

"That would support Mrs. Finlay's words."

"Don't be so naive," he snapped. "Just where do you think he would find more women to his liking? At Keir castle or London?"

"Well, I heard he tried to be a good husband and father at the onset of his marriage."

Hunter let out a brittle laugh. Somehow, the innocence in her voice bade him to discuss a man he loathed. He could not leave her with the impression that his father possessed one ounce of goodness.

"Don't defend him out of naiveté, or worry you'll offend me. He's a *rogue.*"

"I'm not exonerating your father's actions, or saying that I believe Mrs. Finlay's accounting of the situation. Maybe his leaving was the best thing for your mother. By doing what the other wanted, maybe your parents would have been miserable. Maybe your father realized they could never be happy. My father said to do what you believe in your heart, and not what others want you to do."

Hunter cursed silently at her naive defense of Randall. He disliked the picture she was painting, for he saw her and him. "You're making conclusions about a man you don't know."

"No, no I don't, but—"

"Do you know why I thought you were a courtesan?"

She frowned. "Did you think your father sent me here?"

"He shows his concern for my welfare in unusual ways."

Sabrina's eyes grew wide. "Because he's a rogue, he thought you might want a courtesan? That's why you thought I was a courtesan?"

"That thought crossed my mind."

"I'm not sure I like his sense of humor. What else will you tell me about him?"

"Tenacious, aren't you? Are you going to question the contents of each paper that you read?" He nodded toward the crates and hoped to turn the course of the conversation.

"It's your duty to tell me about your life. Don't you want me to be the *perfect* wife?" Her eyes portrayed wide-eyed innocence.

Clever. He'd fry in hell before he'd tell her more. Even if an annulment were what she still wanted, he'd refuse. That alone would serve up enough gossip for a session. When Parliament opened, Hunter didn't want any new scandal associated with his name. The abolition of slavery was too important to him. Besides, Sadlerfield would make him pay.

Until he received a report on Sabrina, how could he counter her attack? Hunter had little ammunition except…her sweet, lying lips. He could think of only one way to stop her questions. Leaning, he placed his hand on her chin and brought his face close to hers. Her body grew taut.

"I don't want to talk. I think I'd rather practice kissing you," he whispered huskily.

A tiny sound came from her parted lips. Desire flickered in her pale blue eyes, but she pulled away from him and grabbed the stack of papers from the table. With a sharp rap, she tidied the edges as if dismissing him.

"You said it's time to go back to work."

He lifted her chin with his finger. "As you wish. That means we'll practice later. Remember our agreement. Perhaps after our dance lesson tonight."

A thin smile etched her face before she lowered her gaze to the papers.

Hunter should have felt victorious, but instead, his pride took another blow. He seated himself in his chair and wondered what she was thinking as she shuffled through papers. Why was he so repugnant to her when he clearly saw desire? Damn if he knew. She puzzled him more than any female he'd ever met. Soon though, he'd know everything about his mysterious wife.

For now, the only way to weaken her control was to seduce her slowly.

The cadence of a waltz echoed off the music room walls. Sabrina never imagined that Hunter could create such a rich sound from merely humming the tune. How could she concentrate on obtaining clues to his past?

With their palms touching, a ribbon of heat seemed to fuse their hands as one. She could hardly breathe for the strange sensations, and stepped on Hunter's toes.

He raised her chin with their clasped hands. "My touch guides you." Hunter squeezed her right hand with his left, then patted her back with his right hand. "When I pull with my right hand, I'm going backward. When I push with my left hand, I'm going forward."

"Push-pull. Yes, I think I understand." Her hands grew damp. The elegant texture of his black frock coat reminded her of the urbane man who lay beneath the expensive cloth. He represented all that she wasn't. Her muscles went rigid.

"Relax." As if he could ease her tense muscles, he wiggled her arm and began to hum.

Considering all that had happened between them, he seemed unduly—kind, which made her quest seem more traitorous.

"At least your trip to Dunfermline has you more comfortable with each other. You even left me to dine alone tonight." Sadlerfield's clicking heels added an odd cadence to Hunter's hum.

Sabrina trod on Hunter's toes. He winced from her misstep. As he twisted his head toward the door, Hunter's fingers tightened around her hand. "What do you want, Sadlerfield?"

"We all know the answer to that question. Do we not?"

Heat prickled her skin as she faced her grandfather. With cool perusal, he regarded her blue printed gown, the cotton not comparable to his impeccably tailored gray frock coat and trousers.

"You are rather clumsy. I cannot believe your father lacked the foresight to teach you. He cheated you just to spite me."

She bit her tongue. Wisdom whispered she shouldn't antagonize him, at the same time love for her father spurred her to move. With heavy steps, she marched toward her grandfather. "Unlike you, Father gave me everything a child should have."

"Don't upset my wife," Hunter said with soft authority.

Sabrina's heart warmed from his defense of her, though their unyielding looks spoke of a different battle, the one Hunter had lost when he agreed to marry her. What were they hiding?

"I think I will stay and watch for a few moments. The mother of my heir must have every refinement."

She winced as if he'd slapped her. Both knew the duke was referring to her mother, too, and she wanted to speak in her defense. With Hunter present though, airing her parents' past would be a stupid thing to do. The information might be dangerous for the twins' sake since he might meet them and then because of the debt, delve deeper into Marga's life.

"The dance floor is getting crowed," Hunter said very dryly. "I'll fetch some music and we'll practice the piano instead."

Cabinet doors creaked. She didn't want to be around either man, and edged to the window. In Hunter's arms, his closeness had sharpened her senses and made her acutely aware of her femininity. Employing her new stratagem to learn Hunter's secret would be difficult. Every touch and look reached her core.

Her sympathy for his childhood aside, Sabrina knew she must remain wary. From her experiences, she knew that he possessed a dark soul, a dangerous passion, a ruthless nature and more secrets than a priest did. She sensed he withheld information. Why would his father, Lord Wick, venture to Australia, a place filled with convicts and few women? He liked the company of ladies! Was Hunter supporting his father out of the goodness of his heart?

Despite her sensibility and the unanswered questions, Sabrina could barely concentrate on her plan to glean information. Ignoring Hunter's virility was impossible.

Suddenly he was beside her and caressed her with his eyes. "Are you ready?"

The sensual look made her mouth go dry. With both men watching her, she rushed to the piano and sat. "You wanted to hear my repertoire, did you not?" Sabrina played a Virginia reel before anyone could utter a word.

"Good God. Is that all you can play?" Her grandfather started to walk toward them, but Hunter stepped in his path.

Sabrina stared at the ivory keys and bit her tongue. "You dislike the colonial music? I like it."

"Teaching her is my job. Your responsibilities ended the day I married her."

"Remember your place, Kenilworth."

"All too well. But yours isn't in here." Grabbing her grandfather's arm, he ushered the duke to the hallway and slammed the door. "Don't think about him. Tonight is for us, not entertaining a meddlesome fool," Hunter said in a gentler tone. "I'll teach you to play a few Strauss tunes."

Sabrina released a calming breath, thankful that he didn't question her grandfather's animosity. Lying would be poor repayment after Hunter had defended her. "I'm not a society lady," she said in a jesting tone.

"You will be though. Remember who you are now."

She caressed the gold-winged lion at the end of the keyboard. In trying to make her into someone she wasn't, he made her long for the things that were familiar to her. She missed her own piano and family, feared for their well-being. Sighing, she pushed aside the ache in her heart. Her reasons for agreeing to the deal were for everything she held dear.

"This Tompkinson piano is beautiful. Will your guests appreciate a few renditions of the Virginia reel if they have enough ale?" she asked dryly, hiding her doubts behind the quip.

Chuckling, he sat beside her on the small bench. "Perhaps." As he played, he passed her a quick glance, then focused on the keyboard. "Do you hear the triple measure?"

She smiled and nodded as she tapped her foot to the beat. Although he wasn't holding her, his thigh rubbed against hers as he pressed the pedals.

Abruptly, he stopped. "You try it."

"All right, but I've never played a tune right on the first try." She limbered her fingers by playing several scales and then began the waltz overture.

"Learning to play a tune by listening to it is quite remarkable. A true gift."

She focused on the keys. Looking at him was dangerous. "That's what my father said, though he wished I'd learned to read music so I could play properly. I've no patience for studying all those dots. However, he always commented on my fine rhythm." Hunter moved again. "Did I miss a note?"

"No. You put fire in all the right spots, and I sense that you have incredible rhythm."

"Fire?"

"Crescendo," he said quickly.

"Oh yes, I see what you mean." The moment her fingers struck a wrong chord, she knew it. "Oh dear."

"Let me show you." Extending his arm around her back, he placed his fingers on the lower keys and played the chords. When he finished, his arms circled her waist. "I think it's time. Kiss me," he said in a baritone voice.

Her heart beat double time. Turning to face him, she met his smoldering gaze and planted her hand on his chest. "Now? We're practicing the waltz tune." She failed to hide the panic in her voice. "My grandfather expects perfection."

He pulled her close so their bodies touched. "You promised. One kiss a day."

Before she could protest again, his sensuous mouth descended on hers. Sabrina inhaled sharply and tried to pull away but he just drew her closer. He kissed her gently and her stomach fluttered, sending waves of unbridled pleasure through her body. Immersed in the feelings, she succumbed and parted her lips. When his tongue touched hers, a whimper escaped her throat, but she liked the sensations rising from his kiss and forgot her stipulations. Desire warred with caution. Then Sabrina recalled everything she knew about Hunter and the agreement they had made.

"That's long enough," she said breathlessly.

As he ran the pad of his thumb over her bottom lip, she tremored beneath his touch. "Why did you pull away from me? I wanted to kiss you, and I know you wanted to kiss me back.''

''I agreed to short kisses. *Short*.'' Rising, she stalked to the music room door. Sabrina hated herself for enjoying his kisses and for losing control. Now he knew she wanted to return his passion.

''Oh, Sabrina? That wasn't a short kiss.''

She pirouetted with her hands balled into fists. ''I accept your apology.''

He grinned devilishly. ''That wasn't even a beginning,'' he said in a low voice.

''It wasn't?'' she asked in a whispered tone.

With a predator's grace, Hunter walked toward her. ''Would you like me to show you now?''

Her mouth went dry. ''Tomorrow. Well, maybe not tomorrow. You said you're giving me a riding lesson.''

Shaking his finger, he said, ''Once a day. That was our agreement. I'll decide when the time is right.''

''Not *once* a day. I said no *more* than once a day. That's different.''

His grin widened. Whirling around, she slammed the door behind her and leaned against the cool stone wall. Her heart pounded. How would she ever manage each day not knowing when he would kiss her?

Still, kissing was better than consummation. Without completing their union, she had a chance at an annulment. She bit her lip. How much patience did Hunter have? How long could she keep him at bay? Could they continue to fool her grandfather into believing they were content?

Slowly she climbed the stairs and entered their bedchamber. It smelled of bayberry. An hour later, Sabrina lay in his bed, and instead of concentrating on learning Hunter's secret, she thought about the virile man. He wanted to kiss her. She wanted to respond in kind. Suppressing the unwanted desire, she reminded herself that the kiss was just a part of their treaty and nothing more.

She stared at the empty spot where he usually lay and

thanked the Lord for the huge bed. A lone candle sputtered on his side table. Picking up her candle snuffer, she whacked the flame and it hissed in the liquid wax. She snarled at the shadowed room and was glad he hadn't come to bed as he had done since their marriage a week past. His presence would only intensify the peculiar feelings his kiss evoked. She must not let passion rob her of her remaining wit.

With renewed determination, she vowed to learn the reason Hunter had succumbed to her grandfather's demand. The great duke had found something with which to blackmail Hunter. Surely she and Hunter could find another way to guard his secret, and not remain in the marriage.

## Chapter Ten

From the stable doors, Sabrina glanced at the paddock railing where Hunter had tied his massive black stallion, Gallus. In the adjacent enclosure, the filly frolicked under her mother's watchful eyes. The maternal act sparked an unnerving vision.

*You are rather clumsy…*

Her grandfather's words reminded her that he demanded perfection. Suddenly she saw her brother, wheezing and becoming so angry at his weak lungs that he'd almost turn blue. She slid her palms down her skirt. Their grandfather couldn't learn that the twins weren't Marga's, even if Sabrina had to—

Crackling hay made Sabrina turn to the docile chestnut mare Hunter guided from a stall. The stable's gray light outlined his white linen shirt and buff trousers, attire that revealed shoulders the width of the mare's back. She focused on the horse instead. "What should I do first?"

"Relax or Honey will sense your distress. Learning to ride is important since coach wheels do break."

"Geoffrey maintains my carriage. He visits frequently so he offers his skill and time."

Under knitted brows, Hunter's eyes darkened. "You forget. We're married. You'll no longer need your precious Geoffrey."

Suddenly she realized she was still thinking of escaping the marriage, while he was planning on a future together. With trembling hands, she stroked Honey. "He'll always be important to me. Do you plan to choose my friends, too?"

He shrugged. "Depends what they're about. Back to riding. Where does your aunt live? I'm sure you'll visit her."

Oh, pickle. He presumed she'd move to his house, but then, a husband would expect that... "On Wilsted Street in Sommers Town."

"That's on the outskirts of London. The only thing nearby is St. James' Burying Ground. What if a wheel were to break? Whom would you wake to aid you?"

She fought a smile, but conscience demanded she defend the souls resting in the cemetery. "That's not humorous."

A lazy grin emerged. "In such a situation, you'd unhitch the carriage and seek help. Riding astride and bareback would be your only choice. Go ahead. Tuck your skirt in your belt. When Pamela arrives, we'll get you a proper riding habit in Edinburgh."

She curled her hands around the wool fabric of her cinnamon-colored skirt. Since Marga created everything Sabrina owned, his plan made her feel like a traitor to her aunt. She held her tongue. Another slip would cause Hunter to become even more suspicious than she sensed he was.

Minutes later, they were in the paddock and he instructed her on proper riding form. As Sabrina circled the enclosure, she could sense his gaze on her legs. Dampness coated her neck under his intense scrutiny.

Through the railing, the filly nudged Hunter's thigh and he stroked her nose. "Well, little one. Finally learn the difference between a crop and an udder?" The filly whinnied and Hunter chuckled. "That's your father." He pointed to Gallus.

She hadn't seen him in such a carefree mood since their initial meeting. His gentle exchange with the filly offered Sabrina hope that she'd find the kind man beneath his veil of secrets. "Gallus. An unusual name for a horse. Does it have a special meaning?"

"It's Scot for daring and self-confident. He's had that air

about him since William…I mean His Majesty, gifted him to me.''

The reins fluttered in her hands. Most people would delight that their husband knew the new king well enough to address him as such. To her, his friendship just represented the power of the new world she'd entered so unwillingly. If she managed to avoid consummating the marriage, how many powerful men would she encounter when she sought an annulment? What if the king were to ask her the reason? She'd have to lie.… Oh, God, how could she lie to the Crown? Honey whinnied, bringing Sabrina's attention back to her mount, now eyeing the stable door with increasing regularity.

After she circled the paddock again, they returned to the stables and Hunter instructed her on saddling a horse. Honey avoided the saddle but, after three tries, Sabrina landed the seat on the horse's back. During her struggle, Hunter smiled lazily and leaned against a stall.

''Obviously, you plan to make this lesson difficult for me.''

''I'd be remiss if I failed to show you every facet. Very slowly, but very completely, as in *everything* I plan to teach you,'' he said softly. His green eyes darkened with seductive promise.

Her heart stopped. ''Did I do this right?''

He checked the equipment and nodded. After giving her a leg up, he adjusted her stirrups. ''Long legs,'' he murmured.

Did he prefer someone petite, like the countess who represented everything fashionable, from her blond hair to her smart ensembles? Inexplicably, resentment stirred. ''My father was almost as tall as you.''

''Don't take offense. Long legs will help you grip. I'll show you just how effective that can be.'' As he regarded her with a hooded gaze, a lazy smile emerged. He dragged a finger down her leg, gently pushed her foot into the stirrup and then traced her ankle where it met her boot.

Sabrina clutched the saddle horn. ''Well, you won't unless you mount callous…I mean Gallus.''

He chuckled, capping it with another slow grin.

Suddenly she realized his words might have a bawdy meaning. Her face burned. As Hunter guided them outside, the mare snorted. "I think this horse wants to stay here." Rubbish. So did she.

"Honey probably senses you're an unskilled rider."

Her poor riding ability paled compared to her inexperience with passion. She failed to understand her body's response to this man and disliked that he could initiate the unnerving warmth in her belly. Atop Gallus, horse and man melted together like one powerful entity, daring and self-confident. Formidable as foe, friend or...lover.

Forcing herself from her wayward thoughts, Sabrina viewed the meadow's russet hues instead. They stopped at a boundary of firs and ashes, their gray branches appearing white against the sky. Turning, Hunter looked toward the valley. At the wondrous sight, she drew a breath of sweet air.

A stone wall surrounded the castle grounds that displayed an array of paths, shrubbery and ponds. To one side stood the conservatory she'd visited. Gardeners were trimming vines from the terrace's stone balustrade that spanned the mansion's width. Other workers were laying fresh gravel or raking debris into piles. As wagons loaded with earth moved slowly around the wall, gardeners shoveled dirt into the weathered holes at its base. In the distance, the firth's blue-green hues glimmered against the horizon.

At once, she understood the reason he'd brought her here. This would belong to his heir. A cold shiver coursed through her. If her plans failed and they eventually produced a son, would the duke interfere with the child's upbringing? She pushed the black notion aside. Maybe she'd never have to worry about that.

"Beautiful, isn't it? My mother admired Capability Brown, a renowned landscaper in his time." Hunter conveyed the joy the garden had given his mother.

Sabrina didn't interrupt him, sensing he was speaking from his heart. A mixture of compassion and sorrow flickered in his eyes. She wanted to nurture the emotion. Besides belonging to his heir, she sensed the estate's restoration would be his mother's memorial. Maybe he was in an approachable mood.

Sabrina licked her lips, now tasting faintly of salt air. "Would she be mortified by our marriage?"

He grinned crookedly. "She'd understand."

What kind of answer was that? "I think I would have liked her. Your mother showed inner strength living without your father."

Hunter's features became unreadable. "If you plan to compare my parents' relationship to ours, don't."

Her shoulders slumped. "Why do you want to stay married?"

His gaze drifted down her torso then up again. "Your posture."

Under his intense inspection, Sabrina slowly straightened her spine. She sensed his regard went beyond her poor riding form and recalled when he had turned his anger to passion. Though his eyes remained a brilliant green, caution warned her to avoid provocation. The last thing she wanted was his kiss. Seeking distance from him, she suggested they canter down to the park.

He agreed, urging Gallus into a trot. Honey followed, but the mare ignored Sabrina's commands and thundered past them in a run. Suddenly a wagon edged out from the wall and into her path. After making an abrupt right turn, she tightened the reins. Honey started to rear. When she relaxed her grip on the straps, the mare raced toward the stable.

Sabrina's bottom bounced against the saddle. The wind loosened her braid. Behind her, thundering hooves approached. Reaching her side, Hunter circled his arm around her waist. His strength crushed her lungs. As she fought for air, he pulled her off the horse and settled her onto his lap.

Hunter tightened his grip. "Are you all right?"

She let out a disgruntled breath. "Stupid horse!"

As stable hands and gardeners gathered to view the spectacle, Sabrina lowered her lids and fought the heat rising to her face.

"What is going on here, Hunt?"

Countess Darlington's voice stopped Sabrina's heart.

Turning Gallus, Hunter faced the newcomers. "Pamela. Brice. Pleasant trip? I'd like you to meet my wife, Lady Kenilworth."

Hunter's friends blinked hard.

Sabrina pasted a smile on her face. From beneath the rim of her hat, Lady Darlington's green eyes widened, and then she smiled. She appeared a few years older than Sabrina and possessed a confident air. Her fashionable green wool traveling gown and pelisse trimmed in black braid indicated her place in society.

Suddenly her winged brows snapped together. "You're Miss Beaumont! You look different with your hair…loose."

Sabrina's body turned rigid, but Hunter tightened his hold as if giving her a warning signal. She brushed a long strand of hair off her face. "A pleasure to see you again, Lady Darlington."

Hunter introduced Pamela's husband, Brice Weston, Earl of Darlington, who displayed a fit form beneath his well-tailored gray frock coat and trousers. The breeze stirred his fawn-colored hair, and his hazel eyes reflected kindness.

"Sabrina! You look like a gypsy. What happened to you?" Her grandfather bellowed the words.

All heads turned. Sabrina lifted her chin. Hunter's body tensed. After hasty greetings, the duke glared at her.

"Remember your station, young lady." Turning to the countess, he said, "She would do well with instruction from you."

The countess arched a brow, then beamed. "Of course, your grace."

Throwing Sabrina a censorious glance, he strolled toward the gardens for his daily walk. She bit her tongue.

"Don't let him upset you," Hunter whispered, giving her a reassuring squeeze.

For one insane second, she relished his strength and settled into the comfort of his broad chest. Warmth from his body penetrated hers. She straightened.

"Darling, do help the poor young woman down," Pamela said kindly. "I can hardly *wait* for an explanation."

After Brice lifted her from the horse, Sabrina adjusted her clothes and threw Hunter a pointed look, but he volleyed with a sensuous smile. Dismounting, he reached for her hand, but she hid it in the folds of her skirt. In a heartbeat, she decided suffering Lady Darlington's curiosity was easier than experiencing more passion. Sitting on his hard thighs with his arms around her was enough touching to last for weeks.

Rushing forth, Sabrina gestured to the house and they started walking. "Would you like to freshen after your long journey?"

"Are you really married to Hunt? The duke's your grandfather?"

The word stopped in Sabrina's throat. "Yes."

"Oh, this is a surprise! You must call me Pamela. May I call you Sabrina?"

The curiosity in Pamela's voice sent a foreboding tremor down Sabrina's spine. To avoid the marriage topic, she said, "Of course. Refreshments?"

"That would be delightful, along with your *explanation*."

"An explanation? Of course. An explanation." Sabrina slipped Hunter a swift glance. He narrowed his eyes.

Thirty minutes later, Pamela and Brice returned downstairs after refreshing themselves. Hunter motioned them to enter the Rose drawing room and a maid, carrying a tray of freshly baked sweet buns and steaming tea, followed. Pink-hued roses woven in the gray Oriental carpet and upholstery contrasted with the mahogany furnishings. His mother's favorite. Recalling when she had decorated the room, his heart warmed, but the vision also reminded him of his blasted father. Quickly Hunter buried the memories and waited for Sabrina in the hallway.

As wool whispered against the stairs, he met Sabrina's gaze. Her gray gown nearly matched the shade of the drawing room rug, but her pale blue eyes gleamed with courage. With her head held high, Sabrina walked toward him. He caught her arm as they neared the drawing room.

"Remember what you owe me, and remember the word *conviction.*"

Sabrina glanced away and he knew what she was thinking. At the stable yard, she had avoided his touch. He'd deal with a kiss later.

"Pretending is very hard for me. Once Pamela learns the reason we married, I can imagine another round of comments. She'll tell her friends. This won't be good advertisement for the shop. I just know this marriage, and this hostess business, is a bad idea."

"Trust me. If you play your part well, I'll be Lord Byron at his best. I'll say I was smitten from the time I laid eyes on you."

She choked. "If you do that—"

"Then the world will know. Any hopes you have for an annulment will raise questions."

When she swallowed hard, he knew that annulment was still on her mind, and he should have been angry. Instead, her downcast eyes beckoned his hand to her cheek. She trembled. As he stroked her soft skin with his palm, a rosy hue trailed his touch.

Taking a small step backward, Sabrina reached for the door handle. He tensed at her slight, which again chafed his pride, but he still offered his arm. Sabrina hesitated, then acquiesced. Her touch spawned a deep need. As he gazed into dusky-hued eyes, he knew she experienced a similar response, which only heightened his desire. Turning, Sabrina quickly opened the door.

Pamela's cup clinked against the saucer. "Finally!"

Rising from a Chippendale chair, Brice approached them and heartily slapped Hunter on the back. "Come, tell us how this all happened. Two weeks ago, you thought only of politics.''

As Sabrina extended her hand, Brice brought her wrist to his lips. She produced a winning smile and the threesome agreed to address each other informally—something that should matter little to her. How long had it taken Hunter to persuade Sabrina to address him familiarly? He jabbed his hands into his pockets. Why should he care?

Brice turned to Hunter. ''Pamela can hardly sit still. Did Gavin's upcoming nuptials inspire yours?''

''Of sorts.'' He and Sabrina sat on a settee across from Pamela.

As Brice seated himself, Pamela looked at them expectantly. ''Hunt, how *did* the two of you meet?''

She nudged his arm. ''You answer and I'll pour.''

Beginning with the shop account, Hunter explained their meeting, telling half-truths until Sadlerfield's arrival. He decided now was the time to speak a few lines from Lord Byron's poem. Because he disliked turning into bed with Sabrina, he had spent the nights memorizing the lines for occasions like this. A man could suppress his needs for only so long.

He brought Sabrina's hand to his lips and summoned his most sensual look. ''A verse from Lord Byron.

''She walks in beauty, like the night
Of cloudless climes and starry skies,
And all that's best of dark and bright
Meets in her aspect and her eyes,
Thus mellow'd to that tender light
Which heaven to gaudy day denies...''

Sliding her fingers from his grip, Sabrina turned to the refreshments but, when she placed a serviette on his lap, her hand brushed his thigh. Desire surged. He wanted to capture her fingers and teach her to explore.

Pamela sighed. "Oh, how lovely."

Nodding, Hunter turned to Sabrina. As she caught his gaze, amusement brightened her eyes. At least his wife knew a lie for a lie, but he thought he did a damn fine job imitating the great Byron.

"Your attentiveness toward each other is *so* romantic!" Pamela sighed wistfully, then faced Sabrina. "I cannot believe you are Lord Sadlerfield's kin."

She smiled thinly. "Neither can I."

"He is a Tory. Hunt is a Whig. For His Grace to sanction the marriage, well... I would have thought he'd kick up his toes with a Whig in his family. Right, darling? Hunt?"

Swallowing a bite of a sweet bun, Sabrina slowly faced him. A knowing gleam brightened her pale blue eyes. "You're a Whig, hmm? We've so much to learn about each other."

"Yes, and so much to teach," Hunter murmured.

"Hunt, have you told Sabrina the reason you returned to England?"

Sabrina needled him with an elbow. "Do tell me, Hunter."

"We've been busy," Hunter said smoothly, and faced Pamela. "That reminds me. Will you help Sabrina select some gowns for Gavin's wedding? She's here without a proper wardrobe."

Suddenly he thought of something he hadn't considered. Would Pamela tell Sabrina what she knew about his past?

Pamela balled her hands into fists and tapped her lap. "Oh, I wish your aunt were here. She designs delicious gowns!"

"He's met my aunt and his feelings for her are beyond prose."

Hunter pierced her with a warning glance.

"She is a wonder. We're wasting time over tea. Show me your wardrobe." Pamela stood and waved her hand with impatience.

Hesitating, Sabrina's grip tightened around her cup. Suddenly she jumped to her feet as if something had changed her mind. The word *conviction* burst forth.

After Sadlerfield's public display of disapproval, something made Hunter take her hand. "You'll be all right."

She licked her lips and turned toward Pamela. "I just brought a few gowns, but maybe we can use yours for some ideas."

A knock sounded and Gavin entered. "I see you've settled in."

Pamela wagged her finger. "Mac! Why didn't you tell us that Hunt had married? We spent two days on the ship with you."

Gavin shrugged. "My mind's a bit dotty. My own wedding, the house…"

Sabrina took a hesitant step forward. "Excuse me, Mr. MacDuff. My aunt. Did she arrive home safely?"

He nodded, displaying cool politeness. "Aye. I saw her to her house. That's what you mean?"

"Yes. Good. I just wanted to know. Thank you."

Gavin's attitude toward Sabrina was as disquieting to Hunter as was his own attraction to her. Inexplicably, her concern about her aunt warmed his heart, but he wouldn't allow her compassion or his unbidden emotions to turn him into a real sap. This aside, he had to live with both people and wanted some harmony between the two. He'd address the problem later.

Pamela linked her arm with Sabrina's, and within seconds, they left the room.

Rising, Brice walked to the cellaret. "You and Lord Byron?"

Hunter understood the double-sided question. For too many years, he had vowed never to marry; convincing Brice would be more difficult than fooling Pamela. His friend possessed a sharp mind and had proved himself an excellent business partner. Undoubtedly, the same astuteness had prompted Brice's silence during tea. "Why not? She likes him."

"Why Sabrina?" He turned to pour the brandy.

"A dram for me, too, Brice." Gavin raked his blond hair.

"She's intelligent and never dull." Hunter smiled, though

her recklessness unnerved him. He had scarcely recovered from her Trojan horse fiasco only to have her thunder past him on a real horse. The recollections stole his breath.

Brice laughed and handed them drinks. "If her entry into the stable yard is any indication, then no, I imagine she is far from dull."

Without hesitation, Hunter held up his glass and a chime split the air. "To Sabrina."

"Do you care for her?"

The words slammed into his gut. Hunter pretended great interest in his drink. After swirling the glass, he sniffed the heady aroma, then sipped the brandy and waited for the liquid to calm his unease. Why did the question bother him? He never expected Brice to question the engagement so closely and knew his friend meant *do you love her?*

"Perhaps differently than the way you care for Pamela. I imagine strong feelings come with time."

A smile melted the disbelief on his face. "That's true. I lusted after Pamela at first."

As if Gavin sensed his unease, he reached into his jacket pocket and retrieved a thick packet. "From Faraday."

Anticipation seeped through his veins as Hunter accepted the letters. He wanted to believe in Sabrina's innocence. Perhaps she had very good reasons for all the things she'd done to him.

Gavin downed his drink in several swallows. "Brice, let's ride to the hunting lodge. You can see my new home."

Hunter thanked Gavin for occupying their friend. After he snapped Faraday's seal, his fingers tightened around the vellum. "Damn her."

# Chapter Eleven

Blackmail.

Futilely, Hunter tried to concentrate on the dinner conversation, but the dark thought overpowered Sabrina and Pamela's chatter, drowned the exchanges between the duke and Brice.

Hunter emptied the wine from his crystal goblet, but the sweet brew did little to ease the bitter taste of Jonathan Faraday's report. Nor had Hunter enjoyed the smoked salmon and venison.

He drummed his fingers on the mahogany table. Did Jonathan's theory hold truth? The report said a new corporation, Andrew Limited, owned the building housing Maison du Beaumont. Sadlerfield's property. Now Hunter knew in part how the duke kept an eye on Sabrina. How long had he known she was his granddaughter?

Faraday had reviewed Sabrina's client book, the name she dubbed her records. Among those on the list were wealthy, well-known gentlemen who had purchased gowns for their mistresses. Faraday questioned the ledger's special column, which showed who settled the bill. He suggested that a lady in crisis might threaten to expose the clients unless they paid her money to keep silent. Why else would she keep records of men's names? Was this the reason she wanted to return to London?

Besides the possibility of blackmail, he forced himself to look at the debt. Had his father and Sadlerfield concocted an elaborate scheme? He wanted to believe she was their victim, like him. Yet, that didn't dismiss the fact that she was hiding something.

Waiting until after supper to confront Sabrina proved a cork-brained idea, but he refused to jeopardize his marriage. He still had his welfare to consider.

For a long moment, his gaze rested on Sabrina. From a twisted loop of hair at her crown, a trailing mass of mink curls framed her finely sculptured face and emphasized her neck's delicate arch. Rather than her serviceable wool dress of indigo blue, he imagined Sabrina wearing an elegant gown. He envisioned her bare, alabaster shoulders draped in a swath of pale blue silk. Desire stirred. He cursed his depravity, loathed himself for wanting her.

"Hunt?" Pamela inquired. "Are you bored? In a day or two, I wish to take Sabrina to Edinburgh. She needs gowns. Is that agreeable?"

Lost in his thoughts and rising carnal desire, he groped for a suitable response but Sadlerfield intervened.

"Of course he will agree. He cannot introduce his wife to society in commoner's attire."

From beneath her lashes, Sabrina stabbed the duke with a dark look and stuffed a bite of ratafia pudding into her mouth.

As Hunter twisted the button on his waistcoat, the metal popped into his hand. He wanted to ram it down Sadlerfield's throat. "How about tomorrow? Since I have a meeting in Edinburgh, we'll spend the day there."

"Lady Darlington, you must excuse my granddaughter's colonialism. She lived in America. I trust you've begun to teach her the ways of a true lady?"

The chime of silver and china stopped. From the chandelier, a drop of wax hit the gravy bowl and hissed. Hunter reached for the button on his waistcoat and realized only a thread remained.

Pamela cleared her throat. "Your grace, you speak as if

Sabrina cannot count to two. From Maison du Beaumont, I know she is quite intelligent.''

The corner of Sabrina's mouth curled. "What's wrong with colonialism? William the Conqueror was French, and he captured England. She wouldn't be the country she is today if not for the French." Pausing, she added, "No need to make excuses for me. My grandfather just forgets his history."

Sadlerfield choked on his wine as Brice grinned. Chuckling, Hunter met Sabrina's twinkling eyes and volleyed with a lazy smile that a lover might give to his temptress. She delved into her dessert, but her pink cheeks were like a salve to his wounded pride. At least she failed to hide the affect of his flirtation.

"Ooh, I know! I will plan a huge soiree to announce your marriage." Pamela clasped her hands.

"Sweetness, you should discuss your plans with Sabrina first," Brice said.

Sabrina ate another bite of pudding. When all eyes turned to her, she shrugged her shoulders. "Gavin's wedding will be my first soiree. To consider anything else is overwhelming."

Sensing Sabrina's unease, compassion stabbed Hunter's heart. "Scottish weddings can be quite rowdy. After the Scotch flows, the crowd will seek merriment. If you make a mistake, use the happy occasion as an excuse."

"Lady Darlington, you have an excellent idea. As Mr. MacDuff's wedding will introduce her to Scottish society, your affair will present Sabrina to London. You've time to turn her into a true lady?" The duke arched a white brow.

Pamela rolled her eyes and chuckled. "Really, your grace, you mustn't tease." Leaning forward, she looked at Sabrina. "Put your concerns aside. As your mentor, I will teach you everything. If anyone questions anything, you *face* him. Boldly. Success in the ton deals with attitude! With a bluff! Right, darling?"

"Pamela's right," Brice concurred. "If you find yourself in an unfamiliar situation, just pretend otherwise."

"I've plenty of attitude, and under pressing circumstances, I can pretend." Sabrina glanced innocently around the table.

Hunter narrowed his eyes in warning. "Sabrina, would you enjoy a stroll in the garden?"

Sabrina looked at him hesitantly. "Now?"

"Hunt! You are such a romantic!" The countess turned to Sabrina. "Go with him! We can entertain His Grace."

Hunter needed little encouragement. As he escorted Sabrina from the dining room, he sensed the reluctance in her stride. "We aren't going for a stroll. I must speak to you in private."

Moments later, they arrived in the study that adjoined his bedchamber. Through the span of windows, moonlight painted a silvery glow on the walls. He ground his teeth and wondered if his life would ever mirror the room's tranquillity again. Hunter lit a lantern. After retrieving the report from his desk, he motioned her to the Chippendale chairs separated by a mahogany side table.

Curiosity replaced the wariness in her eyes. She slid her palms down her skirt. "Is that a report from your solicitor?"

Hunter handed her the papers. "See for yourself."

As Sabrina read, her eyes grew wide and her mouth gaped. "*Due to your wife's financial crisis… However, she has a most curious set of ledgers…and anyone with criminal intent…* Criminal intent!" She slapped the paper on the table. The china figurine sitting atop wobbled.

"Go ahead. Keep reading."

Her hands started to shake. "*She could make a fortune off the knowledge contained within her ledgers. Perhaps she intends to use this information to blackmail…* Blackmail!"

"Just read the blasted thing."

Tossing the page onto the floor, she read the next. "*Perhaps she wished a grander existence and contrived a method to bleed money from her clients. Her marriage to you should grant her the material goods she seeks if this is so.* Bleed money!"

When Sabrina finished the last page, she shot to her feet and threw the papers at him. "You call this an inquiry into the debt? It's a joke! If you believe that nonsense, then you're a fool!''

As he stood, the papers fluttered to the floor. ''Do you hear me laughing? Why would you keep such an odd set of ledgers? He refers to the list of gentlemen and ladies. Obviously, the ladies are their mistresses since they appear unrelated. If society learned about their relationships, men's reputations and their families would suffer. Now, are you blackmailing them?''

Her fists sliced the air. ''You believe him?''

''You've proved yourself very resourceful in the past.''

Stomping up to him, she jabbed his chest with a finger. ''You're reasonably smart. You figure it out.''

Her gardenia scent threatened his sensibility, and he moved away. He planted his fists at his waist. ''Are you blackmailing your clients?''

''You belong in Bedlam. Do you think I'd risk my soul and freedom for a few pounds? You should know better. Think about our marriage. My freedom is what I've wanted. Not your money.'' Her voice vibrated with fury. She stalked to the door that led to her bedchamber.

''Where are you going? You sleep in my quarters. Furthermore, we're in the middle of a discussion.'' He started toward her.

''Discussion! *Maybe* I'll speak to you if you stop behaving like—like a *half-wit.*'' She slammed the door in his face.

*Half-wit?* Hunter drew a deep breath, gathered the papers and settled into a chair. Perhaps she accused him justly. How often had she suggested an annulment? In her desire to return to London, twice she attempted escape. She looked so innocent and her words seemed sincere. Hunter wanted to believe that she wouldn't extort money from anyone. However, she had blackmailed him.

He ran his fingers through his hair. Why did Sabrina muddle his brain? She frustrated and confounded him more than any other lady he had ever met. As he read the details of the investigation again, he wished he had learned more about the debt and Sabrina's past. Uncovering her secret would be the key to holding the marriage intact, and if he failed, Sadlerfield would issue more threats.

The answers always pointed to his father and the duke, a match so unseemly that Hunter couldn't imagine the two in a civil conversation. Was his father in England through Sadlerfield's help? Had the two made plans so his father could retaliate and allow Sadlerfield to get his heir? The continuation of his bloody name seemed to drive him to near-lunacy. What created the animosity between Sabrina and the duke? Not merely an heir, was it?

Suddenly Hunter imagined his child, the boy the duke so desired. After witnessing the way the duke treated Sabrina, Hunter knew he'd do anything to shield his child from the man. But then, he needn't worry now. Sabrina hadn't allowed him his due, either.

Refocusing his thoughts, he looked at the report again. Could the person behind this be a member of Parliament who intended to distract or discredit Hunter's reform efforts? If the debt was intended to be a personal attack on his political beliefs, Hunter suspected his neighbor in Barbados, Sir Lawson, a man who preached the rightness of slavery. Just thinking about the man and his whip brought a rancid taste to Hunter's mouth. He snorted and searched for more potential enemies.

If he needed to spend the rest of his life to find the answers, he would do so. The person responsible would pay.

Rising, Hunter put the papers in his desk drawer and retrieved the rest of the report. *Once I complete the investigation of her personal life, I shall send you another summary. Afterward, we can decide your course of action.* Maybe when Faraday finished his inquiry, and she proved innocent, then Hunter could share his theories with her. For now, to gain her cooperation in the marriage, he must assume her innocence. He'd deal with her secret when he learned its nature. Besides, he refused to chance something happening to Sabrina without knowing his father's whereabouts.

Hunter eyed her bedchamber door. Maybe he had treated her unfairly by assuming the worst. Before he lost his courage or allowed pride to surface, he decided she deserved an apology.

After knocking and receiving no reply, Hunter entered and looked at an empty bed.

Sabrina blinked away angry tears and wiped her damp cheeks with the back of her hand. The lantern flame sputtered, sending shapeless shadows across the conservatory's glass walls. Occasionally, coal chunks shattered against the stove's interior. Even so, the eerie setting seemed less threatening than Hunter's accusations.

"Idiotic report!" However, she understood his reasoning. She had blackmailed him, but that was to preserve the twins' welfare. Despite her good intentions, she couldn't tell him.

With a furious jerk, she plucked another dead leaf off a neglected plant. The leaf crackled in her fist. "Arrogant man!"

She wanted to hate him for keeping her away from everything she held dear. Were the twins crying for her? Her vision blurred. She missed them. Were they all right? Sabrina hugged the jasmine plant to her chest and she caught the flower's sweet fragrance.

Could she ever weaken Hunter's defenses and convince him the marriage would never succeed? Must she remain wed? Knowing the possibility loomed, hot tears rolled down her cheek.

Tasting the salty liquid, she steadied her quivering lips. What fueled his distrust? What was he hiding? Inspiration struck. By gleaning information from Pamela, Sabrina could decipher the enigmatic man! At least the countess had defended her at supper.

She held the jasmine up to rejoice, but suddenly the leaves' hue reminded her of Hunter's sultry green eyes. They promised to burn any sensibility a woman possessed. Her body grew hot just thinking about his lips pressed against hers, and she cursed the unwelcome feeling.

Why was she wildly and inexplicably drawn to him? How long could she fight her attraction? Her freedom seemed so essential to fulfill her duty to the twins, but with every touch and kiss, she could sense he was coaxing her toward consummating the marriage. What was she going to do?

Carefully she pinched off more spent flower petals. "I'm sorry I took my anger out on you, jasmine."

The door squeaked. Sabrina swung around and hugged the pot to her stomach. "What are *you* doing here? How long have you been here?" How much of her raving had Hunter heard?

"Long enough. Disappearing has become a habit of yours," he said irritably as he approached. "Why are you talking to plants?"

Gravel crunched beneath his boots. Silver light reflected off his black hair and a cravat hung loose around his neck. Peeking beneath the sleeves of his coat, snowy cuffs edged with lace fluttered in the darkness. The rest of him blended with the night. Like a breathing shadow, he would hunt her down.

Trembling, she moved toward a table. "They respond better than you."

"I want to finish our discussion." He edged closer. "Have you been crying?" His tone softened.

She had too much pride to admit to any weakness. "No. I was too angry to sleep, so I came here. You shouldn't have worried."

"I should have let you explain your ledgers to me."

"You're apologizing?" When he remained tight-lipped, she gazed at him pointedly. "Are you apologizing? Unless you're in *full* control of your faculties, I refuse to discuss anything."

"All right. I apologize. As for my faculties, they disappeared when you arrived," he said flatly.

Despite his tone, his eyes twinkled with wry humor and

Sabrina sensed his apology bludgeoned his pride. The act made her believe she *would* find a way to break his defenses.

"If you cast aside your distrust, you'd see the hilarity of your solicitor's theory." Fighting a smile, she briefly glanced down at the pot in her hands.

His well-shaped lips formed a thin line. "Tell me about the column of names."

She managed an angelic smile as a prelude to her defense of her client book. "Aunt Marga is horrible with finances and records. I'm the exact opposite. The method reminds me who paid the bill since that person is rarely the lady. From this, I noticed liaisons changing. I never recorded the names with blackmail in mind. Most people have morals. If a gentleman pays for *several* ladies' gowns in six months, I would have to be blind not to notice."

"What happened to your ideals when you blackmailed me?"

She licked her lips. "I've told you. I did what I had to do."

"What happened between you and your grandfather? Why do you dislike him?"

The pot dug into her ribs. "You're digressing from your solicitor's report."

He regarded her pointedly. "Did you question the other notes after the first bill remained unpaid?"

"I just thought you were another wealthy rogue."

As he threw her a frigid look, he jabbed his chest. "It's not I."

She stepped backward. "I've another reason. Marga's children had chicken pox at the time the debt occurred. They had barely recovered when I became indisposed. Marga was unaware that the first bill still existed and accepted the other notes. Before this, our clients had always paid their bills on time. Why should she doubt someone who has an elevated title? Besides, I could hardly go out with spots on my face." Sabrina pointed to the scar near her right ear.

He angled his head for a better look, then straightened. "All right. I believe you."

She stared at him wide-eyed. "You do?"

"When Gavin returned, you seemed concerned for your aunt. Obviously you are very close."

Her heart thumped. "Thank you for accepting my word."

"We have something else to finish."

The husky timbre of his voice disappeared into the darkness. Suddenly he tried to remove the plant from her arm, but Sabrina gripped the container with both hands. "I'm still tending this plant." She failed to hide the desperation in her voice.

His green eyes possessed a look of seductive challenge. "Are you breaking our bargain?"

He was going to kiss her. Panic constricted her lungs. When he lifted the plant from her hands, Sabrina stepped back, but he caught her by the waist and drew her close. She dug her fingers into his arms and tilted her head back to avoid his kiss. "Please."

"Please what? You say one thing, but your body says another," he whispered hoarsely, and lowered his head.

His mouth covered hers with unleashed hunger. When his hands moved up her sides, she moaned, relishing the feelings his closeness evoked. Wanting to feel more of him, she arched her back and wrapped her arms around his broad shoulders.

His long fingers delved into her curls and they tumbled past her shoulders. The pins clattered against the gravel. He parted her lips with his tongue, releasing their bridled passion as hot as the humid air surrounding them. Searing sensations shot through her body and settled in the pit of her stomach.

"You're mine. Don't run off like that again," he said through his ragged breath.

His words stopped Sabrina's heart and the thick air between them lifted. Did she misunderstand his tone? Was that concern in his voice? Had she scared him by leaving her room? Quickly his possessive words overshadowed her thoughts. Nothing scared him.

Moving away from him, Sabrina bumped against the table. Passion could lead to darker temptations, desires she sensed without knowing what they all were, something her body craved. "We're married, but I don't belong to you." That was a lie. He owned her.

"One day you will." With his finger, he gently lifted her chin. "And such a short kiss."

Trying to contain the surges of panic, she hugged her waist and ignored his first comment. "*Short?* What's long?" Why had she asked the dim-witted question? He'd probably insist on a demonstration.

With a twinkle in his eyes, he smiled languidly. "That sort of kiss defies description."

For a second she looked away. "Oh."

"Can you deny that you enjoyed our short kiss?"

Still shaken from the effects of his passion, Sabrina straightened, disliking that he *knew*. His cavalier attitude hindered any trust she might place in him, especially with her heart. Denying that she enjoyed his kiss was unthinkable, but she refused to admit it, either. Their hunger would lead to disaster.

"You wanted me to be convincing. Did I act adequately?" She managed a steady voice.

The veins in his temple twitched but his look turned bland. "Remember to keep up the pretense," he drawled. "Oh, don't mention your Geoffrey to Pamela. She might become suspicious." Hunter waved his hand as if dismissing her.

Suddenly the hot environment took on a disturbing chill. Unwilling to take the time to consider his mood change, she brushed past him. Why press her luck? "I'll be very convincing." The door slammed behind her.

After Hunter watched Sabrina's shadowed form enter the house, he picked up the potted jasmine and relished its sultry fragrance. For a few glorious moments, her sweet lips had smothered the lies, the secrets and all their distrust.

"Pretending?" he said viciously, and crushed the plant in his hand. Her heart might belong to her precious Geoffrey but Hunter knew that her body responded to his. What else was she lying about?

## Chapter Twelve

The barouche clattered across North Bridge then turned onto Lawnmarket. Rising like giant steps toward Edinburgh Castle, Old Town's stone buildings came into view. Sabrina chewed her bottom lip and hoped she'd done the right thing by asking to shop here.

Ahead of the barouche, several men dressed in homespun woolen trousers and ill-fitting coats were leading a horse cart up the hill. People and conveyances fought for space. The air smelled of things old and new—yesterday's supper, whiskey from a tavern's open door, pansy-filled carts, and people doused with perfume. A cloth merchant's ware flapped with a merciful gust of wind.

"With the splendid shops on Princes Street, why do you want to come to Lawnmarket?" Hunter's tone was dry.

Startled, Sabrina wondered if he somehow guessed her intent. "The servants say that a shilling will buy more here in Old Town."

Earlier, she had endured shopping the length of Princes Street for clothing accessories and jewels, which filled the coach behind them. Uncertain if she'd remain in the marriage, she had protested Hunter's purchases. She had detested her afternoon appointment with the modiste, too. A couturiere wearing a competitor's gown was like a brewer drinking the ale made in another distillery, an act of betrayal. Everyone seemed to have forgotten her previous life.

Now she was the wife of a powerful earl, and the time had come to see what her husband was about. In the Darlingtons' presence, Hunter might share more of his life.

"Oh! I love a bargain, but shopping at a market will be a new experience for me." Pamela glanced out the window.

Hunter rubbed Sabrina's cloak. "What do you intend to buy?"

She gazed at his long fingers. "We're shopping here for you. I'm quite done. You've emulated Lord Byron thrice over." She hooked her thumb toward the other coach.

"Gardeyloo!" came a shout from outside.

Sabrina instantly understood the words that meant *gardez l'eau. Look out for the water.* The housekeeper had warned her about the French phrase that the Scots borrowed. The pedestrians' rapid steps clicked on the cobblestones. No one wanted a chamber pot emptied on his head. Suddenly the barouche stopped.

Hunter snapped the shades closed just as a splash hit the coach's roof. The driver swore viciously. As his whip cracked, the conveyance lurched forward.

"Sabrina, are you *certain* you want to shop here?"

"I'm sure. We just have to listen for the warning." Sabrina paused. "Do you plan to help the Scots in Parliament? The newspaper said you're speaking on the Reform Bill today."

Hunter lifted his eyebrows. "How does my business relate to shopping in Old Town?"

"When you attend the political meeting, tell the people we shopped here. Helping the populous will seem more sincere if you show an interest in their failing trades."

"Using a shopping trip to my political advantage? Most ingenious." Hunter's eyes sparkled with apparent admiration.

"Such foresight, Sabrina. You will make a good political wife, just like Pamela." Turning, Brice kissed her on the cheek. "She supports my work, too."

As a sense of belonging warmed her heart, Sabrina questioned again whether she'd remain Hunter's wife. The idea quickly died. Acting in her family's best interest would always come first, and an annulment might occur. At least she knew the reform movement was important to him and couldn't help but admire Hunter's work.

Sabrina's heart surged with hope. Was the newspaper's portrayal of him as a kind man also true? Would he eventually understand her need for an annulment if it became necessary?

Cautiously Hunter lifted the shade. When nothing dripped, he rolled up the covering.

A moment later they stood in the crowded street and nearly suffocated from the sewage odor. Pamela and Brice quickly entered the gift shop behind them. After Hunter instructed the driver to clean the coach, they edged their way to the store.

The shop smelled a little musty, as if the room had captured a slice of the air from years past. Sabrina examined a set of soldiers, the Royal North British Dragoons, sitting atop their greys. It cost a pound. She grimaced at the price and swallowed the lump in her throat. Alec would love them.

"Aren't you a little old for those?" Amusement brightened Hunter's eyes.

She set down the soldier. "I was just thinking my cousin would like them."

As a soft tune sounded, Sabrina turned. Pamela held a stand with a doll sitting at a piano and as the tune played, the doll's head moved. Drawn by the exquisite piece, Sabrina drifted toward the music. Reverently she touched the doll's red satin gown, a miniature of a French dress with ruffles at the hem and leg-o'-mutton sleeves. The piano's intricate details imitated a real instrument.

"This is the most beautiful thing I've ever seen," Sabrina whispered.

Like the soldiers she wished for Alec, she wanted the music box for Christine. An ache settled in Sabrina's chest. Were they all right? Mentioning the children again might draw too much attention. She scanned the shelves for other wares.

"Hunt! This box is so charming. Do buy it for Sabrina."

Hunter took the stand from Pamela, then handed the toy to the merchant. "The lady would like the music box and soldiers."

She grabbed his arm. With the others nearby, she tried for a teasing tone. "Wait! You've already put Lord Byron to shame."

"He's moldering in his grave. Six years, I believe. He won't feel a thing."

"Stop jesting about the deceased."

Pamela hooked her arm into Brice's. "Come, darling. We will let them settle their lovers' quarrel. Perhaps we can find Mac a wedding gift."

Brice chuckled. "I think Gavin just wants his bride."

With eyes shimmering, Hunter whispered in her ear. "Lovers' quarrel? They've half of it right."

His breath warmed her skin but his words made her hot. "No. Buying things for me is one thing, but not for my family."

"Why not? Now they're my family, too." Ignoring her, Hunter pulled out several gold coins from a pouch.

Already he claimed her share in the shop, and his involvement with the twins could only lead to trouble. She opened her mouth and snapped it shut. "They're too expensive for children's toys."

Hunter arched a brow. "How can I announce that I shopped in Old Town if I leave empty-handed?"

"Then buy something for yourself."

"No. I like the idea of buying toys. Doing things like this will help me adjust to having our own child."

Planting her shaking hands on the counter, she pretended to examine the wares again.

"Do you see something else that you'd like?" Hunter lifted her chin with his finger.

She detected urgency in his softly spoken words. He was speaking about himself and their passion. About consummation... What was she going to do? "No. Let's go to another stall."

After depositing their parcels in the barouche, they continued through the arcade. To support the failing shops, Hunter bought anything in which she showed a minor interest.

"Ooh, Hunt! Wilson's stall!" Pamela exlaimed. "They are the premier plaid makers. Buy Sabrina a Sinclair plaid or the Graham pattern to honor your grandfather's title. Well both! Oh, darling. I almost wish you were of Scottish ancestry. You have such attractive le—"

Brice grabbed Pamela's arm. "Let's ask the merchant Wilson if he has Graham's plaid."

"Would you like me to wear one?" Hunter's green eyes sparkled.

Her mouth grew dry just imagining his exposed muscular legs. Sabrina licked her bottom lip. "I suppose you can always use an extra blanket," she murmured.

His mouth curved as if he knew how she would react to him with just woolen stockings covering his calves. As they edged toward the stall, mischief brightened his eyes. Was he flirting with her? Was this his newest ploy to coax her into consummating their marriage? Her neck grew damp.

"I'd rather use the plaid like my ancestors. My Graham side goes far back. One relative, the third Duke of Montrose helped repeal the Highland dress prohibition. A Scot, especially a relation, should reward Montrose's parliamentary efforts. In fact, Graham's motto is *Do Not Forget*."

Despite his seductive taunting, his voice possessed an obvious pride in his heritage. She let out a slow breath. "What about the Sinclair family? Tell me about them."

"Last night you spoke of William the Conqueror." Hunter chuckled. "Your grandfather nearly had apoplexy. Why is that? Why does he think you're too dim-witted to become a lady?"

She lifted her chin. "My father didn't raise me aristocratically. That's all. In the duke's eyes, I'm not perfect. But he doesn't think many people are."

"I almost intruded." He smiled. "But you managed well enough."

Her heart bucked, yet if they continued to discuss her family, he might ask questions about the twins. "You were talking about the Sinclair family, not about the duke's insufferable manners."

"Ah, yes. Baron Walderne de Santo Claro left St. Clare in Normandy and served under William the Conqueror. Others were less noble. The fourth Earl of Caithness imprisoned one son, and while he was in prison, the earl's other son starved him. By then the name had changed to Sinclair."

The story chilled her blood. "What's the Sinclair motto?"

*"Commit Thy Work to God."*

"By helping the people, you're fulfilling the motto?"

"I do what I feel necessary."

"What did your father do to honor the family name?"

"He enforced his rights and produced an heir."

Her breath hitched as if she'd run into a stone fortress. "What hold does my grandfather have over you? Why must you stay married to me?"

His jaw twitched. "No questions about motives, remember? You said that when you blackmailed me."

She looked away. At first, she didn't want to know, worried he would question her reasons for refusing to marry. Now the knowledge was imperative to any plan she conceived for her family's safety.

When they reached the stall, Pamela was examining a Scottish blanket, dominated with brick red and indigo. Thin white stripes crisscrossed through the dark hues. Brice held one with deep green and midnight squares where ribbons of white intersected to form the design.

As if their conversation of moments ago had never occurred, Hunter's mouth curved, sending a glimmer to his eyes. "Which one do you like, Sabrina?"

Suddenly she realized he could control his emotions if he chose and this meant he had vast experience doing so. Now he displayed his passion. With damp palms, she pointed. "The green one."

Brice grinned. "I would give you one of my best horses just to see you donning a plaid."

Hunter laughed. "You might lose a horse."

Their carefree manner reminded her of the first time she saw Hunter with the colt. Would he act like this without the confines of their marriage? If she stayed in the union, would she see this gentle man more often?

What was she considering? She couldn't think in that direction. Yet, this was just one enjoyable afternoon. What was wrong with experiencing a few pleasurable hours? At least she'd learned something about Hunter.

After lifting the blanket from Brice's hands, Sabrina held the garment next to Hunter's green eyes. Suddenly the hue deepened. She recognized his beckoning look and yanked the wool to her chest.

"You're holding Graham's plaid." Hunter ran his hand across the soft wool, and then his fingertips ventured to her cheek. She stood very still, unsure where his hand would drift next.

"Are you buying the Sinclair plaid?" Pamela asked.

"Find another, Pamela," Hunter replied. "I'll buy two of each." Taking the garment, he draped it on Sabrina's shoulder.

She looked down at the swath of wool. As if she had just contracted ague, fever washed through her body. "So, this is the Sinclair plaid? Intense. The colors are intense."

"Like the shades of a fire. Does the plaid keep you warm?"

When she raised her lids, heat spread through her body, and not from the blanket. His languid eyes promised the day would end with a kiss.

"Just buy them." Sabrina whipped the garment off her shoulder and held the merchandise out to him.

"We have a meeting, and you ladies have a dressmaker's appointment." Brice tucked his gold timepiece into his waistcoat pocket and clapped Hunter's back. "You will don a kilt?"

The corner of his mouth turned up. "Aye, 'tis only fitting that I practice a Scottish custom," Hunter said with a brogue.

A vision of Hunter emerged—long muscular legs as solid as granite, the ensemble attached to his virile body with a brooch and a belt. The costume covered less than a *short* dressing robe.

Sabrina's heart hammered. Her mouth went dry. Was this a prelude to the future? Would he come to bed naked next?

As the barouche neared the dressmaker's shop, Hunter's conscience battled with guilt. In minutes, he'd know Sabrina's reaction to his news, and she'd already caused havoc with his emotions and pride. Their kiss in the conservatory represented only one example. During the busy day, he managed to stifle the emotions, but now, the feelings hung heavy on his soul.

Brice's curiosity about the debt annoyed him too. His questions reminded Hunter that other matters needed his attention.

"I wish you had told me the particulars about this debt sooner. You think your father is involved?"

Hunter scowled. "I've other theories, but he favors bringing innocent young ladies into his schemes. You know that." Though he wanted to tell Brice his suspicions about his father and Sadlerfield, Hunter never could. To involve another friend would damn him as an accomplice, like Gavin. Allowing Brice to believe Lord Wick had been working in Australia was best.

Brice knitted his brows. "You usually manage a more detached tone when speaking about your father. What else is troubling you?" Suddenly he snapped his fingers. He grinned in a way that only a man could understand, like a fop about to capture his first light-skirt. "Ah. This is the first time away from your bride."

Hunter fingered the button on his waistcoat. Considering he hadn't even reached the marriage bed, to allow Brice's taunt seemed prudent. He looked out the window. "I'm sure I'll survive."

Survive. The word dredged up the events leading to his

crime. After taking his father to the edge of hell, Hunter had sailed to Barbados to escape the censure of English society, who gossiped about his engagement to Diana. The island people knew nothing about his or his father's past, the first of which he regarded with nipping guilt, and the latter, great shame. How could he admit that running from the scandals represented the most cowardly act of his life?

Despite the ton's raised brows about Diana, the kidnapping was the act that could cost Gavin and him their lives. He must ensure that his marriage would survive. Sabrina didn't want the union and was becoming too curious about his past. What could he do? Now an immediate problem plagued him, too. Brice's astute hazel gaze made Hunter's stomach knot tighter. He had portrayed Sabrina as a victim. How could he in good conscience leave her alone with her grandfather and perhaps his father lurking somewhere?

"I can see you're still nervous about your married state. At moments I can't fathom that you finally wed."

"Neither can I." He looked out the window again. "The next time we come to Old Town, I'll bring a few of my sailors. If someone shouts *gardez l'eau,* they can clear the street for us."

Brice chuckled. "A close call today."

"You know that my managers train my sailors to ride and shoot."

"Yes. In India, they're your outriders, too. Have you had trouble with your sapphire shipments?"

Hunter shook his head. "While we were attending our wives, I sent Gavin to Leith. He's ordering a dozen sailors to Keir Castle. I worry that my father might arrive."

"You are wise to take precautions if you suspect Randall. Did you tell Sabrina?"

"No."

"Secrets already? Good God, Hunter. Learn to trust your wife. That is what marriage is all about."

"I'll get around to telling her about Randall. If nothing comes of my suspicions, I'd scare her unnecessarily."

"That's true, but you are doing one good thing for your marriage."

"What?"

"Continue to court your wife. Spoil her just a little. Like today. I enjoy giving baubles to Pamela, and you make my generosity possible. When I inherited a revered title and little money, you gave my life direction. I'm indebted to you."

"You owe me nothing. You've worked hard, and wealth is your reward." Then his thoughts were no longer on business. He crossed his ankle over a knee and drummed his fingers on his boots.

Spoiling Sabrina? Courting her? *You've already put Lord Byron to shame...* He'd sworn he'd never give her baubles, and today, he had bought her more than most men give their wives in a lifetime. Guilt plundered anew. In his quest to learn what she was hiding, had he stooped to "buying" her secret?

He shifted against the squab and swore under his breath.

"No need to be embarrassed about showing devotion. This marriage business involves constant work."

"I'm aware of that."

But courting as a means to secure his marriage? He tapped his boot. Years ago, he convinced himself that a union out of duty, to produce an heir, or lust would result in a life of misery. Furthermore, a wealthy, titled man would wonder if a woman wanted those things more than she desired the man. Sabrina wanted none of the material rewards and made a good show of not wanting *him*.

He refused to abandon his plan to kiss the truth from her, but he needed an alternate strategy. Though he was making slow progress, he wanted to secure their marriage. More Lord Byron? The plan possessed a more honorable ring than mere seduction. Perhaps Brice's suggestion had merit. The price of a few baubles and finery seemed a small price to avoid criminal charges.

When they arrived at the dress shop a few moments later, Brice helped Pamela into the coach while Hunter escorted Sabrina to the second barouche.

"I've something to discuss with you." When she ignored him, he cast her a quizzical glance.

"A traitor," Sabrina hissed. "That's what I am. A traitor. That dressmaker has none of Marga's brilliance or originality."

During her raving, Hunter remained silent, but once settled inside the barouche between the boxes and parcels, he decided to be direct. "You and Pamela are returning to Keir Castle without us. Our political meeting will continue after supper."

Sabrina's eyes grew wide. "You're leaving me alone with my grandfather and Pamela?"

"She'll not bite. She's enjoying our marriage too much."

Her hands balled into fists. "This is a *horrible* thing to do to me. I might say the wrong thing in front of Pamela. You know I can barely spare my grandfather a civil word. At least return to Keir Castle for supper."

He smiled lazily. "Do you need me, or is it that you'll miss me?"

She drew in a sharp breath. "Need you? Miss you! This afternoon, I *almost* liked you. How could I forget you're usually ruthless?"

Warmth seeped into his soul and his smile broadened. "You almost liked me? Do not forget."

She raised her chin. "Forget what?"

"This." Slipping his hands around her waist, Hunter brushed her lips with his and, when she accepted his mouth, he deepened his kiss. A tiny mewing sound bubbled from her throat.

As he parted her lips with his tongue, torturous sensations enlivened his imagination. *Her bare breasts against his chest. Two bodies fused by desire.* Hunter groaned and shifted from the ache in his loins. He plunged his tongue deeper, seeking the sweet taste of her, hungering for her as he had never yearned for any woman.

Searing pleasure swept through his blood when their tongues met. He nipped and teased her lips as hot breath whispered between them, but the invisible caress fueled their passion. Exploring fingers combed his hair, slipped down his cravat and then massaged his neck. Hunter moaned with unbridled satisfaction.

"That feels wonderful," he said thickly.

"I'm not ready to…" She whispered the words.

The meek protest contrasted with the arch of her body, the way she tilted her head as if inviting him to savor every sensitive spot. Encouraged, he brushed a trail of kisses down her throat then paused. For one guilt-ridden second, he hesitated, but then parted her cloak. She was his wife. Expecting a slap but not receiving one, he unbuttoned her pelisse. The warmth of her skin emanated through the chemise, and reverently, he cupped her breast.

Sabrina gasped but their lips met again and silenced any words. Just as he began to explore the curves hidden beneath the yards of wool and lawn, a bellow from outside jarred his mind back to reality.

"Yer lordship! McGregor's Hotel!" The driver yelled again as the barouche slowed.

With great reluctance, Hunter pulled his lips away from hers, swollen now from his plundering. Passion flushed her cheeks and desire cast warmth in her pale blue eyes. Her gardenia scent seemed to cling to him. She looked so lovely he nearly changed his mind about going to the meeting.

He smiled slowly and reveled in the warm feelings their passion evoked. Yet he failed to understand the reason. Perhaps her willing participation had bandaged his pride.

"You're beautiful. We'll try for a longer kiss next time." When she started to open her mouth, he put a finger to her lips. "I know you enjoyed the kiss as much as I did. Let me part with that knowledge," he said softly.

"If you think you can change the rules, think again," she said, her breath still raspy.

When the coach stopped, he managed a semblance of control and quickly brought order to his disheveled state.

Quickly, Sabrina righted herself. As the passion disappeared from her eyes, the indifference returned. He disliked the look so much that he almost kissed her again. Instead, he kissed the tip of her nose. "Do not forget this moment." Hunter cupped her chin and grazed his thumb over her lower lip, which quivered beneath his touch. He smiled, knowing that despite her impervious facade, she sensed the physical attraction between them as much as he did.

After entering McGregor's Hotel, he and Brice waited until the coach departed. An arriving cabby blocked his view, and as the occupant disembarked, Hunter's body tensed. The man had dark hair and was tall... When the passenger looked up to pay the driver, Hunter let out his breath. The man was not his father.

He prayed that the men he sent to Keir Castle would thwart any dangers. Where the devil was his father?

Brice clapped Hunter's shoulder. "You need not look so distraught. It's only one night you will be away from your wife. Nevertheless, I must agree, sleeping alone is no comparison to a warm and willing lady."

Hunter rammed his hands into his coat pocket. The only road to "warm and willing" seemed to involve courting her. The idea was beginning to taste a little better.

For some reason, the more she opposed his purchases, the more he wanted to buy for her. Hunter had simply bought everything that made her eyes sparkle. Perhaps he thought the trinkets would warm her coolness to his touch. Not coolness. Avoidance. Once in his arms, he could warm her a few degrees, but coming to him willingly remained another matter.

Suddenly he realized the reason he enjoyed the outing. When she did anything with passion, her fervor ignited his. Sabrina even refused his gifts with intensity, though he admired her principles. She made him feel alive, an emotion he had missed for years. Then why did her refusal of his gifts bother him? Damnation. He didn't know.

Unfortunately, feeling anything meant that he left himself vulnerable. Resolutely he pushed the emotions deep into his soul. He couldn't care about a woman who had lied and blackmailed him. No. He was just trying to learn what she was hiding so he could save his and Gavin's necks.

# Chapter Thirteen

The words seemed to stick in her throat. Sabrina had spent a day with Pamela and hadn't found the courage to ask her one question about Hunter. Seeking information about Hunter under the guise of friendship stirred her guilt, especially since Pamela showed kindness. Enveloped in a deep leather chair, Sabrina sipped her cinnamon-laced tea and savored the spice that the Scots added to their brew. Pondering her strategy, she gazed around the library and summoned her nerve.

Across the desk from her, the countess resembled a military general in silk skirts as she planned Gavin's affair, and Sabrina felt like a press-gang recruit fresh from the London docks. Pamela's quill scratched as she continued to scribe her attack. Lists, like strategic maps, littered the mahogany desk. The papers contained duties for each head servant. Wanting the guests to find their suites easier, she'd even named each bedchamber according to the floral painting that hung near each door.

"You seem a bit distracted. Were you envisioning a different decor for this room?" Pamela turned over a guest list. "Or were you wondering what his Grosvenor Square house looks like?"

Sabrina choked on her tea and set down her cup. "I was thinking about his heritage. He's said little about the Sinclairs, but I'd like to understand him better. Will you tell me?"

Rising, Pamela's silk skirts rustled and stirred her lavender scent. She walked to a mullioned window. The blue jacquard drapes framed her form, a perfect vision of what and who an earl's wife should be. Sabrina tore her gaze away and stared at the dusky gardens. Outside, workers were still building canopies on the lawn. She wasn't Pamela and never could be.

Turning, Pamela glanced at her with knitted brows. "I'm not certain if I should tell you, but he might remain mum."

Sabrina's heart plunged to her toes. To urge Pamela to speak, she quickly revealed all she knew about him.

"Making Hunt happy is obviously important to you. You should know about his family. Except for his mother, he's had little joy."

Compassion tugged her heart. "What else made him so unhappy?"

"I'll get to that. Our mothers were best friends. Priscilla was a lovely lady, intelligent and charming. Since she disliked London, we came here to visit. Hunt acted like a big brother." Her face glowed as if she treasured the memories.

Pamela's words reminded Sabrina of Geoffrey, and she smiled in return. "Sometimes, close friends can be like family."

She nodded. "Priscilla either worked in her gardens or painted. Her art hangs in the hallway leading to the guests' bedchambers. That's where I got the idea for assigning each room by the flower's name."

"That's a lovely tribute to her. What else?"

"Randall's affairs hurt her terribly at first, but gradually she found peace, and was a wonderful mother. When Priscilla died, something inside Hunt died. He remains silent about her death." Sadness filled her eyes and she lowered her gaze.

Something urged Sabrina to delve deeper. "After his mother's passing, he must have felt very lonely. Is he afraid someone will profoundly affect him again?"

Pamela smiled warmly. "You have good insight."

Sabrina understood because even now, a part of her heart seemed hollow with her parents gone. However, she still had

Marga and the twins, while Hunter had no family he loved. "I wonder if he'll ever share his feelings with me, such as his mother's death."

"Oh! You mustn't think that he will hide his whole life from you." Pamela rushed over and took Sabrina's hands. "After all, he married you, and until now, Hunt's avoided the altar."

*Blackmailed to the altar.* Guilt warmed Sabrina's cheeks though, intuitively, she knew he needed someone to love him. "I almost need to pull every word out of him."

Pamela rolled her eyes. "In time, he will share more with you. Men are sometimes uncommunicative despite their pasts. That may be their nature. They think we are too weak to bear burdens."

Sabrina chuckled, feeling an odd sense of camaraderie. "Little they know, hmm?" Something inside warned her of their lighthearted banter. What if she and Hunter ended their union? Would their parting ruin her budding friendship with Pamela? Sabrina realized she enjoyed the idle chatter and, for fleeting moments, had forgot her purpose. "What else can you tell me?"

"I never thought he would be the same after…"

"After what? What happened to Hunter?"

A tap sounded on the open door. Both whipped their heads around as Sadlerfield entered. The rich drape of his gray frock coat and trousers made him look quite dapper, but she knew a cold heart lay beneath his exquisite clothes.

He tucked his ebony cane under his arm. "Yes, indeed. I am interested in all aspects of Lord Kenilworth's life, too."

As the lady of the house, Sabrina could throw him out… Prudence prevailed and she swallowed the urge.

"Oh, your grace. This story was on everyone's tongues."

"Do continue, and I will see if I recall. As Sabrina reminded me, I have forgotten moments of history. I presume it is my age." He turned to Sabrina. "Is that not so, my dear?"

Age had nothing to do with anything he said. His mind was

sharp as a well-honed stiletto. "I'll remind you when you stray."

He pressed his lips together and sat on the edge of the desk. Glancing down, he picked up their room assignment list and scanned the names. "Do go on with your story, Lady Darlington."

As Pamela's green eyes darkened, she released Sabrina's hands and sat in a leather chair. "I find discussing Randall difficult because he hurt people dear to me. Society only knows half the tale." She placed a serviette on her lap and reached for her teacup.

Sabrina's heart stopped. What if Pamela revealed something her grandfather didn't know? "Perhaps this isn't a good time for reminiscing. We're working, after all."

"I doubt the story will take long. Continue, Lady Darlington."

"About six years ago, Hunt learned about his own betrothal in the *Times*. The lady was a stranger to him. Randall arranged everything without Hunt's knowledge."

"That's a terrible thing to do!" The intensity of her emotions surprised her as much as the news. Concurrently, a disturbing thought occurred. Her grandfather's actions weren't so different. Slowly she looked at him, and, as if he sensed her regard, he met her gaze. "What do you think?"

Determination hardened his blue eyes and he shrugged. "Sometimes a father just knows what is best for his child. We do not know Lord Wick's reason for acting as he did. Do you know, Lady Darlington?"

Sensing something horrible, Sabrina took Pamela's hand and filled their teacups. She wanted to stop her from telling all as much as she wanted to comfort. "This will make you feel better. Take a sip. Forget the story."

With an unsteady hand, Pamela brought the beverage to her mouth. She took a dainty swallow. "You really should know. Society thought Hunt behaved wretchedly, but that's not true. Do you think he would act dishonorably?"

"No. He's a difficult man to understand and can be arrogant. He shows his gentler side, too."

When her grandfather looked up from the guest list, his eyes gleamed. "You are adjusting to your husband. That pleases me."

Sabrina suppressed the urge to throw the teapot at him.

The cup chimed as Pamela set it on the saucer. "Randall had gotten this young lady with child. Her name was Diana. Can you guess how they thought to solve the problem?"

She quickly pieced together the information and the conclusion. With a balled fist, she pounded the desk. "They *used* Hunter?"

"Yes. They decided Hunt should marry her. He refused, but offered a suitable allowance so she could start a new life. Despite her trickery, Hunt did not want Diana and the babe to suffer. He despises scandals." Pamela's voice wavered.

The duke raised his aristocratic nose a notch. "Sometimes indiscretions require difficult choices and a firm hand."

Sabrina ground her teeth. In ways, the story mirrored her situation. The manipulative elder using his kin to right his wrong. A bitter taste clogged her throat. "Then what happened?"

"After speaking to Diana and her parents, Hunt issued an announcement withdrawing his suit. They were not happy but agreed to some compensation. When Hunt arrived at their home to make the settlement, he learned Diana had just died." Pamela swallowed and paused. "Apparently, she drank several bottles of laudanum, and society believed she killed herself because of Hunt. After that, the ton considered him a blackguard like his father. Hunt made no effort to convince them otherwise."

The ache in her bosom rooted deeper. "That's unfair." Again she looked at the duke, who remained stoic. "Did you know?"

Putting down the list, he waved his hand with a dismissive stroke and stood. "How would I know such details? Nevertheless, I heard about the scandal. Nasty business."

"Yes, Hunt had an awful time of it."

"Interesting tale. Now I believe I will go for a walk and see how the gardeners are progressing. Good afternoon, ladies."

"They're stirring up the soil," Sabrina remarked. "Adding manure. You're rather good at that yourself."

Pamela smiled faintly. "Watch where you step."

The duke glared at Sabrina and left.

She and Pamela sat in companionable silence and sipped their tea but unease crept up Sabrina's spine. Her grandfather was so conservative that she had expected him to make a disparaging remark about Hunter's worthiness. He hadn't. She sensed her grandfather knew this story. Perhaps he just wanted to hear Pamela's version and confirm he hadn't missed anything.

Despite the past affair and Hunter's tainted reputation, her grandfather didn't care. All he wanted was an heir. He would stop at nothing to get what he wanted. Deuced. Did he know about the twins? An old consideration surfaced. Had her grandfather decided he wanted a "perfect" heir? Tea sloshed on the saucer.

Guilt assailed her anew. She recalled Hunter's comment about losing respectability. *Once lost, no amount of money can buy it back.* Most likely, he had also tried to prevent his mother from more hurt. Why else would he provide for such a despicable man like his father?

She suddenly understood in part the reason for their marriage. Hunter wanted to save her reputation. The thought both soothed her heart and clashed with her burgeoning emotions. Given the situation with the twins, she had considered him the enemy, but now knew he had honorable intentions, despite being blackmailed by her grandfather.

After Hunter's forced engagement, she surmised that he questioned every person's actions. Including hers, she thought grimly. Like the gossipmongers, she had thought poorly of him, and worse, she had blackmailed him without thought to his feelings.

If she were a better wife, she could prevent him from more scandal. He needed compassion, not more hurt. Annulment was still on her mind, but while they were together, she could try to make him proud of her.

Maybe her act would help heal his battered heart. If not that, at least she could keep her grandfather from causing Hunter more problems. Despite his flaws, she knew a much gentler man lay beneath the hardened surface, beneath the guilt, beneath his scarred and tormented soul. Being a better wife meant she should perform her wifely duty. She held her breath. Maybe she could do all but that one thing....

Pamela set down her teacup. "We must return to our task or Gavin will have our heads. He wants everything finished before Colleen, his affianced, arrives."

"I appreciate you sharing the story with me."

Warm green eyes held her gaze. "Speaking of that incident was hard for me because I adore Hunter."

Pamela's proclamation stirred Sabrina's turbulent emotions more. With her feelings in flux, she lacked the courage to ask if Pamela was or had been in love with Hunter. Had he cared about her before all the darkness entered his life? Sabrina frowned, disliking the direction of her thoughts.

Like a boom of thunder, the feelings came unbidden, and her pulse quickened. Sabrina realized she missed him. Her cup rattled against the saucer.

"I adore him, too." Unsolicited, the simple words came from somewhere deep within her. So did the wave of jealousy.

A thud sounded, followed by another. Sabrina's eyes flew open. A block of light spilled from Hunter's dressing room and she knew he'd just removed his boots. She was used to his routine. Tonight, would he sleep in his clothes as he had done before? Clasping the bedsheets, she gazed at the empty portion of the bed, and then the single taper that flickered on his table.

She wanted to tell him she'd be a better wife, that compassion urged her to do so. Still, discussing the subject in bed might invite temptation, and she didn't want a misunderstanding. Already she expected him to ask if she remembered the last time they kissed, and that she owed him one for today. With trembling fingers, she touched the lace at her throat.

A part of her wanted to tell him about the twins so he'd understand, but she didn't dare. One slip of his tongue and her grandfather would steal Alec, maybe Christine too; that is, assuming he didn't already plan to do so.

Besides, what if she grew fonder of Hunter and she had to leave him? She shuddered. In her heart though, she knew she was being unfair to him. The best she could do was to show him her intentions by deed. If they remained married, she wanted to establish a reasonable relationship with him now.

Through half-closed eyes, she stared at the dressing room door. Her heart stopped when she saw his bare feet. No trousers covered his ankles. She forced herself to look up, stopped at the hem of his robe and let out a long, silent breath.

After extinguishing the dressing room light, he padded softly across the room. His robe parted with each step and the candlelight was enough to reveal his muscular calves.

She lowered her eyelids but his bayberry scent quickened her pulse. The bed dipped. For a long moment, everything remained still and she peeked at him from beneath her lashes.

As if deep in thought, he sat on the edge of the bed, his elbows resting on his knees. His position drew her sympathy rather than her passion. When he reached for the candlesnuffer, she forced herself to speak.

"Is something wrong?"

Swinging around, his eyes dropped to her hands. "I didn't mean to wake you."

Sabrina forced herself to loosen the grip on the bedsheets. "Did something happen at your meeting?"

Turning away, he placed the snuffer on the side table. "Edinburgh has empty coffers. I donated twenty thousand pounds."

She stared at his broad back, covered in indigo velvet. Though he might be speaking the truth, she sensed something else bothered him more. "That was generous. Did you have another argument with my grandfather?"

He swung his legs onto the bed, tucked his hands beneath his head and stared at the frescoed ceiling. "Go to sleep."

For reasons she couldn't name, his dismissal tweaked her temper. She disliked his attitude. "If you want this marriage to work, you can't ignore me."

"I can and I will."

Avoiding temptation was one thing, but she didn't want him to cast her from his life, either. That would make consummation even more difficult if staying married was her only choice. Besides, she still didn't know what her grandfather held over him.

"Don't be upset, but Pamela told me about Diana. I asked her about your past and she thought I should know the whole story."

Closing his eyes, he worked his jaw. "Neither of you is to blame. Perhaps I should thank her for speaking the truth. What else did she tell you? That I failed to help Diana?" A self-recriminating tone seeped into his soft voice.

Sabrina released the bedsheet and touched his arm. When he opened his eyes, she stared into their green depths. They were the shade of a forest and, like nature, they held as many secrets. "Pamela defends you."

His eyes dropped to the lace around her throat. When he grasped her hand and brushed her fingers with a kiss, she suppressed a cry. The air suddenly grew thicker. In that second she knew he had stifled his passion until she'd touched him.

"How was your grandfather? Did he annoy you very much?" He twisted her sapphire ring.

"No more than usual."

"More innuendos about his desire for an heir?" With the tip of his finger, he traced her hand.

She wanted to bury herself beneath the covers, but knew if he wanted, he could do whatever he pleased, find her wherever she was. Her hand and arm tingled. She had never realized the sensitivity of the soft spot between her fingers. "He thinks of nothing else."

Passion darkened his eyes. "Have you thought about sealing our vows?"

Her heart stopped. "You've been patient with me."

With his other hand, he grabbed her wrist. "How long can we fool your grandfather? A month? A year?"

Suddenly she envisioned him looming over their bed. She swallowed hard, flexed her captured fingers. In that second, she knew Hunter deserved a reason. Both knew and understood their passion. Tonight he didn't taunt her or present her with Lord Byron's prose. He didn't remind her of their last kiss. Only his anger and passion circled her wrist.

"I promised to be a convincing wife. But the other... I'm protecting us. Can you just accept that?"

"Protecting us from what?"

"It's better that you not know."

When he yanked her close, his hot breath veiled her skin. He smelled of brandy and bayberry. "Another lame excuse. First a ring and then Lord Byron's gibberish."

She noticed his taut jaw beneath his unshaven skin, the tiny lines of tension marring his brow. They were all signs of his incredible control. Still panic began to rise in her chest. "I thought you were enjoying yourself. You even amused me with his prose. You promised you would wait."

"Just where should my honor and loyalty lie, Sabrina? Give me one good reason I should keep my word."

Suddenly she realized he would not change their agreement without good reason. He liked his seductive game too much. More, she believed he would honor his promise...if he could.

# Chapter Fourteen

Hunter held her curious gaze and continued to hold her wrist. If anyone did any touching, he would be the one. Until they settled the matter, passion had no place in their discussion.

He didn't know if he should tell her that Gavin was considering canceling his wedding, of breaking poor Colleen's heart in two. He refused to shame his affianced and blamed Sabrina for his position. Unfortunately, Gavin knew that Hunter wanted Sabrina to come to him willingly. If she fulfilled her wifely duties, Gavin believed Sadlerfield would leave her and Hunter alone. To take a wife and then go to prison didn't sit well with his friend. He couldn't tell her the truth without slitting Gavin's and his own throat.

Tomorrow he would talk some sense into his friend, but unfortunately, in Gavin's mind, his wedding depended on whether Hunter could consummate his marriage tonight. If he were a more astute gambler, he would walk away now, but the stakes had never been so high. One more hand…

He narrowed his eyes. "I'm in no mood for games. One good reason is all I ask. If not that then you tell me when."

She lifted her chin and the lace around her neck fluttered as she swallowed. "If I can't?"

With a great effort, he ignored her gardenia scent. "Then I know where my loyalty lies. That doesn't say much for my honor. But neither of us has experienced much of that, have we?'' he drawled.

He expected her to defend her stand. Instead she lowered her gaze and chewed her plump lower lip.

''You'll complete our union without my consent?''

''As your husband, I don't need your permission.''

She rubbed the lawn between her fingers. ''Something happened today and you don't like the choice you must make. Am I right?''

Her pale blue eyes still whispered of her slumber, but keen intelligence replaced the curiosity. He resented it deeply. Her gaze bore into his soul and left him no place to run, but she was keeping her secret. Damn her. The trade didn't seem fair.

''Don't wheedle your way out of this,'' he snapped. ''We're not talking about me. I won't deny that I want you, Sabrina. What happens when I touch you here?''

Removing one hand from her wrist, he gently cupped her firm breast. When she trembled beneath his touch, he expected her to pull away, but she didn't resist. Her nipple began to push against the lawn, and he circled the nub with his thumb until it hardened. No answer came from her softly parted lips, but her heavy lids and swift breath spoke for her.

''When?'' he whispered.

Short breaths whispered through her lips as her breast swelled in his hand. ''Maybe…maybe after we return to London.''

He had thought to court her into acquiescence, the nobler route to her body, but perhaps she should experience a taste of what she was avoiding… By showing her, he'd just bruise his honor without totally dismissing it and could tell Gavin that he'd made progress. To allow his wife to ruin their lives would never be an option.

As he eased his grip on her wrist, he also released her breast. He plucked the bow at her neck.

She blinked hard. ''I ask you to reconsider.''

Hunter managed a sensual smile as he released another ribbon. ''You don't know what I'm going to do.''

Her face blanched, but she gazed at him steadily, not flinching or resisting. Hunter felt like a scoundrel, a naughty boy torturing a defenseless animal. However, she was his wife, and not a very honest one at that. He resented her refusal to confide in him. Pushing his compassion aside, he freed another bow and the heat from her skin accentuated her gardenia scent.

"Are you going to keep me in suspense?"

He summoned a naughty-boy smile. "Even Lord Byron has no words for this."

She shivered, but his desire surged and the untimely ache spread through his body. Slowly he urged her onto her back and parted the lawn that revealed her luminous skin, her high small breasts. He took a rosy nipple in his mouth. A squeal followed by a tug at his hair broke his concentration.

"Don't be afraid. I won't harm you." When she loosened her grip on his scalp, he circled her nipple with his tongue, tugged at it with a gentle grip of his teeth. Sweat beaded on his brow and he shifted, fighting his desire, feeling the ache. Damn.

She began to writhe and her fingers dug into his shoulders, but the pain was minuscule compared to the joy he knew he was giving her. Her breath came in short rasps, and he took her other nipple between his fingers, but continued to suckle until she let out a moan. "Does this hurt?"

She shook her head. "I can…can hardly describe how it feels."

Raising his head, he smiled, and as if she felt suddenly neglected, she opened her languid eyes. "Do you like the feel of passion? Do you trust me in this?"

Her eyes held his gaze with unbridled innocence. "Yes."

The unbidden emotions her faith stirred unnerved him as much as his physical response to her. As he rubbed her nipple, he brushed a kiss against her brow, placed another on her cheek and crushed his lips against hers. She tasted like sweet apples, smelled like an exotic forest, and the essence provoked his lust.

When he lifted his head, a bead of sweat rolled down his temple and dropped onto her breast. How long could he tease her and not want all of her? Her hand drifted up his neck, tugged downward.

"What do you want? This?" He licked her nipple and it immediately rose to his ministration.

"Yes." She arched her back.

Surprised, he captured the nipple in his mouth, and she groaned, pressing into him so that he suckled her flesh, too. Curse the ache in his loins. Damn her responsiveness. This was just supposed to be a little prelude before their consummation, a lesson in passion.

He wanted to tear off her nightgown, to feel her skin against his. Instead, he moved his hand down her stomach. Her hips pressed into his palm, a sign she needed more. Hell. He'd give it to her and prepare her for their consummation. Maybe not tonight, but soon, even if he had to tease her every night for a week. Unfortunately, he'd torture himself, too. Damn her wretched soul.

When he reached the juncture of her thighs, he pulled up her gown, and she brought her legs together as if she knew what he was going to do.

He took a fistful of her hair. "You said you trusted me."

"Anything. Anything but consummation."

His aching body resented her remark deeply. Her permission aside, what the hell was he supposed to do to relieve himself? Spill his seed on the bed? "Draw out your legs."

Slowly she did, but just an inch. He pushed them farther apart. Frustration fueled his passion and he pressed his palm against her mound.

"*What* are you doing?"

"You'll see. Then you can tell me if you enjoyed it. If not, I've other ways to pleasure you."

She let out a mewing sound. "No, this is…isn't so bad."

When he inserted his thumb into her feminine core and teased her nub, she arched, pushed her hips against his hand. "Do you like this?" he asked.

"Oh, yes." She gripped his shoulder harder.

He added a finger, finding her tight with need. Lust sluiced through his blood and he cursed the reaction his body had to her passion. This wasn't supposed to happen. Damn her. His arousal felt only the warm sheets, and they would never substitute for his wife. Inhaling deeply, he smelled her feminine scent. He thrust harder, inserted another finger. Bringing up her knees, she began to rotate her hips, as if instinct guided her passion.

With a frenzied thrust, he pumped his hand and imagined that one day soon, he would be inside her. She was so wet. His seed was dampening the tip of his arousal and he was about to explode.

He could take her now, fill her with his seed. The law and God were on his side and he wanted her as he'd never wanted another woman. Then she cried out, groaning with purring satisfaction as he gnashed his teeth and another drop of seed escaped. Despite his unbidden reaction, he could thank the devil. At least he had not humiliated himself inside her.

Slowly he withdrew his hand, pulled down her nightgown and turned on his back. He would never let her know that his lesson had given him an ache that would not likely subside for hours. That was all the touching his body could endure this night.

Just then she snuggled beside him and planted her arm on his stomach. His muscles tightened again. Her hand was mere inches away.

"If...if doing that will give you pleasure for now, you've my permission to do it again. It was indescribable, as you said."

Though he should have said or done something reassuring, he didn't move. Damn her permission. If he had a brain, he shouldn't have played the last hand. On occasion, he was a man of chance, but he wasn't sure if he could torture himself again.

As Sabrina left the conservatory, she considered calling a gardener to carry her flower-and-water-filled pail to the house.

Gravel crunched by the pond and she paused. Hunter? Heat bathed her cheeks. Could she ever face him again without blushing? Summoning her courage, she continued walking.

By the saints, she had fallen into wanton lust last night and lost control. Odd feelings stirred in her womb as she recalled his experienced hands, his exquisite mouth. Despite not consummating their marriage, she oddly felt as if she belonged to him.

Why didn't he say anything afterward? Though silence hung between them, sleeping next to him was better than each clinging to opposite edges of the bed. The question ricocheted off her passion-numbed mind.

She reached the formal garden and the bucket handle dug into her flesh. Setting it down, she flexed her fingers. They had explored his broad shoulders and back, his silken hair. She shook her head in disgust. Everything reminded her of Hunter's touch, the feel of his hard body tensing beneath her hands.

Sinking onto the bench beside her, she rubbed her palms and sighed. The pine and floral scents renewed her senses and reminded her of her task, but the ordered gardens mocked her life, a world that seemed askew.

She adored a man she was trying to escape. At best, he just tolerated her, humored her as he mimicked Lord Byron. Passion and secrets bound them together. Last night she had trusted him and allowed him to touch her in places reserved for someone special, someone she should love.

What had urged her to commit such a folly? She'd even given him permission to do so again! Was it just her vow to be a better wife? Was it because passion had no rules? She shuddered at the confused state of her life. In fact, nothing that happened last night made sense.

Though he hadn't executed his rights, for a brief moment, he had considered doing so. She had seen bleakness and indecision in his dark green eyes. Loyalty and honor were fierce competitors in his soul.

What problem would cause him to consider breaking his word? If he couldn't solve his dilemma, would he choose loyalty over honor? Who was the person who deserved his unfailing trust? Fearing she might never earn his respect, she experienced a pang of jealousy toward this unknown person.

To insulate the twins, she had blackmailed Hunter, lied to him and done a number of things he might never forgive. What if she told him the truth? No, she couldn't tell him about the twins. He might reveal her secret out of loyalty to another.

She frowned. To allow the questions and sentiments to fester was ludicrous. They smacked of a debutante's mindless wanderings. An annulment was what she wanted. Wasn't it? Besides, he only needed her body, and circumstances had forced him to the quest. Despite all this, her adoration for him remained. Foolish girl!

The twins and her future depended on what she learned about his past, and this should be her focus. What was he hiding? Whatever his problems, maybe she could help and free him from her grandfather.

Gravel sounded again and the duke came into view. He was examining the potted plants she'd placed under the canopies that decorated the lawn. Rising, she grabbed the pail and spun around. She retraced her steps past the conservatory and walked toward the rear of the castle. Water sloshed on her muslin gown and half boots. Pausing, she shifted the pail to her other hand.

Just as she neared the stable, Brice and Gavin entered the paddock, their horses spraying clods of dirt. The earl's coattails flapped behind him as he waved, but Gavin sneered, his dark look blending with his tanned face and arms. His tammy sat atop his blond hair at a jaunty angle, but contradicted the firm set of his square jaw. Before, he'd been distantly polite, but even then, she'd sensed he didn't care for her much.

Gavin stared at her hard then nodded curtly. She clutched her apron but managed a smile.

"Good Lord, Sabrina," Brice said. "You should ask a servant to help. That pail is much too heavy for you." He swung off his horse. "Here, let me take that. I hear you're in charge of the flowers."

"Gardening is something I enjoy and know how to do." When he took the pail, she wiped her damp hands on her apron.

Brice started to walk away, and when she didn't follow, he turned. "Should I give this to Mrs. Finlay?"

"Yes, thank you. She knows to add some sugar to the water to keep them fresh. I'd like to speak to Gavin a moment."

"I think my friend has a bachelor's concern regarding his nuptials. Perhaps you can tease him out of his grim mood."

Turning to Gavin, she smiled again. He dismounted and started leading both animals to the stable. She straightened but refused to let him ignore her.

Mindful of her new vow to become a better wife, she considered winning Gavin's friendship one of her tasks. Pamela had said Hunter and he were like brothers. Perhaps he might have a few answers, too.

He continued into the stable. Undaunted, she followed him. "Is there a special flower that your affianced likes? I can see if we have it in the conservatory."

Finally he paused and turned, his blue eyes so troubled that the color resembled a mounting storm. Stopping, she clutched the post beside her.

"Anything but *bloodroot*," he growled.

For a second the stable began to spin and everything blurred, but reason asserted itself. She should not feel guilty for taking precautions with the twins. "You know?" Her voice quavered.

"Aye, because Hunter forgot what the cursed plant looked like."

"I didn't ask for this marriage."

"Nay, but ye pledged to be his wife. While I understood your worry at first, I can't now. He's been a good husband. Better than ye deserve from what I hear. I'll not stand by and let ye ruin our lives."

Hunter dared to tell this man about their private affairs!

Her breath stopped. Splinters from the post pricked her hand, but then a single word registered. "*Our* lives? How does this concern you?"

"I meant Hunter and you." He whirled around and led the horses to their stalls.

"No, you didn't. Please. I want to know what you're talking about." She followed with long strides.

"Such determination," he drawled. "Now if ye could show the same in your marriage."

Startled by the force of his anger, she slid her palms down her apron. "I'm trying...harder, that is."

Unsaddling the horse, he placed the equipment by the tack wall. The ripe scent of horse sweat, leather and hay stole her meager breath.

He looked up with his mouth set in a grim line. "'Tis not good enough. Sadlerfield doesn't strike me as a patient man. It won't matter to him that Hunter's a good man here." He slammed a fist against his heart. "Or that he wants to help the Scots obtain an equal voice. Or that he wants to rid the world of slavery. The duke only wants his precious heir."

Sabrina lowered her gaze. "I told Hunter that maybe after we return to London. I just need time." Suddenly she realized she didn't have to defend herself to this man. She had sound reasons for everything she'd done. Well, almost everything. She drew her chin up. "You might be Hunter's friend, but I don't have to answer to you."

"Nay. Or Hunter, either. In a short while, ye might say the same thing to a new husband."

Sabrina slid her hands down her apron. "What do you mean?"

"Sadlerfield could get rid of Hunter this quick!" Gavin snapped his fingers.

"You mean an annulment?"

"Nay, I mean this." He made an ugly sound and slashed his hand across his throat.

She let out a nervous laugh. "Really, you do exaggerate,

Mr. MacDuff. I doubt my grandfather would harm Hunter. An heir…''

But then what if they couldn't produce one and not from lack of trying? She recalled her mother's imprisonment, the ex-soldier who had provided the damning words against her mother—and his curious death. No specific proof existed against the duke that he'd been responsible for the soldier's demise. Only her parents' words.

"Say that to your next husband."

The deathly calm in his voice made her heartbeat waver. An eerie sense that he was telling the truth seeped into her soul like a seed taking root. "A criminal…"

"Aye, he would be, just like I am." He held her gaze, his solemn blue eyes darkening with desperation.

Stiffening, she stuffed her trembling hands into her apron pockets. "What did you do?"

"I helped a friend in need."

Suspicions burst forth like shooting stars. "But I'm not married to you."

"Nay, but we're like this, Hunter and me." He clasped his stout hands together, the knuckles nearly white. "Hunter took the vows to defend me!" Paling, he sank onto a barrel and buried his face in his hands. "Oh God. What have I done?"

As understanding dawned, she brought her quivering hand to her mouth. Hunter was sheltering Gavin, and whatever his crime, her grandfather knew the story. Details aside, compassion lodged in her throat. He didn't appear to be a murderer or a vicious man, just a person battling the past. Instinct told her that Hunter would never aid a man without just cause.

"I swear that I'll never speak a word of this."

With his head hanging, he let out a derisive snort. "I'm to believe ye? I must tell Hunter what I did."

"If you choose, but I'll tell you what I told Hunter. I can't do what my grandfather wants now. I'm trying to shield Hunter and myself. If I revealed your secret, then I'd defeat my own cause."

He looked up with red-rimmed eyes. "What's your problem? Are ye in trouble?"

"Adding to your worries is the last thing I want to do. Just like you accidentally told me your secret, the same thing could happen if I told you. I can't do that."

Lowering his head again, he braced his elbows against his knees. "If the duke gets impatient, we could well nigh land in prison. Then what of my poor Colleen? How can a man marry a lass knowing that might happen?"

Despair and foreboding made her stomach churn. An acrid taste seeped into her mouth. She never imagined that her grandfather's desire for an heir might ruin so many lives. She spun around, dampness burning her eyes. "I don't want harm to come to anyone. That's my whole problem."

"You're protecting someone?"

"That's not what I said."

"That's what ye meant. I know what that burden's like. Sheltering someone means ye love him more than life itself. Why do ye think I hesitate to marry my bonny lass?"

She recalled her parents saying that love mattered the most. "Marry her," she said softly. "A short time together is better than no time at all."

The straw crackled behind her and a gentle hand rested on her shoulder. She swallowed the thickness in her throat.

"Do you want to talk about it?"

She quickly shook her head. "If I speak about this, it should be with my husband."

"Then do it. He's a kind man. Ye don't know what ye have now."

"Maybe not." Her voice cracked.

Whose life could she sacrifice?

# Chapter Fifteen

"**W**here is everyone?" Gavin asked as he entered the Rose drawing room. He smoothed the front of his black frock coat and tugged at his cravat.

"I'm glad you're here. I thought you might cancel your wedding." Hunter fought a smile as relief washed through him. His friend felt uneasy dressed as a gentleman, but Hunter wouldn't care if he arrived in cotton trousers. At least he had come.

Just as Gavin opened his mouth to speak, several servants entered, wearing gray livery trimmed with gold braid. One carried a silver tray laden with crystal goblets and wine. He set it on the sideboard. As the under footman tended the hearth, peat hissed and flames stirred the woodsy scent.

When they finally left, Gavin heaved a deep breath and compressed his lips. "Your wife changed my mind."

Hunter raised his brows. "Sabrina? A confidante?"

Gavin conveyed his encounter with Sabrina and bowed his head. "I've dug our grave a bit deeper."

"Bloody hell! I wonder if she'll hold her tongue," Hunter said through his teeth. He paced, looked at the clock. "At least she doesn't know the whole story. Maybe Faraday's learned something about her."

"'She swore she wouldn't tell and looked about to weep.

'Tis her last words that convinced me to marry my bonny lass. Mayhap I can give Colleen a child to remember me.''

He clasped Gavin's shoulder. ''Damnation. Don't talk like that. I'll take the blame before I let anything happen to you. It's not entirely your fault. Sometimes Sabrina looks at me with those eyes...never mind.''

Raising his head, Gavin ground his teeth. ''Ye wouldn't have to worry if you'd just claim your wife and produce an heir.''

Sliding his hand into his frock coat pocket, he curled his fingers around the cool stones nestled within and paced the room. Silently, he cursed his uncontrollable lust, his secretive and sensuous wife, the infamous Lord Byron and, most of all, Sadlerfield. Why did everyone think consummation was so easy?

''Last night I made progress. Maybe I'll succeed soon. If not, Faraday's investigation might reveal her secret.''

Gavin snorted. ''Despite what we might learn, she won't succumb. That's my impression. Something worries the lass.''

He touched the stones again, their coolness no match for his wife's demeanor when she chose to avoid him. Unbidden tender emotions assailed and unnerved him. He realized his investigation had swerved from self-serving interest to a desire to help her. What was she hiding? He slapped the back of a brocade chair.

''Then I'll just have to win her trust. Won't I?'' He had to speak to her about his friend's confession.

Gavin rolled his eyes. ''Aye. Good luck on that score, too.''

Just when the clock chimed six, the door swung open. Sadlerfield entered, wearing another well-tailored black frock coat and trousers made of superfine. The duke had brought enough clothes to last a season, and further confirmed Hunter's suspicions that he had come for a long stay. Trailing Sadlerfield, two footmen stood at attention by the mahogany sideboard, their presence stilling the accusation resting on Hunter's tongue.

Sadlerfield nodded curtly to Gavin, and when he turned to Hunter, his mouth formed a thin line. "Where is Sabrina?"

Hunter pressed a smile in place. "Attending her toilette."

A white brow rose. "Has she suffered any morning illness?"

Gavin let out a disgruntled breath. "I think I need a dram of whiskey." He crossed the room to the sideboard.

Unease slid down Hunter's spine. "What are you doing? Paying my servants to spy on her?" he asked in an icy tone.

Sadlerfield's mouth curved, but his pale blue eyes mirrored his damnable soul and not a shred of compassion lay in their depths. "You must teach her how to read the time. She is late."

Hunter caught the real meaning of his words. He was referring to and waiting for a sign of an heir, not her attendance. Suddenly an acrid taste coated his tongue. With his jaw twitching, he glanced at a footman and motioned for a glass of brandy. "So are the guests of honor. Even Pamela and Brice are fashionably late."

Just as he finished speaking their names, they entered.

"Oh, thank goodness. Colleen and John have not arrived. I told Brice to wake me from my nap and he did not." Pamela smiled at the group.

"With good cause, sweetness."

Hunter accepted the goblet from the footman and skimmed Pamela's dusky silk gown patterned with blue stripes. "You appear to have just come from the finest Parisian couturiere."

Pamela pirouetted and then tugged Hunter's black velvet lapels as if they needed straightening. "You look quite dashing yourself. This is Madame Beaumont's creation."

"You are acting like a hen, Pamela." Brice smiled apologetically. "That's what happens when one is an only child. She swears we will have a parcel of them."

Blushing, Pamela whacked her husband with her fan. "Oh, darling."

"I cannot hold our secret any longer." Brice grinned at

Hunter and puffed out his chest. "Pamela's with child, and we want you to be the godfather."

Hunter choked on his brandy. As he cleared his throat, Sadlerfield uttered congratulatory words. Hunter kissed Pamela's cheek. "Why don't you go tell Gavin? He'll be pleased."

Suddenly Sabrina stepped into the room and stole his breath. Swathed in yards of billowing cream silk, as she was in his dreams, she floated toward him, clothed like a princess and stripped of her practicality.

Though the dress might not represent her true colors, he still felt very proud of her appearance. Compassion surrounded his heart. Attending a formal dinner could not be easy for her with her grandfather present. Beneath the exquisite lady was a simple, proud young woman, and something tormented her to the point where nothing else mattered. He had thought nothing of these things last night.

Guilt gnawed his conscience amid his poignant feelings. That he experienced them at all surprised him, for he rarely opened his heart to a person of short acquaintance. Damnation. He would find a way to help her because he cared.

His friends greeted Sabrina with glowing compliments and they drew him back to his wife. As she moved closer, his fingers itched to touch her, but he put his quivering hand into his frock coat pocket. How would her skin feel when he draped the bauble around her throat?

With a frozen smile, Sabrina nodded to her grandfather and stirred the curls framing her face. The gardenia scent wafted from her skin and stoked his blood. Taking her gloved hand, he kissed her cheek. He could claim her innocence easily after last night, but for now, he clung to his feeble courtship plans. Damn Lord Byron anyway. "You look exquisite. I have something for you."

Just then, voices echoed in the hallway. The doorway framed a diminutive lady with golden red hair, pale skin and smiling gray eyes, features enhanced by the Carmichael colors in her gown.

"Gavin!" Colleen raced into his open arms.

"Aye, my bonny lass! You're a treasured sight for these eyes of mine. 'Tis the longest year of my life." Gavin lifted his betrothed and swung her around, her skirt turning into a kaleidoscope of colors.

Their lack of inhibition made Hunter smile.

Sadlerfield snorted. "Such a display. You would think she is of peasant stock."

Sabrina's pale blue eyes bore into the duke's. "They love each other. But love has never meant much to you," she said in a low voice.

"The heart has little place when one considers an heir. I cannot believe Lord Anstruther accepted an offer from a man of no title. At least MacDuff has a large purse."

Hunter gripped the crystal until the facets dug into his palm. "He has sufficient ties to the Graham name."

"Your grace, maybe Lord Anstruther understands something you don't," Sabrina added.

Talking about heirs and romantic nonsense was the last thing Hunter needed to hear. He leaned toward Sabrina. "Well, Colleen made a grand entrance. That's her uncle, John Anstruther, bolting through the door."

"Laddie! Put 'er down! 'Tis but two days 'til ye say the vows. Can ye not contain your ill manners that long?" When they ignored him, he sighed and ran his fingers through a mop of springy gray curls. "'Tis not important. In time she'll 'ave to listen to Gavin. That's the way of life."

After setting Colleen down, Gavin quickly made the introductions. Hunter couldn't help but feel a stir of envy for the love between them. Quickly he erased the emotion.

Colleen blew an unfeminine whistle and looked Hunter up and down. "Surprise, surprise. You takin' a wife…here I've known you 'alf me life and you dinna invite me!"

Anstruther clapped him on the back. "Aye. Heard a tale 'bout your nuptials. Couldn't stand being the last to wed, eh?"

"Sabrina's aunt had to return to London, so we settled for

a quick and quiet affair,'' Hunter said smoothly, and kissed Colleen's cheek. ''Friends again?''

The freckles across her nose moved with her smile. ''Of course, ye big oaf.''

Clasping Colleen's hands in hers, Sabrina smiled warmly. ''Gavin's a lucky fellow. Cherish every moment you have with him.''

Hunter's blood chilled. She knew Gavin might go to prison.

''Colleen, you're lucky on all counts.'' Sabrina's smile broadened, but sadness hovered in her eyes.

Hunter could see that she envied the romanticism in Gavin and Colleen's relationship. Would the necklace in his pocket brighten her eyes?

''Come, my bonny lass, tell me ye missed me.'' Gavin ushered Colleen to a corner.

Anstruther turned to Pamela and Brice, then bowed, the courtesy displaying his fit frame. He lifted her extended hand to his lips. ''I'm ever in your debt for seein' to 'er weddin' preparations.''

Pamela beamed. ''They make a good match. I love to take charge of anything resembling a soiree, and Scottish weddings are delightful. Besides, Hunt and Mac have always been like brothers. I feel that I have a huge family now!''

Brice leaned into Anstruther. ''With a little one on the way.''

''Nothing is as grand as announcing the arrival of one's heir. Congratulations again, Darlington,'' Sadlerfield said.

Sabrina swallowed audibly and something urged Hunter to take her hand. Her fingers curled around his, so trusting. Long-buried emotions encumbered his chest.

''Let's wish 'em a bit o' luck, Darlington, an' toast your heir, too. Where's that fancy French stuff ye boys drink?''

Hunter motioned for a servant, who served Anstruther a wine-filled goblet and replenished the others. ''To Colleen, a lass who resembles Scottish sunshine,'' Hunter began. ''Always welcome and always warm. To Gavin, a man like a brother to me. Lastly, to Pamela and Brice's unborn child. Of course, I'll be its godfather." That is unless he landed in prison.

"May happiness bless all your lives," Brice added.

Sabrina's hand tightened around Hunter's, though she smiled. The crystal chimed. As Hunter sipped the cool sweet drink, the liquid dissolved the tightness in his chest.

Turning to Hunter, Anstruther motioned for another toast. "To a fine laird and 'is pure bonny lass. I knew ye widna live your life alone."

Anstruther's last words buzzed like an annoying wasp. Tipping his glass, Hunter downed the heady liquid in three gulps, felt the burn settle in his stomach. How had this happened? He shouldn't, couldn't care about a lady who had no need for him.

Anstruther turned to Pamela. "How are the preparations?"

"Splendid! Gavin and I planned a wedding with old and new customs. Let's sit for a moment, and I will tell you more."

When they moved away, Hunter glanced at Sabrina's profile and again her beauty stirred his base needs. His gaze dipped. Barely skimming her shoulders, the creamy silk dipped into full leg-o'-mutton sleeves. The neckline's curve emphasized the valley of her breasts. His fingers curled, wanting to touch her creamy skin, and he imagined her body warming to his ministrations. Remembering the necklace, he released her hand and set his glass on a side table. He reached into his pocket and pulled out the glittering sapphires.

"You should not reward her until you have proof she carries my heir." The duke was ever present.

Sabrina raised her chin. "All your efforts will be for naught if I'm barren."

Sadlerfield's nostrils flared. "Do not jest. Every Barrington, man or woman, has produced offspring."

As Hunter's fingers curled around the necklace, he searched for a Lord Byron verse, but couldn't remember. "I give this to my wife because of my growing feelings." Had he said that? Surely that was Lord Byron. He improvised.

"Love seeketh not itself to please,
Nor for itself hath any care,
But for another gives its ease,
And builds a Heaven in Hell's despair."

Sabrina's mouth twitched. "More Lord Byron?"

"No, William Blake."

"Very poetic," the duke interrupted. "Now, when may I expect news of an heir?"

Sabrina stared at the buttered venison, chicken pie and pickled asparagus still occupying her plate. She itched to throw it in her grandfather's smug face. Instead, she sipped the sweet wine but could sense his constant scrutiny, could hear his question ringing in her head. Was Hunter trying to tell her something by using a Blake poem?

"Sabrina, would a stroll interest you? Perhaps to check the potted plants?"

"Yes!" Did she sound too anxious to leave the group? "I think that would be lovely."

A pristine smile lighted his face. Obviously he wanted to talk to her as much as she wanted to speak to him. Anticipation dampened her palms.

Leaving the group to discuss Gavin's wedding, they headed to the Rose drawing room. After Hunter found a matchbox and lanterns, they left through the terrace doors.

Under moonlight, the canopies and their support posts shadowed the trimmed garden. Long oak tables sat underneath the center structures where Pamela planned to display a wedding feast if the weather allowed. Beside each post were potted plants and flowers. The pruned junipers emitted a refreshing pine scent, easing her tension. Nearby, coal buckets provided warmth. Though enjoying the momentary peace, she longed to return to London. Her grandfather's desire increased her worry over the twins.

As Sabrina examined several chrysanthemums, Hunter hung the lanterns from the canopy's horizontal beam.

"The plants can wait, but what Gavin told you cannot."

She looked up. "I wish you had told me. I swear that I'll never repeat a word."

"No promises, Sabrina, unless you can keep them. We're talking about a man's life." The canopy's shadow hid his eyes but not the desperation in his voice.

"I wouldn't hurt the person who matters to you the most."

Stepping into the moonlight, Hunter crossed his arms over his broad chest. Hot emotion flashed in his dark eyes. "Then why the bloody hell won't you trust me?"

A flower snapped in her hand and she lowered her head. "Don't ask me to tell you anything. I can't. I promised."

"Damnation. Keep my secret as tight-lipped as yours." He heaved an exasperated breath and told her what the duke had said before she arrived this evening. "Your grandfather's getting suspicious."

"I thought if I planted the idea I might be barren…" Her voice quavered. "I thought maybe no one would suffer."

He cursed softly under his breath. "I can tell you want to trust me. Why won't you confide in me?"

"I want to go home." She paused, ran her palm over the chrysanthemum petals. "But I'll stay until you're ready to return to London."

"Then we'll leave after the wedding."

She bolted upright and smiled. "Thank you! You don't know how much that means to me."

"No, I don't." He dangled the sapphire necklace between two fingers. "You didn't accept this earlier. Will you do so now?"

The stones glittered like blue stars and matched her ring. Her chest ached. "Why? You don't have to pretend you're Lord Byron in private."

"I wanted to give you a gift." He paused, then looked up with gentleness in his eyes. "No specific reason."

She fought the tears springing to her eyes. "Sometimes

gifts just come…'' *From the heart.* She swallowed the words. ''From a person's impulses.''

The hope in his tone added to her tumultuous emotions, tore at her plans. She might yet leave this man. As she hesitated, he cupped her elbow, and a tingling sensation shot up her arm, dipped to her toes. ''What are you doing?''

''I'll help you with the clasp, but I need light.'' As he ushered her toward the lantern, the night breeze stirred his bayberry scent.

She fought the urge to bury herself in his arms and tell him everything. ''I shouldn't accept this.''

''Do it just to spite your grandfather.''

''On the other hand, I think I will.''

He laughed, a deep rumble coming from his chest.

As she faced the post, Hunter draped the necklace around her neck. The cool metal rested against her skin, but when his hand brushed her shoulder, she leaned forward seeking distance. With a gentle touch, his callused fingers worked the clasp but also rubbed the sensitive skin at the nape of her neck. She shuddered involuntarily. ''I can manage!''

''Done.'' Grasping her shoulders, he turned her around.

When he looked at her with lowered lids, her heart slammed against her bosom. Wanting to retreat, she grasped the rough-hewn post with her hands and wished she could lift the barrier aside.

Heat ebbed through her veins. Before she could move, his hand cupped her neck and his head dipped. Sabrina let out a startled moan, but his soft lips muffled her pleasured sigh. Passion battled with reason, reminding her that she could lose her heart to this man and they might soon part. Despite the feelings, something inside her soul said this kiss was different. He trusted her with his secret. He wanted to help.

Sabrina slid her hands up to his broad shoulders and his hard frame tensed beneath her palms. His lips smothered hers, hard and hungry. Trembling from an unbidden desire, she arched closer, needing to feel his length, to remember every curve and plane in case they parted. As metal buttons and hard flesh pressed into her breasts, they suddenly felt heavy and warm. She shifted her weight. The movement elicited a short groan from Hunter's throat and caused him to inch closer still.

Through her silk gown, the pole's splinters raked her back, but when he deepened his kiss and sought her tongue, he obliterated her discomfort. Their tongues sparred and, with each velvet touch, passion burdened her insides.

Wanting to memorize all of his body, she reached for the places she had failed to explore last night—his broad chest, and his sculptured cheeks. Would she remember this moment and the feel of him fifty years past? Seizing his cravat, she slipped her other hand beneath the cool silk. His pulse raced under her palm.

"You taste so sweet," he said hoarsely.

Suddenly his tongue found her ear. Soft kisses and warm breath teased her sensitized skin. When his fingers cupped her breast, her breath caught in her throat.

"Let me help you."

"I don't know."

He kissed her breasts, drew his tongue between them. "You were saying?"

Heaviness pooled in her stomach. "What?" she breathed.

"What frightens you, Sabrina?"

Sanity slowly asserted itself and she leaned her head on his chest. For a long moment, she remained in his embrace. His heartbeat thundered and then slowed. He was right. She wanted to trust him and did somewhat. First she had to see if the twins were all right, talk to Marga and Geoffrey. She had no right to reveal her secret without consulting them. "I wish I could explain, but I can't do so now."

As Hunter held her she felt the emotional war so aptly stated in William Blake's poem. Hunter was like her heaven, and the duke her hell.

She looked in the direction of the stables. Beyond the structure, the unmistakable silhouette of her grandfather loomed, the moonlight clearly outlining his cane. For a second she thought another human shadow stood next to him, then it ebbed away. She tensed. ''I think he's spying on us.''

Hunter's offer of help was sounding better.

# Chapter Sixteen

"I take thee…" Gavin's voice quavered with unabashed emotion. Even so, his words floated from the terrace to the crowd-filled garden below. The breeze muffled the sniffling and clearing of throats as handkerchiefs appeared, fluttering like white doves.

Sabrina recalled saying the same words and had to stifle the urge to bolt. Hunter's eyes had been cold and hard, his jaw tense, but Gavin's nuptials came from his heart. Looking away, she ignored the pang of envy.

As Colleen repeated the vows, she held Gavin's gaze. A Carmichael tartan graced her shoulders and at once looked oddly out of place with her ivory silk gown and lace gloves. Unlike her own, Sabrina knew that everything in their ceremony had a meaning.

She leaned against the castle's cool stone wall as tears burned her eyes. Despite his crime, no one who showed his love so openly could have a wicked soul. Colleen and his future lay in her hands. She choked back a sob.

Gavin removed the Carmichael plaid from Colleen's shoulders and took the MacDuff tartan from Hunter's outstretched hands. Lovingly he placed the wool around her shoulders and drew her close. He kissed her far longer than he should have.

The guests thundered with approval. As the fiddlers played a Scottish reel, the sound sent birds chirping from the gardens.

Hunter slapped the groom's back, then kissed Colleen's cheek.

Sabrina wiped her eyes with the back of her quivering hand. Guilt sprouted with abandon. She had the power to insure their happiness. Could she allow Hunter to fulfill their vows and still watch over the twins? Like a soft breeze, his offer to help whispered. Somehow he had helped Gavin until now and had sacrificed his freedom to do so. Could she do the same?

Tentatively she edged toward the newlywed couple and summoned the courage to give Gavin some reassurance that she would not steal his happiness.

"Colleen, we're almost kin according to Hunter and Pamela. I hope we will have a chance to become friends."

She laughed. "Our 'usbands declared themselves as brothers when they were knee 'igh. I call 'em an egg." She jerked her thumb toward Gavin. "'E's the yolk and Hunter's the white. Aye, we'll be seein' each other."

Sabrina smiled at the analogy and hugged her. Turning to Gavin, she lifted her chin. "As Hunter's wife, I'll do everything I can to insure your happiness. That's my wedding gift to you."

A knot dipped in his throat. "Thank you." He started to greet other guests but paused. "Ye're doing the right thing."

Suddenly the crowd dispersed in all directions. Some guests kicked their heels to the fiddler's tune. Gathering her emotions, Sabrina gestured for the servants to serve the champagne. Those not dancing snatched goblets or descended the terrace steps to the tables laden with food. Others lingered to speak with the new couple. Hunter headed straight toward her.

His kilt stirred above his hosiery-covered calves, the stockings emphasizing his sinewy legs. Their strength mocked his carefully arranged pleats, held together by a belt and a brooch. Hanging from his narrow hips, his sheathed dagger nearly disappeared within the folds, but his jeweled sporran winked from a most provocative spot. The closures were no match for the power in his hands. With one jerk, the wool would drift to the floor. Sabrina bit her lip and hoped he hadn't worn the costume with consummation on his mind.

"Did you enjoy the ceremony?" His voice possessed a cheerful tone, his face proud and beaming. He tilted his head. "Tears, I see." Shaking his head, he whipped out a handkerchief and dabbed her cheek. "Not a dry eye among the ladies."

She smiled wistfully. "It was a beautiful wedding—the first I've attended." Pausing, she added, "The second if you count ours. I'm glad he didn't change his mind."

Emotion flashed across his eyes. Regret? Sadness? Suddenly he grabbed her hand, his eyes glimmering like a carefree child's. "We're going to enjoy today. No concerns about anything."

"What about my duties? I should see to our guest's needs. Oh, Pamela wanted me to put some fresh roses in Gavin's suite."

"Later. She can tend things for a few hours. Just one day to call our own. We won't think about what brought us together."

His large hand closed around hers firmly yet gently and he beckoned with his smiling green eyes. Like a lover's caress, his bayberry scent whispered beneath her nose. She couldn't think of one reason to deny him his wish.

One day was all he asked. Another tomorrow might never come. Emotions pulled and, in that second, Sabrina knew her heart wanted to remain in the marriage, though conscience bid that the promise to her mother should come first. As her throat thickened with regret, a surge of guilt followed. Gavin was right. Hunter was a better husband than she deserved. Somehow, this strengthened her resolve. She had vowed to be a good wife, at least the best she could be while they were together.

She forced a broad smile. "You won't let me forget the flowers?"

He laughed and leaned close. "I'll come with you. I've orders to tie a bell under their bed."

She was certain her cheeks flamed the color of her deep mauve gown. ''Whose idea was that?''

''Pamela's. Gavin wanted a wedding of old and new customs. She can be mischievous.''

Sabrina brought a quivering hand to her chest. ''Imagine the ideas she might have given my grandfather.''

''I thought we agreed not to talk about him.''

''At least he can't spy on us when we return to London.''

''I can hardly bar him from calling. The town will know if I do.''

Suddenly she realized she was speaking as if they would always be together. Today she didn't want to think about what she might have to do for her family's safety. From the corners of her eyes, the image of her grandfather grew as he worked his way toward them. Hunter's carefree mood sparked hers. Pressing herself against him, she arched her neck. ''Kiss me.''

He blinked, his green eyes searching her face. ''Did I hear right, Sabrina? No citing the Magna Carta...''

''Forget that silly agreement. *He's* coming. Do your best Lord Byron act. Kiss me.''

Hunter dipped his head and captured her mouth. As he kissed her long and hard, she tasted orange marmalade lingering on his lips. He slid his tongue into her mouth and she accepted greedily, as if giving him unrestrained passion would assuage her guilt. That indescribable heaviness in her stomach blossomed like a rose. Oh, Heavens. She needed to loosen her corset, for the sensation pressed against her ribs, settled on her nipples.

Finally he lifted his head. ''How was that?''

His husky voice sent another warm tremor through her body. When she peeked around Hunter's broad shoulders, she met her grandfather's glare and could almost read his thoughts. *Such a peasant girl's display. Have you forgotten your station?* Yet, she'd only demanded a kiss to curb her grandfather's suspicions. Hadn't she? ''I think he swallowed his lips. I can't see them.''

Hunter chuckled. "You naughty wench. If tweaking him is what you want, I say, let's avoid him the rest of the day."

Just as he finished his words, he pulled her into the dancing crowd that was stepping high to another Scottish reel. After three sets, the pins in her hair loosened and her mane began to tumble about her shoulders. She flicked her head in defiance. The last pins disappeared under booted and slippered feet. Undoubtedly, her grandfather thought she looked like a gypsy, and she smiled like a wayward child.

As blue skies gave way to stars, the bagpipes skirled, their sounds inviting hoots from owls. A waltz tune filtered from the music room, and Hunter drew her into his strong arms. Sabrina laughed as he glided across the slate terrace, into the music room and outside again. He maneuvered around her grandfather, who stood in their path. With an impassioned look, he strolled away, apparently disgusted with their frivolity.

Sabrina glanced at his rigid back. "Maybe he'll retire."

"Which is what Gavin and Colleen are about to do." Hunter nodded toward the couple standing near the terrace steps.

Just then, the music ended, a boisterous roar shook the night, followed by ribald comments from the men and reprimands from the ladies. Colleen held up her skirt as Gavin tugged at her stocking. Her garter hung from his mouth. With a grin, he tossed the cotton streamer over his shoulder and it sailed into someone's outstretched hands. Laughter echoed into the darkness.

Sabrina grabbed Hunter's arm. "Your bell. The flowers!"

Hunter groaned. "Why didn't you cut them this morning?"

"Roses smell better at night."

"I recall my mother saying the same thing." He grabbed her hand and whispered their plan to Brice and Pamela, who stood nearby.

"Go on. We will delay them." Pamela shooed them away.

Within seconds, they were at the conservatory. Quickly Hunter lit a lantern though the hothouse stoves still glowed from earlier fueling. He handed her his dagger. "Use this. The bell's in the stable. I'll be back to help you."

Accepting the knife and lantern, she went to the rear of the conservatory where Hunter's mother had planted a rose bed. The five-foot bushes emitted a mixture of scents—some resembled vanilla while others smelled like spices. Picking up a bucket, she went to the corner where the white roses grew.

While she needed to hurry, she still cut the stems with the freshest blooms. She wanted Gavin and Colleen to remember this night always. The persistent ache in her chest grew. What would she remember if…when she and Hunter took that final step? Her grandfather looming over them? Shuddering, she blocked out the vision.

The door squeaked. Expecting Hunter, she started to speak but swallowed the greeting.

A man with his hat pulled low on his brow entered, and her grandfather followed. Instinct warned her to continue playing Hunter's game. She ducked, held her breath. Gritting her teeth, she extinguished the lantern flame with her knife.

"I told you not to wander around. Someone might recognize you. You are a stupid fool," her grandfather snapped. "I brought you to Scotland for one reason. If Hunter defies me, I want him to see you, to remind him how precarious his position is."

"Do not get too smug, your grace. Hunter went into the stable. Besides, I know him and this place better than you do. Furthermore, I will show my face when I think the time is right."

Peat crackled and drowned her grandfather's reply.

The man chuckled and said, "Do not expect him to bend to your wishes without a fight. He will not scare easily."

"If he values his life, he will. I want an heir. If he cannot sire one, I will find another to replace him."

Sabrina recalled his callous disregard for her mother's life when he left her in jail to die. A tremor danced down her spine and she gripped the knife. With the blade, she deftly parted the rosebush. The man wore a black cloak and pushed his hat back. She pressed her hand over her mouth. The man resembled Hunter.

When the bell jangled, Hunter felt like a leading cow and half expected a herd to wander toward him. He stuffed it into his sporran. Grinning in anticipation of his jest, he took long strides to the conservatory. He had never enjoyed a day more.

Suddenly the conservatory door swung open and two men left. He recognized Sadlerfield for his torch of white hair, but the other man...something about his carriage seemed oddly familiar.

Bolting to the conservatory with his sporran held tightly against his stomach, Hunter's quick breath smothered the bell's muted clang.

He pushed the door open and it slammed against a bench as he rushed inside. His heart thundered in his ears. "Sabrina!"

Hunter scanned the interior, but when she whispered his name, he swung his head to the corner. Within a second, he stood over her. Sitting on her heels, she looked up, her pale blue eyes resembling a frightened animal's. She didn't blink, just stared at him. Between her trembling hands, she held his knife, the blade shimmering under a wedge of moonlight.

Dropping to his knees, he carefully took the weapon from her hands and tucked it into his sheath. "Sabrina, are you all right? Did something happen?"

When she nodded, he captured her in his arms and stroked her curly mane. She crumpled against him, and his urge to watch over her made Lord Byron's chivalry pale in comparison.

"They're...they're planning something. To scare you. Why would they want to do that?"

As he released her, the hilt of the dagger dug into his hand. "Who?" he asked calmly but sensed he knew.

"My grandfather. He wants an heir, but he wants to scare you? Why? That doesn't make sense, and the man with him..."

"What about him?"

Her brow creased. "He looked much like you."

*Bloody hell.* For one insane moment, he thought to run after the duke and his father and demand an explanation. Too many questions rushed forth. How did his father get past the guards without an invitation? Where was he staying? How long had he been at Keir Castle? Prudence cemented his feet to the gravel. One point held all questions at bay: the last thing he needed was for Sabrina to learn the truth.

With a great effort, he forced a steady voice. "Tell me exactly what you heard."

As Sabrina repeated the conversation, he drew his dagger and stabbed it into the ground. He swore viciously under his breath. Sabrina gasped. His worst demons had arrived at his door.

She looked at him with wide eyes. "What does it all mean?"

He took a deep breath and sheathed his knife. "You already know too much. You'd be an accomplice."

She grabbed his arm, her fingers digging into his flesh. "Is this about Gavin? I would never do anything to hurt him or Colleen. So few people ever find their kind of love."

"If I tell you, that's as good as sending you to your death. Now, unless you wish to visit your maker, don't ask me again. Forget everything you heard."

Her fingers fluttered against her throat. "That bad?"

*Worse.* He grabbed her hand and pulled her to her feet. "We're going to be late."

"What are you going to do?"

With the pail in his hand, he ushered her out the door. "Tie a bell under Gavin's bed."

"No. I mean about my grandfather and that man. Who was he? You never told me."

As he tightened his grip on her hand, he lengthened his stride. All he could think about were the affairs and scandals his father had brewed, not to mention the reason for his presence now. "A man you should never trust."

Her feet dug into the gravel. "He's your father."

Damnation. He pulled on her hand. "Like I said. Don't ever trust him."

As they walked toward the castle, the moonlight cast a warm glow over the teetering guests who danced to the bagpipers and the fiddlers who joined in on the tune. Whiskey and champagne flowed, fermenting the air with its heady scent. The bell jangled in his sporran, a stark reminder of what he hadn't accomplished, but this seemed minor compared to his regret. Hunter knew that they wouldn't return to the festivities.

In fact, he doubted that he'd ever allow Sabrina out of his sight again. Wife or not, unwanted marriage or not, she was still an innocent, and the exact kind of woman his father liked. He even reconsidered consummating the marriage until he learned their plans.

If he were to land in prison, he could leave his child in her womb, and Sabrina alone. He was quite dispensable. Damnation. He gripped the pail handle until his fingers cramped. If they killed him, who would help Sabrina defend her secret? No. Leaving her in such a defenseless and frightening position was unthinkable, and this urged him to learn what she was about. Sabrina would fight, but despite her cleverness, she was no match for the duke or his father. After mulling over Randall and the duke's conversation, Hunter concluded his father's presence was to remind him of the kidnapping. Hunter also suspected that they were behind the forged promissory notes.

Now that he knew the scope of his enemies, he could plan how to defeat them. They would rue the day they were born.

# Chapter Seventeen

*London*

"**Y**ou should have gone about your business like the others. I know the way home." When Hunter regarded her with a steady gaze, Sabrina shifted in her seat and pressed her hands on the squab's buttery leather. Since the incident in the conservatory three nights ago, Hunter had rarely left her side. She still didn't understand the reason, but other important things occupied her mind.

"Trying to get rid of me?"

She could hardly tell him she was. "You could have followed my grandfather to see what he's about."

"I'll deal with him in my own time."

Arousing suspicion was the last thing she wanted and pointed outside the coach window. "Those are the burial grounds you joked about, and Sommers Town is just beyond." Unable to face him for fear of more questions, she gazed at the green pastures.

During Gavin's wedding, she realized she wanted Hunter's and her family's safety but feared she couldn't have both. Two vows pulled, increasing the ache in her chest. Without a solution, she knew just one thing. For now, she must keep her promise to her mother. She needed to discuss her problem with Marga and Geoffrey. Alone.

"Is something worrying you?"

If she allowed the consummation, she couldn't imagine ever leaving him. She would endanger her heart. What if they created a child? What if she must flee with the children? Oh, heavens, the complications.

Hiding her worries, she chuckled wryly. "The note I sent from the docks will hardly prepare my aunt. You've arranged to move us to your home. Marga might have something to say about that. She has two children. Why do you think it necessary?"

"I told you. You're close to your aunt and will want to visit. You've ridden a horse once and not too successfully. London is in a political upheaval. Reformists are rioting. Despite everything, you're my wife. They're my family and responsibility."

As she listened to his diatribe again, her stomach rippled with a mixture of anxiety and warmth for his concern. She forced a cheery laugh. "Very chivalrous. You sound like Lord Byron again."

When he had suggested her family move in with him, she'd almost swooned. What if her grandfather saw the twins and noticed Alec's resemblance to their father? Her affairs aside, she sensed the real reason for Hunter's decision centered on Gavin and the danger that threatened them.

He set his jaw. "Lord Byron has some merit."

With her stomach churning, she forced a grin. "Inviting my family to live with you might be a bad idea. You've never lived with children."

Frowning, he narrowed his eyes. "Are you still thinking about an annulment?"

She bit her tongue. "My family's feelings concern me."

Her grandfather's newest caveat still sang in her ear like a devil's chant. *If he values his life…* Although she wanted to probe, she worried that Hunter would counter with questions and uncover her dilemma.

Hunter regarded her steadily. "What about the thing that has driven you to desperation? To hide inside a crate? To shoot a bloody hole in my cloak?"

Stiffening, she worked her bottom lip. "In time...in time, I'll settle the matter. You'll just have to trust me."

"Since you refuse my help, I'll try something else." He grinned as he pulled her to his side.

"What are you doing?" Inhaling, she caught the sea smell clinging to his clothes. His closeness bathed her in his powerful masculinity and enveloped her in security. She trembled, disliking and treasuring the feelings at once.

Slowly he brushed his lips against her brow, then kissed her with more tenderness than he had ever shown. Helpless to do anything else, and not wanting to move away, she returned his kiss. Boldly she traced his lips with the tip of her tongue and settled herself into his arms. He groaned softly and drew her closer. Just then, the coach squealed to a stop.

Gallus, tied behind their coach, neighed. Twisting her head around, she gazed out the window. "I can't see a thing for that brute you assigned as my 'guard.'"

"Cason's a bloody good shot and a fine outrider."

She peered up at the sailor-turned-guard. His blond hair resembled fluttering corn tassels and his harsh Nordic features drew sharp lines against the blue sky. The mounted servant's wool coat bulged from the pistol and dagger strapped to his trim waist. When his stout hand settled on his weapons, she started.

"Trouble?" She turned the opposite direction. Several plainly dressed sailors, transformed into outriders, rode on the other side.

"A funeral procession, Captain," Cason said.

The creaking wagon and clopping of horses signaled their approach. As the mourners walked behind the wagon bearing a pine coffin, the earth crunched beneath their feet. Death's scent tainted the air. Hunter pulled the shutters over the windows and pressed one finger to his lips.

"'Tis not right that 'e should've died," one mourner said.

"I say he was too old to be movin' rocks but 'e insisted on helpin'. 'E clasped his chest and never took another breath. Gone. Just like that." The mourner spit on the ground.

Sabrina raised her brows at the foul sound.

"Should the time come, I'll pitch a rock fer 'im. 'Tis blasted Parliament's fault. Instead of goin' off huntin' grouse and deer, they should pay mind to business here."

The bits of conversation made Sabrina's eyes grow wide. "Hunter. They're ruffians."

"That's why Cason addressed me improperly. I had the crests removed from my coaches. Why make us a target?"

"You could explain your political stance." Suddenly the coach pitched forward and he steadied her with his arm.

"They speak the truth, and are preparing themselves for the Reform Bill's defeat. That tells me the situation and the mood of the populace is becoming more dangerous."

Suddenly she realized the depth of his awareness and the urge to tell him everything rested on her tongue. How long would she have before he pieced her life together?

A few minutes later, they arrived at her small house, a two-story stone structure. "This place could fit into the foyer at Keir Castle," she joked, trying to hide her anxiety.

He glanced at the meadows surrounding the house. "It's too isolated. Your nearest neighbor is a city block away."

"Marga wanted to raise the children in the country. This is still close to London. Besides, we couldn't afford to live there."

When she entered, the scent of baking bread made her take a deep breath. Something tightened in her chest as she regarded the sparse furnishings, a mixture of Queen Anne, Sheridan and styles she couldn't categorize. The unmemorable interior matched the exterior. No one cared who lived here. This was home, at least for a few hours before she stepped onto London's stage. Could she shield the twins in such a setting?

"Irene, the twin's nanny, must be in the kitchen. You may wait in the parlor." Sabrina pointed to the small room on her left dominated by her gleaming piano.

For a second, she stared at the instrument, then tore away her gaze. Smiling at him, she removed her gloves and bonnet as he strolled into the room. He tapped the ivory keys. She slid her fingers over the satin ties, wound them around her hand.

Thumping feet echoed in the hall and she wrenched her gaze from the room. She dropped her hat onto the scarred table.

"Sabrine!" the twins said in unison. Their rumpled night-gowns fluttered behind them as they ran. Alec began to wheeze, and his cheeks flushed pink.

Sabrina caught them in her arms, held them tight and kissed the tops of their heads. Joyous tears lodged in her throat. Their arms clung to her neck and their bare feet snuggled into the folds of her skirt. They smelled like soap and fresh crumpets. "I've missed you so much." She spoke French.

Her brother released his hold. "Are you…going away again?" His French words whistled through his shaky breaths.

"Speak slowly or you'll make yourself sick." She tried to pull him close, but he wrestled away. "Did you fear I wouldn't return?"

"A little, but Mama said—" he took a raspy breath "—you'd never leave us." Alec turned toward the parlor.

"So did Geoffrey," Christine added in French. She took a bite of the crumpet in her hand.

"Then who's he?" Pointing to Hunter, Alec looked at him with curious blue eyes.

Sabrina met Hunter's curious gaze. One hand lay on the crook of his other arm as he stroked his jaw. He stared at the twins. Undoubtedly, he questioned the reason they spoke French. She wanted to tell them not to utter a word of English but remembered Hunter could speak French, too. "Uh. You may speak English since we have company. I'll introduce you shortly."

Suddenly a knock sounded. Rising, Sabrina stared at the entry. Panic compressed her lungs. "Is your mother expecting anyone?"

They shrugged in unison. When Alec started toward the door, she pulled him back and he started to squirm. "No! Stay here!"

Christine ran to the parlor window. "It's Geoffrey!"

Releasing Alec, Sabrina quickly opened the door and looked up at Geoffrey's honey-colored eyes, oddly lacking their usual warmth. Flashing a smile, she pulled him inside. "I wasn't expecting you."

"I called earlier on my way to work. Marga had just received your note about moving."

"He comes every morning," Alec said.

Hesitantly Geoffrey kissed her cheek and ruffled the children's heads. His dimpled smile appeared briefly and fell as fast. As he stepped back, he ran his fingers through his brown hair and the movement parted his charcoal-hued frock coat. He met her gaze. "I cannot believe what Marga told me."

"So you're Norton." Hunter strolled into the hall.

Geoffrey's head jerked around.

"Sabrina! Geoffrey! *Bonjour!* I thought I heard voices." As Marga descended the stairs, her russet muslin gown trailed over the faded green carpet. As always, she had styled her chestnut hair in a coiled braid with curls framing her heart-shaped face, one that showed no traces of alarm or trouble. Pausing, she curtsied. "*Monseigneur*. I am grateful you brought my niece home safely."

"Madame Beaumont." Hunter inclined his head.

Rushing forth, Sabrina embraced her aunt and reveled in her familiar rose scent. "Is everything all right?"

"*Oui.* Reopening the shop requires long hours. I have been taking the children with me."

Understanding Marga's cautious measures, Sabrina stepped back and introduced Hunter to the others. When she gazed at his unreadable look and Geoffrey's bland solicitor's facade, she slid her damp palms down her skirt. Like potential foes, they eyed each other with dark looks, but finally both nodded. Their silent assessment made her uneasy. She wanted them to become friends.

A moment later, everyone found a seat in the parlor. For a long second, the only sound came from Christine chewing her crumpet.

"What do you wish to do about your marriage?" Geoffrey eyed Sabrina with an intensity she'd never seen. Outside the open window, chirping finches filled the silence.

Sabrina licked her lips. "This isn't a good time to discuss the matter."

"This is a perfect opportunity, but without them." Hunter eyed Alec and Christine.

"If you had come to me for the money, your marriage would never have happened," said Geoffrey.

"Geoffrey. Hunter. Please." Sabrina shifted her gaze to the twins and back to him. Though she tried to coax them to go to Irene, they insisted on staying.

"Are you a papa?" Christine looked up at Hunter and took a bite of her demolished crumpet. Crumbs fell on his trousers.

Slack jawed, Hunter finally smiled. "No, not yet."

"*Mes petites,* please tell Irene we have company so she can help you dress." Marga motioned with her hand but the twins stayed.

"Your cousin brought you each a gift from Scotland. Interested? If so, you must do as your mother asks." Hunter raised a black brow.

Sabrina shot him a warning look. Bribery! Usurping her aunt's authority! Before she could say a word, the twins ran toward the hall and Alec started to wheeze.

"Do not run, *mes petites!*" Marga said in French. Rushing to Alec, she dropped to her knees. "Relax. Breathe deeply."

Alec heaved coarse breaths as his tiny hands curled into fists. "I'm…I'm better, Mama."

She brushed his cheek with her lips. "Christine, you and your brother go to Irene."

"*Oui,* Mama." Christine took her brother's hand and they padded softly out the door.

Marga rose, drilled Hunter with a hard look. "*Monseigneur.* Take care what you tell my children."

"They're charming, but shouldn't listen to our conversation. Youngsters are perceptive."

Her aunt's hazel eyes bore into him. "Just remember. They are my children. If necessary, I discipline them."

"What ails him?" Hunter's concern barely supplanted his lack of an apology.

"Severe asthma." Marga dropped into her chair.

With a thoughtful look on his face, he nodded and addressed Geoffrey. "You were saying?"

Facing her, Geoffrey rubbed his brow. "Do you want an annulment?"

She spared Hunter an uneasy glance and met his cold gaze. "I can't take that course. I'm doing the best thing for all concerned by...by staying in the marriage."

"I should have known. Looking for a rainbow?" The cryptic remark didn't hide the sadness in Geoffrey's voice. With clasped hands, he rested his elbows on his knees and gazed at the floor.

Sabrina's unease festered. "Worse things could have happened."

Geoffrey sat back in his chair and gazed at Sabrina with a sorrow she didn't understand. His eyes shifted to Marga. "I know."

As Marga straightened, concern laced her hazel eyes. "*Monseigneur.* I asked Geoffrey about an annulment. Do not hold her accountable."

"No need to dwell on the issue," Hunter replied. "I can't fault your concern regarding family. In fact, have you considered my offer?"

Sabrina inhaled a deep breath and fingered the settee's frayed upholstery. Their proximity to her grandfather would invite trouble but she feared leaving Marga alone. She grabbed the topic to avoid discussing her marriage.

"You're welcome to come live with us. For the children's sake, I think it's better if we stay together, continuity and all." Sabrina wanted to add that Hunter had the resources including armed guards to defend them from her grandfather's latest caveat. Instead, she said, "I still plan to help with the shop. Living in town will be easier for both of us."

The settee creaked as Hunter leaned into the flattened cushions. "You could have a suite of rooms with a place to dabble in your creations."

"*Monseigneur,* why are you offering your home to me?"

"You're Sabrina's family and I assume responsibility."

"That's noble of you, but I do not wish to accept charity."

Panic tightened the knot in Sabrina's stomach. How could she convey her grandfather's threat without revealing Gavin's crime? How could she speak of the twins without announcing their secret to Hunter? "Marga. I want us to stay together. The twins need some constants in their lives."

Hunter shook his head. "This is hardly charity. Do you know you are a blessing to me, Madame Beaumont?"

"*Oui?* How is that?"

"You're a talented couturiere. I want you to create a wardrobe for Sabrina. Would an annual salary and a percentage on the cost of every gown appeal to you? The job is yours for life."

Interest brightened her hazel eyes. "That is a very generous offer. Why?"

Hunter shrugged. "All in the interest of family."

"You flatter me, *monseigneur.* Earning my keep is another matter. The offer deserves some thought."

Sabrina observed their exchange, and though Hunter appeared relaxed, she sensed he captured every nuance in the conversation. Undoubtedly, he memorized every look and word they exchanged. She tapped her finger on the cushion. To what lengths would he go to learn her secret?

Suddenly a horse whinnied then neighed louder. A heart-stopping scream split the air. Finches flew from the tree outside the parlor window. Boots pounded against the earth.

"That sounds like Alec!" Sabrina shot to her feet, as did everyone. In seconds, they were all outside amid sweet air and sunshine.

Still dressed in her nightgown, Christine came running from

the coach. "Mama! Sabrine! Alec's stuck." She pointed at Gallus.

Marga's hand flew to her chest. Her face turned white. *"Mon Dieu!"*

As he sat backward on the horse, Alec clung to Gallus's sides. The stallion pranced and tossed his head. The whites of his eyes flashed. Outriders ran from the water pump where they had been quenching their thirst.

Sabrina let out a terrified cry just as Hunter ran toward his horse. He grabbed her brother by the waist. Cradling Alec in his arms, he spoke soothing words and simultaneously dismissed the outriders with an appreciative nod.

A blue hue tinged Alec's face, his chest caved and squeezed out lacerated sounds. He grasped his nightshirt with a small fist. Sabrina rushed forth with Marga.

*"Mon petit!"* Marga loosened the ribbon at Alec's throat.

With her heart pounding, Sabrina brushed his brow, hot from exertion. "Are you all right?"

Alec nodded, his hands relaxing.

"Don't fight your lungs," Hunter commanded. "Take small bites of air just like you should when you're eating." He propped his hip on the porch rail and placed his large hand on Alec's chest.

She recalled Hunter's generosity and tenderness with the urchin in Scotland. Gratitude and something more enveloped her heart as she observed Hunter's gentleness and softly spoken words. Suddenly she imagined him holding their child. Shaking her head, she focused on Alec again.

"Y-yes…sir." His grated breath mellowed to a wheezing sound and pink began to replace his gray pallor.

"You're a brave young man. Want to stand?"

"I c-can."

Hunter set him on his feet.

Sabrina dropped to her knees and hugged her brother, now smelling faintly of horseflesh. "Are you sure you're well enough?"

With his eyelids lowered, Alec nodded, looking chagrined.

Hunter cleared his throat. "Young man. How did you get up on my horse?"

Alec tilted his head and a smile hovered on his lips. "He's such a g-grand horse, sir. I jumped."

Simultaneously Sabrina and Marga gasped.

"You jumped?" Hunter's brow rose.

"I told you not to," Christine said.

"Well, sir, I climbed on the coach. And—" The eagerness in Alec's voice grew, as did his raspy breath.

"*Mon petit.* Speak slower or you will be sick again."

Alec pinched his brow. "But he kept…kept moving and…I couldn't turn 'round. I just wanted to sit on him." He turned to Geoffrey. "Tell 'em. You…you give me rides."

Geoffrey smoothed Alec's hair. "Riding on my back is different from jumping onto a horse."

Marga kissed Alec's brow, then cupped his chin. "You could have hurt yourself and the horse. And you made yourself ill. Now, apologize to *monseigneur.*"

As his two front teeth gripped his lower lip, Alec looked at Hunter with longing in his eyes. "I'm sorry, sir."

Hunter's green eyes grew solemn. "Admitting your mistake shows character. You should ride something more to your size. I've a filly in Scotland that might be suitable in a year or so."

Alec's blue eyes widened. "My own pony?"

Sabrina riveted Hunter with her darkest look, but felt her heart twist. "He can't indulge in such exercise."

"Owning a pony is a big responsibility. You must learn to *mount* and ride properly, even care for the animal." Hunter glanced at Marga. "Riding at a walk won't overtax his lungs, and will give him a measure of freedom. He's spirited and brave. Let him try to be a boy."

Adoration brightened his blue eyes and his smile spread from ear to ear.

"That's not fair," Christine said. Her tiny voice wavered.

Dropping to his knees, Hunter raised Christine's chin. "Would you like a pony, too?"

She shook her head.

His black brows nearly joined. "Dolls?"

Sabrina's mouth gaped and snapped shut. Why was he courting her whole family? "Don't worry, Christine. Hunter and your mother must discuss this. No one is promising anything."

Alec stared at Hunter with a woeful look on his cherub face. "You *promised.*"

Interest stirred in Christine's blue eyes. "Dolls?"

Her brother frowned. "She can't have…them if I can't have a pony."

As Sabrina glowered at Hunter, she suddenly realized the gifts weren't the problem. The children's attachment to him might be if she ever had to flee with them.

"Come, *mes petites.* Both of you. Do not worry about who is getting what. Why has not Irene dressed you? What were you doing outside?" Marga motioned toward the door.

"We didn't go to Irene. We went to the…coach to find our gifts." Alec's chin hugged his chest, but he glanced at Hunter again.

Marga ushered the children inside.

"My felicitations on your marriage," Geoffrey said softly, and started toward his carriage.

Rising, Sabrina caught him by the arm. "Wait! I still want to speak with you."

He rammed his hands into his pockets. "I never could refuse you." With his head hung low, Geoffrey entered the house.

Her friend's demeanor stirred her curiosity, and when the door closed with a click, Sabrina frowned. "He's acting strangely." Shaking her head, she faced Hunter. "I know you have no experience with children. Within minutes, they brought out your gentleness and generosity, and reduced you to a perplexed state. Courting them isn't necessary."

He grinned crookedly. "They're adorable children."

His softly spoken words squelched her anger and she couldn't quite bring herself to chastise him. She sighed. "Before you speak, you must think very hard about your words. They think every word is a promise."

"I liked Alec's smile. His bravado. He knows he has weak lungs. That doesn't stop him from being a boy. Let him try to be strong. So what if the price is a pony?"

Planting her palms on the railing, she stared down at her gardenia bushes. She tried to imagine her mother tending them and giving her advice as she worked. Only the shiny dark green leaves whispered back. Finally she looked up.

"I've never looked at Alec in that way. We've always tried to keep him quiet."

With his mouth set in an implacable line, Hunter stared at her hard. "You'll kill his spirit. That very thing gives him strength. Alec gets his pony and Christine gets her dolls. I promised."

She looked away. "They're Marga's children."

Grabbing her arms, he spun her to face him. Determination made his eyes hard. "What do you expect me to do when they approach me? Say nothing? Offer only safety, shelter and food? Why are you afraid, Sabrina? That I can open a new world to them? That I might just win some of their affection? They're children. I won't let them think that I'm just a person who lives in the same house."

The taut look on his face said he would not relent. She sensed from his tone and words that he cared what they thought about him. Did she dare hope that he wanted them to be a real family? What if she had to shatter the new bonds? Her throat thickened.

She forced a smile. "I can tell Alec likes you."

"I grew up without a father. All I had was his name to know that I had one. A boy needs a man to..."

"Worship?" Her heart ached for the child within, and fed her guilt. Would Marga allow her to share the truth with Hunter? "I'm sorry. You were being kind."

He shrugged. "One day, we might have our own little girl. Would you like that?" Raising his hand, he brushed a wisp of hair from her cheek. His sultry gaze emphasized his green eyes, now shaded with desire, and he bundled every intimate moment they had shared in that one look, that one question.

As she held his gaze, heat permeated her cheeks. Unless she did as duty demanded, she knew the impossibility of creating a child. Guilt tapped her conscience, but the thought that he wanted children warmed her soul. Perhaps their marriage had hope after all.

Unfortunately, if she gave him her body, she knew he would totally capture her heart. "We'll discuss our marriage later."

"What changed your mind about an annulment?"

"Gavin and Colleen. I must speak to Geoffrey alone. He's waiting."

"Don't take too long. The wagons will be here soon to move the household."

She rubbed her brow. "I sense you don't like him. Why?"

A black brow twitched. "You're wasting time."

"The movers can wait. Geoffrey is an important person in my life. I'll take all the time I need."

# *Chapter Eighteen*

As Sabrina stepped into the parlor, something about Geoffrey's stance crushed her heart. He stood with his back to her, his palms flat against the mantel and his head bowed.

"Geoffrey?"

"Do you think you can be happy with him?" He faced her with a grim look.

"Yes." The word slipped out, surprised her and splintered her thoughts. She ran her fingers along the piano and drummed a chord. "At first, the marriage upset me, but now, I'm trying to do what's best. Why are you so upset about this?"

He heaved a deep breath. "I should have followed you to Scotland."

Considering his mood, a hesitant smile was all she could summon. "I wanted you to come at first, but now I realize you couldn't have helped. Surely, Marga told you. The debt belongs to an imposter. My grandfather planned my marriage. He wants an *heir,* someone to carry on the Sadlerfield title."

Nodding, he looked toward the ceiling. "If I had gone, I could have stopped it. You! In a forced marriage!"

She braced her palms over her ears. "Please! Don't cast any more darkness on the situation."

"Darkness?" He slammed his fist against his chest. "No one could feel more wretched than I do."

Since he rarely showed his anger, his outburst sent a tremor down her spine. "What are you talking about?"

"*I love you.* I have loved you for a long time, and could have told your grandfather we were betrothed."

His declaration stole her breath and brought stinging tears to her eyes. She couldn't bear to tell him that her grandfather would have dismissed the chivalrous gesture. "I didn't know. Besides, that's lying. You're a solicitor training to be a barrister."

"Has that stopped me from helping you? Of course not. If I had declared myself, would that have prevented you from going to Scotland?"

"No." Warm tears spilled down her face.

From his frock coat pocket, Geoffrey produced a handkerchief and brushed it across her cheeks, then pressed the linen into her hand. "Please. No tears or pity," he said in a strained voice. "The mistake is mine. I should have kept my feelings to myself."

She swallowed the thickness in her throat. "Geoffrey, I care about you. I love you, but not the way a woman should love someone she marries."

He snorted. "What about Kenilworth? Do you love him? Equally important, does he love you?"

Warmth invaded her flesh and she looked away. She could give him a madwoman's banter about her dichotomous feelings and passion, but she doubted he wished to hear that answer. She could tell him about the bleak consequences that they faced if they didn't produce an heir. Would Hunter pay with his life as her grandfather threatened? She shuddered. Revealing Gavin's secret would kill Hunter's friend, and she couldn't do that, either.

"I care about him. He wants to make a successful union."

With red-rimmed eyes, he stared at the ceiling. "As low as I feel, you'll always be in my soul. If you need my help, you have only to ask."

"You'll always be my advisor. We'll remain friends."

"If Kenilworth hurts you, come to me for help. Promise me that. He doesn't have an impeccable reputation."

"I know something about his past."

He met her gaze. "You always try to solve problems on your own, so give me your word."

She refused to think about Hunter breaking her heart. "I promise."

Gently he cupped her cheek and then strolled toward the door. "Take care, Sabrina."

The sadness in his voice caused her eyes to water. She dabbed them with his handkerchief, now scented with her tears. "Wait. Do you think I should tell Hunter about the twins?"

Pausing, he turned with a measured move. He held his body straight, displaying his unreadable facade, the iron composure she knew so well. "No. You would gain nothing by telling him. If you had to flee, the authorities might question him whereas I can claim a client's confidentiality. His peers might scrutinize his integrity. You are not committing a crime. However if the unthinkable does occur, I cannot help you. No law in the land will support you."

She wrung her hands and began to pace. Hunter didn't need the authorities examining his life or integrity. He was already an accomplice to a crime. She wanted to tell him the truth, but she didn't dare cause him more trouble.

"If the…the unthinkable happens, and I must flee, what can I do?"

"Leave him?"

"My last resort."

"You cannot break the union unless you have an affair, or willfully abandon him and disappear. Since divorce laws heavily favor the husband, he could end the marriage for those two acts."

She twisted the handkerchief around her hand and stopped in front of him. "Anything else?"

"To annul the union is difficult unless Kenilworth believed he wed an innocent and got a whore."

Every word made her shudder. "I would never consider such scandalous choices just to dissolve this union."

"Then you've no choice but to remain wed. Or if necessary, disappear."

Sabrina brushed his face with her left hand, and his jaw hardened beneath her palm. "Thank you for your advice. You have the biggest heart of anyone I know. You'll always be a part of our lives."

When Geoffrey glanced at the ring on her finger, he stepped back and faced the mantel. "Despite everything, you are still my friend. This should teach me a lesson. Never fall in love with a client. If I could walk away from you, I would do myself a favor, but I can't." Geoffrey swallowed hard. "Kenilworth could prohibit me from seeing you. That would be within his rights."

"I won't allow that to happen."

"Unless Norton dismisses his honor, and asks you to run away with him," Hunter said.

Flinching, Sabrina spun around. What had he heard? "You're eavesdropping?"

Hunter's black look rolled over her like a thundering wave.

From the day they met, she'd wanted to return to London. Now Hunter knew in part her motivation. He'd heard enough to know they'd never reveal Sabrina's secret, but the things he learned almost paled to the Lord Byronic prose still ringing in his ears. Finally he pushed away from the doorway and nodded toward the open window. "My 'eavesdropping,' as you put it, was unintentional. Your declaration is enough reason to listen."

"This is none of your business," Geoffrey said firmly.

"Oh no? She belongs to me. Would you like to see how intrusive I can be?" His possessive words sounded strangely like something Lord Byron would say, but the jealousy raging through his blood was hot and real. Flexing his fingers, he fought the urge to plant his fist in Geoffrey's face. When he hardened his glare, Geoffrey remained unfazed.

Sabrina let out a choked breath. "Hunter! Geoffrey!"

"What do you plan to do? Call me out?"

"Geoffrey! Are you daft?" Sabrina shot him a disapproving look, then turned to Hunter. Pleading filled her magnificent eyes. "You won't call him out, will you?"

"As Norton said, I've a questionable reputation. I've no desire to damage yours." He turned to the solicitor, a man whose loyalty he could admire, except that he loved Sabrina. "Don't let me find you alone with my wife."

Sabrina's shoulders relaxed. "Thank you. You're being very reasonable, but he's a friend and welcome to visit."

"You've heard my last word on this."

Geoffrey stepped in front of him. "Take good care of her, or I might reconsider my values and steal her away."

"Stop while you're still in my good graces. I'll pretend I didn't hear that."

"I will not revoke my words."

Hunter fought his burgeoning admiration for a man who stood behind his pledge. He willed his hands to relax. Nurturing his fragile marriage and sheltering her from threatening forces was all he wanted. "That's your prerogative."

Sabrina placed her hand on Geoffrey's arm. "Visit us anytime. Oh, and I want you to help investigate the debt."

"Of course I will. Send me a note when you're ready to receive guests." Geoffrey nodded curtly and left.

Despite the way he handled the situation, Hunter wanted to stress a point. "I meant what I said about not seeing him alone."

Sabrina rolled her eyes and took a deep breath. "He's hurt and needs to know we can conduct ourselves as friends."

Hunter raked her with a dark look. He could see her point, but she ignored his feelings. Though she wouldn't have married Norton, she loved him in a way Hunter didn't quite comprehend. Suddenly he knew his feelings for Sabrina left him very vulnerable.

He pointed to the door. "My honor allowed him to leave.

Should I demand his return to redeem mine? I should have called him out!"

"No! Please. You did the right thing letting him go. We've enough problems with my grandfather, and *your* father."

Unyielding, unfamiliar emotions cramped his stomach. She voiced things to Norton he had never heard. "You committed yourself to our union. That lessens our problems. I trust you but question his intentions. He loves you."

Spinning around, she started to walk away. "I must speak to Marga."

Hunter grabbed her arm. "Why are you embarrassed?"

"I'm not." Her pale blue eyes held his gaze, and something flickered in their depths. Fear? Pain? Guilt?

Gently he cupped her chin. "What torments you so, Sabrina?"

She parted her lips softly and then closed her mouth. "When the workers come, be sure they handle my piano carefully."

He tightened his grip. "Damnation. You would have made a great war spy."

For a second her body turned rigid, but then she relaxed. Her lazy smile reached his fingertips. "You carry your Lord Byron act too far, sir. Really, all that nonsense about owning me and duels."

Did she think he was jesting? Or was she joking to avoid the topic? Suddenly he ached to kiss the secret from her sassy lips, to assuage the jealousy simmering in his blood. Tilting her chin, he brushed his lips against hers. When she teased his mouth with the tip of her tongue, he groaned and captured the morsel between his teeth. Kissing her harder, he felt her soft lips mold against his. He pressed his length against her, to force her to feel his need, to remind her that they would consummate their marriage.

Her gardenia scent hovered between them and stoked his burgeoning senses, his elemental needs. He wanted to take her right here, right now. Wanting to taste her sweet skin, he kissed her neck and nibbled on her ear. As her arms slid up his back, he slowly waltzed toward the settee, but something tugged on his frock coat. As he jerked his head up, Sabrina let out a startled cry.

*"Monseigneur,"* a small voice said.

Sabrina swiftly moved away from him.

Looking down, he stifled a groan. "Yes, little one?"

Round blue eyes dominated Christine's doll-like face. She smiled. One small hand toyed with her pink sprigged cotton gown. "Somebody wants you. Bunches of wagons are here. Alec wants to play on 'em."

"The workers are here to move your things to my house."

Sabrina placed her palm on her cheek, but nothing could hide her skin's pink hue or swollen lips. "Hunter, Alec's barely recovered from his last attack. Would you watch the children while I speak with Marga?"

"Of course." Pretending nonchalance, he straightened his frock coat.

"Christine, go with Hunter and don't make a nuisance of yourself." Sabrina started for the doorway.

Christine held out her hand. Trust illuminated her blue eyes, which resembled Sabrina's.

*Resembled Sabrina's.* He stared into the girl's pale blue eyes.

"She means I'm not s'pose to get into trouble. Guess you can take care of me."

The proclamation stirred something in his soul, but the sprouting thoughts made his pulse race. She slid her soft hand into his, and he couldn't tear his gaze from hers. "How old are you?"

Christine held up four fingers.

"When's your birthday?"

"Sabrine! When's my birthday?"

Sabrina's step faltered and she slowly turned. "March, darling."

"March," Christine said. "Why?"

"I don't want to miss it. Let's see what Alec has to say for himself." Could a man stoop lower than to seek infor-

mation from two children? No, but he would. The only way
Sabrina could flee was if she walked over his dead body. If
she didn't come to him willingly, and soon, Sadlerfield might
satisfy the gloomy thought.

"Is that when you'll give me the dolls?"

Sabrina paused at the stairs. "Remember what I told you."

"Senility has not set in, Sabrina."

"Maybe I want a pony instead."

"How about a ride on Gallus?"

"Yes!" Christine led him outside into the morning sun.

The sweet, fresh air dissipated Sabrina's lingering perfume
and steadied his pulse. Hunter had lost the round regarding
Geoffrey's visits, and just thinking about the man made his
blood simmer. Yet winning a little girl's trust made him smug.
He looked at her again. As jealousy tightened his stomach,
something inside urged him not to think they could be Sabrina's children. Neither looked liked Marga; their Barrington
eyes didn't lie. He smothered the image of Sabrina with another man. Who was really the children's mother?

"Alec!" Christine tugged on Hunter's hand.

Her shout shattered his thoughts, but he intended to visit
Jonathan Faraday and convey his suspicions. The possibility
of finding a path to Sabrina's secret stoked his pulse to an
erratic beat.

He found Alec hovering by the workers, who were unload-
ing ropes and old blankets. The outriders had joined the movers. After giving them orders, he took the twins on separate
rides atop Gallus. They squealed in delight and demanded a
second ride.

For the first time in his life, Hunter's world seemed almost
whole. He pulled Alec closer to his chest. The children were
another reason to continue his investigation into Sabrina's
past. Guilt nipped his conscience, but he suppressed the emotion. The findings were no longer just a means to coerce her
into remaining in the marriage, but of learning what would
force her to run away.

They rode down the lane and back to the house. A heady

rose garden hugged the structure, and Hunter took in the sweet country air. Sabrina had fought to come home to all this, and now Sadlerfield and his father were planning something new. Hunter glanced around the open land and gripped the reins. Where in damnation was his father? Soon they would be in London.

In London a person could hide in a million places, observe from anywhere.

Sabrina entered Marga's room, one perfumed from dried rose petals filling several glass bowls. The scent reminded her of the peace her grandfather had stolen. Scooping up some petals, she let them fall and stirred the sweet aroma.

Marga's armoire and dresser drawers lay open and gowns decorated her narrow bed. Several trunks dominated the floor. From the small dressing room, her aunt emerged with another load of dresses, a necessity for presenting the right image to their clients. Yet, the shop would be meaningless if they had to disappear.

"Marga. I must speak to you."

Her aunt looked over the clothes. "I am accepting Kenilworth's offer. Or do you think I should wait a few days so I do not appear too anxious?"

Lifting the burden from her aunt, Sabrina carried it to the bed. "So, you were hiding your true feelings. No. Come now. I don't know what the next days will bring." Quickly she relayed her grandfather's actions, including his last caveat.

"*Mon Dieu!* The man is mad!"

Sabrina pressed her fingers to her brow. "Hunter wants to try to make something of our union. As do I. He's been more forthright than I."

With alarm-filled eyes, Marga grabbed her arm. "You cannot be thinking about telling him!"

"He concluded I carry a secret and will continue to ask me. Marga, he offered to help."

Determination hardened her hazel eyes. "*Non.* You cannot tell him. Staying in this marriage is the best way. No one but the three of us will ever know the truth. Your grandpapa will not look my way after you give him his precious heir.''

Carefully folding a gown, Sabrina placed it in the truck. ''He has not bedded me.''

Marga gently placed her hand atop hers. ''You see something in *monseigneur* that urges you to remain married. The rest will not be as difficult as we first thought, *oui?*''

''How can I give him my body when I can't tell him the truth?''

Her aunt clucked her tongue. ''That is a burden you must bear. I will not let anything threaten the twins, nor will you. Perhaps in time we can tell him. Maybe *after* your grandpapa is in the ground. Surely he cannot live but a few more years.''

As guilt assailed her anew, she lowered her head. ''Hunter trusts me.''

''The twins have only us. To them, I am their mother. In my heart, they are mine.'' Marga slapped her hand on her bosom.

Sabrina had never realized just how deeply her aunt loved the twins. The deceit had somehow mutated to something more possessive. She couldn't fault Marga, who was a good mother, one who would feel the pain of losing a child if the unthinkable occurred. ''Geoffrey advises me to remain mum, too. Revealing our secret will accomplish nothing, he says. Did you know he loves me?''

''I suspected, and you should listen to him.''

''I don't have much choice, do I?''

''Not unless you wish your mother to cry from her grave.''

Swallowing the thickness in her throat, Sabrina walked to the window and braced her palms on the sill. Outside the workers were moving her piano onto a wagon. Hunter stood next to it with a twin holding each hand. She pressed her fingertips to the window and traced a circle around his image. ''I'm sorry,'' she whispered.

# Chapter Nineteen

*Grosvenor Square, London*

Sabrina looked at the gardenia bushes again, still intact after suffering a ride from the morning's move. "A little wider, Cason."

"Must be special plants for ye to bring 'em to his lordship's house." The guard pitched the loam onto the nearby heap.

As the earthy smell roused sweet memories, she glanced at the two finished holes, each nearly two feet wide and deep. The empty spot in her heart suddenly ached. Five years ago, they were three sprigs growing in pewter cups. Each day at sea, her mother carried them onto the deck and let them drink the sun and damp air. When the storm came, she wrapped them in a cloth and tucked them into their bag. Sabrina forced herself not to think about her parents' deaths, but about the bushes. They would have a home even if Marga and she had to flee with the twins.

"Yes, they're very special," she finally said. "But I can dig the last hole. I never expected you to help me. You're a guard, not a gardener." She looked at him quizzically. "I'm not even certain why I need you to watch over me."

He grinned, revealing a missing eyetooth. "I dinna ask

questions, milady. In his lordship's absence, I'm not to leave ye alone. Them's me orders.''

"You're very kind." She spared his weapons a cursory glance. Despite his gentle demeanor, Cason's gap-toothed smile and crooked nose said the man didn't avoid a fight. Lord, she hoped he never had to use the gun around the children.

The children…she peered at the veranda outside the small study she claimed as her new office. Her heart stopped. "Did you see my cousins? They were playing with the bucket and trowels I gave them just two seconds ago.''

"That way, milady." Cason thrust his chin toward the center path lined with trimmed boxwood. "They canna get far with the fence 'round the garden.''

Picking up her green muslin gown, she took long strides down the graveled path. At the end, a trickling fountain spilled into a small pond, the soothing sounds a stark contrast to her growing sense of alarm. When she glanced at the water, she noticed the four floating shoes. She sucked in her breath. "Christine! Alec! Where are you?" she asked in French.

"Sabrine!" Christine yelled.

Sabrina hurried toward a group of matching junipers. Bracketing the greenery, beds of pansies sweetened the air, now hinting of rain. She groaned. "Oh dear. You can't dig up these flowers. They're not yours.''

"We live here now. They're ours, *oui?*" Alec dropped dirt over his muddy feet.

She worried her bottom lip. Already the twins mingled French and English when speaking to her, a sign their move was confusing them. "No. They belong to Hunter's mother.'' She grabbed Christine's hand just as her trowel sliced into the pansies. "What happened to your stockings? Where did you leave them?''

"Don't know." Alec aimed his tool at another flower.

Frowning, Christine lifted dirt-powdered cheeks. "Why can *you* dig?''

Sabrina probably shouldn't be rearranging Hunter's garden,

either, but she didn't have the heart to leave the gardenias. "I received permission. Let's collect your shoes, and do not play around the pond. You might hurt yourself." Or drown. She quickly erased the horrid vision.

*"Non,"* they said in unison.

"They're our boats," Alec added, and sat.

She nabbed their hands. "And you'll ruin them. I'll allow you to fill the *big* hole."

The offer made them shoot to their feet, and a minute later, she stared at their shoes. Without going into the water, she couldn't retrieve them.

Christine clapped her hands and squealed with glee. "My shoe's beating yours, Alec!"

"That's cause my ship's bigger. It's a man-o'-war."

"I can't believe you two did this." She could hardly fault their imagination. With a sigh, she dropped to the edge of the pond and unlaced her half boots. She'd hoped to have the bushes planted before Hunter returned from political meetings and seeing his solicitor. The matter of their…consummation still loomed.

"I want to come with you," Alec said. He stuck his hand into the foot-deep water.

"No! It's too cold and you'll get sick. You two, stay right where you are. When your mother returns from the shop and she learns you disobeyed me, she will not like it."

Hiking her skirt, she stepped into the cool water and pitched the shoes on the ground. Tiny splatters made her jerk around.

"No! You should not fill the pond with gravel."

"They're fish," Alec said in French.

Sabrina thrust a hand into the water and scooped out the rocks. From wrist to shoulder, her sleeve clung to her skin. Climbing out, she dabbed the sodden fabric with her apron, but she couldn't do anything about her wet stockings, now sagging pitifully. "Let's fill the big holes," she coaxed.

For a second, Sabrina pondered putting the wet shoes on their feet, but they were so dirty, she just let out a deep breath. She carried all three pairs instead.

Halfway up the path, Sabrina glanced at Cason, who was still digging the hole. The Georgian house, decorated with Palladian windows, rose behind him like a red brick treasure chest. What would the twins get into next? She rolled her eyes and shook her head, but a movement inside her office captured her attention.

As she moved closer, her blood turned cold. Hunter entered the room, and her grandfather followed, his white head contrasting with the waning light. The duke wandered a moment, then picked up her shop ledger off the desk. With heads bowed, they glanced at it, but Hunter pulled the volume from the duke's hands. Hunter turned and met her gaze.

"Cason, take the twins inside through the servants' entrance."

"Sorry, milady. I canna do that. His lordship—"

"Is here. In my study." Panic blossomed.

The guard looked toward the house. "Right ye are."

Before the man turned around, she had dropped the shoes and scooped Alec off his feet. She thrust him into Cason's beefy arms. The shovel clattered against the gravel.

Cason grunted and blinked. "Well, little master."

"The hole! You promised, Sabrine!" Alec squirmed and screamed, the sound resembling a bagpipe's wail.

Her heart thundered in her ears. "You may fill it later. We've a guest, and don't yell. You'll make yourself sick." She captured Christine and plopped her sister in the stunned guard's other arm.

"But Sabrine!" Her plump finger pointed to the inviting hole.

"Come, me tykes. Good little soldiers obey the captain."

Alec's eyes brightened. "I've new soldiers. You'll play with us?"

When the French doors of the office swung open and booted feet clicked on the veranda, Sabrina shoved him. "Go on, Cason. Take them up to the nursery. Irene's putting away their things. Don't let them out of your sight."

"Aye, milady." He ambled off whistling a Scottish ballad.

When Hunter reached her side, she forced a smile and presented her cheek. She couldn't even appreciate his soft lips, the faint bayberry scent or the way his masculine form filled his gray frock coat and snug trousers.

"Back so soon?" She could scarcely think for her grandfather's stare. Had he paid any attention to the twins? Did he notice any resemblance?

Cold blue eyes traveled down her sodden and disheveled length, stopped at her stocking feet and up again. The duke curled his lip in disapproval.

Hunter smiled as humor lit his green eyes. "Did you fight with the bush?"

She glanced at Cason and the twins as he swung open the servant's door. It closed with a firm click. "I...I was chasing...*moles!* Yes! Moles! They were digging!"

Arching a dark brow, he glanced around the garden. "Moles?"

"Bothersome little creatures. Did you have an enjoyable meeting with your solicitor?"

Like a king with his scepter, her grandfather jabbed his cane and looked down his aristocratic nose. "Instruct your gardener to get some strychnine. You should not be cavorting with the lowers. Instead of attending this and the gardener's whelps, you should concentrate on creating your own."

Sabrina did not attempt to correct his error, yet ground her teeth in spite of it. She just hoped Hunter disliked her grandfather's presence enough not to explain, either. "Had you sent a calling card first, I might not be in this state. Where are your manners, sir?"

The duke straightened and tugged his claret waistcoat, the hue a perfect complement to his charcoal trousers and coat. A ruby pin winked from his cravat. He was a distinguished-looking man, and one who never spewed a compassionate breath.

"You look like a *peasant.* An embarrassment. You are a countess. Have you no pride?"

The words sliced through her heart, but it was the memories

those words provoked that brought burning tears to her eyes. Swallowing, she lifted her chin. "Honor thy parents. Does that answer your question?"

Turning to the duke, Hunter's green eyes narrowed, glinting dangerously. "I don't know what fuels your animosity. But take care how you speak to her."

"You are in no position to tell me what to do," the duke replied. "Furthermore, I expect you to manage the chit properly. Given your past, I cannot believe you accept her wayward behavior."

Hunter looked down with a hollowed expression. "Sabrina, we need a bigger hole. Say, six feet deep?"

Despite her grandfather's ominous presence, Sabrina's mouth twitched. "Larger perhaps. Consider the size of his head."

The duke snorted. "I just came from Darlington's house. They are planning a soiree for this Saturday. Remember. This will be your introduction to society, Sabrina."

"You needn't have stopped by. Pamela already sent me a note about the affair."

"Since I am here, I wanted to be certain before I went home. Any evidence of a child yet?"

Despite her damp clothes and the breeze cooling her skin, angry heat stole to her cheeks. The last thing she wanted to do was discuss her grandfather's obsession about an heir. Glancing at the unfinished hole, she grabbed the shovel. "The rain's coming. I should finish my chore."

An ebony cane cracked down on the shovel handle. She started. The vibration traveled up her arm. A large hand snatched the cane.

Her grandfather met Hunter's cutting gaze with an impassioned stare. "Remember your place, Kenilworth."

Hunter whacked his thigh with the staff. "Heed my advice, Sadlerfield. This is my house. Sabrina is my wife. Don't push me too far. Just remember what I'm capable of doing."

The duke's nostrils flared, cracking his stoic composure. Although she didn't understand Hunter's last comment, she sensed that the words carried impregnable power. He was threatening to use his strength to protect her. Her heart twitched.

"You would seal your fate."

"Yours, too."

Tension seethed between the two, and she knew they referred to something darker. Gavin's crime? Her grandfather's latest caveat? Alarm trickled down her spine.

Hunter whacked his leg again. "Apologize. No one calls her a peasant."

The duke raised his nose. "She is a *peasant*. Just like her mother, a wench. It is my son's blood that gives her any worth. If I could, I would breed that French whore's life out of my descendants."

"She wasn't a whore!" Sabrina slapped her grandfather's jaw.

His head snapped to the side. As he pressed his lips together, he looked at her with frigid eyes. "Your mother was walking the streets and offering herself to any man."

"That's not how things happened! But you got your revenge, didn't you? Get out of here!" Raising the shovel, Sabrina was ready to swing.

"Sabrina! No." Hunter grabbed her arm.

She wrenched away from his hold. "He's defiled her memory!"

"One cannot dishonor a brazen woman."

"You should have died! Not them!" Tears stung her eyes.

"Enough!" Hunter pulled her aside.

Even in the waning light, she could see the red mark she left on the duke's cheek. She lifted her chin. Her body shook with rage.

Suddenly Hunter slammed the cane against the duke's chest. The dark promise in Hunter's eyes challenged her grandfather's frigid glare. "Don't take your bitterness out on Sabrina."

"I merely speak the truth."

"My father crushed your pride, and you can't stand it."

A sliver of lightning speared the sky and clouds thickened to a shade of coal ashes. The wind tugged at her braided hair.

When Hunter looked at her, compassion softened his green eyes. "It's getting cold, Sabrina. Go into the house. I'll finish planting your bushes."

She looked from Hunter to her grandfather. The ominous glint in his pale blue eyes reflected something she had never considered. He might steal any child she bore as punishment for what he believed was her mother's sin. Her blood chilled. Did he plan to dispose of Hunter after she produced an heir? Despite the ugly thought, she needed to make her grandfather believe an heir was another try away. Later, she'd discuss her fears with Hunter.

"The light's almost gone. We'll finish the planting sooner if I help. Besides, you've yet to show me our bedchamber. I'd like a personal tour." Deuced, but she sounded like a light-skirt. She'd already seen the house.

The duke's eyes gleamed. "I will see you Saturday. Kenilworth, I expect you to mold her into someone who commands at least *some* respect." He turned and left.

Sabrina dropped her gaze to the shoes. A tear escaped. He had discovered nothing. Despite this, her grandfather's regard of her still bruised her heart.

She speared the shovel into the ground. "May his soul rot in perdition."

# Chapter Twenty

"**D**amnation! Why is Sadlerfield so bitter?" Hunter slammed the door to their suite.

"You heard it all. What's left to say?" Sabrina's voice quavered. "Thank you for defending me."

A crackling fire guided Sabrina to a wing-backed chair, one of two that bracketed the hearth. As rain pelted the windows, she stared at the wedges of glass framed by brocade drapes and her heart cried for her gardenias. Tomorrow she'd deal with the unplanted bushes. No. She wouldn't let the duke kill them too.

"Who do the children belong to?"

Sabrina's pulsed jumped. "Marga. Marga, of course."

"What happened to their father?"

"He died."

"Along with your parents?"

"I don't want to talk about them." With a toe to heel, she kicked off the half boots that she hadn't bothered to lace. Her grandfather's words continued to slice her heart, and she stretched her trembling hands toward the hearth.

"Something happened. I have to know the reasons for his interference." Hunter moved from his chest of drawers to the bedside tables and lit the tapers along his path. He flicked the match into the fire. "How can I defend you if I don't know the truth?"

She looked up at his hardened features. "I managed well enough, and if you hadn't stopped me, I would have broken his ribs." Angry tears sprung to her eyes.

"Tell me." His eyes darkened with his command.

"Unhook my gown."

Hunter blinked. "Why?"

"I want to burn it." Her voice shook. "I want to burn everything I'm wearing!"

Hunter pulled her into his arms, but she spun away. "No! I...I have to do this. I'll never give him a reason to call me a peasant again." She stretched her arms around to her back, desperate to reach the tiny hooks.

"Stop it! Damnation! Talk to me. How long has Sadlerfield pursued you?"

Yanking off her apron, she balled and pitched it into the fire. The flames soared. "Give me your knife. I'll cut off the gown."

"Bloody hell." Stepping behind her, he made quick work of releasing the fasteners. "I feel as if I have walked into a war without any ammunition."

She closed her eyes and forced back the tears. "My grandfather...my grandfather has no tolerance for imperfection. Anyone not of his class is 'the lower order.'"

Moving away, she tore the gown off her shoulders and stepped out of it. With a forceful toss, the crumbled dress flew into the fire, causing acrid smoke to fill the air.

"Are you going to finish the story?"

Reaching behind her, she fumbled with her corset laces. "If he had *his* way, the world would only number a few hundred people. All with blood as pure as his. Impeccably dressed. Perfect manners."

His hand covered hers. "The story."

Sabrina tilted her head back and let out a shaky breath. "A rich and titled man married a poor tailor's daughter. Yes. It's true. But she wasn't a wanton woman."

He released her hands and worked on the laces. "Go on."

Despite knowing that he would continue to probe, something deep inside her urged her to speak. "Father was a commander in the Royal Navy. They'd just defeated Napoleon. He and his friends were celebrating in Paris when they saw Mother."

"How did Sadlerfield deduce she was a…"

With tears filling her throat, she spun around. "Don't say that word! Mother was a couturiere for Empress Josephine! She was beautiful. The others wanted to take advantage of her. Father stopped them and walked her home. Mother was gentle and caring. They fell in love and married."

"Sadlerfield disapproved."

She snorted. Hunter's wry words didn't begin to mirror her grandfather's feelings. "He suggested annulment. Divorce. Anything to get rid of her or my father would find himself disowned. He chose my mother."

Turning her around, he continued unlacing the corset. "Ah, Sadlerfield lost his heir."

"But that wasn't enough." Her voice shook. "He detests the French. The great duke hired an ex-soldier on the sly. This man went to the War Office and accused my mother of being a spy. He managed to put enough doubt in their bloody ears. Unfortunately he died. Most likely, my grandfather had him killed. Father could see the authorities might find her guilty." She choked for the tears in her throat. "Mother was rotting in jail. My father and a friend bribed the guards to free her. My parents fled. Father went into debt to clear her name."

"Bloody hell. I'm sorry. I swear, he won't hurt you."

But her grandfather would, with one cold glare. Stifling a sob, she tugged at her clothes. Finally she felt her corset slip from her body and watched as it arched into the fire. Ashes and flame mushroomed. As the whalebone crackled and popped, she breathed deeply, taking in the pungent odor.

Hunter pulled her into his arms and shook her hard. "You're not thinking."

Tears escaped. "He stole my parents' lives. Now he's taking mine." A sob choked her breath. "He'll steal our…baby."

As his coat of superfine absorbed her tears, he stroked her hair. "He won't."

"Yes, he will. He's...mad. An eye for an eye."

He lifted her chin. "Damnation! Do you think I'd let him do that?"

"But I told you what...what he said. Don't you remember? In the conservatory? What if he wants to...kill you?" she asked through the tears in her throat.

"You think I can't defend myself and my own? That I'm a coward?"

Sabrina cringed with the force of each word. "No."

"I'm glad you have some faith in me. I've dealt with the very thing you fear." Reaching into his pocket, he snapped open a paper. "This is signed and sealed by the king. He will be the godfather of my heir. Our wedding present. William knows the dangers of my political work."

Relief for the child they might have and fear for Hunter collided. Rationality prevailed enough to remind her that he'd outwitted her countless times, faced a pistol and married her to aid a friend. As easily as he'd tricked her into emptying her gun, she instinctively knew he'd cleverly gleaned the king's help. Even now, Hunter exuded restrained power by the gentle but strong hand that held her waist. She knew the power of his soft lips, now precariously close. His green eyes could slice like a saber or beckon with sultry promise, like they did now.

Her heart started to race. The heat from his body penetrated through her chemise and petticoat. Suddenly he lowered his head and captured her mouth with possessive force. When their tongues met, her body burned. Hunter groaned, his warm breath whispering over her skin. As she slid her arms under his frock coat, his muscles tightened at her boldness but she needed his strength.

He shrugged out of his coat. "I want you," he said softly.

"Yes," she whispered. She tugged at his cravat and let it float to the floor.

As he kissed her cheeks and neck, his hands moved to her

shoulders, and with a jerk, he ripped her chemise from neck to waist. She started, but then felt his lips on her breasts. The caress sent a warm sensation into her womb. When his mouth captured a nipple, she grasped his shirt and arched her back, yielding her body to him. His shirt buttons sprang from their moorings.

"Take it off," he said hoarsely. He kissed her cheek, her neck and then he found her mouth.

Eager to touch him, she pushed his shirt off his shoulders, and he shucked the sleeves. His skin felt like buttery kid leather, a stark contrast to his hard muscles.

She tasted her tears on his lips, accepted his tongue. Their bare chests met, hot and damp. He cupped her bottom and pressed her against his length, his arousal evident through the thin layers of remaining clothing. Anticipation rippled through her body.

His hands moved to her waist, and with a yank, he freed her petticoat. When she let out a startled cry, she felt the lawn slide down her legs and pool at her feet. The movement of his arm was like a rope burn on naked flesh, and the raw heat seeped inward. In that second, she knew she couldn't turn back. Tonight he would make her his wife in all ways. She would fulfill her vow to him. Somehow, she would keep the one to her mother. Tomorrow…tomorrow she would think about her other problems.

"I want you to remember this moment," he said between kisses. He withdrew, studying her with sensuous eyes as if waiting for her answer.

Circling his neck with her arms, she planted an urgent kiss on his mouth, his jaw and throat. He would make the ugliness of the past hour disappear. Their passion would open a gift to the unknown, and she yearned to explore everything.

"We'll savor the journey," he said softly.

"Yes, you said something about teaching me everything." The words came out in a whisper. Heavens. Had she said that?

A slow grin formed on his possessive mouth. He leaned against the chair and his muscles bunched as he pulled off his boots. His skin glistened in the soft light. When he looked up and down her length, his smile broadened. His dark hungry gaze licked over her with palatable desire. "You're beautiful."

Her mouth went dry. Remembering that she wore only stockings, she started to cover her bosom.

He grabbed her hand. "Don't feel shame. You're giving me the greatest gift a woman can give a man. Continue," he said in a velvet voice and flicked the waist of his trousers with his thumb.

The soft command heightened her senses, made her aware of his bayberry scent and the heat simmering between them. "Undress you?" she breathed.

Resting his forearms on her shoulders, Hunter loosened her braid and brought a handful to his nose. "Everything. I don't want you to fear my body, or what you will see."

*Everything?* She mouthed the word silently as dread and the unknown made her pulse race, but before she could respond, he brought her hands to the fall of his trousers. She fumbled with the first button. As she worked the others free, his body tensed. His flesh felt hot. More anxious than afraid to see the whole of him, Sabrina slid his trousers down his narrow hips.

He kicked the garment aside. "One string left."

His China silk drawers were all that remained between her innocence and wanton lust. With trembling fingers, she pulled the tie at his waist. The garment floated to the floor. Sabrina stared at his arousal, then his muscular legs, the firelight emphasizing the curves and planes. His magnificent form stopped her heart.

When she met his gaze, a wicked gleam brightened his eyes and the unholy curve of his lips promised an unforgettable journey. The silent vow made her tremble with excitement.

As they lowered themselves onto the feather mattress, it dipped beneath their weight. He brushed his finger on her leg and snapped her garter. "I want to touch all of you."

Stunned by his virility and the ease that he carried his na-

kedness, she succumbed. He slowly removed her garter and
hosiery from one leg and kissed the top of her foot. A tingle
spread through her limbs and weighted her insides.

"I've dreamed about your legs." He looked down their
length and met her eyes. He smiled.

A tiny cry whispered through her lips. Immediately she
recalled his remark about her "long legs" during her riding
lesson. When he removed her other stocking, heat invaded her
flesh. Slowly his hand moved up her leg and his callused
palms sensitized every inch of her body.

"Are you afraid?" Lowering himself onto his elbow, he
lay next to her. Passion simmered between them.

Incapable of thinking, she kissed him instead. He accepted
with a hungry mouth, one that lured her deeper to the unknown, frightening and exciting her at once. Anxious and undaunted, she dragged a finger up the valley of his spine and
cupped his neck. The veins pulsed against her palm. Although
surprised that she could affect him this way, his reaction delighted her. Their chests pressed together, and with every
brush of his skin her nipples ached and hardened.

He shifted his position and for a brief second, Sabrina experienced a profound sense of loss when his lips left hers.
Moving to her breasts, Hunter captured a nipple and she
moaned with satisfaction. His evening beard felt like coarse
wool against her bosom, and it teased her sensitized flesh and
stirred an odd feeling below her stomach. Drifting lower, he
splayed his fingers over her belly, the gesture as possessive
as his kiss. Sabrina arched against his palm.

"Yes, Sabrina. Let me pleasure you," he whispered, his
breath hot against her flesh as he moved to her other nipple.

She captured his fingers. "I want to do the same," she said
breathlessly when his hand resisted. Though unsure of what
she was doing, Sabrina boldly urged him on his back and
kissed his moist chest, tasting of salt and smelling of bayberry.

Hunter groaned. "Not a good idea."

Concurrently she fought for a confident look and a steady

voice. "You rarely like my ideas," she joked, her breath coming fast. "But this was yours. People marry for passion."

*Passion.* Hunter's body burned with each stroke of her hand and each brush of her hair. Sabrina's gardenia scent assaulted his senses. He was like a man too long imprisoned from life. He thirsted for more. When she captured his nipple in her mouth, Hunter nearly shot off the bed. Gritting his teeth, he teased her swollen breast with his fingers. Sabrina groaned and moved her hand over his stomach.

When his arousal stopped her progress, the touch ignited a fresh onslaught of desire, and fire consumed his insides. Every muscle tensed and ached. Damnation, he needed release. He thought she'd withdraw her hand.

Instead, he felt a tentative finger trace a circle around the tip. His whole body throbbed. Sweat clung to his brow. Hunter dug his heels into the mattress but then grabbed her hand. Her curious and passionate nature might propel her to explore him in other ways. Not yet. He wanted Sabrina to experience and lose herself in the passion. And he'd waited too blasted long for this moment to let her spoil it for her or him.

With one hand, Hunter pinned her arms above her head, brought one leg over hers and trapped her. "I'm supposed to teach *you.*"

She looked at him with guileless eyes, their pale blue hue darkened with desire. "Did I do that right?"

How could he describe her effect on him? No woman had tormented him, turned him away, and then still produced an unnamed emotion that crumbled his defenses. "Perfectly." Hunter kissed the smile off her lips then cupped the warm flesh between her legs.

Sabrina tensed. She knew what he was doing after experiencing the intimacy once and should be beyond embarrassment, yet she warmed a few more degrees. "Can't we just do whatever you need to do?"

Hunter saw the fleeting uncertainty in her eyes, the blessed innocence. The twins weren't hers. For one second, relief smoothed his raging pulse. "I'm preparing you." As he spoke the words, he probed the damp recess hidden between soft folds of flesh.

As he gently moved his finger, the thrust made her body reach for more, and she raised her hips as if the movement could capture her inexplicable need. Suddenly he touched a spot that made her buck. He whispered words that should have made her ears burn.

"Open your eyes. I want to see you when I enter you. Too long. I've waited for this too long not to see you."

Sabrina raised her lids, noted his taut jaw and neck muscles. Moisture glistened on his skin, yet the tenderness in his sultry gaze brought a smile to her face. The knowledge that he had prolonged his own desire made her heart bob. Yes. His strength. In passion or battle, she felt safe with him.

"Bend your knees. When I enter, you might feel a little pain."

"Pain?" Sabrina barely finished the word when he gently pushed inside her. She quickly adjusted to the feel of him.

"Are you all right?" His voice sounded ragged.

His sensitivity to her needs was Sabrina's undoing and her heart ached with love. *Love.* The thought took her breath away. She loved him. In that second, she knew her life would never be the same for he had captured her soul. She could hardly think about this revelation with him pressing inside her. "Yes, are you?"

"Am I all right? Yes. More than all right." Hunter gazed into her impossibly beautiful eyes now filled with passion. An unnamed emotion gripped his heart. No one had ever asked him if he was all right in the throes of passion. If she moved one iota, he would lose control. She had given herself to him and spilling his seed now was too humiliating to contemplate. The moment of respite was all he needed.

"Good," she whispered. "You look as if you're in pain."

Hunter smiled, knowing she now belonged to him in all ways. "Trust me. I'm not."

Slowly he began to thrust, tensing as she tightened around him. Gathering his waning control, Hunter increased his momentum as she adjusted to his rhythm. He circled his hips, teased the moist, sensitive fold with his tip and drew a deep sigh from her softly parted lips. "Do you like that?"

Opening her eyes, Sabrina nodded, too overwhelmed by his masculinity filling her insides. Although he had taunted her with their passion, nothing in her imagination had mirrored the splendor or offered the oneness she felt. The bunched muscles of his arms, the veins twitching at his throat, told her that he was withholding his need for her again. Guided by a little practice, a little instinct and her newly discovered feelings, Sabrina wrapped her legs around his hips. She wanted to give in return and mimicked his driving motions.

"That's not a good idea," he said through gritted teeth.

"We've rarely agreed on anything," she quipped. Suddenly his thrusts deepened and she felt that familiar ache build, urging her to move her hips faster. Something hot raced through her veins. He laced his fingers with hers and went rigid. The sensations of their joined release left her heart pounding.

Sabrina emerged from her dizzying pleasure and knew he changed her life. Her body and heart belonged to only him. He had given her something beautiful, more precious than the jewels or gowns he bestowed on her. Sighing, she relished the joy in her soul.

"I'm too heavy?"

She smiled lazily. The scent of their passion mingled with his bayberry scent. "No. You're like a warm and comfortable blanket. Much better than the tartan you bought."

He grinned. With his hand on her waist, he rolled to his side and kept their bodies intimately joined. When Sabrina kissed his chest, the salty taste of him lingered on her lips. In silent acknowledgment, his fingertips caressed her arm.

Her mother was right. When a woman loved a man, giving herself to him wasn't a duty. However, revealing her feelings to Hunter seemed awkward, at least until she was more certain of his. He had, with aching tenderness, brought their bodies together and that was enough for now. Still, through his concern for her during their passion, she knew he cared. Finding comfort in that thought, she snuggled closer. Maybe their marriage had a rainbow after all.

His fingertips drew lazy circles on her arm. "Next time will be better for you."

Sabrina moved her head so she could see his face. As if sensing her gaze, he opened his eyes and looked at her with a solemn expression. She smiled. "When will that be?"

Though his eyes sparkled, his look remained serious. "I thought you wanted me because you were upset."

"That's true. I wanted you to stay with me."

His body tensed. "If your grandfather hadn't arrived, would you have allowed me to make love to you?"

With a supreme effort, she pushed the duke from her mind. Tonight, she wanted only Hunter in her thoughts. She needed his strength. She realized his concern, and her heart warmed at his use of the intimate words. "I needed you." How could she say her heart knew she loved him before her mind did?

"Do you still?"

When he thrust his hip, Sabrina realized he was filling with desire once more. The thought that he again wanted her, offered more credence to the possibility that he cared about her. "Are you certain you're able?"

"I could make love to you all night. But if you're too tender…?" He brushed the hair off her shoulder.

The ease with which he spoke of their passion should have caused her embarrassment. Instead, his casual attitude made her bold. Besides, she no longer had to rein in her passion. Sabrina smiled, then imitated his thrust. "Does that answer your question?"

He covered her body. "I hope you don't regret this. Once I start, I can't stop."

# Chapter Twenty-One

Sabrina opened her eyes to a gray room painted with slivers of light and scented by lingering passion. Resting across her stomach, Hunter's arm seemed strangely reassuring. She stretched like a languid cat and then froze. What if they conceived a child?

Recalling the king's writ, she drew a long breath and, with a trembling hand, she touched her stomach. Thrill and apprehension assaulted her at once. A boy? Her grandfather's supposed heir... Yet a baby might bring her and Hunter closer, strengthen their marriage. If she forged a stronger relationship with Hunter, surely they could fight anything her grandfather decided to do. Maybe Marga would learn to trust Hunter and feel better about revealing their secret if she saw the marriage thrive.

*Don't you think I can defend myself and my own?* Hunter's words reinforced her thoughts. Could he somehow insulate them all? Sabrina sighed, hating the lies the secret forced her to tell, but she could better her situation.

Somewhere within, a challenge beckoned. She lacked the pure aristocratic blood her grandfather coveted, but that aside, she and Hunter could be happy. A grin tugged at her lips. From her efforts, Hunter might love her one day.

"What are you thinking?"

Starting, Sabrina turned her head. Hunter's tousled hair and shadowed jaw added a rugged look to his handsome face. "I'm going to be a better wife."

"Really? How so?" He traced her ear with his tongue.

She basked in the wondrous feeling of him waking up and wanting her. "I'm serious. I intend to show my grandfather that we can make more of this marriage than just an heir."

He looked up and his narrowed gaze sent a tremor down her spine.

"You're using our marriage as *revenge?* Is that what last night was all about?" he asked coldly.

"No. You misunderstand me."

"That's what your plan sounds like to me."

She smiled at him with all the love she felt in her heart. "Last night happened because I needed you."

He studied her with a steady gaze, one that swallowed the lust in his eyes. "We've enough concerns. Don't add vengeance to it."

"We can share happiness, despite how we met. Your work. Being a merchant, I understand their problems. I can help you."

He propped himself on his elbow. "How?"

Taking his question as a positive sign, Sabrina smiled again. "I've read about the Ladies Abolitionist Society and could join. When we're out, I can discuss your work. Even Pamela says that ladies are speaking about the Reform Bill. Unusual since they refrain from discussing politics."

"What else?"

"My debt. I want to find the person who caused it." She bunched the sheet in her hand. Was passion the only thing he wanted from their marriage? No. He wanted to know her secret. The grim thought made her more determined. "Oh, and I want to help with your shipping work."

"No politics or searching for imposters. Sadlerfield might have orchestrated the debt."

As apprehension circled her heart, the challenge grew. Somehow, she would prevent her grandfather from stealing or tainting her newfound happiness. "That's why you spoke to your solicitor?"

Looking down, he dragged his finger along her arm. "We'll see where my suspicions lead. I'm meeting with Jonathan and Norton about the debt tomorrow."

His touch sent her pulse teetering. "Well, that's a start. I'd like to be there."

He moved his finger up her arm. "This is business. You'll stay out of it. Is that clear?"

The authority in his tone was cause enough to abide his demand, though if her grandfather were the culprit, she wanted to help expose him, or blackmail him. By using the knowledge in this way, she might insure everyone's safety. She tucked away the thought and nodded like a dutiful wife. "You'll tell me what you discuss?"

His finger traced her collarbone. "If we learn anything."

Sabrina could scarcely concentrate for the heat searing her skin. "Why can't I help you with your political work?"

"Too dangerous."

"The Ladies Abolitionist Society? They probably just meet and have tea, or something else that's quite harmless."

"Absolutely not. Abolition is a volatile issue like the Reform Bill. They demonstrate, and I don't want you participating."

"I like the idea. An open forum to vent grievances."

"Forget it."

She bristled, poking him in the chest. "I will not. It was because of narrow-mindedness like my grandfather's—"

"You will." Rolling over, he trapped her with his body. "Even if I have to make love to you all day."

His warmth roused her senses, but she threw him a sharp look. "That's really ignoble to use our passion that way."

"I'm not always noble." He kissed her brow. "You might be carrying my child. I don't want anything to happen to you."

His words pumped joy into her heart and she forgot her ire. Did his feelings go beyond caring? Did she dare hope? Not even her dark thoughts about her grandfather and his obsessive desire for an heir could steal this moment. She laced her fingers around his neck and boldly kissed him.

"Distracting me?" he murmured.

She gave him a lazy smile. "Just letting you know that I appreciate your concern…and caring."

For a second an expectant look flashed in his eyes, but then disappeared. "No politics."

Hunter kissed her breast, now gorged with renewed passion, and took the nipple in his mouth. As he teased the other with his fingers, her tips perked and hardened. Closing her eyes, Sabrina basked in the delicious sensation his touch evoked. Her concentration evaporated at an alarming speed.

"Just how do you intend to stop…oh…don't stop."

"That would be cruel." Hunter shifted his weight and found the warmth between her legs. Pressing his thumb against the sensitive nub of her flesh, he stroked her until she was panting and making soft mewing sounds that fed his own desire.

Hunter's arousal ached. Throbbed. Demanded release.

However, the thought that she would involve herself in something potentially dangerous scared him beyond rationality. Given his concern, his painful state defied logic. No outside forces would take her away. She would always be his.

As if to signify his claim, he pressed her nub harder. She writhed and raised her knees, stirring her feminine scent. Damnation. He wished he could steal her secret as easily.

Hunter wanted to drive her reckless plan from her head, even if taking advantage of her passion proved a momentary solution. As he licked her nipples, her sweet taste lingered on his tongue. He'd think of something more honorable later.

When she begged for him, something tore at his heart and simultaneously stoked his guilt. Still, he entered her only thinking of her needs. As she surrounded him, she tugged at emotions long buried. For more years than he could recall, he'd not allowed himself to care about someone. His passionate wife was too determined for her own good, and he wanted her away from any raucous crowd. Anything could happen and imagining his life without her seemed impossible now. Acknowledging this vulnerability made him push harder and deeper as if he could drive the emotion away.

Damn…damn Lord Byron's sentimental nonsense.

Fighting for air, Sabrina felt the intensity of their passion gaining strength. Like a blind and mad woman, she drifted on this wild and turbulent journey. Tugging. Squeezing. Rolling. Finally the ride pitched her over to a nameless place. Yet, she knew she was safe, for Hunter held her hand and never let her go.

Sabrina awoke to an empty bed and didn't know how long she had slept. Bolting upright, she looked at the clock. Four in the afternoon! She grimaced at what the staff and the twins were thinking. A fresh wave of guilt warmed her skin, but as she recalled the conversation that preceded their last bout of lovemaking, she frowned.

"He really did seduce me all day." Sabrina cursed under her breath. Swinging her legs off the bed, she grimaced at the slight soreness between her legs then walked to her mahogany dressing table. A note in Hunter's bold handwriting lay propped against her perfume bottle. She cracked the seal.

Sabrina, I wanted you to sleep. Undoubtedly you will find a warm bath quite soothing. In anticipation, I ordered the housekeeper to prepare one. Ring for her when you wake. I told the twins you had a touch of ague and are resting. They are safely in Irene's care. I'm off to see His Majesty the King and will return for supper. Your servant, Hunter

Ague! Though he had purposely seduced her into oblivion, the thoughtful note took a little bite out of his actions. She refused to alter her plans. Undoubtedly Hunter went to see the king about the political turmoil in London. Well, she could

help, too. She still planned to join the Ladies Abolitionist
Society. Not today, but tomorrow.

Irritated, Sabrina almost tossed the note in the hearth but
quickly withdrew her hand. She remembered he cared about
her and that softened her ire. Lovingly she pressed the note
to her bosom. A keepsake for luck…and rainbows.

With her grandfather and Hunter's father in the shadows,
she needed all the help she could muster.

Hunter's study felt strangely empty, though he had chosen
the classical Sheraton furnishings and decorated the room
himself. A bust of his grandfather Graham stood in an outer
corner and a portrait of Hunter's mother graced the mantel.
Gray clouds painted the late afternoon sky. Despite a crackling fire, the pale light made everything seem that much
gloomier.

He wished Sabrina were home instead of shopping with
Pamela. His wife's presence distracted him, but not nearly as
much as when she was gone, and she had left this morning.
At least Cason had accompanied them. His gaze moved to the
*Times* lying on a corner of his oak desk.

Reports stated that ruffian merchants were preparing for a
fight, collecting stones, and that the king might call upon the
army to stop any rebellion. Just last evening, Wellington had
boarded his home's windows in concern of such an attack. As
the prime minister and a staunch Tory, he was a target for the
angry Londoners—but no Parliament member was immune to
the populace's dissension. Nor was anything bearing the mark
of wealth like Hunter's coach. He snarled and tried to concentrate on his work.

Knowing Jonathan would arrive within the hour, Hunter
read several more documents, but his thoughts returned to his
wife. What was she hiding? Though she had given herself to
him and promised to be a dutiful wife, the fact remained that
he knew she might run away. Unbidden, his body tensed.
She'd told Norton her plans but not him.

Before he'd let anything happen to her, hell would have to

come to his door. She belonged to him. He slammed his quill on his desk. Guilt gnawed his conscience. His continuing investigation of her and Marga paled in comparison with his need to know her secret.

He'd even imposed on his friend, the king, who supplied Lord Barrington's military record. Gliding over his real purpose, Hunter had told King William that Sabrina might want to meet her father's old friends. One day she might. He faulted Sabrina for not trusting or confiding in him, instead putting her faith with Norton.

After meeting with the king yesterday, Hunter had passed William's information to Jonathan. Would he bring him news today? Hunter rubbed his neck. Where was his father? Lust and greed had always motivated the Sinner, and for him to collaborate with Sadlerfield meant nothing had changed. The duke must have paid a hefty sum for the Sinner to return. What the hell was he going to do about Sadlerfield? Gavin and Hunter were still criminals, but at least no one would find Gavin and Colleen soon. They were spending their wedding trip at a hunting lodge. Hunter's stomach started to knot.

The bright light in his life right now was Sabrina. She had come to him willingly and their consummation should have satisfied him but for a question that kept stirring his thoughts. What was her motivation? Everything she did had a bigger purpose.

What did he want her to say beyond the fact that she wanted him physically? Lord Byron's poems echoed in his head. Hunter ground his teeth. The last time he had sought another person's affection, he had received cold greed. He wanted her to say the words of adoration she said to Norton but knew this was a foolish thought, a Byronic musing to the extreme.

A knock on the door halted his sorry reveries.

Woodstone, the soldier-turned butler, stepped inside the study. "Your lordship, Mr. Norton and Mr. Faraday are here to see you."

"Show them in."

A moment later the duo entered and sat across from Hunter's desk.

Jonathan removed his eyeglasses and wiped the rain from the lens. "Tell Hunter what you learned, Norton."

The young solicitor eyed him with a steady gaze, but a hint of triumph lurked in his eyes. "When I was at Maison du Beaumont earlier, I reviewed Sabrina's records. She helped for a while."

Hunter suppressed the urge to knock the look from Norton's face. In manner and heart, he was too much like the great Lord Byron, a man who braved baring his soul, and a man who possessed a fit form and handsome countenance. He had everything that would interest a lady. The quill in Hunter's hands snapped. Nonchalantly he tossed the remnants into the rubbish bin.

Jonathan settled his eyeglasses on his nose, the frames resting against his round cheeks. "All the gowns had the same measurements."

The clue made him forget Norton…and the insane jealousy pumping his blood. "Interesting. Not three ladies. One?"

Norton nodded. "Marga recalled them looking quite different. One lady has blond hair. Another is a French-speaking brunette, and the last, a redhead wearing patches."

"Hmm. I doubt she revealed her real name," Hunter said.

Jonathan gestured to his pile of notes. "We realize that now after my unsuccessful search for birth records today. Undoubtedly false names, the lot of them. If we're lucky, we might find she came to the shop undisguised. That is, as another client."

"I wanted to tell Sabrina. Is she home?" Norton regarded him with an assessing gaze.

Hunter sliced him with a hard look. Just then a light tap on the door sounded. "Enter."

When Sabrina peeked in the door, unexpected joy bathed Hunter's taut frame. The men stood and Hunter met her halfway across the room. She presented her cheek. He kissed her lips instead. Gasping, she warned him with a narrowed-eyed look. Her cheeks pinked. Hunter grinned. After introductions and greeting, he explained the reason for the duo's visit, then gazed at her lips.

She gripped his arm. "An actress! Obviously, she has the experience to change her looks and speech!" She frowned. "Unfortunately, not all our clients reveal their uh—livelihoods."

Jonathan scribbled some notes. "Theaters, playhouses and other dressmakers. We will check them all."

Norton shifted his gaze to Sabrina, the honey eyes warming. "Meanwhile, I will search the remaining seamstress records. Our mystery lady might be a regular client."

Jealousy curled around Hunter's heart, though he realized he couldn't allow his feelings to hinder the investigation. The solicitors spent a few moments dividing the territory from the east end to the west. Anxious to discuss the investigation with Jonathan, he stood. "If that's all then, Norton, go do your job."

"I'll see you to the door." Sabrina gestured to her friend.

Rising, Norton grinned and flipped him a two-fingered salute. Hunter's body tensed. His blood raged. The gesture reminded him of something Robin Hood might have done. Hunter glared at the door even after they left.

"Hunter?"

"What?" He met Jonathan's frown. "Oh. The papers."

"That, too, but I've information about your wife and her aunt. However, not everything you want."

Curiosity suppressed his insane emotions. He planted his palms on the desk. "Well? What did you learn?"

"This is a start, but hardly much for the money you have spent on the investigation. Or that you might spend. Are you certain you wish to continue? Forced marriage or not, you seem to get on well with your bride."

Scowling, Hunter ignored the last comment. The feelings he experienced were so new they defied all logic. "I don't care about the money. Spare no expense. So?"

"No London hospital has records of twins born in March of 1826."

Hunter slammed his desk. "Who was their father?"

Jonathan raised a brow. "Patience, Hunter. I found several of Lord Barrington's military friends. One corresponded with him regularly. Until the autumn of 1825, your wife lived in Charleston, South Carolina, with her parents and aunt."

"Damnation! I don't have time to check that source." Hunter ran his hands through his hair. "Continue."

"Lord Barrington was moving his family back to England. When they failed to arrive, this friend did a bit of checking on his own. A storm. Your wife's parents died. Lady Kenilworth, her aunt and those children survived. Curious about this friend?"

"Of course."

"Young Norton's father, Thomas."

"Bloody hell."

"Thomas owns a small fleet of cargo ships and the government commissioned them during the war. Lord Barrington was in charge of the fleet. They became friends. Your wife knew to seek him out when she arrived."

Hunter cursed under his breath. "How do you know this Thomas fellow won't tell Sabrina we're delving into her past?"

"Have faith. He has no idea. I went to see him on another pretense. To him, I represent a company."

"This best be good. I don't want Sabrina to find out what you're doing. She might just decide to run."

"Do not worry. However, you might have just bought a ship. You did say, spare no expense?" Jonathan raised a gray brow.

A long moment passed before Hunter realized what Jonathan had done. "You told him my company is interested in buying a part of his fleet?"

"I used Gavin's name. When Thomas said he had to speak to his son, a solicitor, I knew of their relationship. Even so, young Norton doesn't know Gavin. I mentioned I was working on a case with his son. A friendly old chap. One thing led to another. Soon the man was telling me about his adventures on the ship during the war. About your wife's father, Lord Barrington. He was returning to England to start a shipping partnership with Thomas. I will meet with him again.''

Hunter almost smiled. ''You're worth every gold crown I pay you.''

''One more thing.'' He retrieved documents from his leather bag and pushed them across the desk. ''These arrived today from the Barbados business packet. Marked 'personal.' From your Australian man of business. Apparently, he believes you are still there.''

He sensed Jonathan's curiosity—an expected response since he handled all Hunter's affairs except his Australian enterprise. His pulse raced. Prudence said he should wait to read the letters, neatly scribed by the man responsible for the Sinner. Hunter couldn't wait. With every passing day, the urge to bring Jonathan into his confidence grew. Landing in prison, and then informing his solicitor of the crime seemed unwise. He had Gavin to consider. Colleen and Sabrina too.

Flicking the seal, he read the contents. ''The bloody bastard!'' His surprise mutated to anger. ''He couldn't have done this without money. Connections. Help. Sadlerfield.''

''Hunter? Why are you raving?'' Jonathan asked.

Dropping into his chair, Hunter buried his face in his hands. ''I'm in…trouble.''

In short, he conveyed what he had done to his father, the reason Sadlerfield had blackmailed him, and the original reason Hunter wanted an investigation into his wife. He had wanted a trump card if needed. Now he just wanted to aid his wife.

''I suspect Sadlerfield and the Sinner are in deep. I believe they are responsible for the debt.''

Jonathan listened quietly, not commenting, but concern laced his gray eyes. ''Those letters?''

Unburdening his soul should have eased his conscience, but a sense of foreboding crept down his spine. Hunter handed the papers to his solicitor. "This is speculation. My father captured a taipan snake, the deadliest in Australia. After killing it, he laid the creature's head on his leg. He made enough noise for the night guard to hear. The man found my father lying on the ground, and thought the creature was alive. He shot a snake, believing that Randall wasn't dead."

A gray brow rose. "Let me guess. The guard went for help and your father walked off the estate."

Hunter dragged his fingers through his hair. "My only regret is that I endangered innocent people, and Sadlerfield found out. I had to stop my father's plan to impersonate me. I refused to take the chance he would go through with it." He paused as the memory returned, stirring old hurts. He clenched his jaw. "For him to respect Mother in death. That's all I ever wanted. That's all he ever did for her, and only because I forced him."

Jonathan shook his head. "Ugly business. Yes, Hunter, if found out, you're in a spot. Gavin, too. Greedy as your father is, he might accept monetary compensation for keeping his mouth shut. We would, of course, put the matter in writing, that his stay in Australia was 'voluntary,' and the money just a reward for overseeing your enterprises."

Hunter pierced Jonathan with a dark look. Blackmail. The thought galled him. His father would have what he wanted after all. A pampered life. But the Sinner no longer acted alone.

As Hunter looked at his mother's portrait, the sadness in her blue eyes made him turn away. "If he's not agreeable and demands justice?"

Jonathan heaved a deep sigh, his rounded chest straining his waistcoat. "We would engage the best barrister in England. You and Gavin committed a felony. A trial by your peers, and if we lose, seven years in prison."

He glanced at his mother's portrait again. "I'll not serve a day for his rotten soul. Or pay one farthing beyond his upkeep."

# Chapter Twenty-Two

Hunter wanted to be anyplace but here—with the exception of prison. As he and Sabrina entered the ballroom, the din lowered, making the orchestra's Mozart tune suddenly sound louder. Scanning the top floor of the Darlington town house, Hunter looked for Pamela and Brice.

At each end of the room, four Corinthian columns soared to the ceiling where they met a glass-and-beamed ceiling. As people moved about, Hunter saw large potted plants, and small tables adorned with chrysanthemums and pansies. A huge crystal chandelier hung from the domed roof's wooden beams. Soft candlelight melted with moonlight, and the stars reflecting against the glass made them twinkle brighter. The atmosphere resembled the outdoors, a place far away.

He knew Pamela's soiree marked a beginning for him, and for Sabrina too. Acting nonchalant about this evening, his first major event into society since the year he finished at Oxford, had been hard. He'd been too ashamed of his father and the reputation that seemed to follow him…like father, like son. His stomach rolled with unease, but paled in comparison to his unknown fate.

The crowd's curious eyes and hushed whispers made him want to bolt. Instead, he fixed a smile on his face. Hunter's experience with the ton steeled him to anything they could say about him.

He glanced down at Sabrina, who appeared at ease and carried herself with dignity. Dressed in Marga's newest creation, Sabrina looked far more beautiful than any lady present. The pale blue chiffon silk gown, a shade deeper than her eyes, nestled in soft folds across her bosom, modestly exposing their curves and her shoulders. In that moment, he felt absurdly proud, and despite his gloomy thoughts, he wanted to dance with his wife, hold her in his arms, inhale her gardenia scent. Yes, he wanted to savor the evening. Who knew when they'd have another like this?

"Do you see them?" Sabrina asked.

"I only have eyes for my wife." He gazed at her lips, then her bare shoulders.

Sabrina's cheeks flushed. The slow movement of her fan diluted the crowd's scent, an aroma similar to a flower garden. Playfully she whacked his arm with her fan. "Mind your manners. We must be on our best behavior."

He grinned. "I've yet to show you my best."

Pamela, dressed in a moss-green gown, called to them and interrupted Sabrina's response. Brice paused to greet a guest.

"We were wondering when you would arrive. I invited everyone who is anyone, from the haut ton to every wealthy and important merchant in London." Turning to Hunter, she ran her fingers over the velvet lapel of his black frock coat. "You look very handsome."

Hunter bowed, then raised her hand to his lips. Pamela, with her blond hair piled in curls and creamy skin, looked like a flower in sunshine. "You've outdone yourself again. This is a splendid affair."

"Come, Sabrina. I'll introduce you around. Hunt? You'll wait for Brice?"

"We'll join you in a moment," Hunter said. The ladies disappeared into the crowd.

Seconds later, a footman approached with a silver salver. "A missive for you, milord."

As he reached to take the note, he instantly recognized the

slanted handwriting scrawling his name. His insides turned cold. "Who gave this to you?"

"The gentleman at the door, milord."

Grabbing the letter, Hunter brushed past the footman.

"Hunter! Where are you going?" Brice called out.

Ignoring his friend, Hunter stuffed the note into his pocket. He froze at the top of the stairs. Dressed in a black hat and cloak, his father raised a hand to the brim. A sardonic smile flashed across his face. He looked as he had five years' past. Memories flashed. Rage tunneled through his veins, but as he raced down the stairs, his father turned and left. Hunter balled his fists.

He broke a path through the crowd but guests stopped him and congratulated him on his marriage. By the time he responded and went to the door, his father had disappeared. Carriages and coaches lined the street. Horses snorted. Cursing viciously, he stomped back to the house.

"What was that about?" Brice asked, meeting him on the stairs.

"Nothing. I thought I saw someone I knew. Let's find our wives, shall we?" He managed to keep a steady voice. What was his father up to now?

As they went deeper into the ballroom, Hunter searched the crowd, his eyes darting frantically. Hunter made slow progress. Acquaintances he hadn't spoken with or seen in years stopped to greet him. The bankers and merchants embraced him without a hint of slight. Elder guests, the ones who knew of his past and of his father's, greeted him with open curiosity. With each passing second, his muscles grew tenser. Where was Sabrina?

Still, for the first time in years, Hunter didn't quite feel like a pariah among the ton. The blackness in his soul seemed to turn a paler shade of gray, even hinting of rainbow hues. Yet his father's presence hovered like a cresting wave, waiting to smother Hunter again.

"Kenilworth!"

He recognized Sir Lawson's voice, his Barbados neighbor

who treated his slaves like animals. Hunter slowly turned. "Yes?"

Lawson's black eyes narrowed and his mouth formed a thin arch. "So you married Sadlerfield's granddaughter. Think you can sway his vote? I think not." He poked Hunter's chest.

Hunter grabbed the man's thick wrist. Just then, a footman passed with a tray of wine-filled glasses. With his free hand, Hunter swiped a goblet and brought the crystal to Lawson's palm. "Drink up, old boy. Wish me happy."

"You're on a fool's mission. Stirrin' the old ways when they've worked for years!"

Without a second thought, Hunter left the man scowling at him. Suddenly he heard Sabrina's voice nearby and caught a glimpse of pale blue silk almost hidden by a pillar. Relief eased through his body. As he edged his way around the guests, Hunter scanned the crowd for his father. Though no face resembling his own appeared, his concern remained. Did Randall intend to do something unforgivable to Sabrina?

When he focused on his wife again, a group of grandames were glancing at her small waist. He smiled. She caught the innuendoes and gestured to her gown.

"Admiring my aunt's latest creation? Maison du Beaumont, on Bond Street. Madame Beaumont has the latest fashion plates from Paris."

Hunter smiled inwardly at her wit and moved next to her.

She turned and smiled brilliantly. "I thought you'd be discussing political stratagems."

As he put his hand on her elbow, he summoned a charming smile. "If you'll excuse us ladies, I must speak to my wife."

Hunter started to usher her away, but from somewhere near, he heard his name and stiffened.

"My goodness, Kenilworth is a handsome devil," a lady said.

"Lady Kenilworth is lucky, indeed. Do you know what happened between her father and Sadlerfield?" the lady's companion asked.

Suddenly the duke stepped into Hunter's path. Sabrina

started, but her grandfather looked over her head. "Why not ask me, Lady Patterson?"

The last lady to speak sputtered. "Andrew, you old goat. 'Tis an age since we've seen you at an affair."

Hunter narrowed his eyes at the duke, who was already focused on the more stylish of the two elderly ladies. Lady Patterson, a woman with a slight face and translucent skin, looked at him expectantly.

"Indeed it has. Allow me to satisfy your curiosity. My son and I differed on political opinions, but I should have yielded."

Leaning close, Hunter said, "Sabrina, you don't have to stay and listen. Besides, I must speak to you."

"Wait. I want to hear what he has to say." Sabrina shook off his arm. "Pamela said to face the ton boldly."

"You're quite free with your story, Andrew. You might as well tell us the lot of it," Lady Patterson said.

Sadlerfield explained his search for Sabrina after surmising she knew nothing of her heritage, and finally praised Sabrina's intelligence for supporting herself. The duke looked straight at her, civility veiling his facade. "Sabrina, you look well."

Sabrina raised her chin. "Anyone can look grand in Aunt Marga's creations."

"If you'll excuse us, we need some refreshments." Ignoring Sadlerfield's raised brow, Hunter escorted Sabrina from the group.

"You're right. I shouldn't have listened."

"Lady Kenilworth!" A dame of Amazonian proportions parted the crowd. She caught her breath. "We're using this affair to garner more support. Tomorrow's our big demonstration."

Hunter suppressed a growl. "Demonstration, Sabrina?"

Sabrina smiled innocently and whispered, "You were in such a foul mood the past several days, I didn't want to tell you."

He gnashed his teeth and wanted to drag her away. Only the fact that society seemed to forget his past and embrace

Sabrina made him hesitate. Without a shred of remorse, she introduced Lady Yarborough, the leader of the Ladies Abolitionist Society.

"I'll gladly help! I'm certain Pamela will, too," Sabrina said.

Lady Yarborough beamed. "Having ladies of your stature join the organization seemed unbelievable. No offense, but you know the old ton. Their privileges and property are uppermost!"

Sabrina smiled. "No offense taken. Parliament argues about the wealthy versus the poor. The issue is human rights. Even if a lady is wealthy, she should have a voice in her affairs."

With abolition a volatile issue, Hunter wanted to divert the attention from Sabrina. Already people were starting to cluster around them. Her support for his cause at once frightened him and made him proud.

"Lady Kenilworth joined the society," Hunter began, forcing a smile, "because it symbolizes a freer voice among all people, including that of a wife. Her *wit* takes my breath away."

His statement sent a rumble of whispers in all directions. Society frowned upon a woman's intelligence, and his declaration called attention to Hunter.

Sabrina slid him a sidelong glance as if she understood his intent. "Lady Yarborough, he's a true prince."

Hunter smiled at her wry humor. "Only doing my duty."

"Sinclair is right," Sadlerfield added. "If my granddaughter had not been intelligent, she would have likely starved to death. If she champions the cause, then I support her wholeheartedly."

Stiffening, Sabrina glanced at her grandfather, but Hunter could see the disapproval in his eyes, a look contradicting his words. He had confronted Sabrina's sudden appearance in society with an offensive attack. If Sadlerfield wasn't Hunter's enemy, he could almost admire the man's boldness. Hunter tensed when he realized the ease with which the duke wooed the ton made him even more dangerous. Compared to Sabrina's past and her kinship with Sadlerfield, the old gossip surrounding himself paled. He only had to recall the duke's threat.

Even if their peers questioned the Sinner's sincerity, they would believe the duke. One word about the kidnapping and Hunter would be in prison. In that second, he realized Sadlerfield had planned the Sinner's appearance, a warning of who held the power. The blackmail might continue anytime, in any form. Impotent rage pumped through his veins.

Lady Yarborough beamed, then turned to Hunter. "To allow a wife her voice. The establishment might suffer apoplexy over your words! My best to you in Parliament."

Hunter forced a smile. At least the attention had shifted from Sabrina and the volatile slavery issue as he intended. The orchestra faded from Mozart to Strauss, the sensuous music a perfect excuse to whisk his wife away. He brought her hand to his lips, then laced their fingers. "Dance with me."

Without waiting for an answer, he ushered her from the ballroom and down the stairs to the second floor.

A few minutes later, they entered Brice's study, a bookshelf-lined room with periodicals scattered on a mahogany worktable. Hunter explained the Sinner's arrival and quick departure.

Sabrina brought a quivering hand to her bosom. "Oh dear. Can you guess what he wanted?"

"No. But you joining the Ladies Abolitionist Society doesn't help matters." Pulling the note from his pocket, he snapped open the vellum. His heart reeled. Anger threatened to paint his soul black.

*We are both full of surprises. Are we not? My felicitations on your nuptials. I'm still pondering a wedding gift. Randall.*

Hunter and Brice followed the ladies around Hyde Park and kept a reasonable distance. At least Sabrina recognized that Randall posed a threat and asked Hunter to accompany them to the park. He wanted to keep Sabrina safe.

"I should have brought the sailors here today. What if a band of ruffians decided to join the ladies? That would change the entire atmosphere. I can't decide who belongs in Bedlam. Me, for allowing Sabrina to attend, or her, for wanting to come."

"They believe in the cause," Brice stated.

Hunter kept his eyes on the group. "Are my political beliefs worth the danger?"

"Has a pair of sweet eyes changed your mind? That's what Parliament needs. Sabrina on the floor."

Although Hunter chuckled at the vision, he still wondered if he should risk one sweet life. The wind slapped his greatcoat against Gallus and the stallion objected with a snort. With the chilly November wind, now brisker as dusk approached, Hunter was glad the ladies were almost done. He focused on the Parthenon frieze atop the George IV Arch, the point marking the entrance to Hyde Park Corner, where the ladies had started and would end their walk.

The group timed everything well, with the social hour now at its height. Carriages rumbled past them and horses kicked up stones, ricocheting off the wooden rail that separated the pedestrian walk from the equestrian path. Occasionally a mounted peeler tipped his blue bonnet to acknowledge the ladies.

Occupants of barouches and cabriolets scanned the group with condescending looks as their drivers maneuvered through the traffic. Others viewed them with amusement and commented that nothing would change the old establishment. Some men, riding atop their park hacks, pushed back their hats to gain a better look at the ladies.

Despite all this, Hunter admired their perseverance. When the ladies reached the iron gates of the entrance, they lowered their wooden placards and clustered around the arch. Some shook their arms as if to ease the stiffness from the cold while others straightened their bonnets.

"Pamela must have a pebble in her shoe." Hunter watched as she raised a foot then leaned on Sabrina's arm.

Brice grinned. "I'll rub her feet tonight."

Hunter chuckled. "I'm thinking of a bath for two."

Suddenly the rumbling of a conveyance and jangling harnesses caused Hunter to look behind him. A hackney raced toward them. Horses and wheels were flinging mud in all directions.

"Get out of the fool's way!" Hunter maneuvered Gallus to the left as Brice turned to the right. Gallus stomped and neighed. Settling his horse, Hunter turned his attention to the departing hackney now barreling for the ladies.

"Sabrina! Pamela! Move!" Hunter spurred his horse toward them, but the crowded conditions around the gate made quick maneuvering impossible. Terror raced through him. He couldn't stop the coach or reach Sabrina. He yelled again.

As she looked over her shoulder at him, Sabrina stared at the approaching coach. Her eyes grew wide. The ladies screamed and scattered. When Pamela lost her balance, Sabrina tried to break her fall. Signs crashed to the ground.

Working Gallus around the chaotic scene of spooked horses, conveyances and people, Hunter edged closer and shouted again. Oblivious to her own danger or perhaps challenging the threat, Sabrina pulled Pamela to her feet. By helping her to safety, Sabrina put herself directly in the hackney's path.

Hunter yelled. His pulse raced. Alarm blazed through him. If Sabrina didn't move, the coach would hit her.

"Sabrina!" Pamela cried. She yanked her arm.

Wooden signs splintered. A flying placard clipped Sabrina's leg. She screamed. The hackney soared by her and through the gate.

When Hunter lost sight of his wife, panic sizzled through his veins. His heart hammered. Then he saw Pamela kneeling over Sabrina's crumpled form.

"Pamela! Is she all right?" Hunter dismounted before Gallus stopped.

Tears streamed down Pamela's face. "I—I'm not sure."

Gently Hunter raised Sabrina's head in his palm and cradled her in his arms. Liquid seeped between his fingers. Her hair felt damp. When he took his hand away, blood painted his skin.

Why this? Why now? So close. Life with her was as close to happiness as he had ever come. Damn his stupidity! He should have acted on his instincts and forbidden her to participate. Maybe if he had come more prepared…with nearly an army at his disposal, why hadn't he used it? Lowering his head, he closed his eyes.

He had failed his wife.

Hunter paced the hall outside his bedchamber. "Damnation. What is taking so bloody long?"

"She is alive." Pamela swiped away a tear.

Hunter refused to consider the other possibility. "I'll kill the bastard who did this," he said coldly. "She's kind. She's good. Too much has happened in her life to deserve this."

"At least the peelers caught the man," Brice said.

"He's somebody's pawn. I'll find the man responsible," Hunter said icily.

Just then the door swung open and a man with an unruly shock of silver hair waved Hunter into the room.

"Will she be all right, Dr. Easton?"

"I think so."

Hunter rushed to her side. Her still form merged with dark memories and a cry of disbelief nearly reached his throat. Dropping to his knees, he laced his fingers through hers. "She can't die," he said in a choked whisper. The words came from somewhere deep within his soul.

"I don't think she will. Lady Kenilworth's head, however, will feel like someone used it for a battering ram."

"Concussion?" Gently Hunter stroked her bandaged brow.

"A real crowner." The doctor rolled down his sleeves and covered his stout arms. "I stitched that ghastly cut. Had to shave a bit of her hair. Aye, and don't panic if she has a weak stomach or experiences dizziness. That should disappear in a fortnight. Have someone sit with her though. If she needs to tend to herself, she'll need help getting about. Aye, and I left a bottle of laudanum if the pain gets too bad.''

Hunter hoped she would never need it. The stuff had killed Diana. Renewed panic spiraled, churning buried emotions. ''She'll be all right?''

''As far as I can tell.'' He shrugged. ''With a head injury like hers, I can't guarantee anything.''

Hunter swallowed hard. Sabrina's skin looked pale, emphasized by the black arcs of her long lashes. Reverently he touched her cheek, the silken flesh cool against his hand. The stillness of her body brought a fresh wave of fear, more powerful, more devastating than when his mother had died. As his chest ached, the pain made him recall the horror of watching his mother die.

They had been enjoying a bright spring day at Keir Castle. He fished as she painted. All she wanted was to show him her picture. After tripping, she had fallen off the bridge…a nightmarish accident. Terror washed through him as if it were yesterday.

When the doctor left to tell the others of Sabrina's condition, Hunter removed his coat and boots. His hands shook. Something deep inside said he should be next to her. *In sickness and in health…till death do us part.*

Gently he climbed onto the bed and carefully lay down next to Sabrina. The gardenia scent reminded him of her passion in everything she did, and he wanted to see her filled with life again. Hunter wanted to be with her when she awakened, and maybe if she sensed his presence, his warmth, she would open her eyes. He laced his fingers with hers, feeling strong in their stillness. In that second, he realized he needed her strength, too. He couldn't lose her. She was in his soul. She had become a part of his life and was his. Not even God could have her.

# *Chapter Twenty-Three*

Pain tugged at every hair root and caused Sabrina to stir.

"Sabrina?"

"Hunter?" His name came out in a dry whisper, but she sensed his presence, smelled the faint, mingled odors of dust, horseflesh and bayberry soap.

Soft lips kissed her cheek. "I'm glad you're awake. How do you feel, princess? Can I do anything?"

She blinked, heard the anguish in his voice. After adjusting to the lantern-lit room, she focused on his face, shadowed with stubble and dark crescents under his eyes. Worry creased his brow, emphasizing the self-recrimination in his tone. Hunter's concern warmed her heart.

"Don't blame yourself for the accident." Speaking made her head hurt.

"Then who? Your grandfather? My father? Ruffians?"

His clipped tone sent a shiver down her spine. "I don't know."

She clamped her eyes shut. Why was the room spinning?

"Hush. Rest." He cupped her cheek.

Seeking the warmth of his hand, she moved slightly. Her stomach swayed. Breathing deeply, she tried to stop the intermittent waves of nausea and the throbbing in her head. "The accident…a warning to you? Your father…what does he want of you?"

"You're in no condition to talk."

Urgency and concern laced his voice, but she acquiesced. She felt as if she had one foot in heaven but wanted him to feel free of blame. "A little bump can't hurt my hard head."

A faint smile emerged. "God willing, you'll recover."

An emotion flashed in his eyes, the same look he possessed when he had found her in the crate. Terror? Had her accident scared him so much because he disliked the idea of living without her? As quickly as the thought emerged, she brushed it away. If panic caused his dark look, the reason came from his protective nature, nothing more.

When she tried to smile, stiletto pain jabbed her head. She squeezed her eyes shut.

He grabbed her hand. "What's wrong? Are you all right?"

The strain in his tone fed her own worries. As the spiking ached subsided, she looked at him with all the love she felt in her heart. "Hold me?"

A wrinkle marred his brow. "Are you certain? I don't want to hurt you."

"You won't. You're better medicine than hot broth."

Despite his size and strength, he gingerly tucked his arm beneath her shoulders and drew her close. Nausea erupted, followed by a jolt of blinding pain. She set her jaw and held her breath until the assault passed. Was death about to boost her into heaven?

Panicked, she clung to his warmth, felt his hard chest and summoned the treasured memories of their lovemaking and brief time together. She embraced his gentleness and the concern that bathed her in security. He had given her something beautiful and she wanted to leave him with an equal treasure.

"I must tell you how I feel." The buzzing made her pause.

"What's wrong?" Alarm hugged his words.

She tried to lift her head to look into his eyes. The effort brought an anvil down on her head. She winced, stifled a cry.

"Something is wrong! What?" He shifted her position and met her eyes.

The terror in his gaze brought tears to her throat. Telling

him of her own worries might worsen his, and to blurt out her feelings for him might seem impulsive. She must ease toward her purpose.

"Are you all right?"

His heartbeat faltered beneath her ear. "Yes."

The cadence of his pulse said he lied. Perhaps he cared for her more than she reasoned earlier. The thought fed her confidence. "My accident. You watched helplessly, as I did when my parents died. Yet knowing they loved me helped me through my grief. *We love you.* Those were their last words."

"Don't think about death." His voice cracked.

"If something happens to me—"

"Don't say that!"

The daggers attacking her head made her continue. Was that desperation in his voice? Her head buzzed. "Promise. Promise you'll take care of the twins and Marga."

He hugged her hard, pressed her head against his chest. "You're not dying."

"Promise me."

"Of course, I will."

The world seemed to tilt and spin. Closing her eyes offered her a brief respite. "You do care about me. That's enough. I want to leave you with something."

"Don't speak of death. Do you hear me?" Hunter shifted, tightening his embrace.

From his movement and pressure of his tense muscles, another onslaught of dizziness erupted. A bitter taste lingered. Despite his erratic pulse and raspy tone, she must prepare him just in case. Sabrina waited until her stomach settled to a wave. "I might not get a chance to tell you this."

"You're speaking nonsense. You'll get well." Hunter cupped her chin and kissed her lips.

Under other circumstances, she would have reveled in his closeness, but the small movement lifted her stomach, too. "I love you," she whispered through the thickness in her throat.

He moved away and his eyes widened. "What?"

The motion made her squeeze her eyes tightly. He sounded

surprised. Had he heard her? She tried to form the words again, but swallowed the bitter taste in her mouth. "I need a chamber pot. Quickly."

Hunter could barely assimilate Jonathan's query into Sabrina's accident, which the magistrates concluded was an unfortunate incident. Since Sabrina's injury a week ago, he'd been so certain that his father or political opponents were at fault.

The possibility of a revolution in London had erupted three days earlier when Wellington refused to support reform. Blackguard ruffians stirred small riots and caused enough concern that the Tories apparently abandoned the prime minister. Yesterday Wellington resigned but the mood of London remained ugly, even with the new Prime Minister Grey at the helm.

Following the events, King William had summoned Hunter for informal advice. His recent return from Barbados and business connections provided him with knowledge that few other peers possessed. At the end of their meeting, William had asked Hunter to ponder ways to settle the populace.

Burdened with problems, Hunter continued reading Jonathan's next report. He could barely suppress his spinning emotions. Raising his eyes, Hunter looked across his littered desk. For some reason, the information didn't surprise him. A part of him had suspected. "Why do you believe this?"

Since Sabrina's accident, Hunter questioned every thought and emotion that crossed his mind. Sabrina's declaration of love surprised, thrilled and frightened him. His life seemed askew. He was so uncertain of his own emotions.

Jonathan heaved a deep breath. "Everything I have deduced is on the last page. Four of Thomas Norton's five sons work for him and he has a parcel of grandchildren running about. I commented on them. Proud of his lot, he pointed to a thin child who had refused his mother's milk. That started me thinking. If the twins did not belong to Madame Beaumont, they would need a wet nurse. I suspect the children's nanny, Irene, filled that need."

Hunter flipped to the end of the report, glancing at it but not reading. Everything was starting to make sense. "He knew about Sadlerfield and his son's falling out?"

"Oh, yes. Before Barrington left for America, they stayed with him and his family. Thomas's father was a barrister. The spy charges. He cleared Lady Barrington's name."

Hunter gripped the papers, suppressing the jealousy and anger that his burgeoning thoughts summoned. "Geoffrey Norton knows. I'd guess he knows everything. Bloody hell! She should have told me. She must be terrified that Sadlerfield would accuse Marga of some crime. Damn him. He already has an heir."

That was the reason she didn't want to marry, to consummate the marriage, the motive that prompted her to escape, and would cause her to flee if Sadlerfield learned. If Hunter guessed right, Marga had worked with Sabrina's mother, too. Now he truly understood the reason she'd made him promise to care for them. The request took some sting out of her secrecy.

"She might have discussed the issue because she needed legal advice."

Hunter tossed the report on his paper-covered desk and rubbed his eyes with the palms of his hands. "I have to tell her that I know. But not until she's well."

"She is feeling better?"

He rubbed his brow. "A bit. She wants to get out of bed."

"That's a good sign. Now, what about Sadlerfield? Do you plan to tell him what you know about the twins?"

He slammed his fist on the desk, the motion stirring the papers. "No. I'd never betray Sabrina. The man is so full of himself that he makes the Thames seem pure."

Jonathan's hands shot out, palms forward. "Just asking."

A knock sounded and Hunter bid the intruder to enter.

Woodstone stepped into the room. "Your lordship. The

Duke of Sadlerfield is here. I know you said he couldn't see Her Ladyship, but he insists on seeing you.''

Hunter sneered. "Didn't you tell him I was busy?"

"Your lordship, he said you would know better than to turn him away."

"He didn't threaten to dismiss you?"

"Sir?"

"Never mind. Send him in." When Woodstone left, Hunter nodded toward the small library that Sabrina claimed. "This shouldn't take but a minute. You may wait in there."

Just as Jonathan left, Sadlerfield entered with his lips pressed in a thin line. "Did you forget who is in charge?"

Hunter shrugged. "I don't worry about it. I know you'll remind me. What do you want? My work awaits me." He swept his hand over his desk, one neglected during the past week.

The duke lifted his nose. "If you had kept Sabrina in her wifely place, you would not be behind on your work. Good God. She could have lost my heir in the accident. Was there any evidence of such a loss?"

Hunter's jaw worked. "No."

"Good. She might be with child yet. My solicitor prepared the paperwork regarding Sabrina's dowry. You do remember? Fifty thousand upon your wedding. One hundred fifty when you and Sabrina produce an heir." He pulled the papers from his greatcoat pocket and laid them on the desk. "Your signature."

"I'm not signing anything until my solicitor reviews it. I'll get him."

"He is here?"

Rising, Hunter strolled to the adjoining door, his hand gripping the handle. "Didn't I say I was working?" He pushed the door. "Jonathan," he snapped.

His solicitor returned to the room and when Hunter turned, Sadlerfield held Jonathan's report. Fear shot through his blood, and he hoped the duke had not read anything. In five long strides, he ripped the papers from his hands. "That's none of your business."

"Children! That report speaks of babes. You knew I already have an heir!"

"That's merely a list of those living under my roof. I sought the king's protection against political ruffians."

"No! I investigated Madame Beaumont and her whelps! The Wesley church has records of their births. May...I believe. That paper said Faraday questioned the children's parentage."

Hunter grabbed the duke's arm and shoved him against the desk. "You see what you want to see. Get out of here. And don't ever set your foot in my house again."

The duke twisted out of his grip. "I do what I want. I own your life."

Clutching the duke's lapel, Hunter dragged the duke toward the study door. "And you're about to begin a new one."

"You told Cook to fix dinner for Hunter and me?" Sabrina allowed Marga to accompany her downstairs. She blamed her light-headedness on being prone and subsisting on broth for a week. "I want something I can chew."

Marga glanced at her with concern in her hazel eyes. "*Oui, ma chérie,* but I am not so sure you ought to be on your feet."

"I'm much better. Truly." Sabrina smoothed her gown of deep blue silk, Marga's newest creation under her agreement with Hunter. She hoped he liked it.

"*Monseigneur* will have my head for agreeing to this."

As they crossed the foyer, Sabrina heard her grandfather's raised voice. "Curse the man! Will he not leave us be?"

Lifting her skirt, she rushed into Hunter's study and slid to a halt. He had her grandfather by his throat. "What's going on?"

The duke twisted free and spun around, his blue eyes cold and accusing. "This!" He jabbed his cane at the papers in Hunter's hand. "You little scheming whelp." He looked past her to Marga and then back to her. "You let a *commoner* claim my heir?"

"Sadlerfield! Be quiet, or I swear I'll cut out your bloody tongue." Hunter rushed toward her.

Sabrina's heart slammed against her bosom. Marga's fingers dug into her arm. The room blurred, but she forced herself to take a deep breath. "I don't know what...what you're talking about."

Hunter put his arm around her waist. "Sabrina, what are you doing out of bed? Marga, you were supposed to keep her company."

"*Monseigneur.* She only wished to have supper with you." Marga's voice quavered.

Sabrina met her aunt's gaze, one filled with quiet terror but not as telling as her ashen pallor. As they'd always planned if discovered, they'd flee with the twins. What about leaving her beloved? Panic curled around her heart, accompanied by a festering ache. Maybe she could continue to pretend ignorance.

She forced calm into her voice. "Marga. Maybe this wasn't such a good idea. I'm not feeling so well after all. Would you help me to my room?"

Hunter brushed her brow with a kiss. "Yes, do that, Marga. I'll come up in a minute."

Sadlerfield thrust his cane on the rich tapestry carpet. "Dribble! They are playing us for fools, Kenilworth."

Sabrina only had one choice. Closing her eyes, she let herself go limp, and felt Hunter's arm tighten around her waist. "Sabrina!"

"*Mon Dieu!*" Marga fanned Sabrina's face.

"I would bet a hundred crowns that she is acting!"

Panic seized her lungs. Bringing her hand to her brow, Sabrina shielded her face. She mouthed the words, "Go. Take the twins." When her aunt nodded imperceptibly, Sabrina added, "Marga, silly me. I'm going to make you late. Didn't you have an engagement with Thomas?"

"*Oui.* I must go."

Sabrina let out a deep breath. Marga understood. When Hunter stiffened, she raised her eyes to meet his gaze. Emotions lurked behind the green depths. Anxiety? Anger? As Marga started to move away, Sabrina gave her grandfather a surreptitious glance.

He impaled them with an icy look. "Madame Beaumont. You are not going anywhere. Either of you. I demand to see the children that Faraday refers to in his report."

She swung her gaze up to Hunter. A sickening feeling burgeoned in her stomach. "Report? What's he talking about?"

Hunter shifted his weight, truth shadowing his eyes.

Her grandfather swiped the papers that Hunter had thrown on the desk and waved them at his solicitor. "This one! The one Kenilworth had Faraday compile."

A horrified cry escaped Marga's throat as all eyes turned to the stout gray-haired man. As understanding pierced Sabrina like a cold wind, she tasted the betrayal, the act so palatable she could hardly swallow, scarcely breathe. She loved this man? Deuced, but how stupid was she? Sabrina forced away the tears and summoned all the tenacity she had left. Despite her shattered heart, she must maintain guardianship of the twins.

"Hunter, I suggest you tell your wife the contents of my report," Faraday said.

"Nonconclusive," Hunter snapped.

Faraday cleared his throat. "Perhaps, but remember your…position, the issue we discussed a week ago. If the ladies admit to nothing, Sadlerfield must provide the evidence. He must prove the children are his kin. If they are, no law can stop him from claiming them."

When Hunter released her and stomped toward his desk, Sabrina wrapped her trembling fingers around Marga's. "What are you doing?"

With a grim look, Hunter pulled the bell rope behind his chair. "Sadlerfield wants to see them. He claims Wesley's Chapel has a record of the twins' birth. If so, you shouldn't fear anything."

Marga's nails dug into Sabrina's flesh. "I beg of you, *monseigneur*. You know my son is not well."

Sabrina could taste her fear, sense an impending doom. "There's no reason. They're Marga's children." She tried to put force behind her words, but the quiver in her voice rose beyond her tone.

"Ladies, His Grace just wants to see the children," Faraday interjected. "I see no harm in that."

A moment later Woodstone appeared and Marga left with him to summon the twins. Hunter returned to Sabrina's side, escorting her to a chair. Sitting, she tried to understand what Faraday had said about Hunter's "position." What did he mean? As she suspected a second ago, the report proved that Hunter was still investigating her past. The ache in her chest spread. Lord, but she wanted to ask questions.

Despite the sickening feeling that hovered in her stomach, prudence told her to remain mum, to deny everything. She had to think of the twins first, and the more confrontation she showed, the more suspicious her grandfather would become. Lacing her hands together, she rested her head on her knuckles.

Hunter put his hand on her shoulder. "Are you all right?"

She nodded but couldn't bring herself to look at him. If all her thoughts proved true, she'd never forgive him.

The twins' chatter brought her head up. All heads turned toward the door as the threesome entered. Trepidation filled Marga's eyes but she lifted her chin, straightened her back. The twins were already wearing their nightgowns. Looking curious, Alec glanced at the assemblage while Christine stayed behind her aunt's wool skirt.

Sabrina glared at her grandfather. "You've seen them. Take them to bed, Marga."

"A moment." Sadlerfield marched toward them, stopping a few steps short of the twins.

Speaking French, Marga quickly introduced the children.

Suddenly her grandfather spun around, his eyes cold. "I knew you were lying. Except for his curly locks, the boy is an image of his father at the same age. I have portraits of him. Any court will see the resemblance.''

Marga picked them up and hugged them to her bosom. She flashed him a determined look, her hazel eyes blazing with anger. ''They are *mine.*''

Sadlerfield straightened. ''The mother is in question, but not the father. Bastard or not, the children are coming with me. From that report, I would guess they are legitimate.''

Marga took several steps backward.

''No!'' Sabrina sprang to her feet and her head spun.

Hunter's arm captured her waist. ''Sit. I'll deal with this.'' Terror stole her breath. ''You? This is your fault!''

With heavy strides, Hunter headed for Sadlerfield and Marga. ''Lay one hand on the children, and you'll see just what hell is like.''

Sadlerfield spared Hunter an impassioned glance. ''You would find yourself in prison.''

''Hunter. You can't help them from jail,'' Faraday said.

Hunter riveted the duke with a cold glare. ''You'll rue the day you crossed my path.''

Ignoring the buzzing in her head, Sabrina rushed to the twins. ''Alec's not well. He could get very sick and die. He has severe asthma.''

For a second, the duke seemed uncertain, then his eyes gleamed. ''Asthma? My first son died of it, too. I suggest you and Hunter create an heir. I am taking the boy to insure you do. Your babe's legitimacy will not be in question, and I will be assured of an heir. The Sadlerfield title will thrive.''

Lifting his nose, he reached for Alec. ''Come with me, boy.''

''Mama! I don't want to go!'' Alec cried in French, his breathing raspy with his last words.

''Speak English, boy!''

His sister started to cry. ''*Non!* Mama! Don't let Alec go!''

Marga swung around, giving the duke her back. ''*Mes petites,* hush. Alec, please, you will make yourself sick.''

''Hunter! Don't let him take me!'' Alec yelled, his breath

wheezing. He stretched out his arm. His small hand reached for the man who, in a short time, he had come to adore.

"Stop wailing, boy," Sadlerfield ordered. "Be a man. Perhaps the other whelp makes you weak. A man should never succumb to tears." He reached for Alec, but the boy squirmed to avoid his touch.

Separate them! Tears welled in Sabrina's throat, accompanied by hot anger. "Don't say those things to them!"

With a grim face, Hunter plucked Alec from Marga's arm. "Remember what I told you about breathing?"

Alec shook his head and clung to Hunter like bark to a tree.

"Breathe deeply. From here." He placed his palm on Alec's stomach. Turning, Hunter's eyes bore into Sadlerfield's. "Since you've no proof, you can't take these children."

Her grandfather held his gaze. "You had best remember your place, Kenilworth. I can take Madame Beaumont to court. Under oath, she must speak the truth. She would find herself in prison."

Marga started to weep and held Christine more tightly.

Sabrina grasped her brother's hand and prayed her excuse would give them the opportunity to flee. "Alec, you're getting cold." Turning, she faced her grandfather. "If you insist on discussing this issue, at least let me put some clothes on them. Alec can get very sick from just damp air."

The duke nodded crisply. "Very well."

Sabrina pulled Alec from Hunter's arms and went to Marga. "I'm taking the twins and running," she mouthed.

Marga nodded imperceptibly and relinquished her hold on Christine, who was still whimpering.

With a shattered heart, Sabrina left and never looked back.

As the hackney rocked and clattered down the street, Sabrina fought her nausea and the pain stabbing her head. The stale odor of cigar smoke added to her discomfort, but nothing compared to the ache in her heart. She told herself she had made the right choice, the only sane thing a person could do.

Despite Hunter's betrayal, she knew her escape might cause him and Gavin grief, even death, but she would never allow her grandfather to take the twins.

Tears stung her eyes and she was grateful the twins had fallen asleep. They wouldn't see her anguish. At least they were safe. She placed her arms around them and swallowed a sob. A vision of Hunter burst forth—his sensuous lips, those beckoning green eyes, his powerful male aura that could sweep her away into oblivious passion. Her body shook from the memories and the loss.

She would never see Hunter's handsome face again, feel his body snuggled next to her when she woke or hear the soft timbre of his voice. Her mind and senses would remember every part of him, even his bayberry scent. She almost wished she would forget. Foolish lady. Though she always knew that she might have to escape, she had fallen in love with Hunter, and nothing had prepared her for the emptiness shrouding her soul.

She had given Hunter her heart and body, and he still couldn't accept her without her past. Why? She recalled the savage part of him, the darkness in him that had propelled him to marry her. The part of him that had promised revenge. With a twinge of guilt, she couldn't deny she had blackmailed him. Despite that, she refused to think he wanted to use her past against her, but the niggling doubt remained.

Warm tears ebbed down her cheeks and she bit her lip to keep from making a sound. Though she professed her love, he had never said the words to her. Why hadn't he? Was his concern a pretense, like his Lord Byron act? Had her instincts led her that far astray? Despite his show of concern, had he sought her secret for his own purposes? Christine stirred, and Sabrina realized she had tugged the tartans off the twins. With shaking hands, she covered them. The tartans…bayberry.

Sabrina cried until just a dull ache remained in her heart. To continue her unknown journey, she needed her wits.

A night watchman whistled as he strolled down the fog-lined streets. When he glanced in her direction, she pressed deeper into the shadows of the cab. She gingerly brought her hands toward each twin's mouth in case they woke and spoke too loudly. They hadn't understood the reason they were leaving Hunter's house, and had asked why Marga wasn't with them. Her heart grieved for them. Sabrina almost felt like a criminal.

She pressed her lips together. Hunter's probing had caused her current predicament and she latched onto her anger, the only thing that soothed her battered heart. Because of him, she had uprooted the twins again. Her plan was to find temporary refuge with Thomas. The twins knew and liked him. Though she hadn't wanted to involve her godfather in her troubles, she knew he would help. He had so many grandchildren running about that no one would notice two more youngsters.

With fierce determination, she ignored the burgeoning ache in her chest and head. She had to think about the twins and what she should do. When she reached inside her valise to fetch her handkerchief, she suddenly couldn't recall if she had brought her reticule. Digging deeper through the few garments she had tossed inside, she felt the cold steel of her pistol. She had never unpacked it from her Scotland trip.

A sinking feeling unfurled when she realized she didn't have a shilling to her name.

## Chapter Twenty-Four

"Have you heard anything? Any of you?" Hunter paced, stopping beside Geoffrey and Jonathan.

Jonathan shook his head as his solemn gray eyes peeked above his spectacles. "I did everything you asked last night. Nothing. No sign of Lady Kenilworth. This lists the men searching." He placed the paper on Hunter's cluttered desk.

"My father and I haven't seen her," Geoffrey said. Easing deeper into the leather chair, he crossed a booted foot over his knee. He looked up, his expression blank, like a barrister facing an opponent in court.

Marga sat with her hands clasped, and the shadows under her eyes emphasized her accusing look.

With sickening realization, Hunter sensed that even if the Norton men or Marga knew of Sabrina's whereabouts, they would keep the information to themselves. Despite his intervention last night, he was as much the enemy as Sadlerfield.

Hunter slammed his fist on the mantel and rubbed his brow. "Damnation. Where could she be?"

"Disconcerting when a wife leaves her husband. My sympathies, Kenilworth." Geoffrey scanned him with a bland look.

Mockery aside, Hunter would bet a fortune that the solicitor knew where she was. Impotent rage sluiced through his veins. He wanted to throttle Sabrina and embrace her at once. Guilt assailed him anew. Her flight was inadvertently his fault. He should have taken her at her word, that her secret involved others' safety, and not probed. Despite her courage, he never guessed that she would flee in her weakened state.

Moving to the window facing the garden, he gazed outside and willed her to appear. The gray skies smothered the late day sun, draping the landscape in premature shadows. He stared at her beloved gardenia bushes and swallowed hard.

Last night he had hired every Bow Street runner worth a shilling, called on his sailors to comb the streets and docks, while he searched, too. No one had seen her. The duke was livid, demanding a quiet search. No one would make a fool out of him, or create a scandal that might tarnish the pristine Barrington name. Hunter curled his mouth in disgust.

The situation forced him to ask Geoffrey if he knew her whereabouts, an act that had cost Hunter his pride. Like a raw wound, the humiliation exposed his heart. Geoffrey loved Sabrina and would do anything for her, of that Hunter was certain. Jealousy coupled with his concern and anger made his blood boil. He gripped the drapes. He had been so sure she'd run to her solicitor or his father, Thomas. Within minutes of discovering she had left, Hunter went to the elder Norton's house, but she wasn't there.

Suddenly Hunter sensed that everyone was staring at his back. How long had he been gazing like an oaf? He released the wrinkled drapery. His lack of control grated his pride, eroded his confidence.

"Bloody hell. She hasn't recovered." Turning, Hunter raked his fingers through his hair. "And to watch two rambunctious children? What if Alec became ill? Where the devil was her mind?"

Finally Marga looked up, dark crescents marring her olive complexion. "*Monseigneur,* I wish my babies were here. However, I know Sabrina will love and care for them." Her voice cracked.

Hunter suddenly realized that even if the twins were Sabrina's siblings, Marga had raised them like her own. The situation mirrored the way his mother had raised and loved Gavin. Still, to entrust the children to someone else took great courage.

He wanted to tell her to trust him, but doubted she had much respect for him right now. By continuing the investigation, he had obliterated any strides made toward winning her confidence. He looked away, back to the garden. With grim clarity, he knew he would search alone. Sabrina's confidantes would remain tight-lipped. Curse the lot of them. He'd find her himself.

"Go about your business." Steel crept into his voice and he planted his hands on his littered desk. He needed to think like Sabrina. As he recalled the things she'd done in Scotland, he swore under his breath.

Geoffrey rose. "Marga. I will escort you to the shop."

"*Merci.* I am not sure I can work, but I must keep busy."

Jonathan clasped Hunter's shoulder. "If I hear anything, I will send a missive straightaway." He turned to Geoffrey. "Should we compare notes on the theaters?"

The two solicitors agreed on a time, and suddenly Hunter was alone. Moving to the oak cellaret, he poured himself a brandy and swallowed a healthy portion, the liquid burning clear to his empty stomach. He refilled the goblet.

With slumped shoulders, he left his study. No squeals of children broke the silence. No wife challenged his decisions, or teased and tormented him. He missed the noise, missed her. An odd emotion surrounded his heart, but he attributed the feeling to his concern.

Entering their bedchamber, he moved to Sabrina's dressing table and picked up her perfume bottle. Hunter squirted the heady liquid, the gardenia scent rousing his senses…and guilt. He had driven her away. The unnamed emotion gripped him anew.

Setting down his goblet, he dropped into a chair and buried his head in his hands. Saving himself had turned into a disaster. Was he any different from his father or Sadlerfield? As he reached for his glass, he saw himself in the mirror. He sneered at his reflection and tossed back a huge gulp of brandy. When he began the investigation, he had intended to use any damaging evidence to blackmail Sabrina into staying in the marriage. With the opposite occurring, shame and remorse assaulted his conscience. *His father.*

Suddenly he sat straighter. Sadlerfield wasn't the man who controlled Gavin's or his fate. If his father never accused Hunter of kidnapping, Sadlerfield would have no hold over anyone.

That meant he must find the Sinner and strike a bargain. His father listened to money. The thought left a bitter taste in Hunter's mouth, and he took another drink. Could he let go of the past? Forget his father's sins? The crystal facets pressed into his flesh. His old anger simmered as he forced himself to mull over the possibility.

Unlike five years ago, parting with a few pounds would be his choice and a better one than giving up his life. More, he could eliminate Sadlerfield's threat and Sabrina's demons.

With renewed purpose, he scribbled a note to Jonathan. Hunter wanted a report on the theaters. If he guessed right, his father was now associated with an actress.

The clock chimed four and he remembered his five-o'clock meeting with the king. Quickly he shed his clothes. As he shaved, that unfamiliar emotion hit him in the gut again. He nicked his skin. He muttered a vicious curse. Blood oozed through the pristine soap. Damnation. He stared at his reflection. *Admit it, fool. You love her.*

"I cannot believe you talked me into this." Geoffrey frowned.

When the coach stopped behind a long line of others, Sabrina adjusted her flaxen-colored wig, the curls bouncing around her neck. The Theatre Royal at Covent Garden stood before them, shrouded in fog and glowing lights.

"Marga was so clever to have Irene bring me a disguise. The twins were so glad to see her. Do I look all right?" She held up a wide-brimmed hat and wondered if the wig altered her looks enough. At least her aunt had put the stained linen to use. It gave her roundness where none existed before.

Geoffrey paused, eyeing her gray wool gown that clothed her stuffed bosom and padded torso. "Not very becoming."

Sabrina dropped the hat and narrowed her eyes. "Lady Yarborough...I mean, Betsy, thought if I looked more like her, people would think I'm a relative. She has a big heart. Because of her, the twins and I found refuge. I wouldn't have gotten a message to you, either. From the sounds of it, Hunter has questioned your whole family."

She swallowed hard, again feeling the despair when Hunter's coach stood outside Thomas's house. Then she remembered Betsy, a kind widow who said to visit anytime. During the abolitionist meetings, they had gotten on well, so Sabrina had taken the chance. She had little choice but experienced no regrets. Betsy embraced her and the twins without questions.

"Sorry. I'm just worried about you."

The pain in his voice reflected his amorous feelings. She refused to encourage him or allow him to believe there was hope. "Please, I have to do this on my own."

He heaved a deep sigh. "Coming with me is not a good idea. I can question the actress."

"That's fine, but I want the money this Miss Rachael Prentice owes. You know I can't go to the bank and I was wrong to take the money from Hunter. He didn't owe it, although I believed he did at the time. Tonight, I'll get the money from the real culprit. I have to do something, to feel in control of my life again. Besides, the sooner I get the money, the quicker Marga can join me."

Geoffrey planted his elbows on his knees, his look beseeching. "Didn't I say I would lend you the money?"

The ache in her heart cried for all the people involved. "I don't know where I'm going, or when I can pay you back. Besides, my grandfather probably bribed every bank clerk to watch all our accounts." She sighed, forcing the lump in her throat to ease. "Betsy already offered me money. Telling her that a powerful man wanted to take the twins from Marga almost made her cry. I begged her not to tell a soul. Everyone has been kind to help me. Lending money to me might cause trouble.''

''Kenilworth has an army looking for you.''

''For his own purposes, no doubt.''

With a supreme effort, she suppressed all thoughts of Hunter. He had betrayed her, put the twins' lives in danger…and had broken her heart by not returning her affections. She decided he had heard her declaration of love, for she remembered the surprised look on his face. When the pain in her heart rose to her throat, she tugged on the contraption weighting her head. ''He won't find me looking like this!''

Geoffrey looked out the window to where members of the Ladies Abolitionist Society were gathering. ''I think you summoned the motherly instinct of every lady in London. Quite a shield we have.''

Feeling grateful he changed the topic, Sabrina peered out the window at her newfound friends, all holding placards with a painted message for reform. Tears welled in her eyes.

''They don't know it's I or what I'm doing. Betsy just told them that a fellow member and her children were in trouble. That she needed to meet someone here. Amazing what women will do when children are in danger.''

''Yes. Amazing.'' He held his gold pocket watch to the lantern. ''Shall we go? The play is about to end. If Kenilworth's men are following me, I hope you pass for a companion.''

With a supreme effort, Sabrina focused on her purpose. Just hearing Hunter's name fanned the pain in her soul. She and the twins needed money. As they left the coach, Sabrina noticed that a group of men had gathered at one corner of the theater. Their worn garb and unkempt state suggested they might have unsavory natures. She lowered her eyes but wondered if they were ruffians or just lowlifes who preferred the wenches that Covent Garden offered.

By the time she and Geoffrey entered the building, the at-

tendees were spilling outside, a mixture of well-heeled patrons
and common people. She kept her face down and allowed
Geoffrey to lead. They edged the way through a crowd of
male admirers flocking to Miss Prentice's dressing room. A
murmur rippled through the assemblage when she arrived.
The voluptuous actress appeared to be in her late twenties,
though Sabrina couldn't be certain under the veil of stage
makeup. After accepting several bouquets of flowers, the actress slipped inside the room.

Waving his hands toward the bystanders, a burly man
stepped in front of the door. "Begone, gents."

The men grumbled and began to disperse.

"How can we get past that guard?" Sabrina whispered.

"An actress never turns down work. Follow my lead."

A few moments later, and just as Geoffrey planned, the
actress bid them to enter. The small room smelled of cloying
perfume, thickened with the scent of carnations and roses.
Rouge and powder pots littered a small dressing table.

"I'll be ready in two breaths, Mr. Norton," Miss Prentice
said from behind a tall screen. Silk rustled. A petticoat flew
over the barrier and landed on a nearby chair. Next came a
corset.

Geoffrey grinned. "Take your time, Miss Prentice."

When the actress stepped from behind the screen, a red robe
covered her curvaceous form. Honey-colored eyes dominated
her heart-shaped face, framed with dark hair that flowed over
her shoulders. Deprived of her stage garb, she still looked
pretty.

"Let me introduce my companion," Geoffrey said.

The actress eyed them curiously, then managed a quick
curtsy. "You want to hire me for a soiree, do you? I'm hon-
ored, sir, but I can't visit long. I've company coming."

Sabrina forced a smile. "Miss Prentice, I represent Maison
du Beaumont. I'll be frank. Did you disguise yourself as three
different ladies and dupe the shop out of six thousand pounds?
All evidence says you did."

The actress toyed with the ties of her robe before she glanced nervously over her shoulder.

Suddenly from behind the screen, a figure emerged.

"I thought I recognized your voice. You are my son's wife. Are you feeling better?"

Sabrina blinked in disbelief. Her pulse raced. "Lord Wick?" she whispered. The world seemed to tilt.

"Blasted. Whoever you are, you just scared the wits out of my client," Geoffrey said with a hard edge to his voice. He put his arm around her waist to steady her.

"Baron of Wick, Randall Sinclair." He made a sweeping bow.

When he straightened, he stared at her disguise, and she gaped back, her whole body trembling.

The room seemed to shrink with the elder Sinclair's appearance. Dressed in an indigo frock coat and trousers, he looked so much like Hunter that he took her breath away. The height and build of father and son appeared the same. Thin lines etched the corners of his green eyes, and gray brushed his black hair at the temples.

Appearing younger than his age added to the aura of his masculinity, but who was the man beneath this exterior? When Hunter's father stepped forward, Geoffrey stiffened. The movement and tap of Lord Wick's heels against the wooden floor accelerated her pounding heart and made her aware of her rude perusal.

Suddenly she recalled Hunter's warnings, the conversation the baron had had with the duke in the conservatory. Deftly she moved her hand into her cloak pocket. Cold steel. The weapon's presence eased the concern trickling down her spine.

Just then, someone pounded on the door. Everyone turned toward the sound.

"Wick! I do not have all night," Sadlerfield said.

Sabrina's blood turned cold. Desperation stirred her senses. She threw herself at the door. From her cloak pocket, she drew her pistol. "You can't open it."

Stepping backward, Miss Prentice's eyes grew wide.

"Sabrina, put away that thing," Geoffrey said.

"No."

Lord Wick glanced at the weapon, his eyes darkening. "Your grandfather owes me money. I imagine that is the reason he requested this meeting."

"Wick!"

"A moment! Rachael is dressing."

Sabrina looked at the baron with all the desperation she felt in her heart. "Sir, my grandfather can't see me here. I beg of you. If you allow it, you'll be a party to murder. You might see Australia again."

Miss Prentice's hand flew to her throat. "Randall. I waited for you. Do something. You can't be going back to that bloody place."

His hard green eyes studied Sabrina for a second. "Very well. Behind the screen. I trust you will refrain from using that thing."

Despite the terror lodged in her throat, she summoned her most vicious look. The baron's show of compassion aside, he had schemed with her grandfather. "If you keep your mouth shut, I won't use the gun."

# Chapter Twenty-Five

The two splits between the screen's three panels offered a place to view the meeting. Sabrina prayed they would conduct their business quickly so she could finish hers. As her grandfather entered, she and Geoffrey peered through the two cracks, ones offering narrow scope. Opposite their position, the dressing table mirror provided a broader view.

Miss Prentice curtsied, then moved to her dressing table near the back door. As if nothing were amiss, she sat and brushed her hair, her gaze occasionally darting to the duke.

Her grandfather placed both hands on his cane. "I will make this short, Wick. I no longer need your services."

Lord Wick tilted his head. "Then you brought the money we agreed upon?"

"You will never see a shilling."

The baron shook his fists. "You manipulative bastard."

Her grandfather shrugged. "I could not let the glorious Barrington name die. You were perfect for my plan."

Miss Prentice tossed her brush onto the table. "That's not fair, you pompous oaf! We did everything you asked. That money was to start a new life for me an' Randall love."

Sparing her a dispassionate glance, the duke turned his gaze back to Hunter's father. "If you choose to cause trouble, I will inform the authorities you blackmailed me. That this whole affair was your revenge against Kenilworth. I will say that I only agreed to guard my name and granddaughter's reputation. No one will believe you.''

Sabrina dropped her jaw. Liar!

The baron kicked her grandfather's cane. It clattered and rolled toward the screen. Sabrina grabbed Geoffrey's arm.

Lord Wick jabbed his finger in the air. ''What about your word as a gentleman? You cannot renege on our agreement.''

''What agreement? I do not even know you, Wick.''

''You are not getting away with this.''

''Yes, I will.'' Turning toward Sabrina, he moved to retrieve his cane.

Sabrina glanced with wide eyes at Geoffrey. Her pulse tripped. She held her breath. He put a finger to his lips.

Heavy steps and scuffling made them jerk their heads around. Again they looked through the thin openings. Sabrina expected the guard to burst inside the room. Hadn't he heard the noise?

The baron grabbed her grandfather's collar. Suddenly the duke whirled around, and with surprising agility, backhanded the baron's face. Miss Prentice shrieked. Stunned, Randall staggered backward.

Sabrina winced, gripped her pistol. For a fleeting second, she considered ending the fight. Prudence prevailed. The twins expected her to return to Betsy's.

Miss Prentice ran for the cane. Grabbing it, she whacked the duke's shoulder. ''Don't you hurt my Randall!''

Her grandfather flinched. ''I can have you thrown in prison for that. Remember your station.'' His tone was frigid.

Hunter's father stalked toward the duke. ''Do not talk to her that way.''

''She is a commoner. Your mistress. A nobody.''

Sabrina tightened her hold on the pistol. Debt aside, Miss Prentice did not deserve the cruel words. A strange part of Sabrina's soul cheered for the actress.

Miss Prentice took several steps backward, her hands now resting on her dressing table. Her fingers curled around a pot.

Sabrina smiled.

"A doxy, am I? You think your conscience and blood so pure?" The actress pitched the jar at her grandfather, hitting him in the temple. Powder exploded, showering the threesome in dust. Glass crashed to the floor.

Horror and humor caught in Sabrina's throat.

"Rachael!" Wick sneezed. "I will handle this!"

"You little wench," Sadlerfield managed to say. "I am ending our deal because I will not be here. The king ordered me south on a diplomatic mission."

Miss Prentice laughed, her tone brittle. "You? A diplomat! More like a tyrant! Give us our money."

Ignoring the actress's tirade, her grandfather turned to the baron. "If I know Kenilworth, he will have her arrested for fraud. As for you, your word is worth nothing to society."

"My son has considerable power. He likes to remove annoyances from his life. Why do you think he kidnapped me and sent me to Australia? I pushed Hunter too far. Do not make the same mistake."

"What I do is my business. His will be to worry about the control I have over him."

As understanding dawned, compassion tilted her heart. Hunter had committed the crime and Gavin was the accomplice. She should have been angry they allowed her to believe the reverse, but now she understood they had taken precautions. They looked after each other because of their love.

Her grandfather glanced at the main entrance, then at himself. He started for the back door. "Good God. Nobody can see me like this." His long pale fingers worked as he tried to brush the powder off his clothes.

Was Gavin and Hunter's situation so different from hers? Had she been wrong about him? Had he done everything because he loved her? Tears threatened and she quashed the hope rising in her chest. She wouldn't see him again.

The baron sneered. "Despite my cheap theatrics, Hunter has not buckled to my taunting. Did you think he would lie at your feet? I told you he does not scare easily. If I guess correctly, you are going south because Hunter influenced the king. Ingenious, I say.''

As the duke's hand reached the door, he spun around. "He is a confidante of King William's?" Shock laced his words.

A corner of Lord Wick's mouth curled. "If I expose you, my son might listen. I wonder what kind of trip he would plan for you."

"You have no influence over Kenilworth. I do not believe you." Her grandfather gave Lord Wick his back.

"Oh, no, you don't!" The actress slammed the cane on the duke's arm. "You bloody bloke! You think I'll wear a noose for you?"

As her heart applauded Miss Prentice's bravado, Sabrina suddenly found herself springing on her toes.

Swinging around, the duke backhanded the actress. She screamed. The baron lunged for her grandfather. Miss Prentice stumbled against the dressing table. Sabrina ground her teeth. She raised the pistol. No one should ever hit a woman!

Geoffrey grabbed her arm, pulled her closer to the wall. He shook his head. She scowled, but prudence won.

Suddenly wood crashed against wood. "Did you forget to invite me to your meeting, gentlemen?" Hunter drawled.

Sabrina drew in a sharp breath.

"Good God! Who is behind that screen?" the duke said.

Sabrina's heart stopped. Geoffrey grabbed her hand.

A fist swept the screen aside. Wood clattered.

Fierce green eyes bore into hers. Her throat was as dry as day-old ashes.

"Hiding! You little devious whelp!" Sadlerfield scowled.

After blinking at her disguise, Hunter's gaze traveled down her length and stopped at her hand. He pinned Geoffrey with a thunderous look. "Interesting."

She yanked her fingers from Geoffrey's hold.

"Randall! The bloke's leaving! Go after him!"

All heads turned toward Miss Prentice, then the back door. The baron raced after Sadlerfield, his boot heels pounding the earth.

In one swift movement, Hunter swung around and pulled her close. He kissed her soundly on the lips. "You stay right here. I want to talk to you." His tone possessed a stony edge. He burst out the back entrance.

Miss Prentice ran outside. "Stop that man! He owes me money!"

For a second, Sabrina could not make herself think or move. The kiss made her lips quiver, her heart ripple. A feminine scream roused her senses. Hunter and her grandfather had found her. All she could think about were the twins. "We'll go out the front."

"I do not want you running for the rest of your life," Geoffrey said.

"I'll never let my grandfather take the twins."

She started for the main entrance but then heard jeering. A vision of Hunter burst forth. If a motley crowd had formed, they might mistake him for an enemy because he was a lord. Her heart careened. Heaven help her, despite everything, she still loved him. Turning, she took long strides toward the rear. "I must see what's happening."

"Kenilworth wanted you to stay here."

She continued toward the door. "Maybe I was wrong about Hunter. What if Hunter really tried to do something about my grandfather? Maybe Lord Wick knows his son better than I do."

Although the fog dimmed Sabrina's view, one look at the crowd gathering near the theater turned her blood cold. Placards stood like gravestones in the air. From her position, the men were just black forms, but she knew from the rising curses and accusations that the commoners had rebelled against upper society. Fists started flying.

Screams and neighing horses filled the air.

"I have to do something! Hunter might get hurt!" Her hand tightened around her pistol, her thumb on the hammer, and she ran.

As she reached the edge of the crowd, she pointed her pistol toward the sky. She pulled the trigger. The crowd raised their heads. The acrid smell of gunpowder burned her strained lungs. "Stop! Lord Kenilworth is in your midst! He wants to help you!"

Someone yelled, "Peelers coming!"

Horse hooves thundered. Through the fog, the peelers' rounded hats emerged.

"Gather the lot of them!" an authoritative voice boomed.

The crowd started to scatter.

Suddenly someone grabbed Sabrina's hand and pulled her through the crowd. A second passed before she realized the person was Betsy.

"Let's go, Lady Kenilworth! We'd not want the bobbies to throw us in jail for inciting a riot. The king's ordered them to do so."

"Wait a minute! My husband!" Sabrina looked frantically about the crowd.

"No time. The men can take care of themselves. Prison will kill any lady. Besides, those two children need you to help their mama."

Sabrina's chest ached, forcing tears to her eyes. "Hunter."

A coach pulled up, and Betsy unceremoniously pushed her inside. Her pistol clattered to the floor. Sabrina braced her hands on the window opening, her eyes searching for Hunter. When the coach lurched, the movement threw her against the squabs. She closed her eyes, but a tear escaped. Perhaps this way was best. The twins needed her.

Pounding horse hooves grew closer.

"Oh dear! A peeler's coming for us!" Betsy yelled for the coachman to give the horses some rein.

A dark form appeared alongside the coach, then a thump and clatter shook the conveyance.

As Betsy cursed at her driver, Sabrina's pulse raced. The coach came to a jolting halt. Something hit the earth with a reverberating thud. The door swung open, crashing against the coach. Sabrina started. Betsy squealed.

"Going somewhere?" Hunter drawled.

Speechless, Sabrina smiled at him with all the love she felt in her heart.

Hunter pulled Sabrina from the coach, thanked Lady Yarborough and sent her on her way. Then he whistled for Gallus.

"Wait! I love you, but I can't stay with you!" Sabrina cried.

Hunter gathered her in his arms. Despite her padding, he felt her body tremble. "Sabrina, I know the reason. At first, the investigation was to learn your secret. I admit I wanted a hold over you. Not later though. You must believe me. All I wanted was to help you. I never meant to harm the twins. You can't leave me. I love you." He didn't hide the desperation in his voice.

She looked at him with wide eyes. "You do?"

He nodded. "Like I can never love another."

"Oh, Hunter, how can we be together?" She gazed up at him with eyes now sparkling from tears. "My grandfather..." A sob escaped.

He stroked her face, the petal softness stirring his senses. His chest ached with emotion, a feeling he had never experienced with any lady. He wanted to touch all of her, to know she would always be with him. "Sadlerfield died. My father caught him, but the crowd wrenched him away. In the scuffle, Sadlerfield hit his head. He's no longer a threat to us. Cason's taking care of his body."

She sagged against him, numb.

Alarm pumped his heart. "Are you all right? Your injury? Do you feel faint?"

Taking a ragged breath, she shook her head. "I'm just glad I no longer have to fight him, and I'll not miss him. He couldn't accept people for who they are. Heritage was everything to him."

"No one will hurt you again."

Gallus clomped beside him.

"What about your father? Do you think he will hurt you?

Something tells me he won't. He's no angel, but not horrible, either. He helped me.''

"I know. I heard."

"You did?"

He grinned as he lifted her up on Gallus. "The guard accepted a gold crown to leave."

"No wonder. I expected him to barge into the dressing room. Do you think your father will bring charges against you? Losing you is something I couldn't bear."

As he pulled himself up behind her, his heart careened against his chest. "Nor I you. I asked him to come to the house. I've an offer for him. You have to trust me on this."

She snuggled against him. "Of course I do. Anyone clever enough to 'send away his annoyances' will think of something."

He pressed his lips together. "That's not a very admirable part of me. Manipulative, in fact."

"Only with a person's welfare in mind. Who were you aiding when you sent your father away?"

"A stranger." Hunter told Sabrina about his mother's death, the confrontation with his father, and the threat of impersonation. Gallus clopped along the fog-lined streets, his hooves a steady cadence that accompanied Hunter's words.

"That was terrible of him. I hope he's learned his lesson."

"We'll see when he reacts to my offer."

Suddenly she straightened, and her padded bottom stirred his desire. "Wait! The twins! I have to go get them."

"Since I don't know where they are, I asked Geoffrey to fetch them. He's gone. Whoever's caring for them should trust him."

"Yes, they will. You don't like him very much. Do you?"

His fingers tightened around the leather ribbons. "I love you. He loves you."

"You're jealous?"

The surprise in her voice made him smile. "Insanely so."

She kissed his jaw. "Fear nothing. You're the Hunter of my heart."

His chest swelled with love. Pulling Gallus to a halt, he cupped her face in his hands and kissed her sweet lips. Feeling her in his arms and catching her gardenia scent validated that she was no dream. Her hand slid up his thigh, stirring his base needs. No. Definitely not a dream. "I've never made love on a horse, but we could…" He nibbled her ear. Hunter could feel her cheeks pulling a smile.

"Get this nag home. I much prefer our bed."

"Thank you, *monseigneur,* for helping," Marga said with a quavering voice after hearing the evening's events. She looked down at the sleeping twins, one on either side of her. The threesome filled the settee, making a warm picture.

Sabrina sat opposite, trying to remove her wig.

Hunter's newfound family fueled his heart with love and pride. From his pocket he pulled the signet ring that he had taken off Sadlerfield's finger. "I believe this should belong to Alec."

Rising, Sabrina looked but didn't touch. "It looks like Father's ring. He gave it to me in case he died. To fulfill my vow to mother, he knew that I might need evidence later. The ring is in my piano. We can keep my grandfather's for Alec's son."

Hunter kissed her brow. "You have more courage than any person I've ever known."

A knock sounded and Woodstone announced that his father was here with a lady. Hunter asked the butler to help Marga with the twins.

When they left, Sabrina smiled. "Are you ready to face him?"

"I let the past go this afternoon."

Throwing her arms around him, she kissed him soundly. "I love you."

He wanted to take every shred of clothing off her, to feel her warm skin against his. Gently he peeled her arms from his waist. "When I finish with my father, I promise you an experience you'll never forget."

She wiggled her brows. "I hope that isn't all bluster, sir."

He laughed. "Go upstairs and get rid of that padding."

A few moments later, his father and the lady entered. Quickly, he introduced her.

"Remember me, milord? I was with Randall the night you took him away," Miss Prentice said.

Hunter nodded. "I asked you here to put the past behind us."

Lord Wick heaved a deep breath. "I never wanted to help Sadlerfield. All I wanted was to come home to Rachael, but I was afraid to ask you. Until I met him in Scotland, I swear I never knew he considered eliminating you."

"You helped Sabrina. That doesn't erase the past, but I do want to show my appreciation."

Hunter searched his cluttered desk and found the papers Sadlerfield had brought over a week ago. "The duke planned to give me two hundred thousand pounds."

Startled, the duo turned toward each other with hopeful looks.

"Part of it was to pay the debt you had incurred. The rest was for her dowry. I'll deduct the six thousand pounds, and the rest is yours. Two conditions. One, your stay in Australia was as my representative for my Asian trade. Nothing more. Two, you live an honest life. Agreed?"

"I am sorry for all that happened. Sometimes a man does not mature until late in life. I will do whatever you ask."

His father signed the papers Jonathan had prepared earlier and thanked Hunter profusely. He knew they'd never be close but at least they'd be civil. Within minutes, they finished the business, and his father and Miss Prentice left. Hunter headed for his suite.

Just as he reached the foyer, Pamela and Brice dashed inside.

Blond curls had escaped their pins. "Oh, Hunt! Is Sabrina all right? I was at the theater. There was a terrible row. Word has it her grandfather died."

Hunter frowned. "Damn lady abolitionists. Despite the

duke's death, Sabrina's fine.'' He turned to Brice. ''I suggest you chain your wife to you. I intend to do the same with mine.''

They spoke for several more minutes, but he couldn't see the point of revealing the events that had led to tonight's fiasco. His future was upstairs.

Just as the couple turned to leave, Hunter said, ''Brice. Have you forgotten our wager? I wore a kilt so you owe me a horse. I want one suitable for a little girl.''

Brice chuckled. ''Oh yes. Perhaps my loss will teach me not to challenge you.''

When they left, he took the stairs by twos.

Sabrina was in a pale blue dressing robe and unpinning her hair. She smiled when he entered. ''All went well?''

''Perfectly. Your dowry is now my father's compensation.''

''Money. It only entered my mind when I thought I might need to run away.''

He pulled her from the dressing table and captured her in his arms. ''Never leave me again.''

''Never. By the by, how did you find me?''

''I was looking for my father, so I followed Sadlerfield. I wanted to eliminate their threat. If I succeeded, I knew Marga or Geoffrey would get word to you. I should throttle you for disobeying me at the theater. You could put a man in his grave before his time. Especially when you yelled and fired the blasted pistol.''

He slipped the robe off her shoulders.

She smiled and kissed his cheek. ''A lady will do anything to save the man she loves.''

The robe fell to the floor.

\* \* \* \* \*